"Cross's bold debut introduces headstrong nine-year-old Zarq Darquel. . . . Turning the fantasy cliché of the underdog girl who dreams of dragon-mastery into a grim but fascinating coming-of-age tale, Cross scratches only the surface of this richly detailed, well-imagined world."

—*Publishers Weekly*

"[A] remarkable debut novel. . . . It is clear that Janine Cross is a significant new voice in fantasy."

—*Cinefantastique*

"Cross's debut novel tells a fascinating story of love and vengeance. Offering a different approach to dragons and dragon lore, the author combines skillful storytelling with sensually evocative details. With particular appeal to fans of the works of Jacqueline Carey and Terry Goodkind."

—*Library Journal* (starred review)

FORGED
by
FIRE

BOOK THREE OF THE

Dragon Temple Saga

JANINE CROSS

A ROC BOOK

ROC
Published by New American Library, a division of
Penguin Group (USA) Inc., 375 Hudson Street,
New York, New York 10014, USA
Penguin Group (Canada), 90 Eglinton Avenue East, Suite 700, Toronto,
Ontario M4P 2Y3, Canada (a division of Pearson Penguin Canada Inc.)
Penguin Books Ltd., 80 Strand, London WC2R 0RL, England
Penguin Ireland, 25 St. Stephen's Green, Dublin 2,
Ireland (a division of Penguin Books Ltd.)
Penguin Group (Australia), 250 Camberwell Road, Camberwell, Victoria 3124,
Australia (a division of Pearson Australia Group Pty. Ltd.)
Penguin Books India Pvt. Ltd., 11 Community Centre, Panchsheel Park,
New Delhi - 110 017, India
Penguin Group (NZ), 67 Apollo Drive, Mairangi Bay,
Auckland 1311, New Zealand (a division of Pearson New Zealand Ltd.)
Penguin Books (South Africa) (Pty.) Ltd., 24 Sturdee Avenue,
Rosebank, Johannesburg 2196, South Africa

Penguin Books Ltd., Registered Offices:
80 Strand, London WC2R 0RL, England

First published by Roc, an imprint of New American Library,
a division of Penguin Group (USA) Inc.

First Printing, April 2007
10 9 8 7 6 5 4 3 2 1

LIBRARY OF CONGRESS CATALOGING-IN-PUBLICATION DATA
Cross, Janine.
Forged by fire / Janine Cross.
p. cm. -- (Dragon temple saga ; bk. 3)
ISBN-13: 978-0-451-46128-5
ISBN-10: 0-451-46128-2
I. Title.
PS3603.R674F67 2007
813'.6—dc22 2006029977

Set in Weiss
Designed by Spring Hoteling

Printed in the United States of America

To my mother and father

ACKNOWLEDGMENTS

For support unlimited, thanks go first and foremost to Linda DeMeulemeester. Sincere gratitude to my editor, Liz, and my agent, Caitlin, for their insights and patience. Thanks also to all the listserv folks at SF Canada; Claire Eddy, for encouraging and challenging me, way back when; John D., my computer guru; and Sean Kerr, who asked me some pertinent questions when I'd reached an impasse, and thus provided me with forward mobility. As always, much love to the Faerie and the Bean, for all the magick they regularly conjure.

FORGED BY FIRE

ONE

"Walk faster if you can, what-hey," Daronpu Gen muttered. "Your head should be on a pike by now."

The tunnel reeked of dead air. No mildew or lichen grew on the walls; the stones were a lifeless gray that leapt briefly into a fluctuating tapestry of shadow and flamelight under Gen's torch before being swallowed again by darkness.

Gen gripped my elbow, urged me on faster. I stumbled. Pain lanced across my fractured ribs and I cried out.

"Steady," he murmured.

"Hurts," I snapped.

No empathy from him. "The bull dragon'll be mounting his last breeder soon, and the crowd'll expect to see your head paraded afterward. We don't want to be caught in this labyrinth when that spectacle doesn't occur, so *move*, girl, move."

The tunnel rumbled.

Earthquake, I thought with a spurt of panic, but realized, even as I thought it, that the rumble was the bellowing of the bull dragon in Arena above us, answered by the cheers of two hundred thousand Arena spectators. A clammy sweat broke over my skin.

It was then that I thought of Dono.

I don't know why; perhaps because I'd smelled the sweat of fear on him as he'd attacked me in Arena, just a short while before.

"What about Dono?" I asked.

I could see nothing of Gen's face beneath the ivory-hued Auditor's veil he wore, save for the whites of his eyes gleaming like the petals of wet lilies, and his pupils, black as beetle carapaces. "He can't hurt you now, Babu. Keep moving—"

"He's dead?"

"Bastard refused to die," a voice gurgled behind me, and I glanced over my shoulder at Dragonmaster Re, who was supported by a man disguised, like Gen, as an Auditor. Blood ran dark as plum jelly down the dragonmaster's thighs; he'd been wounded by the bull dragon's venomous tongue. A great flap of torn skin hung from his chest in a bloody frown. His goatee braid dangled in the wound.

"I couldn't strangle the air from him, so I ripped his throat out with my teeth." The dragonmaster's eyes rolled. "The bastard still refused to die."

"Dono's alive? Up there?" I stopped, looked at the stone ceiling that was so low, Daronpu Gen walked stooped over.

"Dead," Gen said with finality. "The bull will have trampled him by now. Keep walking."

I jerked my elbow from his grasp. "The bull *flies* when mating. Dono won't be trampled."

"Not trampled, oh, no. Not him." The dragonmaster cackled. His head lolled; he was barely lucid from the bull's toxin. "Crawling through the dust I left him, pressed against the stadium's walls; oh, no, not dead, that bastard, not dead."

"Gen," the other would-be Auditor said curtly. "We have to *go*."

Gen jerked on my arm and we were moving again.

"Son of a whore turned against me!" the dragonmaster shrilled, and his voice echoed down the tunnel.

"Shut up," the man holding him growled.

We reached a crossroad of tunnels. One was blocked; the ceiling had collapsed, whether long ago or recently, I couldn't tell. I wondered if there were any human bones moldering beneath that blockage. Or on the other side of it.

Without hesitation, Gen steered us down the tunnel to our right. The air was cooler and slightly damp. I pictured Dono—my milk-brother, the orphan I'd spent my childhood with—crawling through the hot, dusty Arena above, his sight impaired by the wound I'd inflicted on one of his eyes the day previous, his throat mauled by the dragonmaster.

"They'll execute him," I said. "He was supposed to kill me in Arena, and he failed. Temple'll behead him."

"A mercy," Gen said flatly. "There's no place in a stable for a crippled apprentice."

I stopped again. "We have to go back for him."

"Don't be a fool."

My teeth chattered. My head was pounding. My ribs were a fiery, creaking ache. The image of my sister, Waivia, bloomed in my mind. I'd seen her in the stands in Arena, leaning provocatively against Waikar Re Kratt, the overseer of Clutch Re—the same man who'd murdered our father and beaten health and sanity from our mother. A man I'd once vowed to kill. I wondered if Waivia were watching Dono crawl blindly in the dust; I knew she'd do nothing to save him if she were.

It suddenly became essential to rescue Dono. If I didn't, I'd be condemned to wander Arena's dark tunnels until I collapsed and became nothing but moldering bone. I felt sure of it.

So I lied, then, and used the only weapon I had: Gen's belief that I was the Dirwalan Babu, the Skykeeper's Daughter, a woman prophesied to liberate dragon and human alike from Temple's rule. "Dono's a part of it, Gen. I don't know why, but we *need* him. I can feel it in my marrow. We have to go back."

The dragonmaster babbled to himself like a babe drifting into sleep.

Daronpu Gen spoke slowly. "Zarq. You're under the influence of venom—"

"You gave me hardly any," I spat. "Every step I take is an agony; I feel every fractured bone as if I'd drunk nothing more than water."

The torch crackled and threw uneven heat and light across my face, his veil, the encroaching stone walls.

Gen abruptly turned to the man who held the dragonmaster upright. "Take them down to the end of this tunnel." He sounded angry. No.

Trapped. "You'll come to a three-way; take the middle tunnel, turn left at the end. Hurry. Tell the men stationed outside to wait for me."

"You jest," the man holding the dragonmaster said, aghast.

"Move it!" Daronpu Gen bellowed, and he thrust the torch into my hand and shoved past me, heading back the way we'd come. "Wait for me outside, with our dragons."

"For how long?" the man shouted after Gen's back. But Gen had already disappeared.

I'd be fine now; we'd find our way out of the labyrinth, wouldn't be condemned to die in it as punishment for leaving Dono behind.

Then why were my teeth chattering?

Dimly, I knew I was under the influence of venom, was deluded, paranoid, intoxicated, giddy. Didn't matter. Dono *was* family, and I'd be damned if I'd leave him for Temple to execute under the callous eyes of my sister. I'd be damned if I'd be anything remotely like *her*.

We moved faster after that, lurching along in a broken run. Things skittered in front of us, sometimes behind. Once I saw something lumbering into the darkness ahead, knee-height, the yellowish gray of overcooked yolk, with a spine like a knuckled fist. It moved crouched, and smelled like matted fur and oily dander. I had no idea what it could be. My skin prickled.

We followed Gen's instructions, wordless. Even the dragonmaster fell silent. On and on we stumbled. On and on. Through endless dark.

On and on.

Great Dragon, had we missed the turnoff? No: ahead, a three-way. We took the middle route, found ourselves in a narrower tunnel that ascended gradually at first, then steeply. An abrupt end: a stone wall in front of my face, a tunnel on my left, one on my right. I turned left. The tunnel curved, curved, curved. The ceiling grew lower. Lower. We were going in a circle, stooped.

"This is wrong," I wheezed. The heat from the torch I held drew the skin on my face taut. My fractured ribs felt like dragon talons raking my guts.

Abruptly, the tunnel angled away, opposite how it had been curving, and behind me, the man carrying the dragonmaster let out a bark of relief: Ahead of us was light, and I could smell fresh air, green things, and warm earth. Stifling a whimper, I staggered forward.

Stooped, we spilled out of the tunnel's mouth. I dropped my torch and leaned heavily on my knees. A warm breeze licked sweat from my skin. Dragons snorted. Wooden stirrups clunked and bridles jangled.

"There's only three of you," a voice barked. Steel hissed from a scabbard. "Were you followed? A fight?"

A silhouette appeared before me in the blinding light of full day: a man, frowning, holding a sword. He looked from me to the tunnel mouth at my back.

"Gen went back for an apprentice." Beside me, the man who was holding the dragonmaster hacked and spat. "The girl insisted. Give me a hand; this one's fainted."

Squinting in the light, I watched the two men heave the dragonmaster onto a winged dragon while a third held the dragon steady. When they were done, the man who'd carried the dragonmaster through the labyrinth shucked his Auditor's robes; he wore breeches and boots beneath, and had arms like a blacksmith and legs twice as thick. He looked at me and gestured brusquely with his chin at a saddled dragon. I straightened and limped toward her.

Was she a destrier? No. She didn't smell of venom. An escoa, then, one of the winged dragons employed by Malacar's parcel-and-letter dispatch service. All escoas had their venomous sacs removed.

The man with the build of a blacksmith helped me—roughly—into the saddle. Two dragons snorted and shifted on the other side of my mount, tethered to a sapling they could have uprooted with one lunge if they'd wanted to.

From atop the escoa, I looked about. In the distance, rolling orchards stretched toward the horizon, and at the end of the alluvial plains stood a girth of low mountains. We were at the far side of Arena, away from the taverns, hawkers' stalls, and caravansaries of Fwendar ki Bol, the Village of the Eggs. Away from the main entrances to Arena.

To my right, the massive curved walls of Arena towered above us, gray and intimidating.

The dragonmaster revived and muttered invective, but remained atop the escoa he'd been heaved upon. The three men stood beside his mount, watching the tunnel mouth. One kept his hand on the hilt of his sheathed sword.

"There'll be seven of us. If Gen returns with the apprentice," the sword holder said grimly.

Seven couldn't fly upon three dragons. Six, yes. Seven, no.

"Two of us will leave with the girl and the dragonmaster," Blacksmith said slowly, testing his own words for logic even as he spoke them. "One of us'll head for the fields, leave the third escoa for Gen and the apprentice."

Sword Holder's grip tightened on his weapon. "This place will be swarming with Temple soldiers soon."

"The quicker two of us are in the air, the sooner our decoys'll depart. Better chance for Gen to make it."

The three looked at one another in that way men have when they're taking the measure of one another.

The third man spoke. "Reckon I can reach those orchards before the alarm is raised."

All of us looked at the orchards in the distance. Either he was a very fast runner or an optimist. What choice did he have but to be both, given the situation? Blacksmith clapped him on the shoulder and, without another word, the man sprinted away from us.

A muted trumpeting came from beyond the Arena walls, followed by the oceanic roar of spectators. I shivered.

"How long do we wait?" Sword Holder asked, eyes upon the tunnel's mouth.

"Until Gen returns," I said. Both men looked at me. There wasn't much friendliness in either of their expressions. "He *will* come back," I added.

I repeated that silently to myself as we waited, as the escoas grew restless and tossed their snouts and whipped their tails at biting flies, as the air grew fraught with tension. But my refrain petered out as time crept onward, and finally I just sat there, mind as empty and black as the tunnel's maw, while my pulse raced and my mouth went dry.

"We're leaving. Now," Blacksmith ordered, and he spun and came toward me.

"No," I said hoarsely. "He'll come; he has to come—"

"We wait any longer and we're as good as dead. Half our decoys may have been discovered by now. Mount up!" He barked this last at Sword Holder, who swung up behind the dragonmaster.

I'd sent Gen back to his death.

"We can't leave." I started to dismount from the escoa.

Blacksmith gripped my ankle. "If he's alive, he'll join us. If he's been captured, there's no point—"

"Soldiers!" a hoarse voice shouted from the tunnel, and our eyes swung toward it. Gen staggered out. Dono was draped limply across his arms, naked save for a loincloth, dust, and blood.

"Take him, mount up, move, move!" Gen wheezed, and Blacksmith and Sword Holder were instantly at his side. Sword Holder took Dono; Gen leaned on Blacksmith and lurched toward me. "Soldiers following. Seven. Maybe more. The decoys ready?"

"Six escoas, each with a rider," Blacksmith said. "They'll take flight and head south and east the moment they see us airborne."

"Where's Granth?"

Blacksmith pointed to a figure bobbing in the distance.

"Dragon give him the sense to drop and keep still once we're airborne," Gen muttered. "He'll stand a chance of not being seen." He looked at me. "Lie as flat as you can, Babu."

Flying a dragon means lying half-prone along the dorsum, knees locked against scaled flank and leather saddle, feet lodged in the stirrup rungs situated either side of the dragon's spine. Gritting my teeth, I carefully assumed the flying position. Gen swung up, stretched atop me, mindful of my broken ribs, and reached with both hands for the reins either side of the escoa's neck. Sword Holder was already mounted, Dono lashed atop his escoa like a sack of grain. Blacksmith mounted behind the dragonmaster and took up reins.

We exploded into the air.

I watched the ground, looking for the man Gen had called Granth. Didn't see him. I didn't know who he was—where he called home, whom he loved, whether he had children—but found myself praying he'd see us winging westward and have the sense to fall to the ground. Surely, if he covered himself with dust and weeds, he'd be safe from the eyes of Temple. Surely.

I had to believe so.

Dragonflight is romanticized.

In reality it's noisy and exhausting. Cramping muscles locked too long in one position vie for attention with ears that ache from both the changes in elevation and the wind screaming past. One's throat becomes parched from the wind; one's tongue cleaves to the roof of one's mouth. Each breath feels hard-won and insufficient in the incessant wind. Eyeballs feel like desiccated peas. Nostrils burn with dryness. It requires unflagging concentration to stay seated upon a dragon, not to be caught unawares from a sudden list to one side and plummet through sky and clouds to death miles below.

How much more miserable, then, is dragonflight when one is bruised, battle-battered, bone-broken, and ill with hunger and exhaustion.

Our escape from Arena went on so long that by twilight I was beyond fear of pursuit. My fingers felt soft as aloe gel around the wooden hand rungs jutting fore of the saddle, either side of the escoa's neck. I knew I couldn't hold on much longer.

I feared for Dono. He hadn't stirred once from where he was lashed across the rump of Sword Holder's escoa, and the leather bindings holding him in place looked to have loosened, for he slewed back and forth like loose cargo in a storm-gripped trawler.

"We have to land!" I yelled into the wind. "Look at Dono."

No answer from Gen. At least, not one audible. I *felt* his body tense, though.

"Damn it, Gen, we can't let him fall!"

"A little farther and we'll reach Clutch Xxamer Zu."

"*How* much farther?"

His silence was answer enough: a lot farther.

"Dono won't last," I shouted into the wind. "*I* won't. We have to find somewhere to land for the night."

Below us, only mountainous jungle. I waited for a response from Gen; none was forthcoming. Piqued, I fumbled for the reins he held and yanked on them. Our escoa's head snapped left and she listed sharply. I shrieked, felt myself sliding from her back, and Gen bellowed in my ear. Only his weight atop me kept me in the saddle.

After several heart-thudding moments, we righted. Some moments after that he lifted an arm and signaled to the men flying aflank us. We changed our course.

Night fell, and a short while later we landed on the outskirts of a crude village, in a dark smudge of field located in the lee of a mountain ridge. At the far end of the field, a stand of dead trees pointed jagged limbs toward the stars. Beyond lay jungle.

"An unplanned stop," Blacksmith said sourly from atop his champing escoa. "What's this place?"

"A Hamlet of Forsaken." Gen dismounted. In the hamlet a dog barked, was joined by several others. "We'll be safe enough."

"Safe? You're dressed as an Auditor—"

"I know what I'm wearing."

A muscle twitched in Blacksmith's jaw. "You should disrobe."

"They'll have seen us land, me in particular in this moonlight. Better we not try to deceive them." Gen took hold the bridle of my escoa and pulled.

We were met halfway across the field by a clawful of men bearing pitchforks, brands, and drawn bows. Several held yapping dogs on lengths of twine. Our escoas came to a snorting stop. Gen lifted both hands to show they were empty.

"We need a short respite from our journey!" he boomed above the barking of the curs.

A Forsaken man stepped forward. All his joints were grossly swollen and he looked on the verge of malnourishment. As was the manner of all Forsaken, he wore a clay disk through his lower lip, signifying allegience to none but those within his hamlet. He glanced at me, dismissed me as a harmless rishi boy, then looked long at the dragonmaster, who lay muttering and twitching between the shoulder blades of Blacksmith's mount. He looked even longer at Dono, lashed crossways behind Sword Holder. He didn't try to hide the aversion on his face as his eyes returned to Gen.

Gen should've shucked his Auditor's disguise. As Forsaken, these folk would have vowed to live free of Temple influence.

But as the silence stretched taut, I thought again. They were a sinewy, scarred lot, barefoot and ragged, and had a desperate air to them; behind their ring of snarling dogs, they eyed us with a mixture of loathing and want. It was a *good* thing Gen was dressed in the robes, hood, and veil of one of Temple's dreaded henchmen; fear of reprisals from Temple would prevent us from being killed for our possessions.

I was relieved to be mistaken for one of Temple's servants, then immediately disgusted at Gen—and myself—for drawing the fear of Temple around us as a shield against these folk.

"We don't like visitors," the Forsaken man said at last.

"We won't stay long," Gen answered. His detatched tone belonged to someone who fully expected to be obeyed and wasn't concerned about what it cost to acquire such obedience from others.

The Forsaken man wasn't so readily cowed. "You've trampled our seedlings. There's a cost for that."

"You'll be reimbursed."

"Can't wear a scrap of paper on your feet. Can't defend yourself from outlaws or jungle cats with it, neither."

"You'll take what's offered." Gen stepped forward, and I didn't blame the Forsaken for despising us. But Dono needed attention. "We'll require clean water. Boiled and cooled, preferably."

Fire licked along brands. Dogs snarled and strained against coarse rope. The escoas shifted.

With a look of contempt, the Forsaken man acquiesced with a nod. He took his anger out on the nearest cur, kicking it in the ribs. It yelped and cowered.

The hamlet existed behind a palisade of hewn saplings meant primarily to keep out wildlife. The huts within were crude affairs; no light flickered beyond the skins and mats hung across their entrances. Other than the men and snarling dogs flanking us, we saw not a single inhabitant.

We were shown into a hut and given a brand for light. Sword Holder stood first watch, outside our door, with the escoas. Still twitching and muttering but moving without aid, the dragonmaster staggered to a corner and collapsed, limbs sprawled. Blacksmith laid Dono on the floor.

Dono's face was distorted by the gross swelling of his torn eyelid, and pus and blood coated the lashes as thickly as gruel. The purple skin over his swollen eye had split in several places where it was so taut. His throat looked worse. I could see white glistening beneath layers of black dried blood. His larynx? I didn't know. Didn't want to.

He was unconscious, waxen, and breathing shallowly.

"He won't last the night," Blacksmith said.

Gen handed the brand to him and crouched beside Dono. "I fear you're right."

"Do something," I said hoarsely. "Something . . . Djimbi."

Something magic.

Gen's hood and veil glanced at me. "There's no incantation in the world that can stave off death, Babu. Not that I won't try . . ." He held up a hand to forestall my protest. "I'll do what I can, with whatever these folk can spare. But they've more need of their herbs than Dono does."

"You don't know that."

"I've seen enough to know when a man's night draws near."

I was swaying on my feet. Gen nodded at the floor. "Best you sleep awhile. I'll wake you if anything changes."

My torso felt rigid as old bamboo, my guts lacerated by my fractured ribs. Lowering myself to the ground seemed impossible. Gen rose and helped me. I lay on my back and listened for Dono's breaths, but they were so faint, they were drowned by the snorts and rasps of the escoas outside, the dragonmaster's mutters, the crackle of the brand, the stertorous breathing of Gen and Blacksmith. The smoke from the brand was filling the tiny hut; I shut my eyes against the sting.

"Should douse it, what-hey," I heard Gen mutter. "Sparks'll turn this place into a pyre."

I meant to protest. I meant to say that Dono needed light, that we had to hold back the dark. But I was already asleep.

Dono died at dawn.

Gen woke me, held marshy water to my lips, and helped me to Dono's side. "He's going now, Babu. There's no more I can do."

"But you tried."

His white veil stared back at me. A wall.

"You *did* try," I said, angry now.

"You doubt me?"

I held Dono's hand as he breathed his last. It was still bigger than mine, that hand, even in death. Big, calloused, the bones straight and stout. We hadn't held hands since we were children, and then only to play spinning whip.

But whatever had given Dono life and strength had fled. My milk-brother was gone, his hand as cool as clay. I wanted to say something: a prayer, a stanza of song, something heartfelt and meaningful. Nothing came. Nothing.

I wondered if Dono had ever felt regret about sending me to Temple's gaol.

I let his hand slip from mine.

TWO

Home.

The word is powerful, entwined with emotion, layered with memory. Home is where we are formed. We hold it in our minds as an example of what we do—and don't—want for our children, our morrow, our kin. We want a hearth that is warmer, a shelter more welcome. Tweak that, change this. Keep a thing or three the same. The end result, by damn, will be the perfect sanctuary, a flawless home . . . and be forever just beyond reach.

Somehow, I'd convinced myself that I was flying home.

I'd never been to Clutch Xxamer Zu, save in the dreamworld of a vision I'd experienced upon my mother's death. Now, flying with Gen pressed atop me, the wings of the escoa glistening on either side of us like enormous sheets of burnt sugar, anticipation thrilled through me. I was heading *home*, to a dragon egg–production estate that I'd won through an illicit wager at Arena. A place where I'd be safe, and where I could make others safe. I'd tweak one thing, change another, and the end result would be . . .

Dawn stained the sky lavender and pale orange. Miles below us, a sea of jungle buckled and humped toward the horizon. Dawn turned to morn, morning to noon. The topography below altered; mountain changed into plains, jungle into undulating savanna. The warm scent of dust and seedheads was detectable in the wind, even as high as we were. The sun blazed; the air was mercilessly hot and dry. I was insanely thirsty. My body screamed with ache.

Then, ahead of us: a brown smudge, embroidered on one side by the reflection of a river.

"That's it!" Gen boomed in my ear, triumphant despite his fatigue.

Xxamer Zu. *My* Clutch. Home.

I had navel kin there, aunts, uncles, nieces, and nephews on my mother's side. Would they recognize my mother in my scarred, lean body? In my hacked-short hair? In my skin color, which bore not a pigment nor whorl of my mother's Djimbi green?

"Ghepp'll have arrived yesternoon," Gen shouted. "He'll be finalizing the takeover from the former overseer."

Ghepp: the man I'd chosen to govern in my stead, because Temple forbade any but a recognized lord or warrior to command a Clutch. As the son of a renowned Roshu-Lupini, Ghepp met Temple's criteria.

"Fine wine and succulent meats!" Gen roared against my ear. He was heady with our success. "Silk robes and ripe fruits! All yours, Babu!"

And there'd be destriers in my Clutch stables, venomous dragons trained for warfare. So there'd be venom.

Again a thrill coursed through me, this one followed by self-loathing. I'd given up venom, had vowed to be enslaved by its potent charms no more. Curse me for even thinking of the dragon's liquid fire.

The Clutch on the horizon grew larger, faster.

The center of the Clutch was apparent. Jutting up from the grassland knolls were the mansions of the elite—aristocrats who are known, in the Emperor's tongue, as bayen, First-Class Citizens. The mansions were clustered around a temple, the central dome of which loomed from the savanna like an enormous egg in a grass nest. As we drew closer, I could make out the gold-plated minaret protruding from the dome's apex and stabbing lancelike into the belly of the sky.

A patchwork of crop fields surrounded the Clutch, and beyond them, a huge sheet of white.

"Salt pans!" Gen boomed, as if following my gaze. "The Clutch's source of revenue. Ready yourself for landing, now!"

We were there. My new life was about to begin.

Under Gen's guidance, our escoa banked over rooftops, circled wide around the temple dome, and descended into the large courtyard of the messenger byre, which was clearly identifiable from the skies by its checkered red and black roof tiles. In Malacar, only places that can accomodate a dragon bear such tiles.

Blacksmith and Sword Holder landed on either side of us. We'd left Dono's body with the Forsaken and promised them payment for nailing him to one of the trees in their sepulchral grove. I hoped that whoever shot and ate the jackals that would consume Dono's corpse would say the ritual honor-thanks as they cooked the jackals' ribs for dinner.

Every stall in Xxamer Zu's messenger byre was filled with escoas. Some with two.

Good, I thought wearily as Gen slid off my back and dismounted. I own an impressive amount of escoas.

"Give me your hand, Babu." Gen's white veil looked up at me. "I'll help you down."

Think of roasted meat and cold fruit, I told myself, bracing for the dismount. My fractured ribs felt like a hot vise across my torso. Think of clean water and sleep.

I didn't so much as dismount as slide, grunting, into Gen's outstretched arms. A young herald apprentice appeared from the stablehands' cottage at the far end of the byre's long courtyard. He jogged over to us and took our escoa's bridle. Blacksmith dismounted and offered a hand to the dragonmaster. The dragonmaster swatted it away.

"I've ridden more dragons than all the women you've ever ridden, or are likely to," he snapped.

Blacksmith turned his back on the dragonmaster and tossed his reins to the herald apprentice. "Take good care of her, boy. She's flown hard and far."

The boy swallowed, shot a look at Gen, and scrambled for the reins of Sword Holder's mount.

"Did we disturb your noon sleep?" Sword Holder asked the boy, swinging to the ground. "What, are all your fellows abed in this heat, and you left to work alone?"

The apprentice ducked his head and tugged hard on the reins of our three dragons, leading them quickly to the ground floor of the shadowed feed loft that formed one side of the court.

Gen slipped an arm carefully across my back and under my armpits. "Lean on me, if you have to—"

Blacksmith slammed into us. Gen staggered sideways; I fell to the ground with a scream of pain.

Sword Holder cried, "Down, down!" Then his head lurched forward onto his chest with such violence, he was thrown to his knees. Steel glinted from the back of his neck. A war quoit.

Gen and the dragonmaster dove to the ground as an Auditor materialized from a corner of the courtyard, then a second from another corner, then a clawful of them from everywhere. We were surrounded.

"Stay down!" Gen shouted at me, even as he snatched Sword Holder's blade from its scabbard. He rose to his knees as the Auditors drifted toward us. With an unholy Djimbi cry, Gen launched the blade spearlike toward an Auditor. The steel flew with preternatural speed and sank into the Auditor's belly, where it exploded into a shower of blue-white shards. The shards formed a howling vortex.

I belly-crawled through the dust to Blacksmith and yanked at the quoit embedded in his neck. It came out with a gristly rasp. Gen bellowed at me to stay down, and the hair on my nape rose, because I knew a throwing ring was flying at me. I dropped onto my side—the *pain*—and threw my own quoit with all the force and precision my training as an apprentice had ingrained in me. An Auditor's razor-ring spun over my left arm; my own sliced through his veil and sank into his gullet. I didn't wait to see if it felled him; four more Auditors were coming at me, fast, while the unnatural cyclone Gen had spawned ricocheted off a wall and exploded into two more Auditors. The cyclone stopped, became a sheet of white flame: shrieks, the smell of roasting flesh and burned hair. I scrambled for a fallen quoit, spun it around a forefinger, and released it at another Auditor. Missed.

The dragonmaster had Blacksmith's sword in his hand and was running, bellowing insanely, toward an Auditor . . .

How many Auditors *were* there? A whole Host?

We wouldn't make it. The realization was cool and clear. Four Auditors had us surrounded, quoits spinning around their forefingers.

One Auditor jerked once, twice, thrice, hands spasming, quoit spinning off uselessly to one side. The three Auditors beside him likewise convulsed; black tips stabbed through their robes in various places. Their hands dropped as they staggered forward one step, two. A quoit bit into the ground near my foot, sending a clod of dirt against my thigh. A second quoit fell near my knee.

The Auditors fell like cornstalks beneath a scythe. Quarrels protruded from their backs.

I looked up; there, at the far end of the courtyard, near the stablehands' cottage, stood a clawful of men, several bearing bows. Other than them, Gen, the dragonmaster, and I were the only ones left alive in the courtyard. The dragonmaster hacked and hewed at an Auditor's fallen body.

"Dragon and the Snake!" a voice cried, and a bayen man strode toward us from the shadows, elegantly dressed in slit pantaloons the color of ripe dates, his emerald shirt billowing about him as he gestured at the slain Auditors. "Damn you, Gen, damn you a thousandfold! You were supposed to arrive before dusk last night."

It was Rutgar Re Ghepp, the man who'd agreed to deceive Temple insofar as acting as the overseer of my Clutch.

"I've been cut." Gen gasped from where he was rising to his feet. Red was flowering across the white of his left sleeve. "Zarq?"

"I'm unhurt. I think. Yes."

Gen tugged off his veil, breathing heavily, and clamped one hand across a bicep. His black beard, cleaved down the middle and as tangled and unruly as the tufts of hair on his head, glistened.

Not with blood, I thought. Not Gen. Not here. Not in my Clutch.

Rutgar Re Ghepp—now Lupini Xxamer Zu—stood before us, his canted eyes blazing, his high cheeks flushed.

"They arrived late this morning." He sounded defensive. Petulant, almost.

"Could've warned us," Gen said through gritted teeth.

"They locked down the stable."

"Are there more of them?"

Ghepp ran a hand through his black hair and looked about the courtyard. His full lips moved slightly as he counted. "This is it."

"What about in the destrier stables?"

Ghepp snorted. "Empty. This Clutch doesn't own a single damn destrier. Not a one. You're looking at Xxamer Zu's only winged dragons, and most of these were flown in by the Auditors you just killed."

If Gen took note of the *you*, he didn't show it.

The dragonmaster staggered up to us, trailing his bloody sword through the dust. He had foam around his mouth. His ugly chest wound was bleeding profusely.

"What's this, hey? What the *shit* is this?" he shrieked.

"I could ask the same of you." Ghepp stabbed a finger at Gen. "You said you'd make a clean escape. You said Xxamer Zu wouldn't be linked to *her*." His finger stabbed my way.

"Xxamer Zu hasn't been linked to Zarq," Gen growled. "Think, man! Temple sends a Host to every Clutch that undergoes a change of governship after Arena, to supervise—"

"Then why the stable lockdown? Why the ambush?"

Gen's cinder black brows furrowed. "Was it a lockdown? Did you try to send a dragonflier to alert us?"

Ghepp's fine nostrils flared. "I wasn't so stupid."

"Titbrained fool," the dragonmaster snapped. "Your fears turned you witless, and now we've got a dead Host on our hands!"

"Enough." Gen swayed, braced himself. "You know for sure this was an ambush?"

"Look about you!" Ghepp cried.

Gen didn't. "Why was the Host here in the byre with you?"

"We were to tour the outskirts of the Clutch and verify the boundaries—"

"So. No ambush. Just in the wrong place at the wrong time, and they recognized Zarq for who she is and acted." Gen gestured with his jaw at the bowmen watching us from the shadows. "Those yours?"

Ghepp nodded grimly. "From Clutch Re."

"Got eight of 'em?"

Ghepp swore.

"Get those Auditors' robes washed and dried as fast as you can and pick eight of your men to wear 'em. Put the fear of death in that apprentice cowering in the feed barn so he keeps his mouth shut about what he's witnessed, and get me somewhere I can sew myself up, before I bleed out. Scout out the rest of the byre, make sure no one else saw or heard a thing."

"And *her?*" Ghepp's eyes blamed me for the Auditors' deaths and the trouble it would cause him. "You know how *small* this Clutch is, how primitive? There's no bastion here; I've nowhere to hide her. Bring her into the bayen quarter and she'll be recognized by someone who attended Arena. Like *that*." He snapped his fingers, hard.

"Anyone who's at Arena is still whoring and gambling—"

"No," Ghepp said, and there was iron in his voice. "Look at her. She won't pass as a bayen woman or boy. Nor him. Hide them amongst the rishi."

It was Gen's turn to swear. Then he blanched, swayed, and closed his eyes. The magics he'd employed had sapped him of all strength.

"Catch him!" I cried.

Ghepp and the dragonmaster both caught the swooning giant—barely. They staggered under his weight, then, after a curt exchange, laid him down. The dragonmaster fell to his knees, breathing heavily. Ghepp stormed over to his men.

Gen stirred. "Arbiyesku."

"What?" I leaned closer.

"Go to the arbiyesku."

My heart sank. The dragonmaster started to protest, but Gen cracked open an eye and shot him a look. "No one'll look for you there. Understand?" Gen paused. "I'll send word."

I understood, and I knew that, after a moment, the dragonmaster did, too: Gen didn't believe a word he'd said to allay Ghepp's fears. He suspected that, somehow, Temple had linked me to the wager that had won Ghepp Xxamer Zu. He feared the Host had been sent to ambush us.

Perhaps one of our decoys, or the man we'd left behind—Granth—had been caught and interrogated. Perhaps the merchant tycoon who'd backed my wager had turned on us. Perhaps that hunched, knuckle-spined creature in the labyrinth had been human, had recognized me for who I was and overheard me talk of Xxamer Zu. . . .

I could make a thousand speculations. Didn't matter. The facts remained: After drawing weapons against me, a Temple Host lay dead in the messenger byre of my Clutch, and the panicked Clutch overseer was insisting that I hide amongst the laborers of Xxamer Zu.

Roasted meats, succulent fruits, clean water, and sleep were not to be mine. Not yet.

As for any sense of security and home . . .

Within moments of the attack, the courtyard looked as it had done upon our arrival. The unnatural white fire spawned by Gen's Djimbi magics had completely consumed the three Auditors it had made contact with; no bones, no ashes, no smoke to be seen. The only indication that something had recently burned was the lingering stench of charred hair and meat. The other corpses lay concealed beneath bedding chaff in the feed loft, and would be disposed of under cover of deep night.

We won't get away with this. Even at high noon, with the bayen quarter asleep in the heat, people will have heard the shrieks.

In our favor was the terror that Auditors inspired in all folk, bayen and rishi alike. Everyone knew that where Auditors walked, interrogations and screams followed. Even Temple's daronpuis were uneasy around the sacred henchmen veiled in white. So perhaps questions wouldn't be asked. Perhaps fear would keep mouths shut, would put a clamp over curiosity. After all, Malacarites are good at not seeing and hearing the visible and audible. When it suits them.

The dragonmaster lay upon a bale of hay, the gaping wound on his chest bleeding sluggishly. I was aching so badly that I no longer denied to myself that I craved venom. Ghepp had promised to send a healer; one had yet to appear.

I didn't like that I'd been left with no weapon with which to defend myself. Especially as I didn't wholly trust Ghepp. No. The way he'd looked at me . . .

Not just his look. The facts didn't add up. If he and the Auditors had been about to mount up to verify the Clutch boundaries, why had some of Ghepp's men carried bows and arrows? Strange choice of weapon, when soldiers were usually armed with swords. Unless a long-distance defense was required. As was the case against quoits.

And what about those quoits?

Auditors were forbidden to carry ordinary arms, save for the decapitation axes used when performing a holy execution before a Temple tribunal. The only weapon Auditors were permitted to carry—and use in self-defense—were *furgkri*, spinning razor-rings. Quoits.

The Auditors wanted to make their attack look like self-defense.

Had Ghepp known about the ambush, or had it been coincidence that they'd all been in the byre courtyard upon our arrival? What about Ghepp's men . . . had the Auditors known that some of them were armed with bows, or had the bowmen appeared in the byre without the Auditors' knowledge?

Again, I could speculate a thousand possibilities. I doubted I'd ever know the answers. The end result remained the same, regardless: Even here, on my own Clutch, I wasn't safe.

Well after high noon, an Auditor—one of Ghepp's disguised men—brought us a flagon of watered wine, a handful of plums, and a Djimbi woman. The woman wore the blank expression of someone on the brink of terror, and she carried a reed basket upon one hip. I was nonplussed by what she was wearing; it looked to be no more than a bolt of cloth, plum-colored and patterned with black fish bones, that had been artfully wrapped about her from bosom to thigh. Never would such exposure be publicly tolerated on Clutch Re. I wondered if her mode of dress marked her as a whore.

The Auditor gestured toward the dragonmaster, and the woman went to him, set her basket on the floor, and began tending to his wound with visibly trembling hands. He flailed; she murmured to him in Djimbi; he settled and permitted her to continue.

The Auditor withdrew bundled brown cloth from one of his long sleeves and dropped it at my feet. "From the cloven one."

He meant Gen.

Moving stiffly from pain, I picked up the bundle. It was a bitoo, one of those ankle-length hooded gowns deemed appropriate wear for a Malacarite woman. The style—brown, no tucks or pleats, made of serviceable byssus—was popular amongst rishi.

The bitoo had been wrapped about a tunic, which was in turn wrapped about a dowry-sword. In the manner of all dowry-swords, the object was two sticks tied together with red twine to form the quillion and blade of a toy sword. It had been covered with an assortment of hole-punched coins, Temple chits, and copper drippings, all linked together by red twine. It wasn't a long dowry-sword, nor did it bear any silver or gold, but it was impressive enough. It would adequately purchase me and the dragonmaster inclusion in the arbiyesku.

The Auditor crouched before me. I disliked his nearness, his veil, his studied calm.

"What?" I snapped.

He took his time handing me a small roll of parchment. The instructions on it were terse:

> *The dragonmaster is a batagin komikon who's lost his caravan and status in an inopportune Arena wager. You're his roidan yin. Give your Arena cape to the bearer of this note. I'll summon you when I feel it's safe to do so, and provide a token so you'll know the summons is mine.*
>
> *Gen*

So the dragonmaster was to play the part of a caravan owner, and I, his claimed woman. The wound on his chest would readily be accepted, for it was not uncommon for a caravan master to be hurt by one of his surly, overworked dragons.

I shredded the parchment into tiny strips. "Burn them," I said. "And turn your back. I need to change."

For a moment I thought the man dressed as an Auditor might refuse. I wondered if he knew who I was, or could ever guess. Maybe he did know, and simply wasn't unsettled by the knowledge. He took the strips from my hand, stood, and turned.

In the shadows of the feed loft's ground floor, the Djimbi woman bound the dragonmaster's chest wound and helped him into the tunic

Ghepp had provided, while I labored to shuck the cape and modified tunic I'd worn into Arena. My fractured ribs and battle-stiff limbs made the task a nasty challenge.

When I was done, the dragonmaster and I were escorted from the messenger byre. I carried the dowry-sword concealed under my bitoo, and wore my cowl up—*not* for protection against the sun. The byre was located in the daronpuis' quarters, a stockade of blinding white stone buildings, each enclosing a courtyard that was linked to the next by a short viaduct. We passed several opulently gowned holy wardens en route, but with the Auditor at our side, and the dragonmaster and I moving in the stilted lurch of those recently injured, eyes slid over us as if we were invisible. No one wants to look upon the victims of Temple's interrogators. Why admit that Temple practiced torture?

Guarded gates swung open for us; we exited into a dusty market square dwarfed by the Clutch temple. The cobblestones of the market square shimmered in the midday heat. Djimbi rishi bearing bales upon their green-mottled backs crossed the square, moving slowly in the heat. Instead of bitoos, the women all wore strange garments of plum-colored cloth, ragged and worn, wrapped from bosom to thigh. They carried their babes not in cowls upon their shoulders—for they wore no cowls—but strapped their offspring lengthwise across their chests or backs in a sling. I was amazed by how much of their bodies the women exposed: shoulders, arms, legs, all completely bare.

"Walk south," the would-be Auditor beside me said. "Ask directions if you need them."

"We'll need water," I said. Beside me, the dragonmaster stared blankly at the caravansaries and tenements at the far end of the market square. We needed sleep as well as water, and not a long walk to an unknown reception by a strange clan.

The Auditor shrugged. "The Clutch is small; won't take you long to get there."

It took all day.

By dusk, the dragonmaster and I reached our destination. We'd been forced by heat, thirst, and exhaustion to rest in the meager shade of several abandoned huts throughout the afternoon, and though the distance we'd traveled had not been great—the central dome of the temple shimmered behind our backs, still visible across the grassy miles—the journey had seemed interminable.

As we staggered into the arbiyesku, seated men rose from the dusty ground. Women stopped scrubbing pots and plaiting grass fibers and nursing babes. Children ran to their mothers.

I gagged at the sweetish reek of the decaying dragon cocoons stockpiled in the arbiyesku brick warehouse to our left, hastily drew a corner of my bitoo cowl across my nose. Pain knifed across my torso and I gasped and froze. Broken ribs dislike sudden movement.

The dragonmaster scowled as the arbiyesku gathered about us. Like all the other serfs I'd glimpsed thus far in Xxamer Zu, the clan members of the arbiyesku were barefoot and ribby. Most of them had the pitted teeth, canker sores, and black-stained lips and tongues of the rishi we'd passed en route through Clutch Xxamer Zu. The dragonmaster had muttered something about slii fruitstones, sucked to dull hunger.

I was hard put not to gape at the women's mode of dress, too, nor at the variation amongst the color of their skin, for I'd never before come across so many folk in whose veins ran Djimbi blood. Under the crimson-streaked sky, some folk gleamed like polished mahogany, the weird whorls upon their skin the color of patina on old bronze. Others had an umber pigmentation mottled here and there by dull olive. Still others were chestnut, their piebald markings a cinereous green. Not a single rishi had skin the color of mine, that tan that's referred to as fawn when describing bayen, but is called aosogi, poorly cured hide, when describing a rishi.

Nor did any before me possess the pure ivory tones of the Emperor.

A Djimbi woman with a magnificent bosom and a hideous scar that ran along her left jawline stepped out of the crowd. Her skin was the color of wet cinnamon mottled with sage whorls, lighter toned than some of those around her, darker than others.

"I am Tansan," she said. Her voice was bold, the directness of her gaze challenging. She was taller than me by at least a foot. "I'm waiting for bull wings to bless the herd of Xxamer Zu."

I looked from her to the dragonmaster, from the dragonmaster to her. But as if it were normal for a woman to extend the ritual greeting to a stranger while in the presence of men, and as if the name she'd used to describe herself were a typical Malacarite one, the dragonmaster did little more than scowl more deeply.

"May your waiting end," he snapped. "May bull wings hatch." He gestured brusquely at me to produce the dowry-sword, and as I withdrew it from a sleeve, he tersely introduced himself and said we wanted to join their clan.

Eyes locked upon the significant value of the dowry-sword. Children gaped at us. The old folk champed their toothless gums, eyes bright, and exchanged mutters. A Djimbi man carefully took the dowry-sword from my hands to examine it and was at once surrounded.

But the tall, lush-limbed woman before me—Tansan, she'd called herself—wore a wary look. "Why us? Why here? Who are you, that you carry such a dowry and appear at nightfall, aosogi-via?"

Her distrust and acuity irked. Her confidence and closeness irked even more. She was directing the question at me, too, and not the dragonmaster, which was unusual and an annoyance.

I tried to play the part of a demure claimed woman and looked to the dragonmaster for him to answer her.

"You'll either take us or you won't," he snapped. "There's more coin on that sword than you'll have seen in a long time; we can always join a more reasonable clan."

Tansan's gaze flicked to him, then fell back on me. Her eyes were opaque. "Why us, aosogi-via?" she repeated quietly.

I fought to keep irritation from my face, not to stare her down. Not to visibly withdraw deeper into the shadows of my cowl. "I'll be honest, yes?" I murmured. "My claimer has run afoul of some First-Class lordlings over the years, in Lireh; no one will look for us in this Clutch, in this clan. No one."

Lireh was the harbor city of our coastal capital, Liru. It was as far from Xxamer Zu as any place in Malacar could be, both literally and figuratively.

"But why *this* Clutch and why *this* clan, aosogi-via?" Tansan repeated softly.

I felt my nostrils flare and I stifled the urge to clench my hands into fists. "Xxamer Zu is nothing but salt pans and drought," I murmured. "All Malacarites know of it, and none with any choice would seek a life here; *that's* why we chose this Clutch. And this clan? Because you're far from bayen eyes. Nothing more. But there'll be other clans on this Clutch's outskirts; I think we'll join one of those instead, yes?"

I held out my hand for the dowry-sword, and the man who was holding it looked alarmed. There was a brief flurry of Djimbi dialogue amongst them; the dragonmaster interjected several times, as their tongue was his own. Tansan's face closed like an orchid in a deluge.

"You will stay," an elderly man said, taking the dowry-sword and clasping it against his forehead. "Your womb will be ours; our seed will be yours. You are arbiyesku now."

At once the women of the arbiyesku pressed about me, the heat of their dusky skin tangible through my bitoo. Tansan still stood directly before me, immovable, so close that her proud, outthrust breasts brushed against my chest. I don't like people standing that close, uninvited.

I studied her from within the haven of my cowl as the arbiyesku women murmured kinship greetings and pressed their palms to my womb in ritual welcome. Tansan looked a little over my age—twenty or so. Calm, thoughtful, and confident, she studied me with eyes fringed heavily with black lashes. Her lips were full and stained black like her kin's, but free of the canker several others suffered. Her broad shoulders were very straight but rounded softly at the ends.

Suddenly she reached up to my cowl and pulled it back. "Let's see you, hey-o."

Murmurs and clucks as I was revealed.

I would have snapped my cowl back over my head if not limited in movement and speed by the pain of my fractured ribs. Instead, I contented myself by openly glaring at Tansan. She ignored my hostility and continued to study me. I felt like a yearling being examined for purchase.

My neck bore a thick scar that ran from the left side of my cheek down to my collarbone, given me by a dragon's tongue while in Dragonmaster Re's stables. For the sake of unobstructed vision in Arena combat, I'd chopped my black hair short, as a young boy does. My eyes were heavily bloodshot, and the black of my pupils was marbled with white from past abuse of dragon venom. There wasn't a square inch of my skin that wasn't covered by bruises, welts, or oozing scrapes—wounds I'd received in Arena.

The warmth of Tansan's chest, so close to mine, invaded my breasts and surged to my throat. The dragonmaster followed a group of men to one of the arbiyesku huts to exchange ritual greetings in the privacy of a men's domicile.

"You've had a debu life," Tansan pronounced. Those about her accepted the observation with calm nods.

Debu. A derogatory Djimbi word for *cursed*. I'd heard my mother use it, in my youth.

I wanted to slap the certainty from Tansan's face. Who was she—indecently dressed, in clothes so worn they were all but threadbare—to pronounce my life cursed? How dared she—surrounded by kin and kith, safe from the insanity of Arena on this far-flung, impoverished Clutch—declare my life damned?

She turned on her heel, arms balanced at her sides, not a tense line in her body, and walked away. Someone touched my wrist: an old woman carrying a baby in a sling. The whorls on the old woman's loam-brown skin were the color of damp hay, her eyes the color of snails. Her lips and tongue were black from slii stone.

"Come, yes, we'll give you food, water."

The women surrounding me showed the good grace not to remark upon my shambling gait. Ahead of us, Tansan walked erect and loose-hipped toward the wooden stairs of a long bamboo-beam-and-woven-jute structure on stilts: the women's barracks. She walked with the same sultry fluidity as my sister, Waivia.

Tansan seated herself upon the stairs of the barracks, and the old woman with eyes the color of snails left my side to hand Tansan the babe in the sling.

"Sit here, sit," another woman murmured to me. "Join us for evening meal. You are hungry and thirsty, yes?"

I stiffly lowered myself to the ground, failing utterly to hide the pain I suffered in the process. Several women crouched on their haunches around me, staring, their children clustered beside them.

The old woman with eyes the color of snails returned to my side and crouched before me. She thumped her bony chest; the sound was the same as if she'd struck an unripe gourd. "I'm Fwipi. You?"

"I am the hatagin komikon's wai roidan yin," I murmured.

"No, not good, that. A name, a name."

"That's my name."

"Gaaa! That's just a title. You have no name?"

"Kazonvia." Not exactly a lie, as I *was* the second girl to leave my mother's womb.

Fwipi grimaced. "Your name is Secondgirl? Empty name, that. Emperor's ways. You like his ways?"

How annoying, her question. How irritating, the growing crowd as the men who'd accompanied the dragonmaster into a mud-brick hut now joined the women sitting about me. I needed to lie down, couldn't think clearly.

"The Emperor's a despot," I snapped. "He's not worth my piss."

Fwipi sucked in a breath. Several of those about her exchanged looks.

"People who say such things lose fingers, lose tongues," Fwipi chided. "Endangers the lives of us all, such perfidy. Better to hold such thoughts close, hey-o."

Several elders in the clan murmured agreement, and no more was said to me until two women carrying a plank piled with kadoob tubers raked fresh from embers weaved amongst us, offering food.

Instead of taking their place around the outskirts of seated men, the women and children of the arbiyesku sat side by side with them. Instead of waiting until the men had eaten their fill before touching the food, the women and children ate at the same time as they did. Irregular behavior. But I approved. I loathed the custom of women and children eating last.

Not that I ate. A stone-size kadoob tuber, charred and wizened, sat unheeded upon my lap while I stared, exhausted and aching, at nothing in particular. Beside me, Fwipi exchanged a few words with an old man. They spoke in Djimbi.

Fwipi addressed me again, her pitted teeth flashing like speckled black beetles. "You watch only tomorrow. You've traveled far, hey-o, you're tired. Watch only."

The old man beside her nodded and beamed agreement, revealing gums as toothless as a newborn's.

Fwipi placed a dry hand on my arm. Her eyes traveled to the dragonmaster, who was just joining us. "Don't fear him now. You do as your clan sees fit. We'll protect you, yes?"

She thought I'd been beaten by my claimer. I gritted my teeth and forced myself to act the grateful, submissive woman. "Thank you," I murmured, eyes downcast.

The old man stirred. He was holding something toward me, dry, contorted, the color of bone. Maska root. He said something in Djimbi, and though I didn't understand him, the meaning conveyed was plenty clear: *Eat.*

"Thank you," I repeated again, this time with sincere gratitude in my voice, and I took the precious root, swiftly peeled it with my teeth, and began chewing. It tasted like bile.

As those around me ate, children with potbellies and twiggy limbs slowly summoned the courage to draw nearer me. They gathered in a semicircle, openly curious. One of the children cleared her throat, a sloe-eyed girl about six years old, skin the color of a honey-drizzled cake and mottled with small, very faint green whorls.

"What was your clan before this one?" she demanded.

"I belonged to the hatagin komikon, not a clan." I was aware that everyone was listening to my reply.

"Is your claimer mad?"

I bit back a heated affirmative and replied with as much timidity as I could contrive: "He sometimes looks mad, sometimes acts mad. Perhaps he is mad?"

"What's wrong with your eyes?"

"I was ill as a child. The illness marked them."

"Did the illness change your skin that color, too?"

How unusual, to be singled out because of my color. It was not a situation I was used to. I replied slowly. "Where I come from, most rishi look like me. Aosogi, some call this, though bayen with the same pigment like to lighten their skin and make it more fa-pim by calling it fawn."

"Fa-pim, gah! Who wants to be like the Emperor? Bayen are yolk-brained."

Fwipi clucked her disapproval but the girl ignored her, then crouched down beside me. She studied me a moment, frowned, then pointed at the worn garment she was wearing.

"This is a yungshmi." She spoke with exaggerated care, as if I were from the north and spoke Xxelteker. "Yungshmi, yungshmi. You shouldn't hide in that ugly sack, no, no."

"I prefer my bitoo," I replied, lips slightly numb from the root I chewed, the pain in my ribs turning sludgy and dull.

She shook her head as if I were simple.

"Yungshmi," she slowly enunciated. "I'll help you change into a yungshmi."

She leaned forward and shyly touched my hand. Her teeth were not yet chipped and pitted from sucking slii, though her lips bore the telltale black stains. "You don't want to look like an Emperor's woman, hey-hey."

She got to her feet, thrust out her potbelly, and strutted about, feet splayed.

"I Emperor!" she boomed in imitation of the Archipelagic warlord. "I big fat Emperor! I hide my women in sacks, like eels in baskets."

The children around her giggled. She turned, waggled a finger at me, and, crossing her eyes, announced, "To my eyes, you look good in eel sack. Good, good! Tasty eel!"

"Enough, Savga," Fwipi said sharply. "Tansan, you tell this greatchild of mine to guard her tongue. A reckless mouth breaks bones."

Murmurs of agreement from the elders of the clan. I looked to where Tansan sat on the barracks stairs, nursing her babe. Three young men were crouched about her feet.

She lifted her chin. "Let her speak the truth, hey."

Anger spurted through me. I couldn't help it. Tansan was my age, had a healthy babe pulling at her breast, *and* was the mother of the precocious six-year-old beside me; she had a prudent mother, a clan, and not one admirer but three, and there she sat, above and separate from the rest of us, slighting the possibility of danger that might come because of her daughter's words. Tansan had things I had lost or never had, and might never have, and that, along with the memory of her condemnation of my life, stung.

Too late, my emotions went straight to my tongue. "You would let your girl speak and risk her being punished for it?"

Tansan looked at me with an expression of maddening amusement. "I think it was you who were comparing the Emperor to your piss just now."

"I'm an adult; I know the consequences of what I say if I'm overheard. Children are vulnerable—" My throat was suddenly thick. I continued hoarsely. "A good mother gives her child guidance, protects her."

Tansan's dark eyes flashed. "You think her tongue isn't at risk of being split with a holy warden's ax when *you* speak ill of the Emperor? I don't know where you come from, Secondgirl, but here, any within earshot of perfidy share the slanderer's punishment."

An uncomfortable silence settled over my new clan. Tansan and I were staring each other down . . . but I was having difficulty not being distracted by the wet sounds of the babe suckling at her breast.

A small hand tentatively touched my shoulder, and I allowed my attention to turn from Tansan to Savga.

"You're angry at me?" the young girl asked, sloe eyes dark beneath a furrowed brow.

"No." And then, fully aware of the effect my actions would have on Tansan, I gripped Savga's little hands in my own. "How can I be angry at you? You are bright and amusing and pretty, everything a friend might wish for."

Savga's eyes widened. "Really? We're friends?"

I could *feel* Tansan stiffening where she sat upon the stairs.

Looking only at Savga, I solemnly nodded and said, "I hereby promise that I, Kazonvia, will be a most impressive foremost friend to Savga of the arbiyesku Xxamer Zu."

Savga beamed, then withdrew her hands from mine and clasped them together in delight. Looking a little smug, she territorially patted my head for all the other children to see. "Friends," she said. "Me and Kazonvia are foremost friends."

From the corner of my eye, I saw Tansan fluidly rise to her feet and disappear within the barracks.

THREE

Something woke me, and I knew not where I was.

My surroundings were plunged in the smoky gray of predawn. A thatch roof was above my head, and the silhouette of a woman was crouched beside me, a white scar gaping across her mottled jawline in a parody of a grin.

I cried out and jerked away. Pain cut across my ribs. With the pain, memory flooded back, and I recognized the figure before me. She was the scarred Djimbi woman who'd declared my life debu, cursed. Tansan. She was squatted beside me, studying me as if I were a snake she was undecided whether to milk for poison, decapitate, or dismiss as useless.

In the murk of dawn, her eyes seemed to suck in all shadow, so that they were black as venom. The fine, rounded bones on either side of the hollow of her throat flared into the smooth straightness of her collarbone, supporting shoulders, biceps, and arms that seemed shaped not by a rough life of communal agriculture and poverty, but by some sculptor who worked with stone as warm and dark as teak to create only beauty and magnificence.

Her eyes glinted as mine locked on hers. "Leave my daughter alone, debu Secondgirl. Understand?"

The hoarseness of my dry throat helped me match her even tone. "She strikes me as one who makes her own decisions."

Tansan rose to her feet. The easy stance of her curvaceous hips, the strength that resided in perfect balance in her generous proportions as she looked down on me, lent her immeasurable unconscious grace. It was also clear she had iron at her core, and the timbre of her voice as she spoke sent a tremor through me.

"It was my milk that gave Savga life. Nothing you say or do can change that. Where's *your* children?"

She turned and walked away, as supple and relaxed as if I weren't watching, and left through the crooked woven-jute door. I wanted to leap after her and stand with legs braced and eyes blazing and inform her that I *owned* this Clutch, by damn. I was not a debu secondgirl; I was Zarq-the-deviant, the infamous rishi via who had openly defied Temple.

Broken ribs, a body as stiff as a day-old corpse, and the need for absolute anonymity kept me immobile on my back.

As I lay there, seething, women began stirring about me. They rolled up their mats, diapered babies, woke children, braided hair. Gritting my teeth, I tried to sit. Impossible. I felt the blood drain from my cheeks as pain from my fractured ribs torqued about my torso. I closed my eyes and lay there for what seemed like only a short time, gathering the will to attempt rising again, but I must have drifted into sleep, for when I next opened my eyes, the gray of predawn had been displaced by full light, and a child was sweeping the barracks floor beside me, frowning at me for my sloth.

Whisk, whisk! her broom went, flicking at my feet like the tail of an angry boar.

Biting the inside of my cheek, I forced myself to roll over. Struggled onto my knees. From my knees onto my feet. Stood there swaying a moment, wishing for milky maska wine to dull my aches, or even more of the foul root I'd chewed the night previous.

Or, ideally, dragon venom.

A cool hand touched mine, and I looked down into the canted gaze of Savga, Tansan's daughter.

"Foremost friend, you can lean on me to walk. Here, like this, yes?" She draped my arm around her slim neck and smiled up at me, uncertain, eager.

I regretted my rash impulse the night before. It had been wrong to promise her my friendship, wrong to use a child's trust to irk her parent.

"I don't need your help, Savga. Many thanks."

Hurt crossed her face, replaced by stubborness. "I'm strong enough. Come on, you've missed breaking fast with us already. Fwipi-granna says you should watch us work; she sent me to fetch you; now come *on*."

She tugged; the movement hurt, and I could have swatted her for it. Instead I clenched my jaw and minced across the barracks floor, using her small body as a crutch. Descending the rickety wooden stairs to greet the early morn outside bathed me in sweat and left me breathless.

Having eaten and performed whatever ablutions my new clan deemed necessary after rising, the arbiyesku was gathering for the day ahead. The women with young infants were unraveling a portion of their yungshmis from their waists, draping them slinglike across their breasts and settling their babes within. The slii fruitstones everyone sucked clitter-clacked against molars. Fwipi had Tansan's infant strapped in a sling upon her back, and she greeted me with a pursed expression that I took for a smile. No one else so much as glanced at me. I hoped it was because they were too focused on their day ahead, and not because I'd alienated them with my impetuous rebuke to Tansan the night before.

As a group, we approached the dragon cocoon warehouse, me embedded in the middle of a group of children, Savga still acting as my crutch. The dragonmaster was amongst us, looking as surly as a gharial with an abscessed tooth. The front of his tunic was plastered to the wound on his chest and he walked slowly, unevenly.

The smell of the warehouse was thick and oily in the morning's heat. Sun-bleached grassland stretched away from the warehouse in endless undulating miles, until somewhere in the indiscernible distance, sky swallowed savanna. Termite mounds and tussocks of spikeweed knobbed the ground.

Two massive wooden doors riddled with holes stood before us. The arbiyesku split in two, approached the doors, and, with much concerted effort, began heaving them open. The ground beneath my feet reverberated as the great doors shuddered and rolled reluctantly aside.

At once, the smell of death billowed out of the warehouse.

How foul was the stench! So much stronger than I had expected, and it reeking bad enough before the doors had been opened. It was as powerful as a fist in the gut and sand in the eye, and let me tell you, such a smell imprints itself on a person for life, so that ever afterward all scents seem but a component of it: cloying, meaty, musky, as rancid-sweet as spoiled grain.

I staggered back, but Savga shouted, "Come closer, look, look!" and the children surged forward, carrying me with them, propelling me into my new livelihood and the stuff of nightmares.

Those involucres.

They oozed waxy gray exudate; they undulated with maggots. Mound after mound of them, some shoulder height, some only as high as my belly, all of them jammed against one another, disappearing into the back of the warehouse. And the sounds: the crunchy scurry of carrion beetles, the drill-buzzing of a million flies, the hiss of gases escaping the bodies of the living dead dragons, and the deafening rumble of the doors grating open . . .

"Outside!" I cried, trying to turn around and escape the tide of children, but no, I couldn't swim out from their undertow, weak and in pain as I was.

"Look!" Savga squealed. "Those are our carts. Those are our churners. Those are our trowels! And see, along that wall? Our hashing scythes!"

So fine, she wanted me to say of the things she'd called churners, the baffling, upright contraptions standing sentinel along one wall, and of the blades of the oversize scythes dangling from the wall like hung men.

"You come over here and watch," she ordered, and the tide of children pulled me toward those vicious scythes as the adults streamed into the warehouse and headed toward the tools of their trade.

"Stand here," Savga said, propping me against a wall, out of the way. "I've got to work."

The mournful lowing of a dying dragon reverberated from the back of the warehouse. My skin broke into cold-pimples. Plangent and sepulchral, the lowing tolled again.

Images flashed across my mind, memories of senile old bulls stretching snouts to shafts of sunlight on a cool morn in the convent I'd once lived in. I recalled their slow shivers of delight, remembered how they liked to be rubbed around the roots of their olfactory plumes, how they'd grunted in pleasure, their sad amber eyes upon mine. Flickers and blazes of dragonmemory licked over my vision: I remembered my cloaca stretching thin as paper as I strained to lay my first egg, remembered the bewildering agony of undergoing wing amputation as a hatchling.

Ancestral memories, those, shared during the bestial rite.

Dragons were wise and divine, yet they were enslaved beasts of burden. Dragons were predominantly aerial creatures, yet we shackled them in barns and forced them into the yokes of wagons. I felt ill with dread anticipation of what I was about to see, yet I knew that the involucres contained not live dragons, but carcasses, and that whatever was about to occur had been occurring for several hundred years, and that dragons suffered and toiled during life on our behalf so that we lowly mortals might have food and shelter.

Grace. They favored us with divine grace.

Though I had a feeling that what I was about to witness wouldn't contain much grace at all.

One day I'd change how dragons were treated in my Clutch. I would. But for now I could ill afford to draw negative attention to myself. So I would remain silent, and watch whatever was about to occur to the involucres, knowing that someday, somehow, the dragons would live a better life under my rule, and their dead would be honored when encased in their cocoons.

From the gloom where the apparatus of the arbiyesku trade hunkered, women pulled forth carts while children dragged out massive shovels, the likes of which I'd never seen before. The carts the women pulled were heavy and cumbersome, built to be pulled by satons. As some of the women labored to station the carts in a large semicircle near the open doors, others lifted down the massive scythes from the walls and walked, alongside the men of the clan, into the darkness of the warehouse.

My eyes strained to follow them. I found myself leaning forward. There was the dragonmaster, weaving his way through the rows and rows of immobile living dead, his easily identifiable bald pate bobbing in the gloom. Now and then he stopped and pressed an ear against an involucre, bending stiffly because of his wound.

The arbiyesku continued to fan out throughout the warehouse, checking the involucres, their scythes glinting high above their shoulders. They shouted information to one another as they paused and listened to each cocoon, and soon an apparent consensus was reached, for the arbiyesku formed a line midway through the warehouse.

Men and women alike hefted their great scythes from their shoulders. Breaking into song that sounded more dirge than melody, they began rhythmically swinging their blades and moving slowly, steadily, through the cocoons, the dragonmaster amongst them.

Cracking, watery sounds. Sickly, warm odors. The line moved slowly toward the waiting carts, hacking, hewing, creating spills of maggots, deliquescing flesh, and keratinous membranes.

My heart pounded hard against my larynx.

The children hitched heavy ramps to the waiting carts and waited for the ichor-streaked men and women to reach them; when they did, the adults handed them their scythes, and the children promptly took them outside and began slashing the blades through wild grass to clean them. While the children were thus employed, their parents approached the line of ominous contraptions standing sentinel not far from me. Churners, Savga had called them.

The things were upright wooden devices, my height, looking for all the world like double-armed pumps situated on top of boxy wooden platforms, which in turn were stationed above stout casters. As the old men wheeled the things forward, the axle of one broke with a loud crack of wood and clank of metal. There was much swearing as the churner was moved out of the way and tipped onto its side. Metal blades shone beneath the exposed underbelly of the boxy platform.

In pairs, the rest of the adults stood upon the churners, on the platform stationed above the blades of each. They began pumping the handles up and down, up and down, which propelled the churners forward. Like frantic oversize bugs they bumped and rolled over the mess of slashed involucres, churning them into a gray lake the consistency of gruel.

The children returned from outside, scythes polished clean by twists of wild grass. They hung the blades on the wall nearest me—Savga grinned and waved—and took up massive wooden shovels: two children per shovel, or, in the case of the smallest children, three or four to each. The wooden scoop of each shovel was over four feet long, knee high, and slightly concave. Into the mess of churned cocoons the children waded, and they began pushing the paste created by the churners straight up the ramps they'd earlier hitched to the back of the carts.

At some point I went outside to lie down, my body a blinding ache. Savga found and woke me.

"Your skin is the color of a roasted kidney," she said soberly. "You're going to suffer evil sun-sickness tomorrow. That was witless, falling asleep without shade. You're not crackbrained, are you?"

"Water," was all I could croak for a reply, whereupon I fainted.

I woke to cool, wet sensations tickling my forehead. I opened bleary eyes. Fwipi was bent over me, dribbling water from a rag onto my forehead and lips, upon my wrists, over my groin.

"How'll you get better if you do this to yourself, hey-o?" she muttered.

She pressed a gourd of water to my lips and cooed encouragement while I drank. She helped me stand, her body all sinew and bone, as tough as bark. Holding me about the hips, she led me back to the women's barracks.

She didn't come into the barracks but stood instead at the foot of its rickety stairs, gray paste hardening upon her calves.

"We'll deliver the fodder now," she said. "We'll be back sometime after dusk, then clean the carts and clothes before eating. You know how to weave mats and baskets? You do that until we return. Make plenty baskets, plenty mats."

"Deliver fodder?" I asked stupidly.

"Yes, yes. Brooder feed."

She was talking about the pulped involucres. The mess was destined for brooder consumption. Dragon would eat dragon.

Bile rose into my throat.

"Make plenty mats," Fwipi ordered, pointing to a pile of jute strips stacked to one side of the barracks stairs.

Mercifully, I was then left alone.

Yamdalar cinaigours. Dragon cocoons.

Permit me to explain them.

As they near the end of their lives, all female dragons begin secreting death-wax, whereupon they are marched to a cocoon warehouse. Upon reaching the warehouse, each dragon curls up and enters a comatose state, and death-wax production increases tenfold. Within a clawful of days, the cinaigour is completely enclosed in a yamdalar, or keratinous involucre. Temple teaches that in this manner, the imperfect female dragon—imperfect by dint of her gender—prepares to enter the Celestial Realm.

Although the encased dragons appear dead, they are alive for some days; limbs and mouth parts occasionally move within the involucre, and sometimes a mournful, liquid braying is emitted. A dragon must never be killed, regardless of age or condition, for the beasts *are* holy, even if recognition of such divinity is oft conveniently reserved for the rare males of the species. So the cocoons are left in peace.

But eventually, all motion and sound stops within an involucre. A clawful of days after the last visible movement, the dragon has completed her death journey to the Celestial Realm. Then, and only then, the cocoons may be disposed of.

As a member of the arbiyesku, that was now my primary responsibility: disposing of dragon cocoons, each month and every month, without fail.

And that was what I'd witnessed on my first full day in Clutch Xxamer Zu.

I wove clumsy baskets. I dozed. I wove mats. I dozed. I tried not to think about how repulsive the work of my new clan was. The sun relinquished its searing hold over the grasslands and sank into the horizon in a blaze of red.

I was ferociously hungry, but was loath to rummage about the arbiyesku in search of a food cellar. I didn't know my new clan's customs and rules regarding cellars and the handling and distribution of food, and I certainly couldn't afford to alienate them any further than what I'd inadvertently done already.

I sighed and stared off into the gloaming. And tensed.

Running along one of the many grassy paths that radiated from the arbiyesku compound was a child. I lumbered to my feet, ignoring the pain in my ribs. Slowly the figure resolved itself as Savga. She staggered to a panting, beaming stop before me.

"What's wrong?" I asked sharply.

She paced wobbly-legged about me, wheezing as she tried to catch her breath. "Did you . . . miss me?"

"Where're the others? What's happened?"

"They're coming. Slow, slow, always so slow. One of the carts broke and I was tired of waiting."

"Should I go help?"

"Funny Kazonvia, you can hardly walk! And they're a long way away, closer to the brooder stables than here."

"So you came back alone."

She shrugged. "Mama can't beat me till she gets here."

I grimaced. Her folly would hardly endear me to Tansan.

"Let's you and I start the evening meal, yes?" she said. "I'll blow on the embers to wake the fire." She darted toward one of the cooking pits. With a curse, I limped in her direction.

She was already on her hands and knees and sputtering from the hot soot she'd blown into her face by the time I reached her.

"Not like that! Great Dragon, you'll burn yourself!" I stiffly knelt beside her and wiped her face with the hem of my bitoo.

"Not so rough!" she wailed.

I muttered an apology as she wriggled from my hands.

"You start the fire, Kazonvia, and I'll get the dramdacan."

"What?" But she was already sprinting away into the twilight gloom and disappearing into a mud-brick hut that looked much the same as the rest.

Muttering, I awkwardly lay before the dark embers—I couldn't bend properly to blow on them, so I had to lie on my side—and, poking them with a charred stick, started blowing and stuffing twists of grass here and there amongst the quickening coals.

Savga returned, huffing, laden with a stack of dried fish.

"Come, you help me cut the dramdacan. We always cook dramdacan on hashing day. Really, I'm telling the truth. Come on."

Whether she was telling the truth or whether I would be roasted alive for permitting this six-year-old spitfire to chop up the impoverished clan's store of riverine fish changed nothing: It seemed I had no choice but to obey.

I clambered to my feet and staggered to where Savga knelt beside a pitted stone slab. She held a wicked curved blade topped by twin wooden knobs and was clumsily trying to cut a dried fish into slices by rocking the blade atop it. The dried fish rattled and popped beneath the steel like grain burning in a pan.

"Do you know how to use that knife, Savga?" I asked wearily. "You'll chop a finger off if you're not— Look out! Just put that down, now!"

A moot command: She'd dropped the knife and was standing, howling, holding a bleeding hand crushed against her potbelly.

I ascertained that I wasn't going to be killed by Tansan for having let her daughter amputate one of her own fingers; then I stanched the flow of Savga's cut with a ripped-off portion of my bitoo. Once soothed, Savga sat in the dust nursing her hand and regaled me with a grisly story someone called Tiwana-auntie had told her, about a girl with no hands; I resigned myself to chopping up the dried dramdacan as night settled around us.

That was how Tansan found us. First I knew of her presence was when Savga leapt to her feet with a gasp.

"Mama!"

I turned—too quickly—from where I was squatted and fell to my rump with a painful cry. Tansan stood above me, her long legs braced, her hands knuckled on her hips.

"Mama, I had to come back, I really had to, I couldn't leave my foremost friend here all alone with the dark coming—"

"Enough." Tansan held up a hand and Savga promptly fell silent. "You know the dangers of walking alone. Get the switch—"

She looked away from Savga sharply, and stared across the compound. I followed her gaze. For a moment I thought Tansan was staring at the white central dome of the Temple, located to the south of the arbiyesku, in the center of the Clutch. But then a strange silhouette cut itself from the dark and came lurching toward us.

"Go inside the barracks, Savga." The urgency in Tansan's tone made me instantly anxious.

"Don't let them take my foremost friend, Mama," Savga whispered.

"Get in the barracks. Now."

"Promise?"

"Savga . . ."

"Promise?"

"Savga!"

"Mama, you have to promise—"

"Yes. Now go."

Savga melted into the dark. I clambered to my feet.

It was a rickshaw, that shadow, pulled by a sinewy Djimbi man who came to a wheezing stop a short distance before us. Seated in the rickshaw were two lordlings, their silk shirts sloppily unlaced, their pomaded hair tousled. I could smell the maska spirits on their breath from where I stood.

One of the lordlings flicked a hand that was studded with turquoise rings. "Bring out all the women! Bring 'em all out!"

"We're alone, Bayen Hacros." Tansan said the honorific *First Lord Dominant* as if it were a curse. "The arbiyesku is delivering fodder to the brooder stables."

The two men exchanged bleary looks; then one lord lurched to his feet. The rickshaw creaked and swayed and he almost lost his balance. He planted one hand atop his companion's head to steady himself and placed the other on the hilt of the turquoise-studded dagger at his waist.

"Are you lying to us, rishi whore? You know what I do to liars?"

"As is your right, you are welcome to examine every hut and building here, Bayen Hacros," Tansan said coldly, and she gestured at the mud-brick domiciles in the compound, her arm gliding smoothly through the air.

The movement, combined with the lift of her chin and the inhalation of her breath, drew the men's eyes to her chest. It had been, I realized, a calculated move.

Their eyes simultaneously raked over her.

"Think we've found us a suitable whore, Neme," the seated one slurred.

"We'll take the both of 'em, by dragon." The standing one's voice had turned thick.

Tansan took a step forward. "I'll do. You don't need her as well."

I began to suspect what was transpiring and stared at Tansan, appalled. "You can't—"

She turned and *looked* at me. I took a step back from the intensity on her face, the muted rage.

"I promised Savga," she hissed.

"I won't let you keep that promise."

"That's not your decision to make."

"I've already made it."

We stared at each other, neither of us looking at the lordlings making quips in the rickshaw about whores fighting over the privilege of servicing bayen cocks.

"Both of you come, and that's an order!" one of them bawled. "There's more than enough for the two of you!"

Tansan gave a humorless smile that bared only the upper row of her teeth. Her dark eyes were intense as they stayed riveted on mine. "You wouldn't survive the night with them, Secondgirl. We both know it."

"I've got twice the strength you have. Now go in with your child."

She slapped me, and the blow rang down my spine and blazed fire across my broken ribs. My vision swam and it was hard to breathe.

"I made a promise to my child." She grabbed a fistful of my hair and lifted my face to the rickshaw.

"Look at her, Bayen Hacros!" she cried. "This is a woman rotting from the inside out with the mating disease! It's my duty to inform you of her contagion."

By the moonlight, the drunken lordlings were able to see the welts and scrapes and bruises that mottled every inch of my face. "Could be that she's your sister, hey," one of them said doubtfully. "Could be you're trying to keep her from her duty."

"She's no sister of mine." The dislike was sincere in her voice. She released me with a push, and I stumbled and fell. White-hot pain blasted across my torso and racheted up and down my spine.

By the time my vision cleared, the rickshaw—with Tansan in it—was gone, and Savga was crouched by my head, weeping.

"Did Mama go with them?"

I thought I might retch. Tansan had knowingly given herself over to violation. Not for my sake, no. But to keep a promise to her child. I was furious and appalled, and I couldn't help but wonder if I would have had the strength of conviction to do the same for my child, had our situations been reversed.

Yes. Yes, I would have. How to break a promise to one's child, knowing that to do so might result in the death of said child's friend? How to face the anguish and accusation in the child's eyes each day thereafter?

And how could I explain all that to the six-year-old sobbing beside me?

"We should have fought them," I said hoarsely.

Savga's eyes went wide. "Oh, no, Kazonvia. You don't *fight* the bayen when they come trolling, hey."

"Trolling," I said bitterly. "Is that what it's called?"

Savga wrapped her little arms about herself and shuddered. "Will Mama come back?"

I glared into the darkness, where Tansan had disappeared.

"Help me prepare the evening meal." I gestured for Savga to hand me a leathery fish.

And, shuddering, she mutely obeyed.

FOUR

The arbiyesku trundled into the compound shortly before middle-night.

In the darkness I found Fwipi. Tansan's infant was sleeping restlessly in the sling on her humped back. Shoulders stooped, rheumy eyes heavy, Fwipi merely nodded at my hoarse narration of what had occurred. A dark Djimbi man who was pulling one of the carts by means of a yoke about his neck cursed at hearing my news. He wrenched himself free of the traces and strode off.

I wondered who he was to Tansan.

Fwipi watched him disappear into the dark mouth of a hut as I stammered an inane apology.

"With you, without you, she had to serve, Kazonvia." She spat in the dust. "A curse, her beauty."

Thick, pungent smoke from the dragon-dung fagots I'd used in the cooking pit slowly curled toward the vast sea of stars above us. Children whimpered as mothers and aunties woke them from the back of the reeking arbiyesku carts, stripped them of their meager clothing, and began scrubbing their shivering bodies clean in the dark.

"Does Tansan have to go with lordlings often?" I asked.

"Once is often." Fwipi's tired eyes searched mine. "More than once, you stop counting."

I didn't ask more.

The soup I'd made under Savga's direction was thick as paste and bland as dust. No one complained; everyone was too bone-weary for talk. Afterward—when the carts had been scrubbed clean with sand and wheeled back into the warehouse, and babies had been diapered and suckled to sleep—Savga chose to lay beside me in the barracks.

I was startled by, and grateful for, her decision. It would have been unbearable if Savga had despised me for her mother's disappearance.

At Savga's insistence, I rubbed her smooth little back till she drifted off to sleep.

Tansan's infant wailed with hunger and suckled only briefly from another woman's breast, and his pitiful cries kept me awake long into the cool night. When I did start to drift off, I dreamt I was falling down a gaping pit, and I jerked awake, heart pounding. Come dawn, I found myself agitated and exhausted, and in that enervated state, I sifted through the memories of my childhood, trying to recall if trolling had been a practice common on Clutch Re.

Xxamer Zu was but a pocket compared to Re; given the expanse and population of my birth Clutch, it was conceivable that trolling *had* existed there, but hadn't often occurred where I could witness it, for the compound of my birth clan had been located a half day's march from the bayen center of the Clutch. I certainly had no memory of trolling occuring on Re. It was a practice I'd have to tell Ghepp to put a stop to on Xxamer Zu. Immediately.

Come morning, Savga and I worked hulling the remnants of last season's wizened coranuts, so the nuts could be pounded into paste. Save for several old women spinning string from beaten jute fibers, and two old men stropping the blades of several overturned churners, Savga and I were alone in the compound; after a dismal morning meal of the cold remains of last night's soup, the arbiyesku had trudged with hoe and hand plow into the patchwork of arid fields surrounding us.

One of the old women beside us was Tiwana-auntie, a fearsome hunchback with a voice like scree sliding down a mountainside. She was Fwipi's elder sister, and as wizened as an old fig.

Beside me, Savga's entire little body went suddenly as tense as a cur's scenting a weasel. She sprang to her feet, coranuts flying everywhere, and streaked across the dusty earth. Tansan was entering the compound, along the same grassy path the rickshaw had traveled the night before. Behind her, in the hazy near distance, the central dome of Temple Xxamer Zu shimmered like a gigantic dragon's egg.

Tansan held a hand up, as if to ward Savga back. Savga stopped, stood uncertainly. Tansan spoke to her and placed a hand on her head. Wordless, the two approached.

To enter the women's barracks, Tansan had to walk past where I sat in the dust in the barracks' shade. She walked slowly, pain clenched tight within her, but still carried herself with the feral grace of a creature impossible to capture. She didn't deign to look at me, and after a quick glance I couldn't look at her, either. She was as bruised and cut as I. The fishy taste of the congealed soup I'd swallowed for breakfast burned in the back of my throat.

Once again, she looked like my sister, Waivia.

I heard her mount the rickety stairs, heard the rasp of the barracks door swing open on its coarse twine hinges. A pause; Tansan was looking down at me, I could *feel* her eyes burning through my skin.

I met her smoldering gaze.

"This place"—Tansan gestured, taking in the compound, the cocoon warehouse, the rolling miles of sun-seared savanna beyond—"this place will be run by us one day soon. It will be ours, belong to Djimbi, belong to rishi. It will be my daughter's." Her eyes turned hard. "I think you're well enough to work the fields tomorrow, Secondgirl."

With that, Tansan entered the barracks, Savga at her heels, and the door creaked shut. After a pause, the door reopened and Savga clumped down the stairs and rejoined me, her face a thundercloud.

"Mama wants to sleep." She sounded on the brink of either tears or fury.

She chose fury and stared at me defiantly. "Mama's myazedo. She'll do what she says, oh, yes. She'll get rid of the fa-pim muck in this Clutch, and then no one will hurt her ever again."

"Close your fast lips, child," old Tiwana-auntie rasped. "Spoken nonsense kills."

Savga's puffed-out chest deflated. She lowered her eyes, bit her lip, then hesitantly looked up at me.

"You won't tell anyone I said that, hey-o? About my mother being myazedo?"

I didn't have a clue what the word meant. But I smiled reassuringly. "We're foremost friends, Savga. I won't say a thing."

With a tremulous sigh, Savga nodded. "Foremost friends."

"Sit beside me." I patted the ground. "Tell me another of your stories, hey."

Slowly she nodded. But she didn't resume shelling coranuts. She stared at the ground, silent.

"I forget sometimes," she whispered.

"Forget what?"

She looked lost, drained, devitalized. "That Mama hates me."

My response was grounded in nothing but reactionary denial. "Your mother doesn't hate you!"

She shrugged apathetically. "She does every time the lords come trolling. I'm a senemei, hey."

I didn't know what the word meant.

"Three bayen lords took Mama one day, when she was returning from the river, before I was born. That's how she got that scar, fighting them, and that's why Fwipi-granna's claimer was killed, for Mama's defiance. I'm a senemei. Tiwana-auntie says so. Keau claimed Mama afterward, to spare Mama some of the shame of having me."

I glanced at Tiwana-auntie. Her puckered face was a mask.

I thought senemei must be the Djimbi word for *bastard*. Keau must have been the man who'd stormed into a hut last night, when I'd informed Fwipi that Tansan had been taken.

"That's why Mama loves Agawan better than me," Savga continued hoarsely.

"Agawan?"

"My baby brother." A tear escaped an eye. "She hates me each time the lords come trolling. 'Cause I remind her of . . . them."

My heart ached for the child before me, and I suddenly understood why she'd been so delighted when I'd promised to be her foremost friend, why she'd been so determined to stay resolutely by my side since. My entry into the arbiyesku had supplied Savga with a childless woman her mother's age, and she'd fiercely—and desperately—adopted me as her own.

I awkwardly pulled the child onto my lap and held her, reliving the ache I'd too often felt when my mother had turned from me to favor my sister. She felt small and frail within my arms. I was comforting not just her, understand; I was comforting a mirror image of a younger me.

After a moment, she leaned her small head against my collarbone and wept.

The next day was my first in the fields, and it was an inglorious one.

Squint-eyed and in pain, I shambled down row after row of blighted oilseed stalks, snapping off the wizened clusters between thumb and forefinger and placing them in the worn sack I carried upon my back by means of a wide strap across my forehead. I felt gelatinous on the outside, my interior scraped hollow and raw by the rake of my fractured ribs. Every now and then a creaking sound issued from them, accompanied by a nasty, bubbling pain. Not that I let the pain prevent me from working the fields, not after what Tansan had suffered. For the love of the Dragon, I'd work the damn fields.

Savga couldn't understand my lethargy and fragility—she was impatient with my mutterings about fractured ribs—and by noon, she worked several rows ahead of me with two other girls her age, their small fingers expertly decapitating clusters of oilseeds from stalks.

While picking, I could have reflected upon what had happened to Tansan. Could have. Maybe should have. Didn't. I worked with the mindless determination to get through the day and collapse upon my sleeping mat come dusk.

But come dusk, I was not permitted to. It was Naso Yobet Offering Eve; I had to join my new clan in their humble observances. There were flatcakes to share, however hard and thin, and there was the hair of elders to wash. For the first time, my hair was washed by another during Naso Yobet: Savga. She worked at my head with a vigor that left my ears ringing and scalp throbbing.

I remembered washing the hair of my elders, to gain merit. I remembered breaking off segments of flatcake for my childhood friends, Rutvia and Makvia, and placing them in their mouths as a show of friendship and trust. I remembered the smell of clay and the talcum softness of kaolin on my skin as I worked alongside my mother in the pottery shed, making moon-shaped candleholders. On Naso Yobet night, every compound in Clutch Re had been lit up with candles cradled in such holders, and then *whoosh!* We'd blow the candles out at the sound of the Naso Yobet horns resounding from the many temples in the Clutch. In the smoky darkness that followed, we rejoiced, knowing that the Fire Season would be extinguished by the Pure Dragon's breath and no drought would come. Extinguished, just like those candles.

Extinguished, just like my mother.

Naso Yobet had been adapted slightly to suit the lack of candles in the impoverished arbiyesku. Instead of a candle, a glowing fagot represented the Fire Season, balanced precariously upon a rock cupped in palms. The clean, herbal scent of the hair wash made the air smell crisp, despite the smoke from the smoldering fagots. My damp hair clung to my ears, and water dripped over my collarbone and down my spine and belly, pleasantly cool.

From the center of Xxamer Zu, from the four compass windows in the temple's golden spire, unseen daronpuis blew their long Naso Yobet horns. The sound rolled across the fields like the resonant braying of musk stags. The arbiyesku dropped their glowing coals to the ground and crushed them with their rocks. I dropped my own and released my rock atop it. I had no desire to crouch and smash the fagot to ashes, not with my ribs as painful as they were.

The dragonmaster appeared at my shoulder, the glass bead at the end of his goatee braid swinging to and fro. He rubbed a hand over his bald pate in agitation, leaving behind sooty marks. He opened his mouth to speak, then hesitated. He smelled of rotting teeth and tumorous disease.

He thrust something toward me. Grabbed my hand, squeezed hard to open it. He dropped a pebble on my palm.

"To place in the bowl," he said, his words sounding rehearsed. "So the One Dragon blesses our union."

I stared at the pebble in my hand, then gaped at him. He was summoning me to the mating shack.

Did he really expect me to follow? Did he really think I would allow him to pull off my bitoo, place his hands upon me, straddle my hips . . . ? Damn him to eternal mulching in a Skykeeper's gullet, if he thought I'd follow.

He scowled at the look on my face. "Splayfooted fool," he hissed, leaning close, spittle spraying my cheeks. "Not that. Think! Use your tit-soft head for once."

It took me a moment to realize: He wanted a place where we could speak privately.

He'd heard from Gen.

Adrenaline, hope, and expectation instantly enlivened me. Gen had summoned us! He'd secured a portion of the stables, had found a way for me to lie, undetected, with a venomous dragon, that I might again hear dragonsong, that I might divine the secret to breeding bull dragons in captivity. It was time for me to leave the arbiyesku.

People were watching us from the corners of their eyes. Fwipi was watching, sinewy old body taut.

The dragonmaster flared his nostrils, angry that I wasn't giving the appropriate response for a woman who'd just received a summons by her claimer, but I couldn't for the life of me recall it. I'd heard my own mother say it plenty of times to my father during my childhood, after he'd pressed a congle nut into her palm. Numerous times I'd heard other women murmur the traditional response when summoned by their claimers. But I couldn't recall a word of it now.

For a moment I thought the dragonmaster might strike me for my idiocy. His hand, which still clenched mine, tightened hard, grinding my bones together. He twitched, once, released me, turned, and lurched in his simian gait toward the mating shack.

I swallowed and nursed my hand against my belly. Savga slid to my side.

"Will he hurt you?" No doubt she was thinking of the welts and bruises so fresh on her mother's face. She was far too young to be bearing such concerns.

"No," I said, and I smiled. The tension went out of her body, for she could see my smile wasn't forced. And it wasn't; my heart was soaring at the thought that Gen had succeeded, that I would taste venom and hear dragonsong soon. I ruffled Savga's hair, knuckled her crown gently. "Not at all, Little Ant. He won't hurt me."

I smiled at Fwipi to reassure her, too. She looked nonplussed by my blithe grin.

Clenching my hand about the pebble the dragonmaster had forced into my palm—no congle nuts out on the savanna—I wove my way quickly through chatting people, toward the mating shack. I ascended the rickety wooden stairs, carefully and painfully stretched up to the lintel, and placed the pebble within the clay bowl that sat there, so the One Dragon might bless my womb with my claimer's fertile seed.

It was dark and stifling inside the mating shack, and stank of unaired dust. A narrow corridor ran down the middle of the shack, so narrow both my shoulders touched the woven-reed partition walls on either side of me. Another couple was inside; their heavy breaths permeated the air like salty musk, and the shack was rocking slightly from their movements.

The shack was small. It contained only four mating cubicles, plus the necessary men's party room at the back. I knew which cubicle the dragonmaster was sat within by the impatient *tap-tap-tap* of a foot upon the floor. I waited a moment for my eyes to adjust to the dark; then, moving sideways because of the narrowness of the corridor, I shuffled to the cubicle where the dragonmaster was waiting.

I stepped inside and slid the paper-thin partition door shut. The dragonmaster sat on the far end of a pallet, hunched slightly.

"You've heard from Gen," I gleefully whispered.

"What?"

I started to repeat myself, but the dragonmaster impatiently waved me silent. "Forget Gen. We won't hear from him for weeks—"

"Weeks!"

He scowled at the volume of my reply. "The mother of that get who follows you like a puling kitten, what's her name? Who's her claimer?"

My discouragement turned into malice, and I savored the fact that I knew something the dragonmaster didn't. I waited long moments before responding. "Her name is Tansan. Her claimer is Keau. Why?"

"Those three young bulls that sat at her feet the night we arrived . . . who are they?"

"I can find out. I expect the information isn't secret."

He rolled his shoulders and suddenly stood. "I've overheard them talking, those four. They've no love for bayen, or the Emperor. There'll be more like them. I want to know them all."

"Why?" The word Savga had used, *myazedo*, echoed in my mind.

He flapped his hands before my face. "Why, why, why! Have I taught you nothing?"

For an instant I was gripped with the urge to smack his flapping hands aside. Instead I snapped, "You can't put these people in danger."

His eyes bulged. "These are *my* people. Don't think you can tell me what I can and can't do, aosogi get."

Staring into his blood-marbled eyes was like staring into the eyes of some wild creature that lived in a supernatural hinterland. I met his gaze for several long moments before dropping it and muttering, "I know I'm not Djimbi. But they've taken me into their clan. And this is my Clutch. I won't see them come to any harm."

"Idiot whelp," the dragonmaster said, but astonishment robbed the vitriol from his words. "What I do, I do to free us from the tyrant's hold."

I remained silent and continued to stare at his horny feet.

"Fine," he spat at last, and I tried not to flinch. "I'll learn what they whisper amongst themselves yet. You live with the illusion that these people are happy and satisfied. Fine. You live with that around your scrawny neck till it chokes you."

He grabbed my chin and jerked it up so that I was looking at him. Again I was gripped with the urge to smack his leathery hands aside.

"More is demanded of the Skykeeper's Daughter than silence," he hissed. "Much more. I'll light a fire under your feet till it blazes and consumes you. So help me, rishi via, that's what I'll do. I'll force you to fulfill your destiny yet."

We stared at each other, frustration, contempt, and fury showering like firesparks from his eyes, aversion and defiance smoldering behind mine.

He snapped his hand away from my chin. "Move aside," he growled, twitching like a leathery toad skewered on a stick.

"No," I said, and yes, I was afraid of him in such close quarters, madness foaming from his eyes, but no, I couldn't hold my tongue as I should, that cursed insolence I'd inherited from my mother looming, as ever, to the fore.

He went still. I swear his eyes glowed.

"We're supposed to be mating," I said, nostrils flared. "Even the quickest fuck takes a little longer than this."

An interminable time passed, him poised on the brink of dervish anger, battling inner demons for self-control.

Breathing heavily, he moved away from me. Bandy legs braced, hands clenching and unclenching, he waited the approximate length of time it might take a man to sow his seed in a woman's womb. With the stab of a finger at the door, he then indicated we should leave.

His ferine eyes burned through me the entire time.

FIVE

Isolated from neighboring rishi kus by a sea of jute, featon, and fallow soil, the cocoon warehouse was an islet unto itself.

A good place to disappear, that.

Wind. Rodent squeak and child chatter. The swish and whisper of feathery grainheads beneath a hard, empty blue sky. I felt infinitesimally small on those undulating plains, exposed daily to the sun's bone-bleaching glare and the night's myriad stars. Small, but relatively safe from Temple's grasp.

Within a matter of days I grew used to the rhythm of life out there, succored by the illusion that I was experiencing the security of my childhood.

Long before each dawn, I woke to the rousing of the water fetchers, those women whose daily duty it was to walk the many dusty miles through the dark to the Sangsusif Chodo, the Indulgent River, with great urns upon their heads. They returned just as the sun began rising, and woke their children, who would then stumble, yawning, to the arbiyesku's kadoob field, a furrowed tract of land surrounded by gnarled slii trees. With their infant siblings strapped to their backs, the children would till, harrow, weed, and irrigate the stubble-mulched earth, returning with a sack of wizened tubers.

After partaking of a meager meal of cold roasted kadoobs—or sometimes, nothing but silty water—all but the very eldest of the arbiyesku would then go work the surrounding fields. The elders who remained—those lame and bent by age, who didn't walk so much as lurch and scuttle and drag themselves forward—did kwano duty, touring round the stinking warehouse, weaving amongst the yamdalar cinaigours, looking for kwano snakes to behead. They found few, for the kwano snake is a jungle serpent, but occasionally their rheumy eyes located a snake—kwano or otherwise—that had slithered into the warehouse, attracted to the fetor of death, and the intruder was always decapitated in a flurry of revulsion, panic, and fear.

Temple teaches that the kwano snake is the embodiment of evil; the Progenitor, the father of all kwano snakes, is the eternal enemy of the One Dragon. Thus the yamdalar warehouse needed to be daily eradicated of the diabolic snakes—along with any other hapless snake that had slithered into the vicinity.

While the elders were thus engaged, the rest of the arbiyesku tilled arid soil, breaking up weed-choked clods, cultivating the meager crops that sustained them. Gaunt bodies dotted the fields for miles in every direction, brown backs, mottled by stormy green whorls, turning ebon under the sun.

I soon learned that all rishi on Xxamer Zu worked its fields, regardless of guild clan. Occasionally I was exempted from such work if my ribs were exceptionally sore and the work particularly strenuous, but, shamed by the exemption, I kept myself busy from dawn to dusk at other tasks.

With Savga by my side, I wove mats and baskets and repaired the holes in the barracks walls by plaiting new jute rushes amongst the old. Savga chopped wild grass; I mixed it with dragon dung fetched by others from the brooder stables; together we made fagots for fuel. *Slap, slap, slap,* went our palms on the warm, pungent stuff as we formed it into bricks for drying, and when we finished forming fagots, we made a slurry with the remaining barrow of dung and smeared it over the men's mud-brick domiciles, to strengthen and smooth out the exterior. The thin mud dried fast on the sunbaked walls, and we had to move quickly to coat them smoothly and evenly, squinting in the glare, ignoring the buzz and nip of flies and the pulsing heat on our backs.

Savga's presence was bittersweet. On the one hand, I felt her devotion was wholly undeserved, and every day and hour that we were together, Tansan grew colder toward me. But on the other hand, I enjoyed Savga's company and guiltily relished the affection I was stealing from her mother.

Sometimes Savga would shyly slip her small hand into mine during our workday, and the simple, unquestioning trust of that action would hold me in its thrall, as if I'd captured something delicate, vulnerable, and rare. It awed me. I was loath to reject it.

Her warmth by my side each night was a gift, a reminder that not all of life was harsh and merciless. The soft swell and ebb of her little ribs as she breathed in her sleep, and the smell of her—like a smooth, sun-warmed stone, like sugared nutmilk—permeated my sleep and cradled me in memories of my own childhood. I recalled how safe and certain I'd felt, curled each night between my older sister and my mother. I remembered the playmates I'd once had—Rutvia and Makvia—and grew wistful watching Savga whisper serious nonsense to Runami or Wanlen or Oblan, the other arbiyesku girls her age. Because of Savga I learned anew why I cared so much for the fate of all rishi, why I had vowed to one day own a dragon estate where a child could grow up fearless, unaffected by Temple's laws and brutal punishments.

But the cost of encouraging Savga's affection was, as I mentioned, Tansan's biting coldness toward me.

Whenever I was in Tansan's presence I grew clumsy, knowing I should be grateful for how she'd spared me from rape, but feeling only impotent anger over the entire incident. I'd drop things when Tansan was around, spill things, trip, and fumble, and, hotter than the merciless sun, her silent scorn would scorch over me.

It shouldn't have been that way. Tansan was everything I admired: a strong woman and mother, respected by her kith and kin. Her wild beauty was emphasized by her physical strength, by her grace and composure, and yes, I admit it: The sight of her oft drew a flush to my throat and heat to my belly. Too often at nights my dreams centered around her, and more than once I woke in the dark with my heart pounding, my thighs damp, my desire for venom and dragonsong spiked so high from my dreams about Tansan that I felt I'd burst.

The dark Djimbi man who'd stormed into a hut upon hearing my news the night Tansan had been ordered to pleasure the two lordlings turned out to be Tansan's claimer. Name of Keau, he was at least a decade older than Tansan, and as meek and quiet a man as I'd ever met. He never once summoned her to the mating shack, nor publicly displayed affection toward her, and I had my doubts as to whether Agawan, Tansan's infant, had been fathered by him, for the child was as light-skinned as Savga.

The days bled into each other.

The dragonmaster became known as the suwembai kam, the madman, for the way he muttered angrily to himself and twitched. No more lords trolled our fields, and as the sun grew hotter and the meager crops browned, and as food grew scarcer and water was rationed, exhaustion helped me convince myself that trolling was rare. Fatigue and relentless hunger can whittle away all but the need to survive the next hour, the next day, the next week, so that one becomes willingly blinded to the larger obstacles looming in the distance.

With each harsh new day, I tried not to envision Ghepp living a life of ease as the new overseer of the Clutch, had to distract myself from the cravings I occasionally suffered for venom by encouraging Savga's prattle. True, Daronpu Gen had given me many charmed purgatives prior to my entry in Arena, to cleanse me of the desire for the dragons' poison . . . but as the days crept onward, sometimes a smell—the stringent scent of a crushed insect, the sweetish smell of soaking grain—would powerfully evoke the citric, sweet scent of venom, and all at once I'd be dizzy and sweat-slicked and filled with a craving so strong I could have howled.

It was after a day when I'd thrice been wrenched by such visceral cravings that I realized Daronpu Gen's charmed purgatives must have had a limit to them, and that my addiction to venom was returning with a vengeance. Unless Gen secured a venomous dragon for me soon, I'd have to seek out my own source of the dragons' poison . . . regardless of the risk.

I came to this bitter conclusion that evening, as I was sat, exhausted, upon the dusty hardpan outside the women's barracks, my body drinking up the twilight as if it were cool water. Sprawled about me was the rest of the arbiyesku, minus the dragonmaster, who had retired at sunset into a domicile, twitching and muttering vehemently to himself. Beside me, Savga played pick-up-sticks with her friends, Oblan, Wanlen, and Runami. As always, Oblan held her infant brother on her lap; she lugged the child with her everywhere, carting him to their mother only when he needed feeding. Oblan's mother, pregnant again, was suffering terrible roidan yin sickness; thus Oblan's duty as surrogate mother.

The arbiyesku elders were talking quietly amongst themselves about days gone by, remembering aloud how Clutch Xxamer Zu had once been, the population more than three times its current number. They whispered the names of nephews and sons who, rather than stay on in the blighted Clutch, had left Xxamer Zu as adolescents and disappeared. They spoke of siblings, aunties, and children who had been taken by the former overseer and sold into slavery to pay off the Clutch's increasing debts and the Roshu's own reckless gambling wagers. And while they talked, I sat hunched in misery, hating myself for how weak I was against my need for venom, exhausted by the mere prospect of trying to find a source of the stuff.

Why couldn't life be easier? Why always the endless strife and turmoil? This was *not* how I'd envisioned living, when I'd dreamed of owning my own Clutch. How did it come about that even while obtaining that which I'd wanted, I'd fallen so far from my goal?

My eyes drifted toward Tansan. She sat with her claimer, Keau, and the three young arbiyesku men who were constantly at her side. The youths were leaning toward one another, talking animatedly, stabbing the air with gestures. They kept their voices low, but their vivacity broke through now and then by exclamation or curse.

"Look how he's smiling," Savga said, of Oblan's infant brother.

Savga tugged on my arm. "When a baby smiles like that, it's because jealous spirits have taunted it by saying, 'Your mother is dead,' and the baby knows it's untrue, since it feeds at its mother's breast daily."

"Yes, yes," Oblan interrupted. "And when a baby cries, it's because jealous spirits say, 'Your father is dead,' and the baby, not yet knowing the father, believes them."

Hush, I wanted to say. *Will you not be quiet for just a little while?*

But I held my tongue and watched Tansan.

She was passionate in her beliefs; that was obvious by the intense, focused way she spoke, by the weight and thought she put into each word. But unlike her three companions, she voiced her opinions infrequently. When she did, her comments started a fresh volley of debate amongst her friends.

I studied those friends of hers.

The youngest was Piah, a gangly fifteen-year-old with a prominent larynx. He gesticulated wildly as he talked and spat frequently to the side when others were speaking. Alliak was my age, eighteen, and carried anger on his dark, whorled shoulders like a sack of rocks. From Savga's gossip, I knew he'd not yet claimed any woman as his roidan yin, despite his maturity. The third young man was Oblan's father, Myamyo, a cocky, large-eared young man with skin as dark as Oblan's. Savga and Runami always giggled when he spoke to them.

Beside me, Savga suddenly stiffened and ceased her prattle. Two Djimbi men sauntered into the arbiyesku compound, appearing suddenly, casually, from behind a domicile, from the direction of the center of the Clutch. The duo ambled into the compound and exchanged nods and polite greetings with several of the arbiyesku elders. The elders' responses were brief.

Savga slipped her hand into mine. She was looking at her mother with the flared nostrils and intent gaze of a deer scenting the wind for danger.

Tansan murmured something to Keau. He looked away from her and gave an imperceptible nod. She stood up from where she'd been nursing Agawan and walked over to Fwipi. Without a word, Fwipi took the babe from Tansan.

The three arbiyesku men who'd sat beside Tansan rose to their feet and, alongside Tansan, joined the two visitors. Keau rose to his feet and followed. Without exchanging a word, the seven walked past me.

It was then that I caught a whiff of fragrance that punched the air from my lungs and sent my senses reeling.

My eyes watered; my belly cramped. Phantom fire blazed through my sinus cavities as I relived, for one nauseating moment, a bitter taste like unripe limes, but tinged at the corners with an aniseed sweetness unmatched by honey or sugar.

Venom.

But no, I hadn't smelled it, couldn't have; it was impossible. I was merely experiencing another withdrawal attack, like those I'd suffered thrice earlier that day. How the ghosts of our past haunt us when we're most vulnerable.

The attack ended as swiftly as it had begun, and I sat there, limp and chilled, as my vision resolved on Fwipi. She was dandling Agawan on her knee, muttering dourly to Tiwana-auntie. No one had noticed my mute agony.

I looked down at Savga. I knew at once by her shuttered eyes that I shouldn't ask her who those two rishi visitors were, nor where her mother had gone for the night.

But those were questions I wanted answers for, regardless. Because what if I *had* smelled venom on one of those men? Something had triggered my withdrawal attack, some fragrance or another. . . .

Don't be foolish. It wasn't venom. You're addled, deluded. . . .

But what if it had been venom? I couldn't continue to suffer withdrawal attacks; they were getting worse and more frequent. I'd need only a little venom to rectify the situation. I couldn't pass by the opportunity. . . .

I rose unsteadily to my feet and headed for the latrines, but once out of sight behind a mud-brick domicile, I swung wide around the arbiyesku, grateful for the relative darkness due to the thin phase of the moon. Teeth chattering, I wondered what would happen if someone noticed me lurking through the dark, along the grassy paths that surrounded the arbiyesku. Would I be hailed, followed, stopped?

No time to consider it. I wouldn't be able to find Tansan and her companions if I hesitated.

Loping half crouched through the dark, ignoring the tweaks of my healing fractures, I bisected the path Tansan had taken. For a moment I feared I'd lost her already, but no: Some way ahead of me walked the group, silhouettes cut from the dark cloth of night.

Staying low—though the dry, knee-high grasses afforded little real cover—I followed them.

We walked westward, the ghostly central dome of Xxamer Zu's temple bobbing in the distance to our right. After a time, unpleasant odors began tainting the wind, and beneath them the silty smell of the sluggish Clutch river. The aggregate of odors was vaguely familiar, and it took me some moments to identify why: We were approaching the nerifruku, the leather tanners' guild clan. The nerifruku of Clutch Re had been situated not that far from the potters' clan of my youth, and the stench of raw, salted hides, pickling dung, and the caustic fumes from limed carcasses turning to leather in tanning pits had occasionally sullied the air in the pottery compound.

I hung back even farther as the dark silhouettes of the huts of the tanners' clan hove into view. I waited amidst the brittle grasses, heart pounding, as Tansan and her cohorts disappeared amongst the huts.

Did I dare proceed? Why not? I wasn't doing anything wrong.

But even as I thought it, I knew that was a lie. My furtive actions, prompted by my imagined whiff of venom and preceded by the arbiyesku's reserved greetings to the two visitors, were clear indicators that I was intruding where I may not be wanted.

The thought didn't stop me from picking my way carefully in the dark around a myriad of broken water buckets and urns to enter the tanners' compound.

I heard voices raised in passionate discussion. My pulse sped up. Bonfire light flickered from the compound's center, and I smelled dung-fagot smoke and the reek of fermented maska milk.

Slowly I edged my way around a hut and peeked into the center of the tanners' compound.

Young men were crouched on their haunches around a bonfire, or sat upon upturned barrels and urns. On the outskirts of those gathered youths sat the nerifruku: stooped and wizened old women, cavern-chested old men, potbellied youngsters, fathers, and nursing mothers, all bearing grotesque scars on their cheeks. I knew they belonged to the nerifruku by those very scars: Black carbuncle sickness is a disease common amongst tanners, and those who survive are left disfigured and have the ability to strip the foulest hides with no danger of reinfection. Perhaps that intimacy with death, combined with the physical ugliness of the survivors of the disease, was what made the tanners' clan of Xxamer Zu bold enough to host . . . whatever it was they were hosting. Something dark and dangerous, I felt sure.

Though perhaps that was merely my own trepidation coloring my perception. Perhaps the gathering in the tanners' compound was benign, a distraction from the reality that their skills as tanners were largely wasted because the impoverished Clutch primarily needed the tanners to work the salt pans, while bayen lords imported perfumed leathers from the coastal capital instead.

Skills are like crushed grapes: Used well, they become wine. Left untended, they turn sharp and caustic as vinegar. Everyone needs a sense of worth to be worthy.

A pear-shaped maska drum was being passed about. Women, as well as men, sucked from the long metal pipette that protruded from the drum, and the smell of the fermented drink hovered over the air like a film of sour milk.

I watched Tansan and her group join the gathering. They didn't discreetly sit on the outskirts. No. Tansan confidently picked her way to the very center, where room was made for her—though I heard several grumble while she did so, and many of the men shot her annoyed looks.

I didn't have a good view; I crept back through the dark, located an abandoned wooden bucket, and returned to my vantage point. Carefully I climbed onto the upturned bucket.

An adolescent wearing a plait of jute about his forehead was speaking. ". . . should call down the myazedo from the hills. It's time. Past time."

Myazedo. That unfamiliar word Savga had used to describe her mother.

"Foolish words, Shwe," a bull-chested youth snapped. "We need the support of the people first—"

"We have to strike *now*, before the new overseer is established. We can't wait."

"We aren't organized enough yet to hold the Clutch. Temple'll send the Emperor's curs, and they'll rip out our guts."

"When *will* we ever be able to stand against Temple?"

"When we have the choice," a young man sitting beside Tansan said. I recognized him as one of the two visitors who'd escorted Tansan from the compound. Was it he who'd carried the smell of venom upon him? (If, indeed, I hadn't imagined the scent.)

I leaned forward, straining to see his eyes and any telltale marks of venom that they might bear. I almost fell off my bucket.

"And we'll only have the choice when we have our own land," the young man beside Tansan continued. "We'll have choice when we have our own infirmaries, and a place where we practice the old ways alongside the new. A Clutch is blood and veins for the body of Temple. As long as we swim in that blood, we have few choices."

"We should leave our land?" Bull Chest said. "Travel who knows where to set up a Hamlet of Forsaken? *These* are our fields, our harvests. We stay here and fight."

A spate of arguments broke out. Voices rose. Tansan merely listened, heavily fringed eyes roving over the gathering.

When the arguments showed no sign of abating, she rose to her feet. She stood there. Didn't say anything, didn't do anything, merely stood, statuesque, magnificent. For a moment—just a flame flicker of time—her image wavered in the shadows thrown by the firelight. In her stead, I saw a dragon.

Xxelteker sailors talk of shape-shifters, creatures made of sea mist and the blood of drowned sailors. I thought I saw something that night, some portent of dark Djimbi magics, some shape-shifting thing blended from flame light and moon luminescence and Djimbi blood. But the moment passed, and I knew, with a shiver, it was one more symptom of venom withdrawal.

Gradually all eyes turned to Tansan, and the debates raging about the fire petered to a stop. Some of the men—a goodly portion of them—looked annoyed. One called for her to sit.

Tansan didn't flinch. She waited, unhurried, as wind soughed over the rooftops. The stars glittered hard and bright above her, like thousands of teeth in a dark grin.

When she finally spoke, her voice held such intensity that the fine hairs on my neck tingled. "Even if all the rishi of Xxamer Zu haven't heard of the myazedo, they know they need to possess their own land. They know they are hungry. What the myazedo must do is create a situation so the people can rise up together. It is our duty to start this."

"And what exactly do you suggest we *do*?" a man called, his tone derisive.

"Strike the daronpuis' stockade. Disable every winged dragon, save one or two that we hide in the hills. If we cripple the escoas, we break the holy wardens' link with Temple."

"You want to do this without Chinion's knowledge?" one of the women cried. "Without his permission?"

"Chinion is off base. He won't return for months."

"He's at one of his myazedo camps—"

"And maybe doesn't know that the old Roshu lost overseership of this Clutch, and that we now have an untried Lupini as an overseer."

Tansan was correct: Ghepp *was* an untried overseer, and on top of that a Lupini, a gentleman lord, instead of a Roshu, a retired warrior from the Fa-para army, surrounded by his own regiment of loyal ex-soldiers. Ghepp's father had been a Roshu-Lupini, a gentleman lord who, after years of governing his Clutch, won the title of Roshu upon successfully participating in a skirmish upon the Xxelteker frontier. He'd fought in the skirmish alongside a regiment of soldiers he'd trained beforehand, handpicked Re lords all.

Ghepp had none of that.

Tansan raised her chin. "Chinion is not infallible. He should have left a chain of command which would've allowed us to govern ourselves without him."

There were outcries from many of the men in the crowd; she continued, voice strong. "But Chinion *has* left, and any day now the new Lupini will start selling us off to pay the old overseer's debts. We've all heard the murmurs coming from the Clutch center: The poaching will start soon."

"Go back to your suckling babe!" a man called out. "Leave these matters for those who should speak of them."

She rounded on him. "For the last few weeks you've done nothing but dance around this fire with your useless words while poaching season has crept closer. Which guild clans in this Clutch will be affected this year? Whose children will be shackled and sold off? Yours?"

She addressed the crowd. "Will we stand by and do nothing yet again? No. We should claim our land now, while there are no soldiers in this Clutch!"

The young man beside her cleared his throat. "There are soldiers, Tansan. The new overseer didn't discharge all the paras who remained after the Roshu withdrew. As we speak, he weeds through them, picking some to remain armed and employed. And there's another thing, hey-o."

He looked slowly around his audience. "The new overseer is recruiting soldiers from amongst the rishi."

Bull Chest slapped his thigh. "Hey, what a chance! Half of us must join. We'll be given arms by our enemy, and we'll have access to the daronpuis' stockade!"

Excited mutters of agreement from many. Tansan raised her voice above them. "You talk as if we have time! Where is this time, I ask you? The poaching will start soon! How many more nights are we going to talk these same words, chewing them over and over like maht? We need to act *now*."

"And will you take responsibility for this decision?" someone shouted. "When Chinion returns, will you step forward and say, 'I took command after you left'?"

Tansan's eyes reflected the fire. "Absolutely. Wolves don't waste all their time howling. They hunt. We are wolves, and *now* is the time to hunt."

Several men demanded that Tansan sit. A few of them rose to their feet. Keau placed a hand on her arm and tried to tug her back to the ground. Alliak of the arbiyesku stood and raised his voice above the clamor, saying a decision had to be reached that night, Tansan was correct, they couldn't wait any longer—

Something hit me hard in the back. I went sprawling to the ground, pain blazing across my ribs. I couldn't draw in a breath. Dust was kicked into my eyes and I instinctively doubled over to protect myself, but hands grabbed me, hauled me roughly onto my feet, and pinned my arms behind my back.

I drew in an agonizing breath as I was force-marched toward the bonfire.

Discussion in the crowd abruptly died as my captor pushed me forward. All eyes turned toward us, and the anger and conflict that moments before had been ricocheting wildly about found hostile focus on me.

"I found her back there." Behind me, my captor jerked, as if gesturing. "Listening to everything."

Exclamations from faces twisted by scars and outrage.

The man with the bull chest stepped forward. "Who are you, aosogi-via?"

I took a painful breath and spoke as strongly as I could. "I'm from the arbiyesku."

Faces swung toward Tansan, and her eyes turned venom black. I felt for her; it was unfair that she alone was blamed for my uninvited presence when Alliak, Keau, Piah, and Myamyo from the arbiyesku stood beside her. But even in Xxamer Zu, where the Emperor's patriarchal ways had been watered down by regional isolation and Djimbi customs, it appeared that women were still easiest to fault, and men were assumed blameless.

"Is this so, Tansan?" Bull Chest barked. "She's from your clan?"

"She must have followed us." Tansan didn't deign to look at me.

"Why?" The question was directed at me.

I thought quickly. "I overheard talk about the myazedo amongst the children. I wanted to learn more. I'm afraid of this poaching. I'm afraid for the children."

My gambit had been to turn the focus away from me and back to the debate that had raged moments before. Small hope. Bull Chest again addressed Tansan. "You were careless, allowing yourself to be overheard and followed. Can she be trusted?"

Tansan's face was cold as she looked upon me. "She's new to us. But she can be watched. We'll make certain of it."

"You can start by watching her while you remove her from here. If she says one word to anyone, cut her tongue out."

Tansan bristled. "The meeting isn't over. We haven't come to a decision."

"We'll meet again tomorrow."

"A decision *has* to be made tonight—"

"You've brought a possible traitor amongst us! You're not in a position to demand when a decision should be made!"

Tansan's face went hard as granite.

Piah quickly stepped forward. "So we meet again tomorrow, when a decision will be reached. This is good."

"Tomorrow," Bull Chest agreed, but no one in the crowd moved to leave until Alliak grasped my arm and marched me away from the bonfire.

It wasn't until we were well away from the tanners' clan that Tansan spoke.

"Can you, aosogi-via? Be trusted?" Although her words were indifferent and she walked with supple ease, she conveyed the impression of bristling anger.

"You're my clan," I said hoarsely. "I'd do nothing to harm any of you."

Alliak's hand tightened around my bicep, and no one said a word after that. Tansan's question turned out to be rhetorical, anyway; when we reached the women's barracks, she lay down beside me to sleep and bound her left ankle to my right, and her left wrist to my right one.

"There's no need for that," I hissed, glancing at Savga, curled asleep between Fwipi and Agawan.

"I disagree, debu Secondgirl," Tansan murmured.

She closed her eyes to sleep, cool as a crescent moon.

I, on the other hand, lay awake until well past middle-night. Seething.

SIX

I awoke with a start, urgency racing through my veins. Disoriented by panic, I thought I was back in the dragonmaster's stable domain on Clutch Re, and that it was the morning I was to leave for Arena. I stared wild-eyed at the young, potbellied Djimbi girl squatting beside me, grinning.

"You came back," the girl said. "Did Mama return with you?"

I remembered where I was and where I'd been the night previous. I glanced down at my ankle and wrist. The leather thongs Tansan had used to bind us together were gone. "We came back together."

"She's gone to fetch water, then. Fwipi-granna said so, but I wanted to check."

Savga helped me sit. The rest of the barracks was empty, and the sounds of early morning activity sifted through the woven-reed walls. I stiffly rose to my feet. Savga rolled up our sleeping mat, then slipped herself under one of my arms.

"Is my claimer awake yet?" I asked hoarsely.

Savga shrugged. She, more than anyone else in the arbiyesku, disliked the dragonmaster. "Come on, I'll help you outside."

Outside, sunlight was pouring like yolk sauce over the compound, gilding green-whorled limbs and ocher earth alike. Babies crawled about the ground. Women raked charred kadoob tubers from the previous night's coals and darned the holes in the jute sacks the clan used for harvesting. Men examined dented hoes, sharpened scythes, returned from the latrines.

The dragonmaster was nowhere in sight. But Piah was, and Alliak, both of them lurking near the bottom of the barracks stairs. Watching me.

I saw Fwipi sitting upon the ground, Agawan toying with a dead bird laid beside her. With Savga chatting at my side, I stiffly descended from the barracks and, ignoring the two men at the foot of the stairs, approached Fwipi.

Fwipi squinted up at me. A partially plucked pyumar sat upon her lap like a naked, wilted child. Feathers and down were strewn about her knees and feet and across Agawan. Agawan stared at me, little fingers clutched round the foot of the dead bird beside him.

"Sit; pluck pyumar," Fwipi ordered. "Savga, get a sack and gather these feathers."

I lowered myself to the arid ground. Fwipi's fingers vigorously yanked feathers from pimpled bird skin.

"So. What do you think? Is my memeslu girl bad crazy?" Fwipi asked.

I didn't know what memeslu meant—*seditious,* no doubt—but understood that Fwipi was talking about Tansan.

I licked dry lips. I stank of pipe smoke from last night's gathering, could almost taste it on myself. "So you know where Tansan went last night. And that I followed."

"Tansan takes a chance, talking dangerous talk. I've seen people killed for less. She's young, hasn't seen what I've seen, hasn't felt loss and grief and the back of a para's sword."

"She's felt other things." I carefully extracted the bird's foot from Agawan's determined grip and lifted the dead pyumar onto my lap to pluck.

Fwipi scowled. "Many think like her, but are afraid to speak their minds. Too long we've been afraid, and why not? Hiding, being silent, these can protect you from the para's sword. It's not the Djimbi way, to fight, to be aggressive. But maybe Tansan is right, hey-o. Maybe it's time we changed our thinking. But maybe not. Maybe that will only lead to more deaths."

I scanned the compound again. Where was the cursed dragonmaster? I had to tell him about the myazedo meeting, so he could slip into the Clutch center and warn Daronpu Gen; the last thing I wanted was for every cocoa on my Clutch to be crippled by an angry faction of my own people. And with the warning the dragonmaster carried would go the request—no, the demand—that the practice of poaching be stopped. And trolling. *That* needed to be stopped, too.

Piah and Alliak sauntered closer and brazenly watched me. There was no way I'd be able to leave the compound and inform Daronpu Gen myself.

It was then that the children working the kadoob tract came running into the center of the compound, their eyes glistening with alarm, their mouths agape.

"Daronpuis! Paras!" they shrieked.

Holy wardens? Soldiers? Coming to the arbiyesku?

At once, mothers dropped what they were doing, gathered up infants crawling about the ground, and herded their children into the barracks, calling loudly for those within earshot to hurry up, come, come! The old men who had been languidly stropping scythes and machetes moments before scrambled stiffly upright, spat into their palms, and slicked their biceps, that they might look sleek and strong. Fwipi rose to her feet, down spilling from her lap like panicked mice.

"No. Not now, not this." Fwipi's face turned pallid, which made her whorls stand out. "Savga, Savga! Where is the child?"

"What's going on?" I rose to my feet, pulse racing. I looked at Piah and Alliak; they were arguing; Piah had snatched a machete from one of the old men, was waving it in the air. Alliak was trying to wrestle it from him.

"Into the barracks, quick," Fwipi hissed at me, bending and scooping up Agawan. "Take pyumar with you! Fast, now, fast."

Heart pounding, I grabbed the plucked birds by their rubbery feet and followed Fwipi up the wooden stairs to the barracks. I shot a look over my shoulder, seeking the dragonmaster. There he stood, under the lintel of one of the men's beehive-shaped domiciles. Our eyes met across the dusty compound.

"Savga!" Fwipi cried as the young girl came stumbling across the compound, eyes wide. "Quick!"

"We should run," I gasped, dead birds heavy and lank against one thigh. "Hide in the fields."

"Paras would return for us, this day, the next, the day after that. We'd be beaten, then, for making them work so hard. Beaten bad. I saw a man crippled, saw a child's arm snapped like a twig. I watched a woman die from such a beating. . . . No. We don't run."

I threw one last look toward the dragonmaster. He'd disappeared back inside the hut.

A line of daronpuis came marching down one of the dusty paths leading into our compound, their porphyry-and-emerald robes startling against the drab background.

Oh, Re.

I ducked into the barracks.

Inside, the children held themselves very still, some crowded onto their mother's laps, others holding a sibling tight. I immediately thought of pundar, the camouflage technique used by dragonmaster apprentices within Arena, where only stillness and a cape the color of earth protected one from being mauled by a wrathful bull dragon.

Hiding, being silent, these can protect you from the para's sword, Fwipi had said.

How appropriate that daronpuis wore the greens and purples of a bull dragon.

Savga was crouched with Oblan and Runami beside Oblan's mother, who was nursing her babe to keep him quiet. Savga's eyes, shiny as flakes of polished obsidian, darted about nervously.

We moved quickly to the center of the barracks, where the women and children had clustered, as if cohesion could somehow protect each individual from harm. Leaning heavily upon me with one arm, holding Agawan against her with the other, Fwipi sat beside Savga. She wrapped a bony arm about the shoulders of her grandchild and placed Agawan on her own lap. Savga buried her face against her greatmother's long, thin breasts.

"After every Abbassin Shinchiwouk, we dread this." Fwipi's voice was toneless. "Some years our ku goes untouched. Some years we hear that another clan lost a clawful of their kin. Rare it is that no one is visited by poachers after Shinchiwouk. Rare it is that the overseer hasn't lost many wagers in Arena and doesn't need to pay off a debt."

"There's a new Clutch overseer," I said faintly. "There are no debts."

Fwipi stared at me with dead eyes.

What was Ghepp up to?

I could not sit there, blind, while our fates were being decided. I rose to my feet and went to the door, my chest tumescent with panic.

I peered past the door frame. Outside, the arbiyesku's Great-elder, Yobif, was kowtowing to one of three daronpuis in the dusty center of the compound.

Shades of history. Flashes from my youth. I smelled hot metals—copper, iron, bronze, the odors of blood—and remembered seeing my father's severed tongue, dust coated and ghastly, upon the ground.

Stiff and awkward with age, Yobif rose from where he'd knelt, banging his forehead repeatedly upon the ground before the daronpu's sandals. Yobif talked quickly, hands clasped, shoulders obsequiously bowed, smile thin and desperate, head bobbing with every second word. The daronpu he addressed brushed him away with a flick of a bangled wrist.

The paras all wore the nationally recognized uniform of a soldier: boiled leather skirt and plastron, faces corded with sinister cicatrices dyed blue, hair in double topknots that protruded from each forehead like the blunt horns of a young jungle buck.

Alliak must have dragged Piah out of sight. The two were nowhere to be seen. Neither was Myamyo.

A daronpu slid a scroll from a gilded ivory pipe at his waist. The paras withdrew their swords from their sheaths. The blades rasped from their scabbards as if the metal were sighing with expectation, thirsting for blood.

"These named shall now step forth, as Lupini Xxamer Zu requires," the daronpu boomed, and his voice carried clear into the barracks and I heard breaths held, felt fingernails dig into palms. "Arbiyesku Xxamer Zu Korshan's Yenvia, commonly called Runami."

Screams and wails erupted within the barracks. The daronpu continued his recital outside.

"Arbiyesku Xxamer Zu Rudik's Rutvia, commonly called Oblan; arbiyesku Xxamer Zu Keau's Waivia, commonly called Savga—"

I turned slowly, as if swimming through soft lard. Saw six-year-old, cant-eyed Savga with the upturned nose and delicate mole beside her left nostril hurl herself at her greatmother, watched Agawan tumble from Fwipi's lap to the floor. Savga clung tight to Fwipi's neck, wailing.

"—and the hatagin komikon and his wai roidan yin," the daronpu finished, and it took me several moments to understand what he'd said.

I was on that list. I would be sold into slavery.

"Come forth now and there will be no bloodshed," the daronpu said. "For every person that resists, eight shall be punished."

Fwipi's snail-colored eyes met mine. She struggled to her feet as around her women ululated and raked their arms in grief, swaying upon their knees, throwing themselves face-first upon the floor. The summoned girls were surrounded by a tight knot of aunties, cousins, and nieces. Savga, too, was lost from sight amidst a roiling knot of grief-stricken women.

Fwipi stood before me, eyes empty.

"You must stay with them, hey-o. You will be their mother now. You alone can offer them love, shelter them from harm. Know this, Kazonvia."

Savga's Tiwana-auntie was wading toward me, her nostrils flared, her slii-blackened lips tight. Savga clung to her, quaking and shrieking.

I would faint; I was sure of it. This could not be happening, not now, not here, not after all I'd gone through.

Tiwana-auntie stood before me, women swaying and rocking on either side of her, blood from their raked arms on their cheeks, hair from their heads hanging like black cornsilk between their fingers.

Tiwana-auntie's rheumy eyes burrowed into mine, eating at my soul, searing my heart.

Slowly, she pulled Savga from her neck.

"No, no! Don't let them take me. Fwipi-granna, no!"

Savga's weight in my arms: heavy, sweaty, unwanted. Limbs slight and stiff with fear.

"Mama!"

The shriek in my ear sent my senses reeling.

Fwipi touched Savga's head, then turned her back on her grandchild, staggered several steps away, and fell, as if hewn down at the knees. She was caught by bloodied hands.

"You are her mother-only now, Kazonvia," Tiwana-auntie rasped. "Remember this."

Savga was heavy. I could not carry her far. So I set her down and she walked alongside me, sucking in spasming breaths, the chain that led from her wrist shackles to mine clanking and tugging with every step. Through the shackles' crude metal, I felt her stumbling footfalls against the soft skin that covered the small, slender bones connecting my forearms to my wrists, felt her fear and vulnerability. That cold, indifferent chain bound us together as if it were a metal umbilical cord.

On the other side of me walked the two other young girls who had been sundered forever from the arbiyesku: Oblan and Runami. They pressed close to me, shivering, weeping, children chained by metal to a reality no child should face. Two young boys had also been plucked from the arbiyesku. They walked stiffly, reluctant to show their fear but failing to hide it.

The dusty path beneath our bare feet was smooth and slippery with trodden grass. Either side of us, seedpods exploded from feathery grainheads at our passage and sailed briefly through the air before lodging, like tiny arrows, into cloth or earth or hair. The sun glared down, shriveling skin, turning my head glossy and hot. The smell of black leather and the stink of unwashed men emanated from the paras marching aflank us. At the very front of the line walked the daronpuis—three of them—and every now and then the cloying smell of incense wafted from their robes and infested the air as they delicately dabbed sweat from their foreheads with hankies of silk.

In my right hand, clutched tight as hope, I held an object one of the paras had slipped into my palm as he'd shackled my wrists. His eyes had briefly met mine before I'd glanced down at the object. It was a small rusted chain and clasp, the type used to close a garment together, on either end of which was attached to a tiny swatch of material the exact rufous color of the ground at Arena.

It wasn't until he'd snapped a pair of heavy, cool manacles over my wrists that I realized what the object was: the chain and clasp from the vebalu cape I'd worn in Arena. I remembered shucking that bloody cape, with much cursing and groaning, inside the feed loft of the messenger byre.

I clutched the chain tightly. It was a message from Gen. Surely.

I tried to catch the eye of the para who'd surreptitiously given me Gen's token. He avoided my gaze.

The dragonmaster walked ahead of me, chained, his shoulders rolling beneath his tunic like the swells of an angry ocean. He turned to look back at me.

"Gen sent a token," I murmured, lips cold. "We'll be fine."

He snorted and faced forward again.

Savga leaned against me, shuddering, her breath rasping in her throat like strips of jute along arid ground. I didn't know how to comfort her.

We were led along a dusty, cracked path; we stopped at another guild clan. Again, the daronpu read from his scroll. Again, the keening of women, burning as if it were hot wax across my skin, tearing, yanking, leaving a raw welt.

The paras enclosed more children's knobby wrists in metal, chained them one to the other. I clenched the small, rusted token in my palm tightly, squeezed it, strangled it.

This should not be happening, I wanted to cry out. This is *my* Clutch. This a place of safety, of family. This is *home*.

It was not.

This was a line of people shackled together, like animals for barter.

When one woman threw herself, shrieking, at the daronpu with the scroll, a para neatly stepped forward and smashed the hilt of his sword into her face. Blood spurted. Savga screamed. I reeled from the memory of watching a boot heel slam again and again against my mother's jaw.

Eight women were randomly chosen from the bloodied woman's clan and punished for her act. The broadsides of swords flashed in the sun. The sound of metal striking flesh, over and over until flesh was pulped with bruises, seemed louder than the victims' screams.

I lapsed into a daze, moved as if made of wood.

Gradually, the three blinding white domes and the golden minaret of Xxamer Zu's temple grew larger, shimmering upon waves of heat. Buildings crouched about the temple like wild dogs about a bone.

We were being led into the center of Clutch Xxamer Zu.

My mouth was sour and grit-laden. I badly wanted water. Savga shuffled beside me, her face a clot of melted tallow.

We shambled by a cart repair shop surrounded by dilapidated, abandoned huts. Hammers stopped pounding, saws stopped chewing through wood. Eyes like beads of tar followed us in faces free of all expression. We shuffled by an empty caravansary where pigeons roosted in the empty eyeholes of windows; then we passed a series of narrow, rickety tenements pungent with the smells of citrus and yanew bark.

If not for my discovery at the myazedo meeting, perhaps a decision would have been reached. Perhaps they would have rallied and prevented the slavers from coming. I was, therefore, partly responsible for the chains around Savga's wrist.

I turned aside and retched. My bile splashed against the warped wooden planks of one of the rickety tenements lining the narrow street.

The purpose of the tenements was unclear from their wooden exteriors, despite the wizened old women sitting beneath each lintel, sizzling lily-white liquids in large pans balanced upon smoking braziers. The old women looked at us as if we were pashnor ki fa cinai ersen, the handwriting of the enraged Pure Dragon, which is what the wreckage left by a hurricane is called in the Emperor's tongue.

At our passage, a dark rishi woman, her skin the brown of a wet water vole and mottled with whorls of sooty green, came to a slow stop, her empty handcart in front of her. A cluster of youths ambled out of an alley, huge baskets of featon kernels strapped to their backs, their skins a mosaic of browns and greens: umber, ebon, berry brown, burnt-onion green, olive, sage. Their piebald markings looked like verdigris cirri trapped immobile upon flesh, and the expressions on their faces as they caught sight of us went from shock to outrage to careful indifference in a matter of heartbeats. Perhaps they even stopped breathing for several moments.

The paras flanking our chained line walked with hands upon the hilts of their swords, their fierce facial cicatrices furrowed into vulture frowns.

We came upon a thoroughfare, a wide, parched stretch of dirt flanked on either side by mansions. A piebald youth was pulling a rickshaw along the road. Two bayen ladies sat within the rickshaw, shaded by a huge ivory parasol that glittered with tiny mirrors and hundreds of fine glass beads. They didn't so much as glance at us.

Our daronpu led us onto the thoroughfare. My eyes were drawn to the impressive mansions lining it.

The facade of each mansion was impossibly smooth and white, as if carved from bone, though heavily furred at the base with red dust. Balconies and balustrades protruded from the mansions' frontage like wrought-iron ribs, and bloodred euphoria flowers dripped in thick profusion from balcony urns to ground level. The fragrance of the flowers was as coppery and heavy as fresh blood.

Late noon. The sun pulsed like a pustulant tumor.

We followed the thoroughfare for a while, then turned down a side avenue, its hardpan littered with curled brown vegetable debris. Abruptly we came out upon the outskirts of Iri Timadu Bayen Gekin, market square of Xxamer Zu's most exalted aristocrats. Wai Bayen Temple stood at its center.

Beside me, Savga made a noise like a small animal caught by a wild dog. She was staring at the temple with eyes like peeled songbird eggs.

Atop an enormous sandstone plinth perforated with geometrical patterns, the three domes of Temple Xxamer Zu squatted. The largest dome—the one visible from every corner of the Clutch—was topped by a golden minaret. Between sandstone pillars, the temple's three sunken open-sided amphitheaters peeped out like three massive black pupils. The amphitheaters' cool interiors smelled like basins of night, the glass tesserae mosaics upon the pillars within twinkling like blue-white stars.

Standing along the westerly edge of the temple like a regiment of massive, blocky soldiers was a series of stone buildings: the offices, dormitories, treasury vaults, larders, dining halls, and prayer chambers of the Clutch Xxamer Zu holy wardens. The very same stockade where, not two weeks ago, a Host of Auditors had tried to slay me.

The puritanical faces of the buildings were interrupted at regular intervals by severe window casements. At the base of the buildings, stone bridges arched over nonexistent ponds like the humps of a giant, petrified snake. A massive iron fence, fourteen feet high and topped by rusted iron barbs, surrounded the entire stockade.

We stopped before that iron fence.

Gates swung open upon hinges that screamed for oil. The stacks and rows of the stone dormitories glared down at us. We were led over a stone bridge. Down a narrow stone viaduct that sloped beneath one of the stone dorms. The underground viaduct stank of piss.

Did the daronpuis urinate there, too lazy or indifferent to void in a latrine? I pictured them casting furtive looks down the viaduct, hiking the many elegant layers of their gowns above their groins, aiming their pudgy phalluses at the wall, spraying urine doglike over their territory with all the impunity of the untouchable elite.

Savga pinched her nostrils shut with one hand, the chain about her wrist clanking against her chin.

Out of the viaduct, into a courtyard.

Oh, how we gaped!

The courtyard was festooned with succulent vines heavy with lush fruit. Upon ground choked with tiny white flowers, colorful glazed pots brimmed with velvet purple blooms. Fat bees buzzed hither and thither. Massive, shady foliage, leaves the length and width of a child standing with arms and legs spread-eagled, rubbed against imperious spikes of berry-beaded plants. They exuded a tart, turpentine scent, those leaves, that made the air crisp and abrasive.

Flowers like great, golden flutes hung ponderously from glossy white stems taller than my head. Fountains sprayed upon purple-hued leaves, making them jiggle and nod as if they had palsy. Bright orange carp flashed within ponds, looking like wet slices of sunset immersed in liquid blue sky.

We crossed through this wondrous world of moisture and lushness, too stunned to notice our thirst and hunger despite the profusion of water and succulent fruits gleaming at us.

Down another viaduct, our senses rattled by what we'd left behind.

Another courtyard, this beautiful in its austerity. Large, slablike stones had been tipped impossibly upright and balanced carefully, precisely, upon one edge. A daronpu acolyte, stripped to the waist—his telltale green collar lying at his knees like an obedient dog—knelt at the court's center. Blood threaded his back and torso. He didn't appear to notice us as we shambled past, chains clanking. Eyes rapturously locked upon one of the impossibly balanced rocks, he was using a flogger to flail his arms, chest, and back. The sound of the many leather thongs striking his skin was like wet dough being slapped by the seamed hands of an old woman.

Down another viaduct: the smell of dragon dung, the leathery reek of dragon hide.

My heart quickened.

Out into a stable yard.

For a moment I thought I smelled venom. So iron-linked was the smell of dragon to the scent of venom, so strong was my craving for venom, that I could re-create the fragrance of the dragons' liquid fire out of thin air with my need.

"The messenger byre," the dragonmaster grunted ahead of me, and as I looked upon the dragons stabled in each stall, I realized that, of course, these dragons were merely escoas, the nonvenomous dragons employed to courier messages, parcels, and privileged persons about the country. The very escoas Tansan had wanted to cripple.

I was back where I'd started from upon first arriving in Xxamer Zu. The messenger byre.

The soldiers herded us to an empty stall.

No bedding of any sort had been forked upon the flagstone. A trough of water stood at one end.

As the chain that joined us together was removed from our manacles—which were *not* removed from our wrists—we staggered toward the trough lining the far wall. There we knelt and thrust our faces into the still, dusty water and sucked long and deep, drinking our fill.

By night we'd all have stomach cramps. By morn, the air would be thick with the reek of diarrhea.

But we weren't to know that. All we knew at that moment was that we'd stopped walking, that the screams of families being torn asunder had ended, that water slaked our chapped lips and ran like cool algae down the backs of our throats.

And that, for the moment, was enough.

SEVEN

I sang to Savga and Oblan and Runami—my three unwanted children—through the night.

"Sen fu lili, sen limia . . ."

Love songs, they were, imprinted on my memory from years of crawling about the feet of potter women as they worked and sang, while my toothless, infantile gums chomped away on a stale holy cake, my little fingers carefully picking up treasure to be examined: a pebble, a pot shard, a dead moth.

"My soft honey, my temptress . . ."

While children clutched their empty tummies and cried out or wept in their sleep, my voice drizzled like a golden glaze over the clay-cold stall that imprisoned us.

Stomach cramps come middle-night. The futile scramble to find a place to void. The shame and stench of upset bowels erupting like volcanoes onto flagstone.

Still, when I was not occupied, I sang. When she could, Savga sat curled upon my lap as if she were a baby, and with both arms I held Oblan and Runami close to me. And I sang.

"Sen wai kavarria, gunashti tras hoiden nas."

Oblan kept asking for her baby brother. She had slept each night with him cradled against her belly; she'd carried him each day while fetching water and hoeing. Unable to fully grasp the enormity of her situation, she focused her concern on her baby brother. *Who will look after him while Mother is busy, Kazonvia? Who, who?* She was almost frantic with the thought that he was cold, untended, unfed. This from a child about to be sold into slavery.

"My first obsession, I am unfit to live with while love-crazed."

Dawn seeped into the night, staining the walls ashy gray. The first flies began to buzz about our foul prison. My tailbone was bruised from where I'd been sitting on the cold floor with Savga's weight pressed upon my lap. My legs felt bloodless; they didn't belong to me.

A daronpu acolyte appeared outside our stall's iron gate and spoke with the four paras who'd stood guard over us the entire night. I stopped singing. The few rishi women who'd been chained along with the rest of us rose up, pleading for food for the children, clean water, a latrine.

"The arbiyesku's hatagin komikon and his wai roidan yin have been summoned by Lupini Xxamer Zu's First Chancellor!" one of the paras barked above the pleadings of the women. His voice was raspy with the fatigue of standing guard all night. "Come forth now."

Savga clutched my neck.

I swallowed. My tongue felt made of splintered wood. I looked toward the dragonmaster, where he'd sat crouched upon his haunches all eve near the stall gate. He rose to his feet. His blood-marbled eyes looked opaque in the predawn gloom.

"Come forth!" the acolyte demanded, impatient and imperious, pleased, as an underling, to be momentarily in a position of power. He tugged on his green scapular, straightening it. Picked invisible lint from it. "Don't keep us waiting."

I tried to rise. Savga shrieked hoarsely and clamped herself to me.

"I won't leave you; I won't," I murmured into her hair. I couldn't rise with the weight of her and her terror. One of the arbiyesku's boys helped me up, though his little hands were hardly capable of the adult task. Oblan and Runami rose alongside me, pressing close, silent, clutching my soiled bitoo tightly.

Like a wounded six-legged beast, we lurched toward the stall gate. Savga squeezed my waist so hard with her legs, where she clung to me like a baby monkey to its mother, that my ribs ached.

The acolyte glanced at the dragonmaster, then looked with disgust at me and the children.

"They stay here," he snapped, flicking the air with beeswax-polished nails.

"Please—" I began.

"Put that thing down and come forth!"

The acolyte looked younger than me, milk-sopped with a life of ease, his fa-pim skin extraordinarily pale from years of copying scrolls upon parchment by candlelight, away from all sun.

"The Lupini has summoned me, yes?" I said, voice low. My stomach torqued painfully. "Can't these three come with me?"

His throat and cheeks flushed, as if dark wine were spreading like a stain over his skin. He turned to a para, punched the air with his indignation. "Behead the children! Bring her out."

"No!" I cried, and everyone within the stall shrieked, wailed, covered eyes and ears. Could he order such a thing, he, a mere acolyte? Apparently, yes. Would he be obeyed?

The para nodded brusquely.

Apparently, yes.

Oblan and Runami gripped me tighter in their terror. I turned to them and spoke quickly, pawing at their hands, trying to pry their little fingers from my bitoo, while Savga held me even tighter and pressed her face into my neck.

"Please, listen, let go of me. I'll come back, I promise; let go, please."

The para opened the gate, withdrew his sword.

"Go, go!" I shrieked at Runami and Oblan, smacking their arms, pushing them, hitting them. "Listen to me! I'll come back for you; now go!"

They ran from me, slipping, stumbling, and dived behind the legs of others.

You will be their mother now. You alone can offer them love, shelter them from harm. Know this, Kazonvia.

I turned, heart pounding against the backs of my eyes, and faced the para. I wrapped both arms about Savga, holding her tight against me. She shuddered.

"Savga," I whispered into her hair. "I have to go now. Please. They'll hurt you if you don't let me go."

She shook her head. The hair of her crown was soft and fine under my chin. "You won't come back."

"I will," I said, meaning it, really meaning it, yet almost choking on the promise, for I knew that once I left that stall, I would never see her or Oblan or Runami again.

"We're foremost friends," Savga breathed against my neck, her little ribs heaving beneath my hands. "Don't leave me."

Filled with despair, I looked at the para, met his eyes, made inhuman, so deliberately, by his monstrous facial cicatrices. And I remembered how Tansan had given herself over to violation, and protected me from the same, for the sake of the child in my hands.

"You will have to cut the arms from my body to separate us," I whispered.

The para's eyes widened; then he turned for instruction from the acolyte, who looked as if he would snatch the sword himself and start hacking at me.

The dragonmaster spoke.

"We waste time, woman!" he barked at me. "Must we lose our heads from the First Chancellor's rage at being kept waiting, all for the sake of one child? Must this acolyte be whipped, this para demoted? Bring her along and be done with it; let the chancellor do what he wishes with the thing!"

I stared at him and a low, hollow sound echoed within my ears, as if I were standing at the bottom of a deep well, and I wondered, then, what he really felt about children, about all the children he'd seen mauled to death in Arena during his reign as dragonmaster of Clutch Re. Perhaps he *forced* himself to dislike children, to be able to continue each day, to be able to do the things that were required of him as a dragonmaster. Perhaps his dislike of children was a front, was his only defense in a world made merciless and bloody by the Emperor's Temple laws. Impatience with children was his shield.

One he was now ingeniously using to protect me.

The acolyte stiffened, reminded by the dragonmaster of his lowly status. He gestured for me to step out of the stall. I obeyed and kept my arms tight around Savga. The stall gate clanked shut behind us.

The acolyte spat at my feet. His spittle was the color of dark meat, looked like a giblet. He spun about and started across the stable court. Hunching his shoulders, the dragonmaster followed.

After a moment, so did I.

Not once did I look back to where Oblan and Runami watched my departure with unblinking eyes.

Is that how you felt, Mother, when you chose Waivia over me? Your belly heavy with despair, your eyes swollen with unshed tears? Did you, too, choke on your own betrayal, comfort yourself with the fierce vow that no matter what, this one child, *this one child,* you would not turn away from, not now, not ever?

Is that a little of what it feels like to abandon a daughter?

Into the daronpuis' quarters, along cool stone halls so narrow two could not comfortably walk abreast. The white stonework gleamed as if varnished; I thought of white coranuts, hulled and bobbing in a pan of hot fat. Small, smooth concavities dimpled the walls, each tiny basin home for an exquisite ivory carving of a dragon. Those were not normal dragons, no: They were nippled, bosomy, teated, pigeon-breasted. Their tails were burled and phallic. Some statuettes were convoluted, kinked into a helix. Others were cuneated, all sharp angles and pointed triangles. Each looked the work of a dawahat komihan, an ivory-paring master, and worth many dragon eggs.

I had to place Savga down, limited by the strength in my arms and back, and she slid otterlike down my torso, clinging still. I kept a hand upon one of her bony little shoulders as we lurched along, joined at my hip.

The musky smell of incense impregnated the air, and sticky brown beads of it clung to the upper walls; trail marks of the stuff ran down the stone as if the white walls were sweating sap. Every now and then we passed a shell-shaped recess, a grotto where a daronpu might stand aside to let others pass him in the narrow corridor.

We passed mouthlike doors, oval, made of beaten tin, stamped with images of featon sheaves, dragon eggs, and pomegranates. Some were locked with great bolts and latches. Temple needed to guard against its own, it seemed.

We stopped at one of those tin doors. The acolyte opened it, ducked through. The dragonmaster followed, Savga and I at his heels.

The room we entered seemed lumpish with overstuffed pillows, the walls furry with ponderous tapestries. I could scarce draw in a breath, so airless and dusty was the room. The stale smell of disuse filled my mouth and nostrils like thick wadding.

Two paras flanking the inside of the door we'd just come through glowered at me with twin repugnance. I flushed with shame for the brown stains upon my bitoo, for the stench of me and Savga, yet I also lifted my chin in defiance. If not for the paras and their ilk, I wouldn't *be* in such a disgraceful state. They'd created my filth; let them gag on it.

"That's the one," a voice said, and I scanned the pillows and tapestries and found, standing amongst the nubby confusion of colors, the Wai Vaneshor, the First Chancellor, clothed in red robes, the trim around his neck and sleeves and hem blue silk. The gray-bearded man looked disturbingly familiar.

"This is the hatagin komikon who owes money from debts incurred at Arena," the First Chancellor said. "I'll deal with him and his claimed woman from here."

The acolyte shot a smug look at the dragonmaster, then me. *Now you'll get your comeuppance,* the look clearly said. As he swept by, Savga burrowed her head under one of my arms. The acolyte flicked his thumbnails against his earlobes as a gesture to ward off evil—as if a hungry child and her filthy surrogate mother had the power to harm him.

He departed. The First Chancellor addressed the paras. "Wait outside. I'll summon you if need be."

They obeyed.

The door shut with a sharp, glassy sound.

"For the love of wings, Babu, what's happened to you?" the chancellor rumbled. I stared at him.

And, as if gazing across a desert at a figure made hazy by shimmering waves of heat, the chancellor slowly resolved into a recognizable figure. Daronpu Gen.

He stood stooped, like a wizened old man, and his unruly cleft beard had been chopped off and groomed into a neat gray arrowhead. His head was tonsured and age-spotted, and his skin was no longer bark-brown but ivory, as impossibly fa-pim as the Emperor's.

"Gen?" I gasped.

"Keep your voice down, blood-blood! That door is listening." He furrowed gray, atypically groomed eyebrows. "Have you been ill? You stink worse than rot."

"Your skin's the wrong color," I said, stupid with bafflement.

"Watch what you say!" He pointed to my side. "Who's the rishi via?"

I looked down, was somewhat startled to see a young girl standing beside me. But only for a moment. I remembered where I was, what had transpired, and suddenly I was spuming with outrage.

"What are you *doing*?" I cried, taking several steps forward. Savga held me back, ballast, millstone, anchor.

"Voice down!" Gen ordered.

I flared my nostrils and dragged Savga toward him, wading over dunes of dusty pillows. "What's the meaning of this, stealing people from their kus and wrapping them in chains?" I held up Savga's manacled wrists and shook them. "You treat children like this?"

Gen looked suddenly as ill and beaten as Fwipi had, back at the arbi-yesku barracks. "Ghepp gave me little choice, Babu. If there was another way to buy what we need, to pay our debts—"

"There *is* another way; there must be!"

"I've thought of many, but Ghepp—"

"I own this Clutch, not Ghepp."

A weary look flashed across Gen's face, but I ignored it, trapped in a hemorrhaging pustule of wrath. I gashed the air behind me with a finger. "Those walls out there are covered with figurines worth a small fortune. How dare you tell me you have no choice; how dare you sell children instead of those!"

"Those figurines belong to Temple," the dragonmaster said. He stalked over and stood beside me, radiating hostility. "We sell those and we antagonize every daronpu on these acres. The uproar will be heard clear to Liru."

"Don't think I haven't fought this," Gen said, his voice old, his eyes pleading.

I would not grant him a shred of empathy.

"Sell off some of our brooders," I demanded, hands clenching into fists, using the word *our* like a sword.

"We've barely enough food in this Clutch as it is. We can ill afford to lose a single egg producer, let alone the amount required—"

"Manioc, then."

"The unharvested crop is already presold."

"Rishi are not slaves!" I cried. "We're not indentured serfs to be poached and traded like deer!"

The dragonmaster waved aside my outcry and addressed Gen. "You trade the children for a dragon, yes? A young destrier?"

Gen nodded. "Ghepp has managed to purchase a venomous yearling from Clutch Diri for our purposes."

"Diri?" the dragonmaster cried. "They suffer scale plague! If that destrier carries the disease, Xxamer Zu's brooder herd will be decimated."

"We intend on keeping it isolated," Gen growled. "No Clutch in the Jungle Crown would sell us a destrier. We had little choice but to go to Diri. Kratt is ill pleased that his half brother won Xxamer Zu in Arena. He's using his influence so that Ghepp hasn't a single ally with the overseers of the Clutches in this jurisdiction."

The dragonmaster scowled. "Kratt suspects foul play."

"Of course! The man's not a fool. Against preposterous odds, Ghepp laid an outrageous wager, backed by an anonymous source. Such a wager doesn't go unnoticed, hey-o! Even now, Kratt's trying to learn where Ghepp found the resources for it. He'll learn before long that Malaban Bri backed our bid."

Gen glanced at me. "And Kratt knows you escaped Arena alive, what-hey. He's inciting Temple and the populace into a fever over you; says you're demon spawned, intent on subverting tradition and corrupting youth to commit bestiality. Your name is on the lips of every Clutch Re rishi right now. The capital is in a foment, a froth, a boil!"

"I have always been unpopular with the public," I said boldly. But my pulse turned erratic.

"This is different, girl. Kratt's made you a symbol of evil and himself a holy crusader driven by repentance. He's using the fact that he once supported you as evidence of your powers of beguilement." Gen wagged one of his fingers at me, as if I were a child. "It's because he fears your Skykeeper, hey-o! He knows who you truly are; he knows what power you have at your disposal. Like a thundercloud, you are, and he fears the lightning you can shed!"

My stomach went hard and sour. I *didn't* have such power at my disposal. My sister did, and she stood at Kratt's side. Kratt wanted to eliminate any threat of losing the Skykeeper. He wanted, therefore, to eliminate me.

Again, the dragonmaster impatiently waved away Gen's remarks, as if swatting the air clear of flies. "When will the destrier arrive from Diri? She'll take months to train. We've no time to waste."

"She'll arrive the week following delivery of . . . of our bartered goods," Gen said, eyes flitting upon me but unable to touch upon the manacled child at my side. "That's why I brought you both here—"

"No," I said. "I refuse."

"Refuse *what?*" the dragonmaster sneered.

I slapped his cheek. Yes. I struck the cheek of the man who, not long before, had achieved Savga's unharmed presence at my side. The man who had, a mere year ago, whipped me, derided me, demanded I commit bestiality with a dragon, and cowed me with fear.

The imprint of my hand stood white as poached albumen upon the dragonmaster's piebald cheek. I felt every bead of blood within the dragonmaster and me realign as my action altered the balance of power between us. His face turned the color of muddy water. I wouldn't let him indulge in a moment of his anger. I met Gen's eyes and held them with all the force of iron manacles.

"I will walk away from you, this Clutch, and your schemes and dreams if you go through with this, Gen. You return every last one of these rishi to their clans, understand? We'll pay for the destrier another way. I will not lie with a dragon purchased with the lives of children."

"For the love of wings, girl—"

"Do it."

"*How?* I can't shit bullion!"

I thought of all the wealth I'd passed in the corridor, all that white wealth locked untouchably in the carved bone and stone and horn of the statuettes. And I thought of the white, dust-furred bayen mansions I'd passed while being led, shackled, to Temple Xxamer Zu.

"Those mansions on the thoroughfare," I said. "What are they made of? That egg-white stone."

"The facades are alabaster. Marble perhaps." A wary look crept over Gen's face. "I'm no stonemason. I can't be sure."

"Demolish one of those mansions," I said with finality. "Sell the contents and have the facade stone carved into fine caskets for salve, into perfume flacons. Into statuettes and drinking pipettes and urns and hair combs—whatever trinkets are fashionable amongst the aristocrats in Liru. Trade those for a destrier."

"Yolkbrained screw!" the dragonmaster raved beside me. "It'll take months for such to transpire—"

Without looking at him I held up a hand to cut off his tirade, and I spoke only to Gen. "Do this. Do this, or lose me."

"You ask me to hold mist in my hands."

"Mist is made from water. You can hold water."

"If Ghepp is pushed toward something, he curls up like a banded noony, all armor-plated and impenetrable. The man barely believes you're the Dirwalan Babu, and he's ambivalent about pitting himself against Temple."

"Do it, Gen."

He closed his eyes and pressed his knuckles to his forehead. He kept still for a long, long time. Finally, he looked at me.

"There is a bayen family here," he said, weighing each word slowly. "One that would not protest too much if relocated to the coast under much pomp and circumstance. Perchance Malaban Bri might find an illustrious post in Liru for the lord of that family. We could demolish their house here, use that marble. . . ."

"Good."

"There'll be repercussions from Ghepp."

"Yes."

He rubbed his cheeks, looked old and frail. But because he was a good man, because he *wanted* to acknowledge the child beside me, Gen took a deep breath that inflated him beyond his disguise as a wizened old man, and he nodded.

"Fine, Babu," he said, and he reached out and placed a broad hand on Savga's head. "It will be done."

Using his rank as Wai Vaneshor Xxamer Zu—First Chancellor to Lupini Xxamer Zu—Gen was able to arrange the release of every poached rishi without consulting Ghepp. Under the artificial guard of two paras hand-picked by Gen, the dragonmaster was taken to the defunct and empty destrier stables of Xxamer Zu, there to begin making an inventory of its tack and what needed repairing. One of those paras was the soldier who'd slipped me Gen's token upon my arrest from the arbiyesku.

I insisted upon accompanying Gen in returning Oblan, Runami, and Savga to the arbiyesku.

Gen ran a blunt-nailed finger over the bridge of his prominent nose. He looked tired and resigned. "Yes, yes." He sighed. "As you say. Into the cart with you."

He'd managed to appropriate several carts for our purpose. The brooders yoked to them were ribby and pot-gutted. If I'd had any room left within my emotionally spent psyche, I'd have been aghast at their condition.

Instead I turned a blind eye, climbed into the back of one of the carts, and settled myself between Runami and Oblan. Savga curled onto my lap. Her body was tense with expectation, and she breathed in gulps. All the children were silent and breathless, all desperately hoping that what Gen had promised them—the return to their guild clans—would indeed transpire.

That's the one thing that upsets me most, to this day. The fragile silence of desperate children.

A few of the captured young boys, however, sizzled like unshed lightning bolts. Now that their freedom was being returned, indignation emboldened them. They muttered, they glared, they cursed Ranon ki Cinai, the Emperor, and Lupini Xxamer Zu, not caring that the same armed paras who had marched them to imprisonment still surrounded them with blades drawn.

Gen was aware of it. Before the last rishi child had clambered into a cart, shivering and sweating from belly cramps, Gen rose from the bench of the cart he would drive, inflated his chest, and bellowed, "Lupini Xxamer Zu is a just man, an ingenious overseer. His refusal to deal in the trade of rishi to clear this Clutch of its previous overseer's debts has granted him the wisdom of the One Dragon, and not but several hours ago did he devise an alternate means to pay off those same debts! I would not earn the wrath of such an ethical man, lest you tempt him to rue and revoke his decision."

Even though he wore the tonsure and gray beard of an old man, Gen suddenly looked the fierce giant he was, and I'm sure it wasn't just I who envisioned him with windswept cinder black brows as he met the eyes of each young boy, one by one.

Such a fine speech cowed the boys, and they fell silent. We began our journey.

The air was muggy, congealed with humidity and odors. Clouds loomed on the horizon, shoals of brooding gray. As if sensing their approach and its impending enclosure, the sun was molten with fury. In the back of the cart, the children and I were languid.

He was wise, Daronpu Gen, where I'd been naive. I had expected tears and joyful reunions. But no. There was anger, so much anger, directed at Gen and the acolytes he'd pressed into driving the other carts. Anger not that the children were being returned. No. Anger that they'd been taken, an atrocious act committed with such impunity. It was good that the paras accompanied us. Only the threat of their swords prevented Gen and the acolytes from being pulled from their benches and mauled.

It was dark by the time the meaty, rancid stench of the arbiyesku reached my nostrils, and those clouds on the horizon had belly-crawled closer, cloaking a great swath of stars in black. Runami, Savga, and Oblan were dehydrated and filthy, and they sat slumped beside me in the back of the cart.

Our procession of carts—all empty now, save the one Gen drove—rolled into the arbiyesku compound, axles squeaking like crickets. We came to a stop. Everything was silent. Beside me, Savga's breath sounded as loud as a bellows.

Shadows rose up from the ground outside the women's barracks, and more shadows emerged from the doorways of the mud-brick huts. Slowly, those sooty wraiths drew closer. Starlight stabbed down like the points of hundreds of rapiers, imparting the illusion that whorled, piebald skin bled liquid silver. Eyes stared at us. Waiting.

Hoarse and weary, Gen repeated his speech about the new Lupini's revulsion for trading in humans and his ingenuity at discovering an alternate means of paying for the previous overlord's debts. But whereas in the morning his words had rung with authenticity, they now sounded contrived and vapid.

The two arbiyesku boys in the back of our cart slowly clambered down. A para removed the manacles from their wrists. One of the boys—eight years old at most—spat at the para's feet, then slowly turned and melted into the shadowy crowd.

I struggled to stand and help Runami, then Oblan, then Savga rise.

A para leaned over the cart to unlock our manacles. They fell like black, broken skulls to the ground.

A woman in the crowd cried out Oblan's name. Oblan burst into tears and extended her little arms out to the dark. I lifted her down to the ground and she ran, knock-kneed and weak, toward a shadow. She was snatched up, clutched, kissed, surrounded, squeezed, petted. The mingled sobbing of child and mother, the murmurs and mutters and weeping of aunts and uncles, was a sad joy dancing on the wind.

"Runami, Runami, my child!"

Runami hurled herself off the cart, dodged between two of the paras that fenced us in, and was united with family once more.

Wearily, I climbed down from the cart and lifted Savga down. I buried my face against the soft, small folds of her neck and inhaled her warm-bread smell. "Go to your mother, Savga."

She stood by my side, swaying with exhaustion, looking out at silver-sheathed shadows merging and dividing before us.

An eerie silence and stillness settled over the arbiyesku. The guild clan of the cocoon warehouse stared at Savga and me, their eyes miniature moons.

I pushed Savga toward her people.

She called out for her mother.

Silence.

A woman stepped forward, an old woman. Tiwana-auntie. "Tansan left. She took her son and claimer with her. My sister left with them, and Alliak. They're gone."

I tried to understand her gravelly words. Tansan, gone? Fwipi, gone?

"Where?" was all I managed.

Tiwana-auntie looked away from me, shrugged. "Too many children have been taken from the arbiyesku. Too many children from all the kus in this Clutch. No one can blame them for leaving."

Savga's hand slipped into mine. I stared down at her, incredulous, horrified. She looked up at me with eyes punched in and bruised.

"I'm hungry," she whispered.

I licked chapped lips, struggled to find the words to tell her what she no doubt already understood. I crouched down to her level, placed both hands on her shoulders.

"You have family here, Savga. Tiwana-auntie. And friends, Oblan and Runami—"

"You made the chancellor bring us back. You'll find my mother." Her eyes didn't waver from mine.

I swallowed. "Savga . . . I don't know where she's gone."

She sighed, closed her eyes, and slowly leaned against me. "Carry me."

I picked her up, her legs dangling against my knees, her small toes brushing my calves. She weighed far more than I could carry. I wondered how I had ever lifted her earlier that same day.

I staggered forward a pace. The fence of paras swung open like a gate. Tiwana-auntie stepped toward me, arms outstretched to take Savga. The veins on the backs of her wrinkled hands looked like rivulets of silver in the moonlight. As her wiry hands enclosed Savga's waist, Savga's weight eased a little in my arms.

Savga stiffened. And screamed.

Her scream split open the night as if it were the belly of a dark jungle cat, and the moon and stars turned into crimson droplets, I swear they did, and the bloated black clouds creeping ever closer were suddenly lurid, and all of us—Temple acolytes, hired mercenaries, mothers, fathers, children—were bathed equally in the bloody culpability of the loss of Savga's childhood.

I clutched her to me, begged her to stop screaming, closed my eyes against the ruddy ichor spilling from moon and starlight. I rocked her, I shook her, I wept.

No matter what, this one child, this one child, I would not turn away from, not now, not ever.

Her scream didn't so much end as die; the secret places in her heart bled out. And when the exsanguination of her soul was complete, I was able to open my eyes. The unearthly crimson light that had bathed us all equally in blame and shame and rending loss had turned thin as serum. Gradually, the glaucous rays of moon and stars drizzled down upon us, once more turning us slate-colored, leaden, into living stone.

Tiwana-auntie looked at me and muttered something in Djimbi, and I knew my heart was ransomed until death, that everything I thought and did would from that moment onward revolve around the child in my arms.

I hoisted Savga onto my hip. Her legs latched around me. With one last look at the silver-stippled clan of my daughter's youth, I turned away.

I was a mother now.

EIGHT

Once close to Temple Xxamer Zu, Daronpu Gen sent the acolytes and soldiers back to the daronpuis' compound without us. He turned our cart down a narrow avenue lined on either side by tall, rickety wooden tenements that looked, in the dark, as if they were flat, without depth. Charcoal etchings upon black wood.

I remembered walking down the avenue earlier that day, remembered how the old crones who'd sat under the lintels of each doorway had watched us from faces as withered as tinder fungus, with eyes that had looked at us as if surveying the handwriting of the enraged Pure Dragon.

Rishi families were squatted outside the tenements, cooking meals upon smoking braziers in the humid night. Children played in the street. At our passage, people fell still and silent, became mere shadows in the dark. Overhead, several great, black clouds skulked closer. There was a nasty pressure in the air, as if everything living were being slowly, inexorably compressed between the dark morass of cloud and the unyielding fist of the earth.

Candlelight crept between the age-warped planks of some of the tenements. Here and there a silhouette moved behind the planks, visible only in staccato, needle-thin stripes. Striated glimpses of life, those.

Gen reined our sluggish brooder to a halt in front of one of the flimsy buildings. The brooder blew foam from between her gums and twitched her bony tail. The diamond-shaped membrane at the end flicked across the tip of my toes and slapped against the cart.

"What is this place?" I asked.

"Noua Sor," Gen replied. Poultice Zone, which meant nothing to me. He dropped his voice, aware that eyes watched us and ears were listening. "I know one of the inhabitants here. Let me speak with her, hmm? I believe you and the child will be safe here. Yes. Safe."

"You're not taking us to the stables?"

"Stables, gaa! There's no point, not now that we won't have a destrier for months to come. And I'll sleep easier if Ghepp doesn't know your location. He'll be ill pleased with your demand to stop Xxamer Zu's slave trade. Damn you, and damn him."

My eyebrows rose into my hairline. "You think he'd *harm* me?"

He sighed, weary. "Save this discussion for inside." Before I could argue, he tossed aside his reins and jumped down from the bench. The cart rocked and creaked in rebound, and the brooder shifted in her yoke. Gen had to bend to duck through the coarse door leading into the tenement. A conglomerate of odors swirled out before the door clacked shut behind him—the nutmeg bite of yanew bark, the heavy musk of ferret, the soft scent of rose attar.

A ribby, one-eared cur slunk close. The brooder's forked tongue flicked out, quivering. She slapped her tail adder-fast against one scaled flank as warning. The whipcrack startled the cur and it darted away. Several children came close—but not too close—and stood in a cluster some way in front of the brooder, ogling me. In the dark, the green whorls on their skin looked like large smudges of wet grime.

The door to the tenement creaked open again. Gen came out.

"It's arranged. You'll board here until I've smoothed things over with . . ." His voice trailed off as he became aware of the listening group of children. He nodded at Savga. "I'll lift her down, what?"

Savga stiffened. She was not asleep, after all. Only feigning it.

"I'll carry her." I slowly eased her off my thighs so that she lay stretched upon the bench. The sweaty patch where her hot cheek had been pressed against me felt at once cold without her presence. Gripping the worn wood of the cart, I climbed down cautiously, not quite trusting my legs to hold me up. Gen's hand cupped my elbow to support me as I stood there, swaying a moment.

Without a sound, Savga flowed into my arms and melded to my skin.

She was too heavy to carry, but I wouldn't ever again make the mistake of trying to pass the burden of her to another. Pressing her little body against me, I staggered after Gen as he turned and pushed open the tenement's narrow wooden door.

The moment I stepped into the gloomy interior, I was assaulted by the same odors that lingered outside, only intensified: musk, yanew, attar, sulfur, moldering wood, greasy sleeping mats, sweat, and another odor, peculiar, like mashed sweet corn. A coarse trestle table practically filled the small room. Upon it sat a tallow candle, wheezing inky smoke into the air. Two crude cabinets stood sentinel at one end of the table, leaning against each other like fat old women exchanging secrets. At the other end of the table, nearest us, stood a crone dressed in a frayed yungshmi, the ubiquitous garment for rishi women on Clutch Xxamer Zu. The crone's exposed legs were so thin, her knees looked swollen. Behind her, a narrow rectangle of inky darkness suggested the existence of another room.

"Where's the rest of your family?" Gen asked.

"Jungle scavenging," the crone answered. "They'll be back in two days, maybe eight."

Gen nodded as if this made sense to him. "Discretion, prudence—these things are necessary, understand?"

The old crone beside him smacked raisin purple gums together. "Our house discreet, hey-hey. No fast lips here, singing to the wind, oh, no." She moved, crepitant, and lifted the candle from the table. "Follow me."

Gen gestured me forward. I hefted Savga's weight to a better position on my hip and followed the crone. Gen lumbered behind me like a great boar enclosed in a wicker cage.

The crone led us up steep, narrow stairs that wobbled and scolded with each footfall. The top of the stairwell ended at the back wall of the tenement. To the left crouched a small room, to the right, another. In lieu of doors, long strips of barkcloth hung suspended in front of both rooms. The crone turned to the right and shoved the barkcloth strips aside. They rattled along the pole they were suspended from like the bones of gyin-gyin chimes.

"This is for you, all this." She grandly swept a joint-swollen claw across the room, which was no larger than a mating cubicle, four feet wide by eight long, though it boasted a shuttered window and a chamber pot.

Light from her candle oscillated upon the gap-planked walls. I imagined spiders burrowed between the cracks.

A water urn stood upon a single sleeping mat that had been unrolled upon the floor. Half of a congle gourd, polished from years of handling, sat beside the urn. A kadoob tuber, a slice of paak, and a tiny crescent of lemon sat in the gourd.

From where he stood on the top stair behind me, Gen peered over my shoulder. "They'll need more food than that, blood-blood! For what I'm paying, you can supply it. This and ten times more."

The crone champed her gums together and nodded brusquely.

"Leave us the candle," Gen ordered. "We'll be a while. Bring the food up later, hey."

The crone handed the tallow candle to me. Hot wax dribbled down my wrist. I held it away from Savga and stepped into the tiny room. Gen followed me, squeezing by the crone on the stairwell. He drew the barkcloth strips closed.

We waited, motionless and silent, while we heard the crone descend the stairs.

He took the candle from me, crouched on his haunches, and set the candle on the floor. He steepled his fingers against his beard; it shone like wet pewter in the sooty light. I put Savga down, then slowly eased myself onto the floor across from Gen, legs trembling from fatigue. The soft, swollen smell of affluence surrounded him: laundered clothes, milky skin creams, roasted meat, stiff new leather.

Savga slunk onto my lap. She held herself intensely still, face buried against my chest, then shivered in a brief burst. I thought of a leaf shuddering after a raindrop strikes it.

"You'll require a few things, Babu, if you're to live here for some time," Gen said. "Clothes, maybe creams . . . ?"

I thought for a moment, then spoke quietly. "Scrolls. From the daronpuis' compound. About the history of Xxamer Zu."

Surprise, hesitation, and concern flitted across his face.

"I'll hide them. No one will know."

He nodded slowly.

"And you'll look for them, yes? You'll have the road leading from Xxamer Zu checked?" I was talking about Tansan, her claimer, her infant son, and her mother, Fwipi.

"Useless, that, but I will. Wasted effort, like trying to see the wind."

I knew he was probably right. Savga's family was Djimbi. The savanna and jungle would show no tracks of their passing.

"We could use another sleeping mat," I said, "and a needle and thread, so I can repair Savga's yungshmi."

"I'll get her a new one."

"No. I don't want her to stand out from the other children here."

He acknowledged the wisdom of my answer with a nod.

We looked at each other for a while as candlelight made dark hollows in both of our faces.

"Tell me about Ghepp," I finally asked.

He sighed and rubbed his hands over his face—something he'd done a great deal that day, as if his worries were coating his hoary cheeks in heavy layers, threatening to smother him. Candlelight made the age spots on his tonsured head ripple.

"Ghepp needs to be handled very carefully," he muttered between his thick fingers. "Think glass, what-hey."

"What does *that* mean?"

He withdrew his hands and frowned at me. "It means he wants to learn from you the secret to breeding bulls in captivity, so he's willing to indulge us. To a point. But he's also dubious of your ability to learn anything from a dragon. He has doubts, many doubts, bats and swallows and pigeons of doubt all flapping inside him."

"He told you so?"

"Not in as many words!" Gen scowled. "Look at who he is, Babu; see with your wit instead of your eyes! He's lived his life in the shadow of Kratt, knowing that because of a quirk of his father's, a firstborn bastard would inherit Clutch Re instead of him. He's lived with that shame while Kratt has lived with promised eminence. Tutors and scrolls and ballads were Ghepp's teachers, all cradled in the women's wing of Roshu-Lupini Re's mansion. But Kratt? Ha! As a boy he was succored by swordmasters, chancellors, dragonmasters! Folk of a different ilk. One must tread carefully when dealing with a man such as Ghepp, a man who harbors both fear and dreams of greatness."

"Does he know your plans for rebellion?"

He nodded. "They're not just *my* plans. Others are involved: foreign émigrés, merchant tycoons, retired Roshus, paras who've defected from the Emperor's army . . . all planning for and dreaming of decolonization. Think I would have succeeded in convincing Ghepp to take the risk of laying that wager if I were acting alone in this? No more than I could convince a worm to attack a bird! The rebellion is greater than you know."

At that moment, the scope of Gen's seditious network paled in comparison to the bitter truth that was sinking into me.

"This isn't my Clutch, is it?" I quietly asked.

Gen studied me with eyes as glossy as burnished teak. He softly laid one of his great hands over mine. It was warm and heavy.

"When you broached the idea of securing this Clutch for Ghepp, a great mist that had hung before my eyes parted, and I saw this Clutch as key for the rebellion. When we get you a destrier, when you learn the bulls' secret during the bestial rite, then everything else will fall into place, hey-o."

I thought of Tansan. "Have you heard of the myazedo?"

He withdrew his hand. "Stay clear of such things, Babu."

"Why?"

"Bandit warfare. People looking to plunder and rape the aristocrats. That's not what makes rebellion successful, blood-blood!"

I thought of all the impassioned Djimbi who'd gathered at the tanners' clan. They'd spoken of ending poverty and starvation, not of committing plunder and rape. With all his connections amongst the politically empowered and the elite, Gen's view was skewed.

Or maybe not.

What did I know?

The full weight of the day's events pressed down on me, and I remembered how exhausted I was. "I'll stay away from them." I murmured the lie with ease, believing it in my fatigue.

Gen picked up the tallow candle and toyed with it, pressing his thumbs into the soft wax and leaving behind tiny half-moon indentations. "You haven't done Ghepp any favors by your demand to stop the slave trade, understand. The rishi will merely be wary, and when their wariness ends, they'll turn demanding. As for the bayen lordlings of Xxamer Zu, they'll be puzzled by the bizarre decision. Apprehensive. Stinking mess, what."

He put down the candle with a scowl and we looked at each other in silence. I pointed to Gen's skin, still so bafflingly fa-pim. "How'd you do that?"

He spoke as he exhaled, exasperated by my question. "The cloud asks the rain how a monsoon is made! I employ the same Djimbi cosmetics as you do, hey-o."

I frowned. "I don't understand."

He stared at me. Slowly a look of wonder passed over his hawkish features. "Can it be that she doesn't know? Does the pundar not know when the pigment of its skin has changed, to blend in with its surroundings?"

"Don't talk like that. You sound deranged."

His eyebrows raised; then he reached for my right hand. Savga recoiled and pressed against me. Gen ignored her fear. He slowly turned my hand this way, slowly that.

"Tell me, Babu," he murmured. "Tell me the color of your skin."

"Aosogi," I said, deliberately choosing, in a spate of unease, the insulting Archipelagic descriptive of poorly cured hide. "Tan."

His great thumb stroked the back of my hand. "Aosogi," he murmured. "Tan."

The candle sputtered, released a jet of inky smoke.

My pulse quickened as I stared into his eyes, dark lagoons whose murky depths rippled as if concealing hidden life.

"Tell me, Babu," he said softly, "what is the true color of your skin? You said before that you trusted me. If you spoke the truth then, tell the truth now."

I withdrew my hand from his. "Don't be yolkbrained. You can see for yourself what color it is. Aosogi."

He shook his head: no.

My mouth turned dry. "Yes."

"No, Babu. Your skin is mottled. Piebald. Like the blood that flows in your veins."

My heart stopped. Thudded abruptly into life again. *Thud. Thud. Thud.* I shook my head, tried to speak. Wanted water.

I remembered, then. Remembered how, throughout my childhood, I'd seen my mother as having the same aosogi skin as me. Remembered seeing my half sister, Waivia, the same way. Remembered dismissing the insults I'd overheard some of the adolescents of my birth clan mutter about my haughty, voluptuous sister, remembered dismissing them as being just the typical, groundless insults one hurled against one's antagonist: Mottled Belly, jungle deviant, dragonwhore.

Then, when I was nine years old, in her agitation over my being exposed to dragon venom by the dragonmaster of Clutch Re, my mother had revealed in an outburst that she was of the same ilk as the dragonmaster—a Djimbi. A veil I'd not known existed over my eyes had fallen away, and I'd seen my mother for what she had been. Piebald. Djimbi Sha.

Not many months after that, the same sort of outburst by Waivia had ripped away another charm that had lain over my eyes since birth, and I'd seen my half sister for what *she* was. Djimbi Sha. Mottled Belly.

Unlike me.

Or so I had thought.

"It is a most powerful enchantment that surrounds you. Like a shield, Babu! So powerful it prevents you from being wholly you. Your moonblood doesn't flow, does it? Dammed, it is. That's how powerful the enchantment is. You'll never bear children while it's wrapped about you. You didn't know of it, girl?"

I couldn't release the simple *no* that was caged in the back of my throat.

"The person who coated you with it would have had to practice and perfect it before achieving such a fine result. Not an easy pot of paint to mix, what-hey! Years ago I marred the skin of three Clutch Re makmakis in my attempts to make this paint. It's only the lucre I compensated them with, and the shrouds those servants of the dead wear, that allow them to go about their lives without being reviled for the improbable pigmentation I gave them."

"I'm not Dj—"

Fast as an adder, Gen moved and clapped a great hand over my mouth. Savga flattened herself against me with a cry.

"Don't say it!" Gen ordered. "It'll weaken the strands that hold the enchanted web about you."

I clung to Savga as she clung to me. She panted against my breast like a terrified cat.

Slowly Gen pulled his hand away from my mouth and sat back on his haunches. Where his hand had pressed against my lips, I could taste the bitterness of incense oil.

I became aware of how tightly I was holding Savga, my fingernails digging into the soft skin of her upper arms. I released my hold. Swallowed. "But . . . how? How can you see what I can't?"

"I have my ways."

"And others?"

He exploded air out his nose, deriding the possibility. "You've no concern there, hey-o. The web woven about you is strong. It extends beyond the color of your skin. The warp and weft of your very essence have been interwoven with the enchantment. Your smell, the whorls and lines and taste of your skin, they've all been disguised. Even someone well skilled in Djimbi ways would have a difficult time detecting you for what you are. If I'd not spent half my life looking for you, *I* wouldn't have recognized you for what you are!"

I stared down at my hands, so familiar and yet suddenly so foreign to me. "And what am I?"

"The Dirwalan Babu," Gen said. "The Skykeeper's Daughter. And a saroon."

I looked up again.

He once more steepled his fingers against the perfect tip of his groomed beard. "You are the result of a pairing of a munano, a half-blood Djimbi woman, with a fa-pim man."

"My father wasn't fa-pim."

"Not ludu fa-pim, no. Not landed gentry of dragon-blessed pure blood. But in terms of breeding, the Emperor considers anyone of Archipelagic descent who is untainted by Djimbi blood to be fa-pim. Truth! It's only the Mottled Bellies who are clachio."

Clachio. Filth that must be eradicated. A holy woman had used that term a decade ago, before cutting away my womanhood.

His words slithered about inside me like flukes, slick, fast, debilitating. "Munano. Saroon. I don't understand."

"There were few Djimbi on Clutch Re. You'll not have heard such words before."

"No," I faintly agreed.

"On Clutch Re, Archipelagic blood dominates, carrying with it all the hues of the myriad island folk the Emperor has conquered over the centuries. Aosogi being the product of matings between the original inhabitants of Messer and its fa-pim conquerors."

"Messer . . ." I said stupidly.

"The second-smallest island in the Archipelago, known as Lud y Auk in the Emperor's tongue."

I didn't know what else to say. My head felt as clotted and dense as the clouds gathering outside.

Gen shifted. "Now, Babu, I should leave you. I've much explaining to do to Ghepp. Damn stinking mess, this."

He rose to his feet, became a tower of red raw silk. The swish of his robes set the candle flame dancing and shadows undulating. I felt, for a moment, as if I'd fallen into a bloodred well.

Gen placed one of his broad hands on my head. His touch was gentle, firm. The illusion fled.

"Peace, Babu. Those words—saroon, munano—they're just words."

But they weren't. They were instruments of control, tools for subjugation.

Until one loses one's freedom, one never really knows what it is.

I dreamed that night.

A dream with few images, jelly and bloat, dense as clay, cold as mud. Ravens shrieked in my sleep, and thunder exploded from a white ocean of sky. Waivia stood before me, the black juice of crushed walnuts running down her hair, her arms. She was the color of a carrion wolf: tar black.

Mother stood beside her. Her eyes had been gouged out. Her mouth gaped, and I knew, without hearing her, that she was calling for Waivia, unaware that Waivia stood beside her.

I woke with my face pressed against Savga's crown, my mouth full of her hair.

Gagging, I pushed away from her and floundered into a sitting position. My head roared with pressure, felt like a grossly bruised melon. I passed trembling hands over my face.

Outside, the dark skies groaned under the weight of peevish clouds.

I stared at the coarse walls, the knots and grains and splinters dissolved by gloom. My heart lisped and squelched in my chest. The air smelled of sweat and unwashed clothes, of rotting teeth and spoiled grain.

I thought of my dream and I knew why my mother's haunt had stalked me since Mother's death, urging me to locate Waivia.

The warp and weft of your very essence have been interwoven with the enchantment. Your smell, the whorls and lines and taste of your skin, they've all been disguised, Gen had said of the enchantment that veiled me. And now I knew: Waivia had disguised herself from Mother, using the same pigmentation charm that hid my true identity from strangers. Mother had woven *my* charm about me and thus had been able to locate me when she was a haunt;

Waivia had woven her own charm about herself, after being sold to the glass spinners, and Mother had known it not.

Thunder slammed against the roof, rattling shingles.

I remembered, vividly, the way Waivia had looked the last time I'd seen her in my childhood: taller, yet slighter, as if she had been stretched and could hold herself together only by hunching her shoulders and walking in careful, precise steps. Bruises splotched her arms. Her upper lip was split and bloody, both eyes half-closed and purple. She'd been repeatedly violated as a sex slave.

The last thing I need is to be known as a Djimbi whore's bastard, she'd cried before pushing Mother, and Waivia's own Djimbi roots, out of her life, to protect herself as best she could for the harsh reality of her future. After that, Waivia must have employed Mother's pagan arts to disguise herself, to ensure that Mother couldn't find her and that others would see her as fa-pim and accord her a measure of respect that kiyu didn't usually receive.

Feasible, that. Waivia had been an extraordinarily bright child, quick to learn, showing singular skill with all she attempted. Given her segregation within the danku and the hostility shown her—the too-clever piebald bastard from Xxamer Zu—I had no doubt that Mother would've taught Waivia all she knew about Djimbi magics during Waivia's youth. It would have been a bond between them and a weapon in Waivia's arsenal for survival. A weapon Waivia had eventually used against Mother, in her need to put her Djimbi heritage behind her.

I found myself on my feet, charged with agitation from the epiphany.

Mother had abandoned me to my fate in Arena, whereas before she'd always come to my rescue, in the form of a Skykeeper, so that I might live another day to seek Waivia. In Arena, I'd seen Waivia myself and had realized Mother would come to my aid no longer, for she'd found my long-lost half sister and she had no more need of me.

Wai-ebani bayen, Waivia had said to me, when I was nine years old. *Foremost First-Citizen Pleasurer. That'll be me.*

She'd always believed she'd one day be Kratt's pleasurer. With her bewitching beauty and her disguise of fa-pim skin, she'd achieved her ambition. And what better way for a Wai-ebani to retain her position of prominence than to bear a son?

Waivia was carrying Kratt's child.

I heard Gen's voice again: *Your moonblood doesn't flow, does it? That's how powerful the enchantment is. You'll never bear children while it's wrapped about you.*

Waivia had annulled the spell about herself to conceive; thus Mother had finally been able to find her. What cared Waivia of her Djimbi ancestry now, with Kratt's second son in her belly and a haunt that masqueraded as a Skykeeper at her summons? What cared Kratt of Waivia's true skin color, given those same things?

Thunder again, dry, angry, growling in its impotence. Every organ in my body trembled. I pressed a fist against my chest. The runty thunder of my heart seemed outrageously bold.

I lifted the shutter latch. At once a gust of sultry air snatched at the shutter, whipped it open, banged it against the outside wall. I leaned out to catch the shutter, ribs smarting against the window ledge. Wind lashed my hair against my cheeks, flung it into my eyes, wind as warm as sunbaked grass at dusk, wind that soared and swirled over thousands of miles.

I wondered if Waivia, perhaps unable to sleep from the uncomfortable weight of the child in her womb, was listening to the rush of that very wind, was feeling its sultry anger. I wondered if the babe inside her started with each boom of thunder.

As second son to a Clutch Lupini, I wondered if the babe stood a chance of inheriting a dragon estate, despite his skin color.

Silly me.

Waivia would employ her Djimbi magics upon her child. The infant would be fa-pim, would have skin as pure and ivory as the Emperor himself, because, of course, Waivia would want her son to be the overseer of an egg-production estate. Though I doubted she'd stop at one Clutch. She was ambitious, Waivia.

She was, I realized, someone I feared almost as much as Kratt.

Savga cried frequently during the rest of that night, elongated moans uttered while she slept. I stroked her slim arms, held her small wrists, pressed my lips against her sweaty brow while outside thunder reverberated across the vast skies.

Dawn came, and with it the sound of bare feet descending the clattery stairs. Rustles and banging below. The creak of door hinges. Silence again. I draped an arm protectively around Savga's waist and drifted into murky sleep.

The rumble of cart wheels and the squeaks of a rusty axle woke me sometime later. Our room was unbearably humid. Head clotted with exhaustion, I swallowed some water from the urn, staggered from the mat, and fumbled with the window shutters. I pushed them aside. Curdled clouds the color of mold hung low in the sky. The air was sodden.

Across the narrow avenue, in front of a tenement two doors down from ours, stood a rickshaw. The piebald youth between the shafts set the rickshaw down, then leaned heavily upon his knees and proceeded to cough as if trying to expel his ribs.

Two bayen women dressed in gauzy bitoos climbed down from the rickshaw. They both held parasols that enclosed them down to their shoulders. One parasol was the green of an angry chameleon, the other the orange of a ripe pumpkin. Silk threads in matching colors sinuously embroidered the women's bitoos, twining from hem to bosom and disappearing beneath the parasols like buttressed roots supporting trees. The two women ducked into the tenement, still enclosed within their parasols.

I turned from the window and looked down at Savga. Sweat plastered her bangs against her forehead, and her cheeks were flushed. Her eyes looked bruised and sunken, even in her sleep. Her soiled yungshmi had come unknotted from the small of her back during the night and was twined about her torso like a snake that had tried to swallow a too-large meal.

Sometime while we'd slept, a small pile of plum-colored cloth had been pushed into our room. I bent, picked up the worn fabric, and shook it out. It was two yungshmis, creased and impregnated with the distinctive nutmeg-and-cedar pungency of yanew bark.

I shucked my filthy bitoo and, using the cleanest corner of it, dampened it with a little water from the urn and washed myself. I then wound one of the yungshmis about my torso and between my legs and knotted it in the small of my back, as I'd seen those in the arbiyesku do. I felt half-naked with my limbs so exposed. But clean.

Savga jerked awake, then thrashed about as if fighting an unseen assailant.

"Savga, shhh, quiet! I'm here." She stared at me, panting and shuddering. "I'm here," I repeated. Slowly I extended my arms. Slowly she crept into them.

She leaned against me, her little ribs heaving, and laid her head upon one of my shoulders. I smoothed her fine hair, snarled at the back from her unquiet sleep, and rocked her slightly. I braced myself for her sobs.

They didn't come.

Disturbing, that, like the silence that follows a scream, as if the air itself has been shattered.

Uneasy, I spoke against the soft curl of one of her ears. "You must be hungry, yes? We'll wash a little, then go downstairs for food. Hmm?"

No response.

I pulled her away from me. Her eyes belonged to someone old and ailing. I could scarcely look at them. Carefully, a little awkwardly, I undressed and washed her, then helped her into the second moth-eaten yungshmi. The entire time her eyes followed me, tracking my face with unnerving perseverance. But she spoke not a word.

When we were finished, I smiled uncertainly at her. "That feels a little better, yes?"

No answer, not even a shrug.

I held her shoulders. "I lost my mother when I was a little girl, too. I know how you feel, Savga; I do. And it's all right to be angry at her, understand? Your anger won't take away the love you feel for her. Don't fear that. That'll remain, always."

She looked at me, face slack, eyes watching, seeming to wait for something. The impossible: the return of her mother.

"I'll carry you downstairs," I said, releasing her shoulders. I hoisted her onto one hip, brushed by the dusty barkcloth strips of our room, and descended the scolding stairs.

The crone stood at the great trestle table, crushing the hulls of coranuts in a wooden screw-press. Amber oil drip-dripped into a waiting cruse. She glanced up at us, then nodded brusquely at two bowls of cold gruel at the very end of the table.

"My thanks for the loan of these yungshmis," I said. I lowered Savga onto one of the stairs; her eyes followed me as I retrieved the cold gruel from the table.

The crone grunted. "Can't have you stinking up the place, hey-o. Smelled worse than maht, you did."

"I'll wash our clothes today," I said, a little stiffly. I pushed a bowl toward Savga. She didn't take it, didn't so much as glance at it. Her eyes were rooted on my face.

I set the bowl on her lap and squeezed beside her on the narrow step. I ate stoically, ignoring the cold blandness of the boiled featon grit and the persistence of Savga's gaze.

I watched the crone work as I ate. She finished with the screw-press and carefully set the cruse of amber oil to one side. Using mortar and pestle, she pulverized a great pile of carmine petals into a fine pulp, then drizzled some of the amber oil into the bloodred paste. She whipped it thoroughly with a strangely pronged utensil and scooped the mess into a fine rufous cloth. My eyes roved to the two great wooden cupboards leaning against each other. I wondered what was stored within them.

"Was a time, in my youth, this house made great good medicines, and everyone knew the skill in Yimtranu's hands," the crone said as she knotted the cloth closed. She began squeezing the bag of oiled pulp. Slowly the bag turned the color of liver, and beads of red seeped through and dripped into a dented metal bowl. The crone's contorted fingers turned red as she continued to work the bag. "Fine elixirs we made, and poultices. Not nats for coloring bayen lips."

Nats: worthless frippery.

"But nats earn more chits than tisane and linctus, hey-o. Rishi can't afford such medicines anymore, no, no. They get sick, their only medicine is hope. And bayen don't trust Djimbi remedies. They get sick, they eat useless little rocks that they buy from Liru. So old Yimtranu makes nats instead."

Yimtranu sniffed sharply, and despite her age I saw in her a pride as fierce as Tansan's as she glared at me.

"And I don't earn chits by housing ebanis for lords and ladies and daronpuis to play with. I'm not like the others in this alley. *This* family has its dignity, hey-o. Honor. We know the old ways. We respect them." Her look turned sharp. "The Wai Vaneshor tells me you're not his ebani."

"I'm not," I confirmed.

With a snort, she went back to mangling the pulp bag.

I finished my gruel, then tried to cajole Savga into eating some of hers. She didn't so much as refuse as just sit there with lips closed, immobile as stone, her eyes relentlessly carving into mine. With a sigh I set the untouched gruel aside, hoisted her onto my hip, and carried her to the local well to wash our soiled clothes.

The last words I'd heard her utter had been back at the arbiyesku, when she'd asked me to carry her, when I'd picked her up and tried to hand her to Tiwana-auntie and she'd screamed. *Carry me.* That's what she'd asked for. So I carried her. I carried her to the well to wash our clothes. I carried her in my heart, under my skin, her silence aching in my breast like a broken bone. I carried her lethargy in my limbs, and her grief in the prayers that I whispered to the Winged Infinite as I slapped our wet clothes against the laundering slab adjacent to the well.

Fa cinai, ish vanras yos via rinu, miir eirmis depin lasif. Pure Dragon, in the strength of this child's mourning, may her weakness for life prevail.

I carried her back to the tenement while overhead the clouds hung stubbornly in the sky and thunder rumbled across the gray plains. I longed for the wind of last night, for the relentless pressure from overhead to burst apart with claps of thunder and bolts of lightning and monsoon rain. I longed for Savga's unwavering gaze to leave my face, just for a moment. I longed for her to speak.

Back at the tenement, beneath the lintel, Yimtranu was sizzling a lily white liquid on a smoke-blackened brazier.

"Cock quickener, this," she grunted bitterly. "For bayen balls."

She gestured with her chin into the humid interior of the tenement. "Something came for you. Bald Djimbi man delivered it a while ago, sent by your sissu, maybe."

Sissu: remunerative lover. She meant the Wai Vaneshor, Gen.

"The Wai Vaneshor is not my sissu," I said sharply. Her expression was wily; she'd been testing me, checking that what I'd said earlier—that I wasn't an ebani—was true.

"You wouldn't stay here if he was, aosogi-via." She cackled. "No fuckie-fuckie in this house, no, no. Wai Vaneshor or not."

Her pride was both irksome and admirable.

I stepped around her, Savga riding my hip, and ascended to our muggy closet of a room. Ribs aching, the small of my back creaking from carrying Savga, I set the silent child on the floor. Her bruised eyes bored into me. I noticed her lips were chapped and split.

"Drink something, Savga," I ordered. "You haven't had water all day."

She remained still and silent, eyes unwavering. I crouched, lifted the urn to her lips.

"You can't starve yourself. That won't bring your mother back. Drink." I tipped the urn. Her eyes stayed on mine as the water trickled uselessly over her closed lips and down her chin and neck.

Anger born of frustration burned in my gut. I wanted to shake her and cry: Life is under no obligation to give us what we expect, girl! So just bear the intolerable and do without the indispensable and fight back! Fight, Savga, fight.

But I didn't say such. She was too young, the words too sharp in their truth. And perhaps Savga *was* fighting, in her own way. She was using twembesai gon-fawen, obstinacy-that-is-gentle, to deny the reality of her situation.

I turned away from her and unrolled the new sleeping mat Gen had sent over. Inside the mat was a needle and thread, as well as a new yungshmi.

Damn Gen—I'd *told* him I didn't want Savga to stand out from others her age. I shoved the new yungshmi to one side.

The rolled cloth clunked as it hit the wall.

I looked at it a moment, then pulled it toward me. Unrolled the bolt of fabric. Found inside a bamboo casing glossy with beeswax, yellow with age, hard as anklebone. I turned it over and read the hieratics carved in the old wood: *Sut-cha ki Tagu Nayone Xxamer Zu.* Sixty-numbered volume of Xxamer Zu registry.

The cork bung was friable. Dry bits of it crumbled to the floor as I unstoppered the casing. The musty smell of old parchment wafted out, carrying with it the faint scent of incense. A fat sheath of rolled parchment was nestled inside. I could barely work it out of the casing.

I peeled off the topmost parchment as if peeling the outer skin off an onion. It was new and crisp, the ink upon it ebon and pungent with perfume. It took me a while to understand the unfamiliar hieratics gracing the top right corner: Census Annals. I glanced down the three columns of hieratics that had been written in a precise, cursive hand beneath the title.

It was names, all names.

I carefully peeled off another parchment, this one also new but not as stiff, as if it had been handled more frequently. More names.

Seventeen pieces of curled parchment later—each piece more aged than the last—I came across a long scroll that wasn't just a list of names. A petal-arrangement title adorned the upper right hand of the parchment. *Kanyan-gai ki Hoos a'ri Chan,* it said. The Scientific Law of Human Chattel.

Thunder rolled across the rooftops. The planks beneath me trembled. Despite the hour of the day, the room was as gloomy as dusk.

> *These being the grades of miscegenation found within the boundaries of Malacar, and the appellations assigned to each:*
>
> *When a man of fa-pim blood plants his seed in the garden of a Djimbi woman, the resultant bud shall be known as a munano. A saroon comes from the pairing of a fa-pim man and a munano, a ginar from a munano and a Djimbi. A sesif comes from the pairing of a fa-pim man and a saroon, and a farasin from a munano and a ginar. A sasangai comes from a ginar and a Djimbi, a memeslu from a fa-pim man and a sesif, and a senemei from a fa-pim man and a memeslu.*
>
> *Any Djimbi who labors upon a Malacarite Clutch is justly considered a freeborn serf. However, pairings between all grades of Clutch Djimbi are against Temple statute, for such unions perpetuate the aberrant Djimbi bloodline. Therefore, if two Djimbi should beget*

> *offspring, mother and progeny become the property of the Clutch overseer, to dispose of as and if he sees fit, and the future increase of such chattel shall likewise be forfeit to overseer and Temple, be they sired by a man of fa-pim or tainted blood. Be it known that Djimbi chattel have no standing in a grievance court in any Clutch or on any lands governed by the Emperor Fa.*

By declaring all Djimbi freeborn, yet by creating a law the Djimbi couldn't help but break, the Temple of the Dragon had foisted the responsibility of slavery upon the Djimbi themselves. In effect, Temple was declaring that the Djimbi enslaved themselves by breaching Temple statute when they mated within their own race. Bondage was therefore transmitted like a birth defect from mother and father to child and grandchild, through the generations.

I looked back at the parchment.

> *Miscegenation can be forgiven all those of fa-pim blood, for which of us has not petted one of the pretty little senemeis belonging to a neighbor as a handmaid? Truly, it is the duty of every fa-pim man upon Xxamer Zu to seek out such comely gardens and sow his seed frequently within them, registering such unions in the census annals, so that should any offspring result, he may be rewarded for his duty when said offspring are harvested, in later years, by overseer or Temple. The resultant flowers that grow from such unions bear a hue much more pleasing than the starkly mottled shades that result from coarse piebald pairings, and thus a man not only assists in decreasing Clutch debt, but increases the quality of the property owned by his Clutch overseer.*

I stared at Savga.

Her skin was the color of wild honey, her whorls faint, small, and few. I remembered she'd called herself a senemei. I'd assumed she'd been employing a Djimbi word for *bastard*. But no. She'd been employing one of the Emperor's words for a grade of human chattel, one of the more *pleasing* grades.

I remembered, too, the scroll the daronpu had read from, before Savga and I had been chained and led away from the arbiyesku. I uncurled the first piece of parchment I'd come across, the one pungent with fresh ink. I looked over the names, carefully this time, then uncurled the second piece of parchment, and a third.

I found what I was looking for: Tansan's name, and beside it, the name of the three bayen lordlings who'd violated her, nine months prior to Savga's birth.

What would those lords have done with the reward had I not prevented Savga from being sold into slavery? Split the lucre three ways?

In a different ink, in the third column adjacent to Tansan's name: *Arbiyesku Xxamer Zu Keau's Waivia*. It was annotated to include the common name Savga. Cruel irony that they'd listed Savga as Keau's firstborn, knowing full well she was a by-blow from one of the three bayen lordlings. The registrar had listed her as such merely as a means of identifying her and Tansan.

The names of Runami and Oblan were also on the list, as well as those of the two arbiyesku boys who'd been taken alongside us that day. Seventeen pieces of parchment, including the one I held, listed names of women who had been violated by lordlings doing their duty for their Clutch overlord. Seventeen pieces of parchment, belonging to a scroll numbered sixty in a series. No wonder the youth of Xxamer Zu disappeared into the jungle, the city, Hamlets of Forsaken. No wonder Xxamer Zu's population was a third of what it had once been.

Again, I wondered if such harvesting had been practiced in Clutch Re. But no: Djimbi rishi were uncommon on that vast estate. My mother had been one of a tiny minority, as Waivia had been.

I remembered, then, what Fwipi had called Tansan. *My memeslu daughter.* I'd thought, at the time, that memeslu had meant *seditious*. No. A memeslu was the result of a pairing between a fa-pim man and a sesif, a sesif being yet another grade of interbreeding. A fa-pim man had therefore sown his seed into Fwipi's womb. Tansan, too, was a bastard child. As was Fwipi.

I'd thought that by having my own Clutch, I would find a sense of belonging, create a world of safety and security. I thought I'd have, finally, a home. But it wouldn't be as simple as that. I had to *make* myself a home, alter age-old practices, defy even more Temple laws. Change things. Fight.

Again.

I abruptly shoved the scrolls aside and rose to my feet. I didn't need to know how many more of the children and adults in Clutch Xxamer Zu were bastards, to be harvested in the future to pay off the overlord's debts.

Just knowing that such harvesting existed was bad enough.

NINE

That evening I suffered another venom withdrawal attack, one so fierce that my guts felt mauled. Convulsions racked me, and my bitoo—which I'd changed back into late afternoon—was instantly damp with perspiration. My heels drummed against the floor, my back arched, and my eyes rolled into my head. The convulsions woke Savga from the restless sleep she'd fallen into; with her knuckles rammed into her mouth, she watched my brief, frenzied struggle.

As I lay drained and shivering in the wake of the attack, I thought she might talk. But no. She remained mute. She pushed herself into a corner of the room and held herself tightly.

I despised my body, that it could, with its base responses, betray both me and a child so recently devastated, and I was furious with Daronpu Gen that he hadn't forewarned me that his charmed purgatives would be effective for a limited time only.

"I'm fine, Savga," I croaked. "I just need some . . . medicine. Maybe Yimtranu will have some."

The idea at once held massive appeal. Surely Yimtranu had something in those ancient cabinets of hers that would dull my cravings. Distilled spirits, maska root, dream-mushrooms, poppy extract . . . She'd told me herself that her house had once made great good medicines.

As wet and unsteady as a newborn fawn, I got to my feet, and, leaning heavily against wall and post, wobbled the few paces to the top of the attic stairs. Candlelight flickered below, and I could hear Yimtranu talking to someone. A man. I summoned my strength to descend the rickety stairs—and was frozen in place by what Yimtranu was saying.

". . . need more dragon's milk. Usual quantity, for the usual fee."

A rumble from the man, followed by a curse from Yimtranu.

"He plays a dangerous game, raising the price," she croaked. "Well, go to him; see if you can bargain the toad down. If not . . . walk away. He'll lower in a week or two, rather than risk his master discovering his stolen hoard."

Another rumble from the man, followed by the clink of coins, footsteps crossing creaking planks, and the groan of a door opening.

My mind raced. If Yimtranu was reduced to making cock quickeners for bayen lords so she could feed her family, it was feasible that she was illicitly using dragon's milk—venom—in her products, because of its powerful aphrodisiac qualities. And it sounded like the man I'd just overheard was the one procuring the venom for her.

I flew back into the room where Savga still sat in one corner, and wrenched the latch off the shutters. I flung them open and leaned far out. There walked a lone figure, down at the end of the alley, about to turn a corner.

"Stay here," I gasped to Savga, whirling around. "I'll be back by morn."

The fear in her eyes cut me to the quick.

"I'll come back," I insisted, but the fear remained. Irritated, I bent, heaved her onto one aching hip, and clattered down the stairs.

"The child's soiled herself," I called to Yimtranu as I passed her. "She needs to be washed."

"Only whores walk about at this time of night," Yimtranu snapped at my back, but I was already through the door, Savga bouncing on my hip.

Outside, I readjusted my hold on her and ran for the end of the alley. Turned the corner where the man had turned. Passed a cluster of old men playing dice on the ground. Passed a young boy pissing against a wall while a cur circled about him, whining.

We reached a crossroads of alleys. Heaving for air, I stopped, looked left, looked right. . . .

There he was. Surely it was him, his lean body bent slightly, as though he were walking into a wind. I took a shuddering breath, switched Savga from one hip to the other, ignored my protesting ribs, and followed my quarry down the alley. Then down another, keeping to the shadows, ignoring the looks of any I passed.

We came out, suddenly, onto the dark and empty market square of Xxamer Zu. To the right of us loomed the Clutch Temple. My quarry was crossing the square, heading toward two abandoned buildings.

"Can you walk for a while, Savga?" I panted. I felt cruel asking, for she was wan and hadn't eaten all day, but my ribs were a screaming agony, and I didn't want to lose the chance to discover where I might find a supply of venom just for the sake of carrying a child. . . .

She gave a small nod.

I quickly set her on the ground, grasped her hand, and towed her across the empty market square.

Our feet slapped against the hardpan, still warm from the day's heat. Wind sent a ball of dead grass tumbling a short way across our path; a cluster of men gathered outside a tavern jeered at us. Savga looked at me anxiously.

Foolish, a voice hissed in my mind. *You should have left her behind. Go back, before you both get hurt!*

My quarry disappeared down an alley between the two abandoned buildings. I tugged Savga after him.

She sucked in a sharp breath at the darkness and closeness of the alley, which reeked of human excrement. Every instinct within me shouted that we should turn back. Instead, I gripped her hand tighter and pulled her into the dark.

The scurry of a rat. The snores of a vagrant. Savga whimpered.

"We're almost there; keep going," I murmured.

We came out onto the bayen thoroughfare. Oblivious to his two female shadows, my quarry was turning into the garden of a bloom-covered mansion that was ablaze with light.

"Quickly," I said, pulse racing. I could *feel* the venom calling me. I dragged Savga along at a stumbling pace, keeping my eyes glued upon the mansion that was so alive with light and music.

I paused at the fore of the mansion's dusty drive. In the dark, the white facade of the building was eerily spectral, and the lights blazing from every room sent attenuated fingers of shadow flickering over the jumble of rickshaws that were gathered outside, around a leaf-littered fountain that looked as if it had never spouted water. A profusion of flowers, black as ink in the night, spilled from the balconies ringing the mansion's upper floors. The smell of roasting onions and game hung in the air. Laughter, heady cigar smoke, and the music of cymbals and mizifars spilled from the open windows of the mansion.

A revel was in full swing inside. I suspected that either the host or one of his guests had procured venom to add to the festivities, and somehow Yimtranu's messanger had been alerted to it.

"Around the back, servants' entry," I muttered. "Savga, keep silent, even if spoken to. Understand?"

Her eyes were as shiny as glasses of dark tea, and her little chest was heaving hard. She pursed her lips and nodded. She was shivering. I grabbed her hand, threw back my head, straightened my shoulders, and marched down the drive.

Pebbles crunched under our feet. The gambling rickshaw pullers glanced up. I ignored them and continued on my way to the back of the mansion.

A bayen woman on a balcony was giggling and batting away the groping hands of a lord, but her giggles had a sharp, breathy edge to them, and her struggles against his persistence looked more real than play. He was undressing her.

"Keep walking," I murmured to Savga.

We rounded the back of the mansion and came to an abrupt stop. A huge open-air kitchen teemed with activity in front of us. Fires blazed beneath spits; Djimbi men chopped wood; women bustled around brick ovens and trestle tables. Knives flashed; feathers from plucked birds flew. Children darted hither and thither, fetching and carrying braces of dead songbirds and buckets of water. The smell of hot pastries, sizzling garlic, human sweat, and roasting meat swept over us. Beside me, Savga reeled.

I frantically scanned the activity. I'd lost my quarry.

I cursed, then cursed again. But I wasn't giving up yet. I tugged Savga forward.

Young rishi women—senemeis, all—were carrying filled platters from the outdoor kitchen down a short flight of stairs and into the mansion. They were dressed in clean bitoos of sheer, white linen, and the swells and curves of their breasts and rumps teased the eye as they walked. *My* bitoo hardly compared to theirs, nor my lean, hard body to their curves . . . but I'd be damned if I was going to let that stop me.

I marched up to a trestle table, bold as you please, and reached for a platter. A large, perspiring Djimbi woman was arranging raw chilies and cubes of fried dragon egg white around a whole roasted iguana that sported a charred mango in its gaping mouth.

I picked up the platter, even as the woman was placing more cubes of fried egg white upon it.

"It's not ready," she snapped, wiping the back of an arm across her forehead and leaving behind a streak of soot.

"My master demands it now." I lifted my chin imperiously. "This girl and I provide a certain type of entertainment for him that he insists must be accompanied by a meal of roast iguana. He's been waiting too long for it already."

The big woman glanced with scorn and pity from me to Savga, then turned her back on us, too busy to engage in argument.

"Stay near me, Savga," I hissed as we wended our way through the melee and down the dank stairs, into the blazing light of the mansion. One of her hands clung to the back of my bitoo as she followed.

I suspected that the upper level of the mansion was where the bedchambers existed. During my youth, some of the bawdy songs the women of danku Re had sung while they'd made clay pots in the studio had been of bayen revels such as these; we children would later reenact the scandalous behavior of the drunken rich, converting by imagination the tops of crumbling compound walls into the bedchambers of aristocrats.

Venom, if it were being illicitly used, would be found upstairs, alongside beds and privacy.

There was another kitchen inside the mansion, crammed with rishi. Pots clattered, steam billowed, orders were barked above the cacophony.

Holding the platter high above my head, I pushed my way through the swarm, following one of the white-clad senemeis bearing a laden platter. Through the chaos of the kitchen she unknowingly led me, and up a flight of stairs. We walked pressed against one of the cool stone walls of the stairwell to allow passage down for a stream of white-clad young women bearing empty platters.

At the top of the stairs stood two huge, muscled rishi men, ridiculously tricked out in crimson turbans and matching loincloths. They stood on either side of the stairwell, arms crossed and thick legs braced, their backs to us. I plunged on.

I reached the top stair and stepped out into the blaze of light and heat cast by the hundreds of candles of a glass chandelier that was suspended from a vaulted ceiling. Bayen lords and ladies in elegant dress swirled beneath those lights, while rishi children, crammed in tiny iron cages that swung from the ceiling, waved huge plumed fans over the heads of the aristocrats below.

A meaty hand grasped one of my biceps and brought me to an abrupt stop.

"No entry," one of the huge Djimbi men guarding the stairwell said. His face was implacable, his eyes indifferent. His lower lip had been pierced with a gold ring.

I lifted my chin haughtily and repeated the lie I'd told the cook.

The guard blinked basilisk eyes. "No entry."

"I don't think you realize whom you are rejecting," I said frostily. "I'm the Wai Vaneshor's Wai ebani, and he's summoned me, this girl, and this food, and is expecting service—"

"No entry."

I was quivering inside. But, driven by the knowledge that I was close—so close—to a source of venom, I plunged on.

"You cannot forbid me entry!" I said, raising my voice. Djimbi women clad in white glanced my way as they hurried down the stairwell behind me. And, too, a lord and lady turned and frowned in our direction.

The mountain of muscle that was still holding me in his relentless grip turned and bent a thick neck toward a very young rishi girl—no more than eight years old—who sat to one side of the stairwell. She, too, wore white, as well as an expression of fear.

He barked something at her; she leapt to her feet and nimbly darted into the crowd of aristocrats.

If Daronpu Gen wasn't present—and there was no reason to assume that he would be—not only would I be denied access to the mansion (and the venom hidden within its fine walls), but I would suffer severe punishment for my lie and intrusion.

As would Savga, behind me.

It was as if a brittle sheath of glass that had surrounded me up to that point shattered, and I realized, for the first time that evening, the extent of my madness.

I turned to Savga and mouthed, *Run*.

Her grip tightened on my bitoo and her lower lip thrust out, even while she looked terrified. She shook her head in refusal.

"Curse you, Savga, *go*. Run so fast you won't get caught. You know where to go."

If he heard, the mountain restraining me showed no indication. Bless him, he was Djimbi, and would allow the young girl behind me to escape my fate . . . if she had sense enough to do so.

"Savga . . ." I started to hiss, but the grip on my arm jerked me so that I was facing forward again.

And staring direct into the eyes of Rutgar Re Ghepp.

His dark hair was slightly tousled above his slender brows, and his full lips, centered below high ivory cheekbones, were parted in astonishment. His eyes, the color of chestnuts streaked with gold, rapidly turned dark as he overcame his surprise.

He studied me, chiseled nostrils flaring like an agitated dragon, and he looked away. I think we were both remembering the last time we'd faced each other over a courtyard of dead Auditors. Behind Ghepp, a cluster of lords and ladies had gathered and were looking at me with disgust and indignation.

Ghepp faced the mountain of muscle who was restraining me. "Take her outside," he coolly ordered. "Two of my paras will escort her to the stockade. I'll deal with her later."

Behind me I felt swift, sudden movement.

I didn't dare look over my shoulder and draw attention to the six-year-old girl escaping down the crowded stairwell at my back.

Two paras marched me across the thoroughfare. I stole a glance at each of them and recognized the one on my left; it was he who had pressed Gen's token into my palm, the day Savga and I had been taken from the arbiyesku. His presence reassured me a little, though the set of his jaw and the way he refused to meet my eyes were unnerving.

They marched me down the very same dark alley Savga and I had sprinted through a short while before. I wondered where she was, prayed she'd had the sense to return to Yimtranu's for the night and would then leave, come dawn, for the familiarity of her arbiyesku.

Sorry, Savga. Sorry.

Motherless and grieving, she'd been taken by me straight into danger. She was alone in every sense of the word now, and I shuddered at the image of her small, wan body navigating the dark alleys around us. A drunk, or a pack of hungry curs, or a man with base desires and no scruples could easily catch her and be the death of her. I was sickened and appalled with myself for putting her into that situation. She was only six years old.

Upon the command of one of the paras flanking me, the huge iron gates to the daronpuis' stockade were opened and I was marched within. I was led across a humped stone bridge. Up a flight of dank stone stairs. Through two great, shiny doors of stamped tin. Along a sconce-lit corridor beaded with sticky incense, past stamped-tin doors and many kinked and cuneated dragon statuettes cupped in dimples in the white stone walls. Several times we came across a daronpu or an acolyte who was forced to hastily retreat to the nearest shell-shaped recess so that we could continue.

I was shown, without a word, into the same airless, cushion-strewn room where I'd met Daronpu Gen in his disguise as Wai Vaneshor. The door clanked shut behind me. A bar dropped across it with a metallic clang. I imagined the paras stationing themselves on either side of the door.

I sank onto a pile of nubby cushions; dust billowed up thickly about me. Coughing and sneezing, I stared at the single narrow casement high up on a far wall. It was miserably hot in the room, and a bad odor hung in the dense air, as if a bird or a mouse had recently found its way into the room and died.

Languid shadows slunk along the walls as the sultry night stretched onward. My bitoo clung to me with sweat. My temples pulsed with headache. I was parched. The pressure from the cloud-heavy skies outside pressed against the back of my neck, as if the air were trying to force me to kowtow before it. The skies groaned with unshed rain.

Still, I waited, silently praying, over and over, that Savga was safe and unharmed, back at Yimtranu's.

In the dark, the profusion of cushions about me looked like misshapen creatures, hunkered down and watching me. Briefly I was overcome by the terrifying illusion that I was back in the viagand chambers, imprisoned in Temple's hidden jail, and that everything had been a dream: my escape, my return to the dragonmaster's stables, my fight in Arena, my time in the arbiyesku of Xxamer Zu.

"Don't be foolish," I growled at myself, and I stood, shaking, and waded through the musty cushions to piss in a corner.

Outside, thunder rolled across the skies, a heavy reverberation that vibrated my back molars. I pulled my bitoo away from my skin and torpidly flapped it, to cool myself. No good. I slumped against a wall and slid down to sit at its base with my legs sprawled. I felt as if I were a melted candle.

Eventually I heard noises outside my door. Orders were curtly given. There was the clank and hiss of a door bolt being drawn back. The door swung open. I stood.

Lantern light streamed into the room, dust motes dancing in the beams. A man's silhouette entered, and the door clicked shut behind him.

My eyes adjusted to the light. Ghepp stood in front of the closed door, holding the lantern high. He hadn't yet seen me. I stepped forward. Lantern and silhouette swung in my direction.

"I would have thought you more intelligent," Ghepp said, each word bitten off like a sour plum. His voice was hoarse, as if he'd been arguing all night.

I approached him, careful not to stumble over the wretched cushions strewn calf-deep about the place. Silence a moment as we stood before each other.

"What were you doing?" he asked softly.

"I was looking for Gen—"

"To wreak more havoc with your asinine demands that I refrain from trading in slaves?"

I tried not to clench my hands, forced myself not to snarl back a heated reply. "Bayen Hacros, I would remind you of our goal. The trading of slaves will become unnecessary once I learn the secret to breeding bull dragons in captivity. If you'd only hasten to purchase a venomous dragon, we'll achieve that goal more quickly."

In the lantern light, flecks of gold flickered in Ghepp's eyes. "Do you forget with whom you're speaking?"

"Forgive me, Bayen Hacros," I said quietly, and I dropped my eyes momentarily before raising them again. "But perhaps you forget with whom *you* are speaking."

"You overestimate yourself, rishi via."

"*You* underestimate *me*." I strove to keep the tremor from my voice. "I *am* the Dirwalan Babu."

"Remind me what, exactly, that is."

"You've seen the Skykeeper I control. You know what I can do with it."

"I've seen the creature once, on my bastard brother's Clutch. I've never seen the creature appear where he is not."

I stared at him. "You think Kratt controls the Skykeeper?"

"I have good reason to believe so."

"Ridiculous—"

"No!" he snapped, and I suddenly remembered what Daronpu Gen had said of him: *One must tread carefully when dealing with a man such as Ghepp, a man who harbors both fear and dreams of greatness.* "Yesterday my brother deposed the Lupini of Clutch Cuhan and incarcerated the

Lupini's entire family. Temple sanctioned my brother's appropriation. Know why?"

There wasn't enough air in the room: I needed to sit; I needed to leave.

The lantern threw heat and light across Ghepp's face. "A Skykeeper's been frequenting Clutch Re. According to my brother, the creature's absconded from you to support Kratt in his quest to eradicate Malacar of your presence. He claims Lupini Cuhan was your ally. A legitimate reason for him to depose Cuhan, hey."

Waivia had used my mother's haunt to Kratt's benefit.

"Where's your otherworld bird?" Ghepp continued, and his voice was a whiplash. "Why've I yet to see evidence of it in *my* Clutch? Why didn't it appear when the Host attacked you?"

"There was no Skykeeper at Clutch Cuhan," I said hoarsely. "Your herald carries propaganda from Kratt—"

"Summon your Skykeeper. Show me your otherworld bird."

"We've no need of it."

Ghepp tilted his head to one side, plunging half of his face into shadow, so that I stared at a one-eyed man, a half-faced creature. "I recall that Kratt once forced you to summon your Skykeeper, back on Clutch Re. He had you whipped. Should I do that?"

I shook my head: no.

"Then call your bird. We'll have need of it when Kratt comes for this Clutch."

"He won't."

"Call your damn bird!"

"I can't." I forced myself to keep contact with his eyes. "Gen made me halve my ability to call the Skykeeper, made me share my power with him. Now I can only summon it when he's present."

Ghepp's lips curled in disgust. "How convenient that he's not here."

"Not . . . here?"

Ghepp spun on his heel and strode to the door. He opened it and gestured abruptly with his lantern. Shadows swooped and swung like mad pendulums across the walls.

"Take her to the cell blocks," he ordered the guards outside. "Tell no one."

By the gray light that seeped beneath the heavy wooden door to my cell, I could guess when it was day and night.

Gloom.

Darkness.

Gloom.

Darkness.

More gloom and more darkness.

Four days passed.

By then I was certain I'd been abandoned in the underground cell. I'd heard no coughs, mutters, nor snores beyond my cell, and I'd seen no feet shuffling back and forth, nor any shadow flung by torchlight, beyond the crack that ran under the bottom of my door. The soldiers had simply deposited me in that stone room, barred the door after them, and departed, ascending the dank stairwell they'd marched me down.

Other than Ghepp, they were the only ones who knew where I was. The thought was not comforting.

I slept. I woke. I counted the length and breadth of my cell in footsteps. I thought of Savga and prayed that she'd found her way back to the arbiyesku and was safe with Oblan and Runami. I wondered why the lot of us had not been brought down to this cell block the day we'd been taken as slaves, and could only guess at the various reasons why: because the intent had been to fly us out to Diri, in bunches, to trade the very day following; because in a dragons' stall, trough water was available, whereas in the cell block, acolytes would have had to carry heavy buckets down the dank stairwell to slake our thirst, and what a bother that would have been; because the cell blocks were unknown to all but a few.

That last reason seemed most likely. Ghepp wanted me not just imprisoned, but hidden. He wanted me incarcerated somewhere where I could die and molder undisturbed, should Daronpu Gen never reappear to champion me as a prophesied woman of power and change.

I tried not to think of that happening—me dying in that cell—nor of Kratt and my sister. I also tried not to think of how hungry and thirsty I was, nor of how my madness for venom had led me into that dungeon. And because I was trying not to think about my craving for venom, that became all I could focus on.

I thought of dragonsong and the sublime numinosity I'd experienced while hearing it, and I was filled with a yearning so powerful, for something so out of my reach, I despaired. My head ached. I suffered stomach cramps. I trembled, I sweated. I started to convulse, then vomited. Thirst raged within me.

When the withdrawal symptoms passed—an hour later, a day, it was the same—I dragged myself to a corner and wished for unconsciousness.

Footsteps sounded outside my door.

The wooden bolt slid open with a splintery rasp. Door hinges creaked, like chalk ground between teeth. Torchlight flickered across the floor of my cell.

Someone stepped in.

A soldier, with double topknots of hair protruding from his head like the small horns of a young buck. He stooped and placed a battered metal jug of water on the flagstone floor and dropped something small, perhaps a roasted tuber, beside it.

The soldier straightened slowly. He was big, bearish, and filled the doorway. He wasn't one of the two who'd marched me down into the cell. His great chest slowly expanded and contracted. He was waiting for his eyes to adjust to the dark.

A guard didn't feed a female prisoner late into the night, after days of ignoring her, unless he had a particular motive for doing so. I held myself still.

He grunted as he picked out my form, then kicked the door closed behind him.

"Come here, rishi via." He lifted his leather loinskirt and withdrew his phallus, a club of meat clearly visible against the black boiled leather of his uniform.

My breath came quicker. He stood waiting. He expected me to obey.

Better to do it, a weary voice said within me. If you fight, he'll beat you senseless and take his pleasure after. Compliance will spare you the beating.

Slowly I rose to my feet, leaning on the wall for support. "You want me to undress?" I asked tonelessly.

"No." He jerked his phallus forward, as if he could shorten the distance between us and speed me toward him by the action. "Jus' come here, hey. Now."

I shuffled toward the guard. Knelt. Gripped him.

"With your mouth," he grunted, but he wasn't speaking to me, because I wasn't there anymore. The person I'd valued had disappeared the moment I'd led an orphaned six-year-old girl into the night, in a quest for venom. It wasn't me feeling the tackiness of his unwashed phallus, wasn't me smelling the seaweed stink of him as I worked my hands up and down his sheath.

He groaned, moved his hips. Sucked in a breath, grabbed my hair. "With your mouth, whore, with your mouth."

Wasn't me closing lips around him.

I wasn't there.

But suddenly I *was* somewhere else: in the viagand chambers, where I'd suffered months of brutal degradation, where I'd witnessed the frequent rape and beatings of the imprisoned women, several whom had died before my eyes.

Rage exploded within me, and I bit down.

His bellows thundered through the dungeon, and still I didn't release, even as my mouth filled with coppery blood. He yanked on my scalp, trying to wrench me off by my hair, and then I tore away from him without quite opening my mouth, ripping flesh from him as I snapped my head back. Then, just as swiftly, I slammed my head forward again, into his bloody groin. He released me and grabbed for himself even as the air whooshed from him.

As he staggered back, I lunged for the jug of water he'd set down by the door. Leapt up. Hauled back with both hands and swung the jug as hard as I could against the side of his head.

He staggered sideways, gel-legged. One of his bloody hands reached for the ear I'd struck; I smashed the jug into his face, dropped it, and wrenched open the door.

I slammed it shut behind me and fumbled with the wooden bar. Dropped it into place.

I stood there a moment, breathing heavily, heart galloping. Howling, the soldier threw his full weight against the door. I leapt away. Again, another thud. The bar I'd jammed across the door creaked nastily.

I grabbed the torch from the wall bracket and ran.

Along the short length of the cell block, up the dusty, cool stairwell, the shadows of the stairs above me looming overlarge in the torchlight.

Giddy, I reached the top of the stairwell and came out into a courtyard that was hushed and dark beneath a black-clouded sky. Several men stood waiting for me. I froze with fear.

They didn't move. I didn't move. Long moments passed. The air was heavy as sodden cotton, the wind that blew sluggish. Overhead, thunder rumbled.

I abruptly realized that those hulking silhouettes were slabs of rock, tipped up on their edges and settled into impossible angles. I recognized the courtyard, then, from the day Savga and I had been stolen from the arbiyesku. This was where an acolyte had knelt, flogging himself ecstatically.

I tossed the torch down the stairwell behind me and started for the opposite side of the courtyard, slinking around its edges, melding with the dark.

Then I stopped.

Why had I suffered the horrors of Arena and survived, if only to hand the Clutch I'd won to a man uninterested in justice for the rishi he governed? A man who, at the first sign of trouble from his half brother, had thrown me into a cell?

I'd be damned if I'd allow my fears to govern how I acted any longer. I'd create my own laws from now on. Why come so far and only go half-way? Better I die blazing in fire.

No half measures. That would become my guiding principle from now on.

My nefarious temper would be my strength. My impossible dreams my guide. No more would I hesitate. No longer would I listen to the base cravings of my body for venom.

No.

No more half measures.

TEN

Silent as starlight, I went back a ways through the courtyard, weaving amongst the solemn, upright boulders, seeking the viaduct that led to the messenger byre. I slipped down a dank viaduct and came out upon an unfamiliar court of stone benches, all facing a stone pulpit.

That wasn't where I'd expected to come out.

I retraced my steps, found another viaduct farther along the courtyard of upright boulders. I followed it. Halfway down its dark length I smelled manure and maht, the regurgitated crop contents of dragons. I'd found the messenger byre.

I paused at the threshold of the byre court. A vast black shoal of cloud was swallowing the moon at one end and disgorging stars at the other, and the sky growled like a great, uneasy dog. The wind was cooler and lively, a dust devil swirled across the courtyard, carrying flakes of chaff with it. I half expected to see Auditors drift specterlike from the darkest corners of the court, as they had done on the day I'd landed in Xxamer Zu.

Don't, I told myself. No ghosts here.

Dragon stalls lined two walls of the court. The shadowy humps of sleeping escoas filled six of the stalls. To my left squatted a small stone cottage with a thatch roof: the stablehands' residence. From the size of the byre, and the number of escoas present, I speculated there would be three stablehands in the cottage at most.

No bowmen standing there to rescue you this time. My teeth chattered.

An open-air tack hall stood to my right, under an arcade. The tack hall and the stablehands' cottage formed one side of the courtyard; the stalls formed two; and the granary and hayloft where the dragonmaster and I had hidden completed the square.

Move, girl, move. You're wasting time.

My legs felt locked, especially up in my thighs. Fear really *can* cripple.

Moving stiffly, the hairs on my scalp tingling, I slunk into the tack hall. Across the court, the escoas slept undisturbed.

I lifted down a set of reins and draped it over my neck. The leather was impregnated with beeswax and the rich scent of dragon; the smells triggered a furious venom withdrawal attack that dropped me to my knees and left me dizzy and disoriented for long moments after it passed.

Great Dragon, I can't do this.

But I would. I had to. No half measures.

Trembling, I staggered to my feet, lifted down two more sets of reins, draped them about my neck, and found in a fusty cabinet a curved paring knife, the kind used to trim the calluses from a dragon's claw pads. I wiped the sweat from my palms. Gripped the knife. Approached the stablehands' cottage.

Calm and easy, I told myself, and shivered with nerves. Calm and easy.

I placed a hand upon the heavy wooden door and tacitly asked the splintered timber to be quiet. Wasn't the wood I should have begged for silence. It was the hinges. They cackled at me. I froze.

"Who's there?" The voice was young, sleep-frogged, and frightened. After a pause, a tremulous whisper: "Kaban? You left the door open."

I stayed where I was, heart hammering, hand tight around the paring knife. Inside the hut, a series of wet snores. Overhead, thunder rumbled.

"Kaban?" Again, the summons was hesitant, as if the speaker wasn't sure whether he wished to wake the snorer or no.

The snores faltered, then whiffled on.

I pressed against the door, straining to hear. The soft padding of bare feet approached. Closer. Closer.

Calm and easy. Calm and easy . . .

I waited until the footfalls were as close as I wanted before I shoved the door open, hard. It thudded against a blockage. A yelp of pain; I stepped around the door, into the hut. A youth stood several inches from the door, naked as a babe, his hands clutched over his bleeding nose. Even as he gaped at me, I stepped behind him and touched the point of my knife to his throat.

"Say a word and I'll cut you ear to ear. Put your hands behind your back."

The boy did so, shivering. He was bony, about thirteen years old, and he readily submitted to having his arms trussed behind his back with a set of reins, even though his arms were sinewy with muscle from long hours spent mucking out stalls, and he could have proved a handful if he'd had the mind to. I suspected he was the same unlucky stablehand who'd witnessed the ambush attempt of the Auditors.

Two hammocks were strung from bowed rafters in the middle of the hut. One was empty, a dark tunic balled into a pillow at one end. Upon the other hammock sprawled a heavy man whose eyes were closed and mouth was wide open. He was snoring lustily, and his tunic—which had the crest of a herald embroidered over the left breast—was torqued about him. He was rank with the stench of semen and wine, and another smell hung faintly in the air, the fetid, sweetish smell of human excrement.

I shoved my bound captive closer to the empty hammock, knife nicking the skin on the boy's throat. He shuddered mightily. "Quiet, now. Not a word."

With one hand I snatched the balled tunic from the empty hammock. "Don't move." I pushed him facedown over the hammock and swiftly hacked a strip from the tunic. "I'm going to gag you."

I could see each segment of his spine, the boy was so bony. It was then that I noticed the ugly welts on his buttocks, as if he'd been pinned down and bludgeoned mercilessly. There were bite marks on his back. Rivulets of blood, dried and flaking, coated the insides of the boy's thighs. The smell of semen and excrement came from him.

I knew, then, why the boy was submitting to me so readily, and it had nothing to do with fear of what he'd witnessed some fourteen days ago in the byre. He was used to submitting to others; the other stablehand regularly beat submission into him.

I had a brother about the boy's age. Somewhere.

"What's your name?" I asked softly.

"Ryn." It came out a thready whisper.

"I'm not going to hurt you, Ryn. Promise. This is what we're going to do. I'm going to saddle every escoa in this byre and we're going to fly them out of here, you and I."

I turned him around to face me. His eyes were huge, and his ears projected winglike from his head. I nodded at the torn remains of his tunic. "That's the emblem of an apprentice herald. Have you flown an escoa before?"

A nodding of the head: yes.

"Are any of the escoas stabled here from elsewhere?"

Yes.

"How many of them? One? Two?"

So quietly I had to lean forward to hear him, he muttered, "Two."

Hmm. That was less than ideal. Stealing the dragons that belonged to another Clutch was worrisome. It meant that heralds who expected to leave come dawn, or in a few days' time, would be missed by their home stables when they didn't return.

No half measures.

I tugged on Ryn's knots, checking that they were secure. I slipped the gag across his mouth and tugged it tight. "Outside, then. I'm going to tie you to a stall while I saddle the escoas, understand? First I'm going to do something about *him*, in case he wakes."

I plucked a heavy candlestick from a coarse table shoved in a corne of the room and stood over the drunk's hammock for a moment, watc ing drool slide down one of his slack, stubbled cheeks. My heart racing so fast, the brass candlestick in my hands seemed to throb my pulse.

All I had to do was hit the man. I certainly had reason enou so, remembering the marks on Ryn's body. But I found it har

a sleeping man senseless, however repungant that man was. I hope this says something good about me.

Didn't stop me from crashing the brass against his forehead the moment he sensed my presence looming over him and began to open his eyes, though. The sound the candlestick made against his forehead was soft and resonant.

Shaking badly, I dropped the candlestick and used one of the sets of reins draped over my neck to tie the drunk's heavy hands and ankles together. I wove his bindings in and out of his hammock, so that when he regained consciousness he'd be unable to rise. It was as I was hacking a strip from his tunic to gag him that I briefly entertained the thought of castrating him with my paring knife. Dismissed the idea, though. Too messy.

Ryn seemed twice as scared of me after I'd finished binding the drunk, and he shivered as I placed a hand on one of his bony elbows and guided him outside.

The night air now smelled muddy and rotted, and the wind had turned blustery and cool. The clouds looked like bloated corpses dressed in the tattered remnants of shrouds, floating upon a river of stars.

We crossed the long, narrow courtyard. Ryn flinched as I stood him against a stall's cool iron gate, and trembled while I tied him to it. The escoa within shifted, uneasy, but not alarmed. Not yet.

"I'm not going to hurt you, Ryn. And I promise I'll bring you back to this byre one day."

His eyes slid from mine. He didn't believe me, was on the verge of tears. Thunder boomed in the distance and echoed across the savanna.

I opened the stall, lifting the heavy metal latch slowly to prevent clanking noises. Murmuring to the escoa within, I pushed the stall door open, forcing Ryn, who was tied to it, to shuffle into the stall as the gate swung on its hinges. Once inside, I knotted my paring knife onto my hip using a twist of my bitoo, then set to work with hands slicked with nervous sweat.

One Dragon, keep me safe. Don't let anyone come into the byre, not now.

I unscrewed one knob off the end of the nose barbell that was attached to the bridle draped across my neck. With one hand firmly upon the escoa's snout, I slid the barbell through the hole that had been punched into the cartilage between her nares. That done, I screwed the knob back on, swiftly adjusted the leather straps of the bridle over her snout, then led her out of the stall, licking my lips that had gone terribly dry, trying to steady my breath that was coming too quickly.

The escoa was a docile beast, used to unfamiliar people and strange stables from her work carrying packages and riders to assorted destinations. She readily followed me across the courtyard to the tack hall, moving in her harelike dragon lunge, eyes bright, forked tongue flickering between her gums. I lashed her reins to the saddling bar, lifted a heavy leather-and-wood saddle from a wall rack, and heaved the saddle over her back.

The saddle wasn't as streamlined as a destrier's, and instead of one surcingle, it had two bands that required tugging snug beneath dragon belly. The extra work aggravated me no end; time was running short; anyone might appear at any time; the night would be drawing to a close too soon. . . .

I shot a nervous look across the yard at Ryn, who didn't appear to be fighting his bindings. Shot a look at the dark maw of the viaduct that led into the courtyard. Shot a look at the stablehands' hut.

I finished with the first escoa, then led a second dragon from her stall, tethered her to the saddling bar, and readied her for flight.

Faster, Zarq. Move faster. Don't keep looking over your shoulder. Concentrate on what you're doing.

I had two escoas saddled and ready. I could escape now. But four escoas still remained in the byre, and I wanted to cut off Ghepp's access to the outside world. . . .

No half measures.

I reeked of fear, was slicked with sweat, and the muscles at the back of my neck were rigid from where I was clenching my jaw so tight. I approached a third escoa, forced myself to methodically saddle her. Then a fourth. Fifth. Sixth. Toss wing bolts and hobbles into every saddlebag. String the dragons together, snout to rump, the reins from each nose barbell tied to the saddle horn of the dragon standing before it.

Stop looking over your shoulder. Quit dropping things. Stay focused; force your hands to stop shaking so you can tie that knot. Where'd I put that damn bridle? It was here a moment ago. Stay calm, for the love of wings!

As a dragonmaster apprentice, each morning I'd watched the veteran apprentices lead the destriers in a long line to an exercise field. The destriers hadn't been tethered together, but the dragonish habit of walking in a line, in the clawprints of the dragon that proceeded it, had inspired my plan.

The escoas grew frisky with the prospect of flight. Their ear slits dilated as they looked about, and their tongues—pink, forked, and venom-free—flicked from between their gums as they scented the night air. They began unfurling their wings.

Someone would hear them. Even above the rumbling of thunder, even despite the late hour.

I looked as if I had palsy, I was trembling so badly. I glanced again at the viaduct, again at the cottage where the drunk was bound. Jogged back to Ryn, riding the knife edge of my own terror.

"Now comes the tricky bit," I panted. "I've only flown a dragon as a passenger, so we can do this one of two ways. I can ride the lead escoa, you can ride the one behind me, and we can both pray that I don't kill us all. Or you can ride the lead escoa with me as passenger, and we can pray that the five escoas behind us will follow. What do you say?"

I removed his gag.

"We need Kahan for this," he said hoarsely.

"We do this alone."

Ryn looked at the waiting line of snorting, frisky escoas, though it could barely be likened to a line at all now. The escoas were pulling one against the others, against the barbells I'd inserted through their noses and lashed to the dragon in front of them. As docile as they were, in a few moments the whole string of them would work themselves into an agitated knot.

"I'll ride lead." Ryn gasped. "But you should ride the one behind me, urge her airborne. The others'll follow, but you've tethered Ickwi after the lead, and sometimes she's stubborn at takeoff. She'll need urging."

"We'll put Ickwi in front, then." But even as I said it, I knew I'd run out of time. The dragons were throwing their hips into the snouts of the ones behind them, twiggy tails lashing this way and that, dewlaps inflated. Ickwi, the second in line, was unfurling her wings and flapping them, sending dust swirling. I was gripped with the sudden urge to run. Run fast, run far, and don't stop till dawn.

I turned back to Ryn. "You ride lead and I'll ride Ickwi. I've got a strong arm and a good aim; if I think you're flying me where I don't want to go, I'll throw my knife and sink it right through your ribs, understand?"

The paring knife was curved, and would no more fly true and sink deep than a crooked arrow. But Ryn's fear had left him no ability to reason, and he nodded.

I untied his hands. They were as cold as the iron stall. Side by side we approached the escoas. Both of us were trembling and darting looks nervously into dark corners.

"Where do you want me to fly us?" Ryn asked breathlessly as we approached the frisky escoa second in line, the one Ryn had called Ickwi.

"To the arbiyesku."

He stared at me. He'd expected a longer flight.

"Wait till I mount Ickwi before you untie the lead from the bar." I extended a hand to Ickwi. Her tongue flicked out, cool as silk upon my arm, and she watched me with bright, lizard-slitted eyes.

"Fold," I ordered, and I rapped her shoulder girdle hard with my knuckles. Slowly she furled her wings and tucked them to her flanks. "Leg up."

She shifted her weight and crooked a hind leg up, as if she were holding it fastidiously off soiled ground. Using her lifted knee as a step, as I had whenever I'd mounted a destrier to groom when in the dragonmaster's stables, I swung onto the dragon, slid forward to her neck, and lay prone along the saddle. With shaking hands I grasped the smooth wooden hand rungs jutting alongside the escoa's neck, then rammed my feet into the stirrup rungs at the rear of the saddle, either side the escoa's spine. Her saddlebags hung from her neck like pendulous fruits.

"How do I urge her airborne?"

Ryn stared at me as if I were yolkbrained. "Pull against the reins and drive your heels against her spine."

"My reins are tethered to your saddle."

"Oh . . ." He chewed his lower lip and shrugged. "Pull back on the hand rungs, then, and kick hard."

"Do we take a run at the flight, or spring airborne from standing?"

"Only destriers can spring airborne from standing."

"So we'll have to urge our mounts into a run."

"Yes."

"This courtyard long enough?"

"Not for a train of six." He swallowed, glanced at the stablehands' cottage, looked as if he wanted to bolt.

"Untie the lead and turn us about," I ordered. "And don't try to run from me, Ryn. I've no desire to bleed the life from you, but if I have to, I will. Just do as I tell you, and I won't hurt you. I vow it."

He was as naked and thin as a skeleton, standing unclad before me, shivering. Just then thunder exploded overhead, a furious clap that slammed like a giant mallet against rooftop and earth. The escoas shied, and one of them trumpeted in fear.

"Quickly, Ryn! If we're caught now, both of us'll die beneath an Auditor's blade!"

He whirled, untethered the lead escoa, and led her at a trot in a wide circle to the end of the courtyard that was directly opposite the stablehands' hut. My mount followed, snorting and tossing her snout. The reins tethered to the escoa behind me went briefly taut; then the third escoa followed. And so on, down the line.

This is madness, I thought to myself, envisioning all of us tangled in the courtyard, dragons trumpeting in fear, wingspars snapped, barbells ripped out of nares, necks broken.

Ryn climbed gingerly aboard his mount. He looked back at me and opened his mouth as if to shout something, and my insides went cold as death, but then he clapped his mouth shut, turned forward, and dropped into flying position. He looked like a freshly whittled arrow lying slender and bare between his escoa's unfurled wings.

Let's go, let's go, let's go!

Ryn's mount hare-lunged toward the far end of the courtyard, and I kicked Ickwi hard on either side of her spine to urge her to follow. There was a gentle tug on my saddle from behind, and then we were all loping across the courtyard, toward the stablehands' hut, and Ryn's mount was lunging swiftly at the fore of the line, her great wings lifted high and beating the air, spread so wide they encompassed half the courtyard, and then she gathered herself and sprang airborne, and Ickwi gathered herself beneath me and she sprang skyward just as her neck shot forward, the reins between her and the lead escoa taut as a bowstring. There was a violent jerk on my saddle from the rear, as the reins between Ickwi and the escoa next in line went taut, and suddenly I knew we'd not survive this; there was no way—

But no. We were airborne, rising over the stablehands' hut, skimming over the daronpuis' building so close I swore I heard Ickwi's scales rasp against stone, and then we were rising into the skies in jerky stages.

The daronpuis' quarters fell away from us. We gained altitude, Ickwi's wingbeats growing even and steady. No jerks or tugs came either fore or aft of my saddle. The white domes of the temple loomed below, and at my shoulder height, the tip of the golden spire jutting up from the temple's central dome flashed by.

Wind, noise, the lurch and list and heave of muscle: dragonflight. I was terrified. I'd fall off without an experienced rider pinning me into my saddle. I was sure of it.

Clinging hold, chin pressed against dragon neck, I dared turn slightly to look behind me. There were four escoas tethered in the string after us. Incredibly, I'd done it. I'd stolen my own escoas from the messenger byre.

Below us, the shingled rooftops of the Noua Sor tenements appeared, a dark patchwork of peaks. We continued south, then began descending rather steeply. The arbiyesku warehouse flashed by below.

The ground rushed toward us. Fast. I tensed, clung tight to the hand rungs. Gritted my teeth. Closed my eyes.

"Slow down!" I screamed, and then we landed. Dragons slammed one into another and bawled. I was thrown from the saddle, hit the ground hard. Dust billowed around me. Agony in my ribs. They were fractured anew; I was sure of it. I couldn't move, couldn't think. . . .

Through the dust I saw Ryn leap off the lead escoa and reach for Ickwi, who was rearing, frothy blood foaming around her nose barbell. Ryn held her reins firmly and cooed to her. Gritting my teeth, I struggled to my feet, took a shallow breath, and lurched toward the escoa tethered behind Ickwi.

Her barbell had been wrenched almost entirely free of her nose; the steel dangled over her chin, sheathed in a skein of bloody phlegm. A jagged flap of flesh hung from her destroyed nares, cluttered with shards of cartilage and bone. She was half rearing, eyes rolling, a foreleg hanging askew as if boneless.

I fumbled with her barbell, managed to unscrew one end, and slid it from the mess of her nose. Cartilage rasped in a gristly way as I pulled the barbell clear. She snorted bloody foam at me and settled, shuddering, on three legs, her fourth tucked close to her breast. The bitter reek of agitated dragon fogged the air.

I stared at the line of mutilated dragons behind her as wind blew gustily. What had I done?

Dust and dead grass lifted into the air in violently whirling funnels, then blew raggedly apart. The darkness about us suddenly turned starkly silver from a sheet of lightning. Thunder reverberated for long, long miles over the sea of savanna. Blood dripped from ruined nares.

Bolt their wings together. Hobble them. Get them restrained.

I went through a saddlebag, withdrew hobbles, dropped them on the ground. Found the wing bolts. The escoa shied a little, and the dragon tethered behind her screamed. I grabbed one wingspar and rapped it with my knuckles.

"Fold, hey! Fold!"

She obeyed, trembling as she gathered wing leather over dorsum, the reek of her like wet copper in my mouth. Once her wings were folded, I inserted a clamping bolt through one of the coin-sized holes that had been punched through her wing leather, slid the bolt through the saddle loop, and clamped it shut. Did the same with the other wing.

Good. Now she couldn't unfurl her wings; they were bolted shut to the saddle.

I stooped beneath her breast, gritting my teeth against the pain in my fractured ribs, and stroked her oily dewlaps. I was about to hobble her; then I stopped. No need. She had a broken foreleg; she was going nowhere.

Ryn had calmed and restrained Ickwi. Wordlessly he unscrewed the nose barbell from the hideously damaged nares of the fourth escoa in line. I went to work on the fifth.

When we had all the escoas restrained, I faced Ryn, my hands slick with dragon blood. I was reeling a little. "I'm going into the arbiyesku," I gasped. "Turn around so I can gag and bind you again."

"I'm not going anywhere. You don't need to bind me." He shivered in the wind, which blew wildly about us, swirling first one way, then blasting another. Far behind Ryn, over the jungle mountains in the distance, lightning spasmed. Thunder rolled toward us, then erupted with three great claps. Both of us flinched, and the lathered escoas shied and tossed their snouts.

I made a decision, hoped I wouldn't regret it. "I'll bring you clothes when I return," I wheezed; then I turned and loped toward the arbiyesku, ignoring the knives of pain and creaking, bubbling sounds issuing from my ribs.

In the far east, greenish light was spilling across the black table of night. Dawn was coming.

I staggered into the arbiyesku compound, clattered up the stairs of the women's barracks, and barged through the door. Shouts of alarm, muffled thuds, silhouettes bolting upright from the floor . . .

"Savga?" I called. "Savga?"

A shadow hurtled through the dark and flung itself at my knees. I staggered back a little under the impact, then knelt to grip her tight.

"Thank the One Dragon you're safe," I murmured against her neck as the women of the arbiyesku surrounded us.

"She said you were taken by soldiers," said a shadow with a voice that sounded like scree sliding down a mountainside. I looked up: Tiwana-auntie.

"I was, but I've escaped. I need to speak to someone from the myazedo. Quickly."

Stillness and silence from the women surrounding me.

I suppressed the urge to scream with impatience, slowly stood, and spoke as calmly as possible. "I've stolen the escoas from the messenger byre. They're not far from here, near the cocoon warehouse. I need help bringing them to the myazedo in the hills."

Savga was the first to speak in the stunned silence. "You're taking me to Mother?"

I hadn't planned to, not at all. But there was little to be done. Savga was present, and I was going to the myazedo where her mother might be. Ergo . . .

I nodded tersely. She flung herself around my knees again and sobbed with raw abandon. I placed a hand gently on her head.

"Please," I said to the humped shadow and glistening white eyes that was Tiwana-auntie. "We have to move now, before the theft is discovered."

With a grunt, she shouldered by me and led the way outside. The men had woken at the alarmed cries of the women and were crowded around the foot of the barracks' stairs. As I started to descend them, I saw someone familiar standing amongst those men, his bald pate identifiable under the starlight.

"What are *you* doing here?" I cried.

"Things are happening, girl—"

"Where's Gen?"

"Wish I knew." The dragonmaster spat. "Something's gone bad; I can feel it."

My spine prickled. "I thought you were in the destrier stables, readying a stall for . . . for . . . a destrier."

"Gen told me where he'd hidden you and the puling kitten. When he disappeared I went looking for you, only to find you gone, too." He sounded outraged, as if Gen and I had planned our respective disappearances.

I took a deep breath. "We need to get to the myazedo in the hills. Tonight. I've stolen the escoas that were stabled in the messenger byres. They're hobbled behind the cocoon warehouse, on the savanna. You can help fly the escoas out now that you're here. They were . . . injured in getting this far."

Eyes stared at me, stunned. Thunder blasted the sky, and the stairs I was stood upon shook.

"There's a storm," Tiwana-auntie croaked. "The Wet starts."

"We can't stay here."

"Dawn comes. You might be seen."

"Not if we leave *now*."

The dragonmaster stalked toward the stairs, shoulders hunched. "Have you lost your reason, or do you speak truth?"

"They're behind the warehouse; I swear it."

"How many of 'em?"

"Six."

"How'd you fly them out by yourself?"

"I took an apprentice herald as a hostage and tethered the dragons together by nose barbell."

"No wonder they've been injured," he said, disgusted.

"Better six injured than no escoas at all. How many have *you* managed to procure?"

"Procure," he said acidly. "Steal, is the truth of it."

"They're my dragons. Can't steal what you own. Now, are you coming or not?"

A rhetorical question. We both knew he would.

ELEVEN

The storm was a living thing. It howled, it bucked, it clawed. Whips of rain flailed my cheeks and blinded my eyes, and gusts of wind slammed against me and the dragon I flew, pitching us first one way, then another. Wing leather shuddered as if it would tear. My fingers felt lacerated. Foam blew from my mount's nostrils and splattered against me, soft, hot, bloodied. Suddenly my dragon slewed sideways. We stalled, and for a moment we were plummeting. The dragon tethered to the back of my saddle bawled and fought our downward plunge. My escoa's wings heaved up and down, battling the wind, the rain, the pitching sea of air about us. Then we were flying once more.

Another savage gust of wind. The dragon behind us yawed from side to side, and my dragon pitched and reeled and floundered. Her muscles bulged as her neck strained far forward, as if she believed she might free herself of the anchorlike drag behind her if only she reached far enough. The muscles in her powerful shoulder girdle shuddered. Her desperation and fear were palpable. I had to release the dragon tethered to our saddle or she would be the death of all three of us.

I fumbled for the paring knife I'd knotted into the fabric of my bitoo, back at the messenger byre. A difficult maneuver, one-handed, on a pitching dragon, while rain hurtled down like ceramic shards.

Mo fa cinai, wabaten ris balu. Purest Dragon, become my strength.

I had the paring knife. Clenching the saddle with knees and thighs, I stretched down to my left knee, to the leather saddle loop to which the dragonmaster had tethered my spare escoa by means of a makeshift neck halter. I slashed at the tether. Missed.

A fork of lightning hissed across the clay gray sky, turning the world briefly, starkly white, and a hundred or so feet below us jungle flashed as bilious green as a wildcat's eyes.

I slashed again. Steel sank into leather. Another gust of wind slammed hard into us and we slewed to the side. My paring knife went spinning from my hand.

The slashed tether went taut, then snapped, snaking away from us like a wild whip, and the sudden release from the dragon behind us was as if we'd been cast free from a mooring, and my escoa flew strong.

I raised my head slightly and squinted in the driving rain. I couldn't see Ryn behind me with Savga huddled beneath him, her wrists tied tight to the saddle rungs to keep her seated. I wasn't sure how much time had passed since I'd last glimpsed them. Nor could I see the dragonmaster ahead of me, Piah gripping his waist. When the storm had devoured us, all had become confusion.

We'd left the arbiyesku mounted upon three dragons, just as a sickly dawn had begun to seep through the parasitic clouds swarming the sky. I flew solo. I'd wanted Savga to fly with the dragonmaster, but no, he'd needed Piah behind him, to give directions to the myazedo camp as best he could from the bizarre perspective of an aerial view. Ryn, as an apprentice herald, had more experience than I at flying dragons, so I'd deemed it safer for Savga to fly with him than me.

All I could think of now was Ryn's bony back and his youth, and how foolish I'd been to entrust Savga's life to a thirteen-year-old boy.

Thunder slammed like a cudgel against my head. Lightning sizzled and forked, charging the air with a metallic tang. My skin tingled nastily, as if I'd been stung all over by a clawful of scorpions.

I could hang on no longer. I would plummet to my death, I was sure of it.

Land, I willed my dragon. Land.

But far below, the jungle was a great, hirsute green fist defiantly clenched shut against us.

Lightning flashed, and in the brilliant white glare rain looked like milk and wing leather like wet, rippling alabaster, and the fingers of my hands, bone. I was plunged into gray murk again, murk that may have been dawn or late morn or may even have been noon. Impossible to tell.

Another deafening boom of thunder exploded around me with such force I felt the noise as an intrusion within my chest, as if the raw muscle of my heart had been touched.

My mount suddenly dropped her hind legs down and craned her neck skyward. I was all but vertical, standing in my stirrup rungs, and I shrieked as I lost my grip on a hand rung. I was tipping backward. . . .

Wings shredded the air on either side of me, great leather sheets flapping furiously, and we landed, not with a hard jolt, but with a discernible rebound, as though the ground were exceptionally resilient. Foliage slapped me as my escoa dropped to all fours, her muscles clenching, twitching, and flexing as she sought her balance. Rain pounded around us in furious gusts, and wind soughed over the surrounding bush and trees.

Shuddering, I sat up in the saddle and squinted through tree branches into the sky, shielding the rain from my eyes with one hand.

"Savga!" I bellowed. "Ryn!"

Nothing above but foaming, curdled cloud, driving rain, and seething wind. I looked behind us, to see if by chance we'd been followed.

Great Dragon.

My escoa had landed on the bough of a cliff-clinging tree, and the bough jutted out over a valley of dense, windswept jungle. Treetops moaned and swayed far below us in the wind, while the tree we'd landed on creaked, and branches bobbed up and down and lashed this way and that, and leaves fluttered and slapped, and twigs cascaded to the hanging garden of snarled vines and hanks of moss and parasitic plants far below us. The ground wasn't visible.

I lay in the saddle and melded to leather and wood. I breathed shallowly, hesitantly, as if the rise and fall of my chest might unbalance my dragon.

She moved. Her wings were widespread, like a grounded bat, the claws at the ends of both wing tips wrapped tight around slender offshoots from our bough.

Lightning flashed.

My dragon moved again, tentatively, clumsily, and the slim branch she held in her left wing tip claws snapped. We listed sharply to one side. I screamed. Thunder boomed.

Beneath me, the escoa's muscles flexed and clenched as she struggled to balance on the bough. She found her footing, settled her weight over her hips, and released the branch on her right.

After a pause, she flapped her wings a few times to shake off rainwater. She drew them in and folded them as best she could over her back. I welcomed the wet, leathery embrace; it held me better in my saddle.

She squatted down on the bough, phlegmatic. Shook water off her arrow-shaped head. Waited.

There was nothing to do but stay in my saddle and wait along with her.

The deluge eased up, thunder rolling into the distance. The rain stopped. Time to search for Savga.

I hastily finished eating the kadoob tuber I'd dared to withdraw, with meticulous care, out of a saddlebag; Tiwana-auntie had insisted we pack food with us, and I was now grateful for her foresight. The starch of the raw vegetable squeaked against my teeth. My escoa craned her neck snakelike over her shoulder to stare at me as I crunched, but I didn't give her the remains of the tuber. I'd made that mistake moments before, having given her a whole root. She'd rolled the kadoob around her mouth several times, then dropped it, either classifying it as inedible, or because she'd been unable to eat from the pain of her mutilated nares that had been ripped from the barbell through her nose. The tuber had dropped down, down, down into the jungle valley below us, disappearing as a speck into the sea of green leaves.

Wasn't the root I saw fall. In my mind, I saw a six-year-old girl.

I choked on the last of my meal. My escoa gave me a baleful look and turned forward again.

Trying not to look at the wind-tossed green far below, I inched my arm along first one side of the escoa's neck, then the other, and retrieved the dangling reins. They were attached to the makeshift neck halter the dragonmaster had rigged. I didn't know if the escoa would obey any commands given her via means of that halter. An escoa was used to obeying the tugs of a nose barbell.

I wanted my mount airborne. She wanted to rest. I wanted to get off our precarious perch. She wanted to stay. I kicked her hard along her spine, again and again, and finally she unfurled her wings and sprang into the air.

There was a brief, terrifying sensation of freefall before she flapped lazily a clawful of times and settled into a glide.

Jungle below, jade and verdant. A rolling valley of it, rippling like ocean swells. I shivered hard in the wind.

"Savga!" I bellowed. "Ryn!"

I wanted to go lower, but how to make an escoa descend? Press forward with knees? Pull down on reins? How could I make her turn in one direction or another?

A dark green-and-rust blur on my left, in the air. Dragon. My heart leapt. Then plummeted; the dragon was riderless.

Please, not Savga . . .

I prayed it was the escoa that had been tied behind me. Over and over I prayed, *pleasepleaseplease,* while images of Savga's still and shattered body, sprawled jellylike over the crown of a tree, rose into my mind with such horrifying clarity I feared I was seeing a vision of what had actually occurred.

My dragon was descending.

Ahead of us, a river. One of the tributaries that fed into Clutch Xxamer Zu's river, perhaps.

Was my mount heading back to the Clutch? I was as good as dead if she were. By returning to her home byre, the escoa would unwittingly deliver me straight into the hands of every holy warden in the daronpuis' stockade.

I glanced behind me. The riderless escoa still followed. No sight of Ryn and Savga. No sight of the dragonmaster and Piah.

Please . . .

I no longer knew what I prayed for.

Sludgy, sage green water flashed below us, obliterated from sight here and there by bowers of trees and hanging moss. We descended lower. Floating caimans submerged into the river as we swept over. A white egret poised on the root-tangled bank took flight.

I would jump. Better to risk surviving the fall into the river than the return to Xxamer Zu.

My escoa stopped flapping. She glided long and smoothly over the river's milky green back, and, for a moment, the wind died. Completely.

Silence, save for the delicate whisper of flight. A song of strength and freedom and hope, that. A song that encapsulates the distance to the stars, the greatness of the skies, the marvel and immensity of life. For a heartbeat I knew peace. For a heartbeat I was suspended in that silent glide, no action expected of me, no decisions required. The lush, silent profusion of creation had inhaled, and I and my dragon were suspended in that pocket of time before it would exhale.

Perhaps life is made sweet by the knowledge that it will never come again.

The moment ended, and I knew I must jump from my mount or ride helpless on her back to Xxamer Zu. I released the hand rungs and tensed to swing off her back. I was gripped by a raging thirst, and I knew the dryness came from terror.

A great fallen tree stretched across the river ahead of us. Turtles, or perhaps frogs, frantically plopped into the water at our approach. My escoa altered her position, was suddenly back-fighting the air and lowering her legs, and I scrabbled for the hand rungs instinctively and jammed my feet back into the stirrup rungs.

We were landing.

We touched down on that great fallen tree as lightly as dew. I shuddered and thanked the Infinite Winged for the mercy shown me, and then I leaned over my escoa's neck and retched. After several moments, the escoa trailing behind us touched down at the other end of the trunk.

My escoa cocked her head to one side and eyed the river suspiciously. She tilted her head at a different angle, examined the water some more. Inspection complete, she snorted, folded her wings over her back, knelt on her forelegs, and bent to the river for a drink.

Time to dismount.

Trembling, I squirmed backward to her rump, which was elevated from her stooped drinking position, and slid out from under her wings. The log was slick underfoot from the rainfall, but wide enough that I could readily balance. I reached into the saddlebags—several inches of cold water sloshed inside them—and withdrew a pair of brass wing bolts. While the dragon drank, I bolted her folded wings to her saddle. A fly alighted on her; her withers shuddered and her tail slapped against her flank. Still, she remained crouched over the river, sucking in long, slurping gulps of water. She was still drinking as I approached the escoa perched on the far end of the fallen tree.

I moved briskly, with false confidence. I feared the escoa might vault into the sky, and it was imperative that I catch her, for should she return to Xxamer Zu, Ghepp could dispatch a herald upon her to the Ranreeb and alert him of the theft of all Xxamer Zu's winged dragons. The myazedo would descend from the hills into the jaws of a regiment of Temple's rabid dogs.

The riderless escoa lifted her snout from the water and eyed me warily as I approached her. Beads of blood dripped into the river from her maimed nares, and when I saw that mangled snout, hope blazed within me, that most powerful and mundane form of magic unique to all humans, for Savga and Ryn had been mounted upon the one escoa that had *not* been injured during my escape from the daronpuis' compound. This, then, was not their mount.

Tears of relief sprang to my eyes.

Be alive, Savga. Be safe.

The riderless escoa looked as if she were considering lunging for the skies. Her maimed nares distorted her entire face, so that she looked snub-nosed and warthogish as she warily regarded me.

"Hey-o, fold up. Fold up!" I commanded sharply, even though her wings *were* folded over her back.

The show of authority was enough to stay her; she dropped her head to the water again and noisily sucked down water. The muscles in her neck rippled with each swallow, and her dewlaps glistened with raindrops. The viridity of the surrounding jungle and the milky green of the river turned her hide into scales of jade, the rufous flecks subsumed under green. I placed a hand firmly upon her muscular shoulder girdle.

She'd lost her saddlebags during the storm. I had no wing bolts for her. After a moment's thought, I wrestled with the makeshift halter rigged about her neck and managed to untie the rain-swollen knots. I laced the reins through the two brass-ringed holes punched into her wing membranes and bound her wings together that way.

With both dragons rendered flightless, I drank, and with each swallow I thanked the One Dragon for hope, my life, the escoas, the possibility of tomorrow. Somehow I knew Savga was alive. Yes, I knew it. She was alive and hale, and though some might argue that my belief was denial, or desperate hope, or a delusion necessary to retain my sanity, I say that one doesn't need to look upon the moon to know that its light is what one sees by at night. And the spirit of a child shines as distinctly as celestial light. Even at great distances.

I'd journey upriver, I decided. Unless I was far, far inland from the savanna, and unless the river flowed in another direction entirely from the Clutch river, downstream would only lead me to Xxamer Zu. I'd journey upriver and trust the One Dragon to lead me to the myazedo.

And, come the morrow, if my faith-led journey had brought me none the closer to the camp of insurgents, I would take to the sky in hopes the dragonmaster or Ryn would see and retrieve me. But for now, I would walk. My escoas were spent, and I had little desire to brave those glowering, roiling skies again that day.

I let the escoas decide which side of the riverbank to walk along. My mount chose the bank closest to her, and the other one plodded after her with stolid calm, as though still tethered to her. Thus our course was decided.

The skies remained overcast and peevish. The wind died. The air turned sultry. Gnats and flies and mosquitoes swarmed around us as we wove through frond and ivy and palm leaf, stumbling over knots of exposed roots and rotting deadwood. Dragonflies skimmed over the river, and toads plopped from the banks and disappeared beneath skeins of algae. Several times the lead escoa's head shot forward, viper fast, and her tongue lashed the back of a toad as it sprang for the river, but never did she catch one. If her venom sacs had not been removed, I warrant the jungle would have been several frogs poorer for her accuracy that day.

My bitoo hindered my progress. I knotted it up around my thighs. Occasionally I cupped my hands around my mouth and bellowed for Savga. I thirsted and drank from the river, and ate another kadoob tuber, and pulled a leech from my calf.

The heat continued to rise, and as it did, great black clouds began amassing upriver, shouldering aside their gray cousins and exerting a heavy pressure upon the earth. I slipped on a fat, slimy ring of toadstools and fell to my knees. The dragons stopped behind me, and, after a pause Toadhunter pushed through bracken and creepers to kneel at the riverbank for a drink.

Warthog remained where she was standing and flicked her tongue in the direction of a nearby tree. The tree's buttressed roots arched smoothly from the jungle floor like giant green ribs, and some seventy feet above our heads, through a dense canopy of liana vines and hanging moss and hairferns, I could just make out the tree's lowest branches.

Warthog flicked her forked tongue again at the tree, her pupils and ear slits dilating. She lunge-hopped to the steeples of root soaring ten feet up the trunk and poked her narrow head into one crack, then another, becoming more animated with each foray between the roots.

Her head disappeared right into the tree, and her neck followed, and she shimmied up to the buttressed trunk until she looked decapitated at the shoulders. Evidently, the tree was hollow.

After several moments she withdrew her neck and head, a giant snail the size of a durian fruit clamped in her jaws.

She dropped the giant snail upside down at her feet. The snail laboriously began righting itself. The escoa cocked her head and watched it intently with one lizard-slitted eye; then her snout shot forward, wickedly fast, and she had the meat of the snail between her razor-sharp front teeth. She shook her head side to side in a short, furious burst, reached up to her snout with a foreclaw, and slowly pulled the snail from its shell, stretching the glaucous slug until it was the length of my arm. She lunged forward, severed the length of the body from its shell-embedded tail, and gulped the meat down.

I stared. Again, she inserted her head into the tree. Toadhunter swung away from the river, snout dripping, and watched Warthog retrieve and devour yet another giant snail. Toadhunter joined her, and they both strained and pushed against the hollow tree as if trying to squeeze themselves between the roots and climb inside.

A hatchling might be able to do that.

No. A hatchling *could* do that.

A memory suddenly leapt at me, bold as sunshine, and for a giddy moment I remembered being a hatchling, and scrabbling face-first down the hollow of a tree from its lightning-blasted crown, feasting on whip-scorpions, giant millipedes, a blind baby squirrel in a nest, and a snail twice the size of my head.

But after gorging myself, my leathery belly was so swollen and taut, I found I couldn't turn around to climb back out. I was lodged.

I shrieked for my mother. Over and over I shrieked, and the trunk of the hollow tree suddenly shuddered mightily. I smelled my mother as her neck and arrow snout snaked down the hollow tree. Her teeth clasped me none too gently around the neck, just above my shoulder blades, and she heaved me out of the hollow, dragging shreds of rotted wood and mushrooms and lichen along with me, nigh on ripping off my wings in the process.

The image left me breathless and reeling.

The memory had been as clear as the dragons foraging in front of me, far and away more coherent than any dragonmemory I'd experienced when hearing dragonsong. Sharper, even, than some of my *own* childhood memories. It was as if a thousand scattered shards from a smashed urn had suddenly coalesced into a whole in front of me.

In that fantastic moment, I was surrounded.

They peeled off of tree trunks, detached from fountains of fern, unfurled from the loamy ground, slid out from between lichen-stippled roots. A rotting log hairy with moss and slimy with mushrooms rose onto legs, spear in hand. The escoas shied; the standing log—the *woman*—held up a hand and spoke to the escoas in a mellifluous flood of Djimbi. The words soothed like warm yolk sauce in an empty belly, enfolded like a down-padded quilt on a blustery night. I heard not words but the sounds of images: a babe suckling at breast; sunlight twinkling on a dewy web; a deep green pool surrounded by a rainbow spray of water, cast by a thin waterfall crashing from a thousand-foot cliff. The escoas not only calmed; they looked entranced. I tell it true. Their eyes glazed over and they looked as witless and impotent as goggle-eyed pyumar birds. The speaker clucked her tongue thrice, and the escoas blinked, then resumed foraging for snails, as if the strangers who had emerged from bracken and soil with weapons in hand were as unremarkable as the surrounding creepers and vines.

I was still on the ground, where I'd landed from slipping upon the toadstools. Warily, I rose to my feet.

There were six of them that I could see, though I wasn't trusting my eyes; there may yet have been more present that I couldn't discern from root or trunk. And they were Djimbi. Freeborn Djimbi. *Pureblood* Djimbi.

Their whorls blended in perfectly with their surroundings, shadings of moss green and palm frond emerald dappled with the rich, wet brown of loam and the grayish brown of peeling tree bark. The women wore crude loincloths only, like the men, made of shagreen. Their breasts were small and high, their nipples and areolae a dark, wet ivy. Great hanks of hair the exact pale green of hanging moss hung to their waists; the men were hairless, their pates as smooth as the tree roots about us. All of them were lean and sinewy, their arms and legs long. The untanned leather loincloths they wore were no more than a waistband strip of granulated leather with a flap attached fore and aft; their hard, lean buttocks were visible.

Two men and one woman held spears, and the others each carried a small quiver of blow darts slung across their backs. One woman with eyes like chips of jade had a wicked blade tied by a thong to her loincloth. As well as spears, the two men carried damp leather sacks, around which buzzed flies and hung the odor of fresh blood.

Hunters.

The Djimbi woman who'd sung to the escoas spoke to me. She looked arrogant and menacing, her spear sharp, her eyes and nose hawkish. Her long, long arms were hard with sinew and muscle. Every terrifying tale I'd heard about the Djimbi came rushing to the forefront of my mind: They kidnapped Clutch babies and fed them alive, limb by severed limb, to dragon hatchlings; they were cannibals who used human skulls for bowls and cups; they knew dragons in the most abominable of ways, inserting fingers and tongues and cocks into leathery orifices.

I didn't understand what the woman was saying, not a word. I could recognize that she was speaking some form of Djimbi by her telltale glottal stops and singsong cadence, but the words themselves were unfamiliar to me.

"I don't understand," I said hoarsely in the pidgin language that passes for common Malacarite. I repeated myself in the Emperor's tongue. To no avail. The Djimbi woman merely reiterated what she'd said, her lyrical words as sharp as thorns at the ends.

I wanted water. No. I wanted maska spirits.

The Djimbi woman turned to her companions. They held a brief conference, gesturing from the dragons to me. A decision was reached. The Djimbi woman addressed me again.

Her words I didn't understand, but her gestures were clear: *Take hold of your dragons and follow us.*

It's hard to argue when one shares no common language, and the sight of spears and blow darts makes a powerful inducement to agree. Bristling at her imperious mien, but wise enough to realize my anger was just a vent for my fear, I tied Toadhunter's neck halter to the back of Warthog's saddle and, with a whack on Warthog's hide to get her moving, I followed the Djimbi away from the river and deep, deep into the jungle.

TWELVE

For a day and a night I followed the Djimbi, and for the bulk of another day after that.

We didn't sleep at night. No. The jungle turned moldy gray with dusk, then plunged into deep, sinister black, but the Djimbi continued walking. I stumbled over an unseen root. Then again. Then again. One of the women ahead of me moaned.

Her moan was gravelly and belly-deep. It went on, and on, and I found myself holding my breath, waiting for it to end, but still it droned on. The hairs on my nape stood on end. Behind me, one of the men barked, a coughing hack I'd heard once in my youth. He continued to bark, punctuating the woman's ceaseless moan, and others joined him with their own harsh croaks and explosive coughs. I stumbled again, not over a root. Over fear. The Djimbi were evoking barbaric magics to travel by.

Pure One, protect me.

When last I'd heard such aberrant moans and barks, my mother had done battle with a dirge-summoned python intent on death. She'd evoked magics of clay and birth and creation, and the python had winked out of existence. But my mother wasn't with me to offer protection against *this* pagan dirge.

About me, frond and vine and steepled root answered the threnody by sliding against one another. I could hear it, a croaking, raspy slithering, but all movement was just beyond the periphery of my sight. I saw only the intimation of black moving beyond black as roots and creepers and bracts and stalks knotted and uncoiled and joined again in an unnatural, night-shrouded orgy.

I had been plunged into a netherworld where the insentient brooded, the eyeless watched, the stationary stirred, and the sexless fucked.

It was as black as pitch on the forest floor. Far above, the oppressive tonnage of the jungle crown moaned and rasped and sighed like the wooden hulls of a thousand boats adrift on a murmuring sea. Fore and aft of me, the dark forms of my escoas shuffle-lunged with heads hanging. From the corner of one eye, I thought I saw the dragon behind me warp into a yamdalar cinaigour, the slick keratinous involucre as bluish gray as a blind eye as it floated in my wake. But when I spun about, I saw only a dark silhouette of a dragon moving through black.

How puny and clean my mother's magic seemed compared to the subtle, serpiginous movement of root and vine around us. Instead of fighting the dark with invasive light, the Djimbi embraced the ebon obscure, and the darkness itself cleared creeper and root from our path and guided our footsteps.

Surrounded by dirge and imprisoned by dark, I was compelled to follow the Djimbi, and foliage parted before me like dark legs spreading wide, directing me into a wet, hidden center.

There comes a point where fear turns into a sterile land without horizons, and to cross such a blighted expanse, one must crawl into the deep quiet of oneself. I crawled into that inner space and remained there till dawn.

A deluge heralded sunup. Overhead, the canopy heaved and roiled. We were submerged beneath an angry ocean of leaf. Little rain penetrated the dense hanging gardens above, and that which did pattered down as sporadic rainfall. We ate chunks of raw meat carved from the grisly slabs in the sacks the men carried. They were hunters, my captors. Predators.

My dragons were failing, both of them. The grisly wounds on their noses had become infected from the dirt of their foraging, from the insects that had swarmed around their heads the day previous, and from the sultry jungle heat that breeds illness and disease. Clusters of hard nodules had appeared overnight on their snouts, fist-sized and turgid, and the dragons showed no interest in their surroundings.

We stopped to piss. The Djimbi spoke tersely amongst themselves. Longstride, the woman who'd entranced the escoas with song and whom I'd named for her long, lean legs, pointed angrily at my back. She wanted me to carry the dragons' saddles myself, to spare them.

I hated the way her amber eyes blazed at me from beneath her green mane of hair. I hated her sinewy strength, her certainty, her feral grace. Hated her warranted disgust over the state of my dragons.

Hated, most, the fear she induced in me, and the fear of not knowing where she was taking me or what would be my fate.

Truth be told, I would have carried those damn saddles if I could have, not just to spare the escoas but to bolster my courage through bravado. If I hadn't been left in a cell without food or water for several days prior to being assaulted by a storm and then taken captive, I would have met Longstride's challenge and thrown her contempt back in her face by carrying first one saddle for half a day, then the other till nightfall. I'd once had the strength for such, and the brazenness. I knew I'd have them again. But to attempt to haul those saddles in the state I was currently in would have been humiliating and futile, and I was levelheaded enough to bitterly realize it.

It was while I was stewing with resentment and guilt and fear that I was attacked by a rebound moment and plunged into the furious agony of venom withdrawal.

It came upon me suddenly, or perhaps not; hard to tell when one is crushed by exhaustion and hunger and immersed in rancor. I was trudging alongside poor Warthog, who was mired in that kind of misery that shuts out all else except the imperative to put one foot relentlessly in front of the other, and next I knew I was on my back, shuddering violently, sweating, gripped with agonizing belly cramps, my back arched like a bowstring. The jungle canopy swooped and circled above me. My fingernails clawed soft, damp loam. My heels drummed against the ground; then I went slack as a gutted bird. I retched. My eyes streamed tears.

Another spasm cramped every muscle in my body, and I went rigid, then convulsed on the ground, loam in my mouth, leaf mold smeared over my cheeks, ivy tangled about my neck.

I was vaguely aware of the Djimbi gathering in a wide circle around me.

It was then that I smelled it, as I writhed and corkscrewed on the ground: the wicked anise-oil sweetness and citric tang of venom. The smell was as real as the agonizing cramps gripping me.

I bolted upright with a hoarse cry. The Djimbi stiffened. "Where is it, where?" I cried.

Longstride tossed something into my lap: a leather bladder as withered and deflated as a eunuch's scrotal sac. The Djimbi exchanged a flurry of comments, then drew closer and squatted on their haunches about me, save for Longstride, who looked down with an arrogance I longed to smack from her face.

My hands shook so badly that I twice dropped the bladder as I lifted it to my mouth. I sucked on it as if it were a teat.

The taste of venom exploded on my tongue. Longstride leapt toward me and barked harsh words. I looked up at her, vision oscillating. Her blurry image gestured angrily at the escoas. She wanted me to use the venom on them.

"You don't understand," I said hoarsely. "*I* need this venom."

Utter disdain on her face.

No half measures.

I bellowed in frustration. Spewing invective, twitching like one deranged, I staggered upright. I stood there swaying a moment as the few precious drops of venom I'd ingested flickered like weak candlelight in my blood. I hated Longstride, the way she looked at me with such scorn.

"I need to make a poultice," I rasped. "I need . . . brallosh leaves, or gruel, or something."

I made angry stirring motions with my hands. She understood.

I can't recall what the poultice was made from; there is a blank section in my memory, whitewashed by the rebound attack of venom withdrawal. Perhaps my captors retrieved roots from my saddlebags, or dug them from the ground and masticated them to a paste. Perhaps they foraged for the snakebane lichen that grows like tiny inverted orange cups on the underside of dead logs, and which, when immersed in water, turns into a spermy slime that heals certain snakebites. Truly, I don't know what they brought me.

All I know is that the bladder of venom was stuffed by one of the Djimbi with dollops of a gelatinous poultice. The woman with eyes like chips of jade pulled the drawstring shut and massaged the bladder with muscular hands, and then it was time for me to spread the poultice, with its precious infusion of venom, onto the escoas' nares.

I did it with my bare hands. The paste oozed between my fingers, scented oh-so-blessedly with the dragon's poison. I luxuriated in slowly rubbing the poultice over the scaled snout, savoring venom's tingle on my skin. My eyes closed as I worked. I yearned for dragonsong. I envisioned Tansan, naked, beneath me.

The Djimbi didn't hurry me. No. They watched, engrossed. Perhaps an hour passed before I turned away from the dragons, who stood with doughy yellow masks on their nodule-distorted snouts, eyes bright and wide, as if they were surprised but couldn't recall by what.

Longstride spoke. She towered over me, heat rising off her. Her ivy green nipples were hard as spring buds. She splayed one of her hands across my breasts and against my groin. She spoke, and her voice was husky, and her serum-colored eyes—like watered amber, like golden broth—burned into mine. She withdrew her hands, lifted a lock of my hair, and severed it with a slash of her spearhead. She wove the lock into her moss colored mane.

I didn't know what her actions meant, didn't know how I should respond. Didn't know if a response was even necessary. Yes, one was: She was waiting.

I shrugged. "I don't understand." I repeated myself twice, again in Malacarite, and the third time in the Emperor's tongue.

The silence following my words stretched overlong. I didn't know what to do. Uncertainty built into smoldering dread.

Longstride drew herself to her full impressive height, the arrogance on her cheeks compounded by outrage. She snapped something at me, stabbed a finger in my face. Brief conversation amongst the Djimbi, and one of the hunters directed a question at Longstride. She turned and curtly responded. The hunters looked at me as they exchanged words with Longstride. A flat-faced man with hooded eyes must have made a barbed remark, for the other Djimbi looked away from him. Longstride's nostrils flared, and she barked something at him and raised her hand as if she would strike him. He snapped something back but turned away. She spat on the ground behind him.

Then she looked at me with an expression that could be interpreted only as fury.

We continued through the jungle, Jade-eyes at the fore. By evenfall, we reached their home.

A cluster of huts stood amongst the great trunks of towering trees, some huts made of bamboo, others of rawhide. Their simplicity suggested impermanence, mobility.

A firepit smoldered. An enormously fat woman was seated before it, her massive breasts covered with gold necklaces. I gaped. I'd never seen so much gold upon anyone before. Around the mountain of her shoulders a fine leather cape hung. The clasp was silver.

A crowd of lean, tall Mottled Bellies clustered about me and the dragons. The women all had long hair, save for the very young. The men, right down to the youngest boy, were all bald. Above a clamor of voices, Longstride spoke to the seated fat woman, who seemed to be a person of status. Maybe a medicine witch, or the tribe Great-elder. A combination of both, perhaps. A matriarch.

I was shoved forward. The matriarch's eyes roved over me and she spoke, rubbery lips blurring her words. Embers clucked and hissed in the firepit between us.

Longstride spoke and gestured at my escoas. The dragons were shifting uneasily, eyes rolling from the press of people, poultice flaking from their snouts. The matriarch gestured me forward.

A sea of hands propelled me toward her. Longstride shoved me to my knees at the matriarch's feet. The ground was damp under my kneecaps.

The matriarch wore no loincloth. The smell emanating from between her thighs was potent, musky, overwhelming. She leaned over, her many gold necklaces—there must have been at least forty of them; it was a wonder her neck wasn't bowed beneath the weight—jingling softly against one another. With sooty fingers she grabbed my chin. Studied my face. Barked something to Longstride. An ember was poked from the fire and brought over, balanced on a spearhead, and I gasped and tried to pull away. The matriarch's grip was relentless.

By the light of the ember, she studied my eyes.

She looked at mine, and I looked at hers, and there passed between us a dark, powerful knowing: She knew about the bestial rite; she'd *performed* it a number of times; and she knew that I, too, had performed it more than once. We had the same eyes, see. Our dark pupils bore shards of white, as if embedded with tiny stars. Our sclera was not white, but a mass of red filaments, of bloody rivulets, of venom channels.

She released my chin and muttered something. Voices blazed around me. Longstride shouted something, her spear raised in the air. She looked around, her hawkish features challenging. Silence. The matriarch spoke. Again, everyone murmured one to another, voices building in volume and expectation to a babble of excitement.

Longstride hauled me to my feet, jaw set with determined triumph. She held my arm tightly. The crowd was dispersing rapidly, and my escoas were being led away.

Longstride spoke, then shook my arm angrily. I looked up at her—she was *too* tall—and realized she'd addressed a question to me.

"I don't understand," I said again

She repeated herself, arrogant pride blazing from her eyes. I hated that superior look.

All my fear channeled into fury, and I jerked my arm from her grasp and stabbed a finger at the rumps of my escoas, where they were being led behind a bamboo hut. "Those are *my* dragons; bring them back *now*."

Longstride gave a feral grin. She spoke and splayed one hand over my breasts and pressed a clenched fist between my thighs, so that her knuckles were against my sex. Again, she waited for a response. I gave her one.

I spat in her face.

She drew back slowly, cold, eyes molten. Those who had remained around the fire hissed. The matriarch shouted out a stream of words. She was angry at me. No. Outraged.

I was grabbed from both sides and flipped onto my back on the ground. I landed hard, was stunned for a moment, and then pain radiated from my ribs. I bucked and heaved and swore and thrashed. More people descended upon me, and the matriarch continued to shout orders, and I was hauled a short way from the fire. My arms were spread wide, my legs spread apart. A swarm of people descended upon my pinioned limbs and knotted thick vines around my ankles and wrists. Stakes were hammered into the ground beside my hands, beside my feet, either side of my neck, either side of my waist, and I screamed and shivered and thrashed and snapped with my teeth, and perhaps I cried, yes, perhaps. But if I did, they were tears of fury, not resignation.

I was tied, spread-eagled, to the stakes in the ground. My waist, too, was lashed down. The vines across my throat went on last. When I bucked against them, I cut off my own breath and was nearly strangled.

I stopped fighting and instead screamed invective and hollow threats.

The fire was banked. Sparks leapt into the starless dark of the jungle canopy high above. Smoke drifted between the trees, wraithlike in the light of the leaping flames. I could feel the greedy heat of the fire.

The matriarch was helped up from the ground by two lanky adolescents. The matriarch summoned a young girl to her side with a flick of a pudgy hand; the young girl listened, then ran into the gloom beyond the firepit and disappeared into a yurt nestled beside the riblike buttress roots of a tree.

A woman wearing a mask suddenly loomed over me. My curses and screams shriveled up in my throat.

The mask was scaled and in the arrowhead shape of a lizard, topped by a storypole at least five feet high. Grotesquely distorted faces had been carved into the storypole, and instead of tongues protruding from the leering faces, dark bones swung from rope. The bones clattered together like gnashing teeth.

The mask had no mouth, just a great suctionlike cup, white as bone, soft and wobbly as unset rubber.

Another masked woman joined the first, then a second, and a third. Soon I was encircled by masked women with suckers for mouths, and the heat from the blazing fire was cut off from me by the wall of their bodies. Bones shivered and rattled upon storypoles.

The women linked hands and began whispering a chant. As they whispered, they began bouncing lightly on the balls of their feet. Their breasts jiggled, and firelight and shadow flickered.

Their words sped up. Their bouncing accelerated. Soon their words tripped over one another, and the bouncing turned into shuddering. Linked hands jerked like fish on hooks. The chant became a wordless, frenzied panting. The women convulsed, hands still linked. The ground itself juddered beneath me.

After several long moments of mesmerizing juddering, the sucker mouths and storypoles and women encircling me melted away. I don't remember the women stepping back. I don't remember them returning to the firepit. It was just as if . . . they melted.

At once I felt the full heat of the fire blazing in the pit several feet away.

My skin would burn. I could feel the fine hairs on my arms curling tight and shriveling from the heat.

A man knelt beside my head, grabbed my chin, and cranked my face to the side, away from the fire, so that I was looking toward a woman who stood some eight feet or so away, near the base of a tree. Her back was toward me. She was wrapped in a cape. She wore a mask of some sort, though I couldn't yet see more than the barest outline of the back of it. The mask bore no storypole.

How did I know it was a woman? The breath of enchanted women had just surrounded me, and the cloying scent of the matriarch was a briny musk in the air. This was a night of swarthy, sinister women's power. The caped person poised some eight feet from me was indubitably a woman.

The man who had knelt beside me released my chin and drifted away. I stared at the caped, masked woman with foreboding.

She threw back her head and ululated at the starless dark canopy above us. The sound ripped up and down my spine. The tribe of Djimbi, watching from shadow and by firelight, ululated back. The woman threw out her arms dramatically. I saw, then, that she hadn't been draped in a cape. No. She was winged. Like a bat. Like a dragon.

The inhuman abomination turned, slowly, bobbing in a strange, primitive dance. The mask she wore was carved into the arrowhead shape of a reptile, its bulging eyes painted with the lizard-slitted pupils of a dragon. That was what she was: a she-dragon, a winged sister, a divine human lizard-serpent spawned by magic. She was naked and sinewy, her leathery membranes stretching from wrist to hip.

The impossible creature came toward me, wings widespread. I could no longer swallow, was having difficulty breathing.

The she-dragon circled me, moving in her primitive jerky dance, head cocked to one side, then the next, in a parody of how a dragon examines potential prey. She stood right over my face, straddling me so that I was staring between lean muscled legs into the night sky of her sex. Her great wings flapped on either side of me, stirring leaves and fanning sparks from the fire. She threw back her head and skirled.

The bloodcurdling cry was exactly like that of my mother's haunt when she'd taken the form of a Skykeeper. Exactly. A sound dredged from brimstone fury and the corpse-riddled fields of nether.

I inflated my lungs and screamed back. I think I called her a bitch, or a whore, or a deviant. I think I told her to fuck herself, screw her mother, give her ass to dogs. I may have screamed it all.

My words were mere air.

She stepped over me, bobbed away from me. Stopped. Began swaying forward and backward on the balls of her feet, head hanging lower, lower. Her wings drooped. She looked as if she were wilting. She dropped to her knees. Tucked her dragon head between them. Enfolded herself with her wings. From somewhere in the dark, a gong tolled. Eight times.

The masked women reappeared, rising from ground, peeling from trees, materializing from dark air. They formed three tight circles around the fallen she-dragon, facing outward.

The three rings of women slowly began snaking around the wing-shrouded she-dragon, each ring moving in counterflow to the other.

The bones dangling from their storypoles clattered as they moved. The women began their panting chant again that escalated to a long-drawn hiss.

From the darkness of the surrounding night, from the throats of the watching tribe, came an answering invocation, raucous, pierced here and there by short, sharp whistles. A deep booming started, like that of a toad, only fuller, deeper, louder, and far more resonant: the heartbeat of an otherworld monster rising through sludge and swamp to be reborn in the night.

The tribe's invocation accelerated. The women ringed around the she-dragon snaked about her faster, faster. The deep reptilian booming quickened in the night, altered my heartbeat, pounded against my temples, pulsed between my thighs. Faster and faster noise and motion went, louder and louder grew the hissing of the women, building to an unbearable peak, and I thought my head and heart would explode with the pressure.

Silence.

The triple ring of women: gone.

My heartbeat throbbed against the roof of my mouth.

Slowly the wing-enfolded she-dragon began to shudder. Her wings parted with a shredding sound; the stench of necrosis filled the night air. Maggots spilled from the crack between her parted wings and belly-humped blind and naked on the ground, hundreds of them, white and damp and obscene.

Slowly the she-dragon rose to her feet.

Slowly she turned to face me.

Her wings glistened with damp, as if she'd been freshly pulled from a womb or freshly hatched from a shell. She stretched out her wings, stretched up on her toes, stretched to her full great height—

—and that was when I saw she was female no longer.

The winged creature came toward me, and the antennae plumes on its head—for yes, it had risen from the ground with the plumes of a male bull attached to its mask—shivered gracefully with each jerky step. Again the creature stood over my head, straddled my face, and this time when it skirled I was silent with dread presentiment.

That was when I smelled it.

Pure, undiluted venom.

I cannot adequately describe the emotion that swept over me next. It was something greater than relief, darker than hope, stronger than need. It was, perhaps, what a sailor might feel after the planks of his ship have buckled and snapped in a raging storm, after he's been plunged into foaming salt water, when he feels himself being dragged, for the last time, below hungry waves, and he catches a glimpse of land—only eight strokes away, almost within reach—and he knows that at least after his death, his body will be returned to shore, and home, and the element of his birth.

Perhaps this describes what I felt as I smelled the venom emanating from the creature above me. But perhaps it doesn't.

The he-dragon danced around me.

The tribe began chanting again, only this was a chant I knew from past experience; this was a song I'd last heard in the dead of night in an impoverished convent situated below limestone cliffs and a hammering waterfall. It was a song that evoked the sensuality of orchids in full bloom, the velvet lushness of wine blossoming warmly through limbs. It was a song of a jungle cat's sinuous muscle and the pounding crescendo of drums in harmony and the crack and whoosh of flames leaping higher. Words caressed me like fingertips, lapped over me like tongues, pressed against me with the soft fullness of breasts and hips and buttocks.

The he-dragon continued to dance about me. He held a knife in one hand. With a lilting whoop, he knelt and sawed one of my ankles free. He stood and circled around me again.

It was then that I noticed that his wings were tied onto his wrists and forearms and biceps. It was then that I noticed he had high, small breasts with nipples the color of wet ivy. And he had hair, a great mane of it hanging to his waist like a tangled fall of dry moss. Entwined about a strand of that mane was a lock of hair as dark as my own.

This was no *he*. It was a woman.

Longstride.

The tribe continued to plait me in its hedonistic song. Longstride whooped, knelt, and sawed my other ankle free.

I recalled what one of the aged convent sisters had said to me, prior to my committing the bestial rite for the first time: *No one is exploited; no one is forced. It is a divine exchange between beast and woman.*

When the last vine had been cut away from me—arms free, legs free, neck and waist released—I chose to remain where I lay, legs spread. Waiting.

No one is forced.

Longstride dropped her knife at my feet and straddled my waist. Slowly she lowered herself to her knees, the muscles in her sinewy legs gleaming as if oiled. She reached down between my legs.

Entered me.

While her tribe watched and sang, Longstride thrust venom into my womb. Her arms and legs quivered, and I could hear her panting beneath her mask. After I climaxed, I rolled her onto the ground, straddled her hips, and used my fingers to ride her, too.

Beauty is terror. Whatever we deem beautiful, we tremble before it. And what is more terrifying and beautiful but to lose control completely? To throw off the chains of mortality for but an instant and look naked, terrible beauty right in the face? I was consumed by fire.

I soared high on venom and lust, and though I didn't quite hear dragonsong—how close it was! how frustratingly, wondrously close!—I climaxed again, with an explosion that ripped down every nerve in my body, and I threw back my head and howled.

I reached for the knife Longstride had dropped. Lunged for her head. Sawed a lock of her hair from her mane. Braided it into my own.

Then I slid off her, weak and trembling, dizzy and puissant, and as I lay there on the ground, yearning for dragonsong, transported on the wings of venom, I realized I had something others might deem far, far more powerful than the dragon's enigmatic song.

I knew the secret to breeding bull dragons in captivity.

THIRTEEN

Abscesses. That's what the nodules on my dragons' snouts were. Great, hard abscesses of prurience. When lanced and squeezed, a curdled material slowly came out, like boiled albumen that had been coarsely minced.

My escoas were drugged at daybreak by means of several blow darts shot into the soft folds of their dewlaps, each blow dart as small as a young porcupine's quill. The darts had been tipped with peshawar, or what Xxelteker sailors call h'xar, redivivus moth oil. Or at least, that's what I supposed the darts had been dipped in; that was what we'd always used in the Clutch Re stables to subdue loose and fighting destriers.

The women tending the escoas debrided the necrotic tissue around the dragons' snouts with swift confidence, nimbly picking soft splinters of deadwood and shards of bone and cartilage from the exposed tissue. I watched them closely as they worked, in case I had to repeat the procedure.

It was as I was bent over their heads that I realized why the women's hair was the exact pale green of creeping moss. They'd woven the stuff amongst their locks in such profusion that moss and hair were one. I felt foolish that I'd not noticed it before.

Throughout my youth I'd heard greatmothers and aunties tell lazy children in danku Re that if they didn't get working, they'd turn into moss, just like the idle tree sloth. As with all effective threats, some truth resides behind their words: Sloths of a certain age are green from the creeping moss that has entwined itself amongst their hair during their protracted bouts of motionlessness. I've heard tell that sloths encourage moss growth on their young by coarsely weaving strands of it over their offspring. For camouflage, perhaps. Now that I could see the women's green hair for what it was, I found it hard to believe I'd hitherto not recognized it as largely moss.

Just as the escoas started to come out of their drug-induced stupor, the women flushed out the knuckle-sized holes they'd created, using a solution the color of Longstride's eyes. They filled their cheeks to bulging with the solution and sprayed it out in a strong blast through their teeth. By way of fingers held up and brusque gestures, I was ordered to flush the gaping holes clean four times daily. Four gourds were filled with the solution and tied to the escoas' saddles.

By late morn, the peshawar wore completely off and my escoas were mobile. The matriarch ordered three of the hunters who had found me to take me away.

I repeated the word *myazedo* many times, but received only disdainful looks: What *I* desired was insignificant.

I remembered what Fwipi had said, back in the arbiyesku: *It's not the Djimbi way, to fight, to be aggressive.* Nothing could be so far from the truth when describing my captors. They were every inch warriors, predators, fighters. If more Djimbi tribes had been like them, Emperor Wai Soomi Kun would never have established an Archipelagic empire four hundred years ago, in the land known now as Malacar.

Longstride stood beside the matriarch to watch me leave, her chin lifted, her eyes fierce. Weeping sores covered her hands, from where she'd thrust venom into me during the mock-bestial rite; clearly she'd not been exposed to venom before. I knew all about those sores, because she'd woken me before dawn to show me the appalling blisters, grinning tightly, nostrils flared and pupils tiny with the pain. I had a few blisters of my own—lentil-sized and surrounded by angry skin—but had, of course, much more tolerance to venom than Longstride.

She'd dropped a gourd of what looked like mashed black mushrooms on my lap, and a slab of bloody meat. I ate the earthy pap and raw flesh in solitude, having slept the night alone in the matriarch's yurt—though the numinous flight of my soul while I'd been enwrapped in venom's embrace had been as far removed from sleep as Longstride was from benevolence. There was something in the mushroom pap reminiscent of the purgative Gen had given me to drain the desire for venom from my blood, for the cold tremors that had seized me upon awakening abruptly stopped.

Led by my Djimbi escorts, I traveled for a day and a night away from their camp, journeying back to where my captors had first found me.

Or so I assumed that was where we were going. One part of the jungle looked much like another, and we seemed to be retracing our steps.

But no. Late morn of the second day, we came out of the jungle onto a windy bluff. The Djimbi gestured at my escoas, then toward the canyon and river below us.

"Myazedo," Jade-eyes said.

Hey-o. We had one word in common.

"Myazedo," Jade-eyes brusquely repeated, gesturing at the ravine. I understood. I was to fly down there and find the myazedo camp.

Thanks were on the tip of my tongue, but the arrogant pride on Jade-eyes's face halted my words. She had brought me there not because I had wanted it, not because I had asked for it, but because it had been *her* desire to do so. My gratitude would have earned contempt.

I wondered, then, why the matriarch and her people had performed their rite on me, why they had expended time and energy to bring me to the myazedo camp. When I'd left her, Longstride had still been wearing my lock of hair plaited amongst hers, and I still wore a lock of hers. When I'd cut her hair and braided it with mine during the rite, I'd felt as if a transaction had been completed.

Yet now there lingered a feeling of debt still owing.

A breeze riffled the edges of Jade-eyes's green mane as she looked down at me from her sinewy height. The sharp angles of her dark-green-and-teak-brown face were predaceous and proud. I disliked the idea of being beholden to her and her people.

I turned my back on her, tightened the surcingles of the escoas' saddles, and tethered Warthog to Toadhunter by means of a crude rope that had been given me by the tribe. Warthog was tractable, and I expected her to follow me into the air without trouble. Still, I tethered her for assurance.

Both escoas had misshapen snouts and were breathing stertorously through their mutilated nares, though their wounds were already visibly healing. As wind tossed volleys of raindrops from the leaves of the trees behind us, the escoas snaked their necks first one way, then the other, as they surveyed the riverine canyon below. Their forked tongues quivered between their gums as they scented the air. They were alert and passably fed after the numerous giant millipedes and land snails and night-blooming orchids they'd foraged from the jungle. They were ready for flight.

By the time I was mounted on Toadhunter, my Djimbi escorts had melted into the jungle.

Toadhunter needed little urging to fly into the canyon, for neither she nor Warthog had had anything to drink since our capture. As I'd hoped, Warthog followed promptly into the skies, taking off the moment Toadhunter sprang from the bluff. We flew side by side.

It no longer terrified me, flight. Perhaps I was even a little exhilarated by the surge of muscle beneath me, the ripple of wing membranes outstretched in a glide on either side of me, the chill of the air and the sight of jungle swaying and rolling below like a multihued green ocean.

We were over a river, then *whoosh*! We listed and dropped a little as we soared over the long, long cataract plunging down into the canyon. The air was noticeably cooler in the ravine as Toadhunter descended.

I saw no fire smoke coming from the jungle forest that lined one side of the gorge. But the myazedo would be smart enough to cook only at dusk and before dawn, when smoke mingled with mist and was indiscernible from cloud.

Ahead of us lay a small stony beach cupped around one side of the deep pool into which the cataract thundered. Toadhunter back-fought the air, legs lowered for landing, and I half stood in my saddle, legs flexed for impact, hands tight around the saddle rungs but arms not locked. With a rasp of sliding stone beneath her clawpads, Warthog touched down beside us in perfect synchrony. I was inordinately proud of how smoothly we landed.

All three of us drank long of the cool, green water.

That was a far different river from the one where Toadhunter had landed after the storm. After eddying and swirling through the deep pool below the waterfall, the river poured down a rocky chute, surging and breaking in whitecaps over boulders and fallen trees. The rock walls of the canyon we stood in were green with moss and ferns, and everything dripped, not just from the deluge that had hammered down from the cloud-clotted skies at dawn, but from the spray of the waterfall. The canyon was sheer rock wall on the far side of the river. Behind me, a belt of forest a mile deep ran along the river as the walls of the canyon rose up behind it in forested tiers.

I rendered the escoas flightless with rope and wing bolts. As they continued noisily sucking water, I climbed over rock and boulder and fallen tree, then wandered along the forest's edge. I found what I was looking for: The trail had been compacted by many feet, over many years. I returned to the escoas, waited until they'd drunk their fill, then led them along the path.

I found the camp within a stone's throw of the river. It looked much like Longstride's village—nomadic, functional—a cluster of bamboo huts interspersed among the trees. No people were visible.

"Tansan!" I called out. "Savga!"

"Here, cut me free!" The voice was hoarse with fury. I recognized it at once.

Glancing uneasily about the deserted camp, I tied the escoas to a tree, then followed the shouts to a leaning bamboo hut. I pushed the door cautiously with a foot. It was latched shut, wouldn't budge. I lifted the wooden latch and the door swung open on creaking leather hinges. A flood of hoarse curses flowed out of the gloom.

My eyes slowly adjusted to the shadows. The dragonmaster sat against the far wall, hands tied behind his back, ankles bound and strung to the ceiling so that his legs were slightly elevated. His neck was held fast to the wall by what looked like a wire garrote. A knife swung from the rafters, tied with the same rope that bound the dragonmaster's ankles.

Chill pimples broke out over my skin. My back crawled. "What happened?"

"Don't stand there, yolkbrain; cut me loose, cut me loose!"

"Who tied you like this?"

"Are you deaf?" His eyes bulged from his head. Ugly weeping bruises encircled his throat like a black collar. "Cut me free, you ass-screwed whore."

"A honeyed tongue, as always," I said sourly. I ducked into the hut—it was no larger than the room Savga and I had shared in the Noua Sor tenement—and worked at the knot around the knife. "Who did this to you?"

"That brooder bitch from the arbiyesku, the mother of that puling kitten you're so fond of— Ahh!"

He yelled as I cut the rope that held his ankles and his feet thudded hard against the floor. He shifted on his buttocks—his tailbone must have been mightily sore from that awkward feet-in-the-air position—and panted as he struggled to overcome the pain of blood rushing back to his feet.

I knelt before him.

He glared at me. "You did that on purpose."

"I'm sick of how you talk to me. Time you changed your ways."

"Rishi whore," he rasped, chest heaving. "There'll come a day when you'll rue that; on the wings of the Dragon, I vow there will. You and that brooder bitch—"

I slapped him. He gagged as the garrote cut into his throat. "Her name is Tansan," I snapped. "What happened to Savga, that Tansan did this to you?"

"The brat's fine," he gasped. "With her mother."

"You brought Savga here?"

"Who else?" He coughed, a hoarse, parched sound. "Water."

I considered making him answer my questions first, but then stood. He'd talk more with his throat lubricated. I went out to the escoas, emptied a gourd of medicinal solution into my mouth, sprayed the solution over the wounds on the dragons' snouts, then took the emptied gourd down to the river. By the time I returned to the bamboo hut, the dragonmaster was slowly flexing his legs.

I held the gourd to his mouth.

He snarled. "What's in it?"

"Water. It held medicine before. Drink." I tipped it to his mouth. After a moment's hesitation—eyes boring into me with fury—he drank.

With each swallow, the garrote cut against his bobbing larynx and his eyes flickered with pain. I felt somewhat contrite, that I was forcing him to drink with the garrote around him, but I dismissed the idea of releasing his neck until he'd answered my questions.

If I'd even release him then.

When he'd drained the gourd, I gave him a moment to recover himself. He spoke without prompting.

"Your puling kitten insisted you'd come. The brooder bitch that birthed her says the kitten sees through the Winged One's eyes sometimes. So I was made to wait here for you."

"Tansan. Her name is Tansan. And the girl is called Savga."

He snorted. He'd never use their names.

"Savga said I'd come here?" I repeated.

"Her teat-nurse says the girl has dragonsight, but it's a lie, to hide the bitch's own weird powers and ill will against me. She left me here to die, simple. She's a scheming, duplicitous blackheart, and not all what she seems to be, either. There's something about her that reeks of the unnatural—"

"She's a strong person; you hate her for it. You prefer subservience and timidity in women."

"Open your eyes, girl! There's more to that woman than what's apparent. I've seen the way these myazedo obey her; she uses dark magics, I'm sure of it."

I remembered the illusion I'd briefly experienced at the tanners' clan, during the myazedo meeting: the hazy, bonfire-lit image of Tansan taking the form of a dragon.

"So what if she sometimes uses Djimbi magics?" I snapped, uneasy. "Are you and Daronpu Gen the only ones permitted to know and use them?"

"Her talents are veiled, her purpose unknown. She can't be trusted."

"Don't be stupid. She's doing what you've only dreamt of: freeing her people. Petty jealousy turns you against her. Now, where have they gone?"

He took his time before answering, muscles working in his jaw. "Xxamer Zu."

"When?"

"Two days ago. If not for you flying direct into the storm, we'd be with them now."

"You flew direct into the storm, not me," I flung back. "I was following *you*."

"You talk shit, girl. Before the worst of the storm hit, I'd landed. You flew straight over us, no matter how your puling kitten screamed for you to stop. You were looking right down at us. We all saw you."

"I what?" His imprisonment had tipped him over the edge. "You landed where?"

"On an escarpment, beside the egg-train road from Xxamer Zu to Fwendar ki Bol."

I'd seen no such escarpment before the storm had hit us, had seen neither the dragonmaster nor Ryn land their dragons upon it. I certainly didn't recall looking straight down at them, nor hear Savga screaming for me to stop.

And yet . . . all I *could* recall was our departure from the arbiyesku, and how the lightning flickering in the distance had looked almost hypnotic, and how the thunder booming overhead and the wind gusting savagely about had folded me into the soul of the storm itself, after which I'd known nothing but fear and the keen desire to survive.

"We waited for you till the worst of the storm swept down on us," the dragonmaster hoarsely continued. "Then we took cover in the jungle. Even then you didn't return. So we went on, followed the egg-train road afoot till the boy steered us off and brought us here."

The strangeness of my flight into the storm was swept away by what the dragonmaster had said.

"The boy? *Ryn* took you to the myazedo?" I said, baffled.

"Not that boy, the other one! Piah, Piah, use your tit soft brain!"

"Piah is hardly a boy," I snapped. "Is Ryn still alive?"

"If you can call his cowardice life, though I'll grant the flea provides information readily enough, concerning the layout of the daronpuis' stockade."

"Ryn hasn't been hurt, has he?"

He sneered. "The boy's so scared he answers questions before they're asked."

"I promised him he wouldn't be hurt."

The dragonmaster shrugged, deeming my promise unimportant. I wanted to slap him again. Instead I felt behind his neck, to where the wire had been twisted tightly around a bamboo pole. "The myazedo took the dragons with them, yes? And they'll have planned to attack Xxamer Zu at night."

"*This* night," he growled; then he swore as my fumbling caused the wire to cut through the bruised, tender skin on his throat. Too bad.

"We can reach them," I said, thinking aloud. "We'll fly low; we don't want to be seen by Ghepp. He'll have watchers scanning the skies for incoming heralds, waiting for an escoa to arrive with a delivery from elsewhere so he can turn it around again and alert Temple of the theft of his winged dragons."

I slowly peeled the wire away from the dragonmaster's throat. He held himself intensely still as I did so, and I knew it must have been hurting. When the bloody wire was free, I told him to bend forward, so I could cut the bonds from his wrists, where his hands had been tied behind his back.

"What about the overland route to Fwendar ki Bol?" I asked as I sawed at the rope. "Has anything been done about it?"

"The bitch sent runners out," he croaked. "Armed."

Good. No heralds would get through overland. I could only hope that no dragonfliers from elsewhere had flown into Xxamer Zu during the interval between my stealing the escoas and the myazedo's impending attack.

"And the escoas? Their wounds?" I asked.

"I dealt with them. They'll survive. One's lame."

The dragonmaster's bonds fell away, and he slowly eased his hands forward, onto his lap. He regarded them for several moments in silence. Then he spoke in a tone that I'd not heard before, low and hoarse, and it rasped against my nerves like a serrated blade against a block of limestone.

"She'll pay for this, hey-o. Oh, yes."

He meant Tansan. A chill shivered down my spine.

"You won't lay a finger on Tansan, you hear? She probably had no recourse but to tie you up."

"No one ties me up without suffering for it." His eyes were bloody and sharded with unholy stars.

I stood up and pointed the knife Tansan had left for me at him. It quivered a little. "You hurt Tansan and I'll finish the job that garrote started on your throat. Understand? I'm going out to the dragons now. When you're ready, you can join me."

Outside, I fussed with the saddles while I waited for the dragonmaster. Twice I had to wipe sweat from my palms. Each time I transferred the knife I held from one hand to the other before drying my palm on my bitoo. I didn't put the blade down, though. No.

I should kill him, once he's flown me back to Xxamer Zu.

I recoiled from the thought. Cutting the throat of one of my own—even the dragonmaster—was the work of a traitor. A despicable, unprincipled act. Something Temple would do, not me.

The dragonmaster appeared at the doorway of the hut.

He stood there a moment, allowing his eyes to adjust. He looked smaller, his legs more bowed, than when I'd last seen him in daylight. The skin on his thighs and torso hung in loose folds. His chest had sunken in. The glass bead at the end of his chin braid was missing and the plait had begun unraveling in a frizzy mass.

I'd alert Tansan to the dragonmaster's vow of vengeance. That would suffice.

"Tell me about the myazedo," I asked as he came stiff-legged toward me. He looked as if he were walking on razors. It must have been painful, the return of his circulation. "Their numbers, their ages, how well armed they are, how disciplined."

"They're warriors," he said. "Some of 'em have lived in these hills for years, training, fighting, planning, waiting. Two of them could kill every komikonpu in my stables in one night."

Clutch Re isn't your stables anymore, I thought, but the message he'd wanted to convey was clear: The myazedo had muscle and wit sharper than the most experienced of the dragonmaster's apprentices. That was impressive, indeed.

"They know the layout of Xxamer Zu like the back of their hands," he continued. "They'll take the place with ease."

"How many of them are there?"

He was breathing heavily, and I wondered if he'd be able to stay atop his mount. My doubt must have shown, for he scowled and spat at my feet.

"You're no sight, either, girl. You look like the slightest wind will knock you over."

"Their numbers," I said, ignoring him.

He ran a hand over Toadhunter's neck and scratched around one of her ear slits in the manner that all dragons love. He murmured to her, and she nuzzled him with her wounded, riddled snout.

"Thirty-two of them, with five out on the Fwendar ki Bol road. There's more within the Clutch. Upward of sixty, so the bitch says, though how much use they'll be is questionable. Count on the thirty-two to do the job."

"Thirty-two?" I cried in dismay.

He looked at me contemptuously. I saw Longstride in him. "Thirty-two warriors with surprise and stealth and a good plan on their side can easily take Xxamer Zu. I doubt a one of them'll be fatally injured in the process."

"If they're the warriors you say they are."

"They are," he said, eyes raking over me, comparing me and finding me far lacking.

"Then we'd best join them," I said curtly. "Quickly. I've got information I have to tell them before they go in. Now, d'you need help mounting?"

If not for the knife I held, he would have struck me for my insolence.

Instead, he struggled aboard Toadhunter.

FOURTEEN

In the gloom of twilight, the dragonmaster and I flew over the jungle. A fast, fine rain was falling, the kind of spitting shower that soon escalates into the pelting torrents of a squall. Far below us, foliage looked indistinct in the gloaming, as if frond and vine were made of beads of water that were blending with the rain and twilight.

We flew steadily, and as inky darkness enfolded us, we left behind the loamy, crushed-leaf smell of jungle below. Gradually the smells of savanna began wafting up to us through the pitch-black: the scent of parched soil, of sunbleached grass, of termite hills and heat-cracked stone and the expansive smell of endless rolling miles. And, too, we left rainfall behind. On the plains, wind and black, depleted clouds taunted the dry land below. No thunder rumbled. No stars were visible through the mantle of cloud.

The flight seemed both long and condensed, like a enormous snake curled tightly around itself. Every nerve in my body thrummed; we *had* to get to the myazedo before they attacked. The escoas weren't making progress; we were suspended in darkness, held motionless in ebon wind. My hands locked tight around the wooden rungs of the saddle and I ground my molars anxiously.

Then ahead of us, in the black: a splotch of gray bobbing in the darkness. Xxamer Zu's temple domes.

"The Clutch!" I cried.

"I'm not blind," the dragonmaster growled against my ear. We were both astride Toadhunter, with Warthog tethered behind. Neither of us would risk having me ride Warthog alone, in case she broke free of her tether and flew straight on to the byre.

Moments later we landed on a grassy hill, several miles from the Clutch. The myazedo was gathered on the lee of the hill, dark shapes lying upon dry grass, blending with crushed weeds, poised to slip over the hill and lope across the prairie miles to the Clutch that was visible as a patchwork of various blacks in the near distance. Xxamer Zu's temple domes leered in the dark.

The escoas were with the myazedo, four shadows of musky animal bulk that snorted and clawed the earth with impatience. In the darkness, their folded and bolted wings looked like great spiked parasites quivering on their backs.

I slid from Toadhunter's back as a small body came hurtling toward me, legs pumping.

My heart constricted painfully as I scooped Savga up and held her close. She smelled good, like trust and small, grubby hands. I wanted to hold her forever . . . but I put her down. I had no time to spare.

"Where's your mother, Savga? I have to speak with her *now*. It's very, very important."

She turned and gestured; Tansan was walking toward us, all dusky curves accented by the spear she held. She came to a stop several feet away from me, calm, balanced, the straight, strong flare of her shoulders squared perfectly with her hips. The gruesome scar that ran along her chin glistened in the dark.

"Savga told me how you influenced the Wai Vaneshor to free those he'd poached for slavery," she said, tone neutral.

I waited. Her eyes were opaque, her face inscrutable.

"You are more than you seem, debu Secondgirl."

"The boulder calls the pebble hard," the dragonmaster acidly said beside me.

Tansan's eyes flicked toward him and her lips thinned. She didn't address him, but looked back at me. "Who are you, Kazonvia?"

"The story's a long one, and this isn't the time or place. But I'm with you. Know that. *I'm with you.*"

She studied me. I met her gaze and tried not to champ my jaws in impatience; she had to decide herself whether I was to be trusted; otherwise nothing I said afterward would matter.

After a long pause she nodded once, curtly. "I believe this. You are with us."

I released a held breath and opened my mouth to speak, but she cut me off.

"We're ready to move. The two runners that we sent ahead of us entered the Clutch last night and sent word to our myazedo within. The runners returned to us today, after dusk. The myazedo within is prepared. Two brands will soon be waved from atop a tenement: our signal to move.

"We each belong to a group, and each group will complete its set of tasks. Some of us will surround and infiltrate the daronpuis' stockade, seal exits and entrances, while others kill the daronpuis within. As for the soldiers, we know where they're posted, how many of them there are, how they are armed, and who amongst them is disciplined and skilled. Maybe some will join us. Maybe not. We'll learn soon enough. A few of them will most likely be loyal to the new overseer and not lay down arms. These, we will kill.

"Some of us will sweep through the bayen thoroughfare. Weapons will be gathered and chancellors and bayen lordlings will be killed. Women and children will be spared—"

"Wait," I interrupted. "The Clutch overseer can't be killed. We need him alive."

She raised an eyebrow in question.

"His name is Rutgar Re Ghepp, and he's half brother to Waikar Re Kratt, Lupini of Clutch Re," I explained. I kept one eye on Xxamer Zu; if those brands were waved before I'd explained all this to Tansan, and if her warriors entered Xxamer Zu and killed Ghepp before I could prevent them, everything I'd learned from Longstride's rite would be for nothing.

"Several days ago," I rapidly continued, "Kratt appropriated Clutch Cuhan under the auspices of Temple, on the grounds that the overseer there was hiding me. Kratt knew I wasn't on Cuhan; he was merely flexing his muscle and using that excuse to become overseer of one of Malacar's largest Clutches. The next Clutch he'll strike will be here, where I *am* located . . . unless his brother can keep him at bay by parleying with him. We need Ghepp alive, to stave off Kratt's attack for at least the next eight weeks."

Every muscle in Tansan's body went intensely still. "You are someone important indeed. But I fail to see what advantage eight weeks will be to us."

"If Ghepp can keep his brother and Temple off our backs for eight weeks, I can guarantee us power, wealth, and innumerable allies. I can do this, Tansan. But I need eight weeks."

Beside me, the dragonmaster let out a hiss. "You *know*. You *know*."

I didn't look away from Tansan's obsidian eyes. "Yes. I know the secret to breeding bulls. And I need eight weeks to prove it."

Tansan's eyes raked over me, and they were no longer opaque; they were lambent, alive with fiery radiance. They were the eyes of a feisty dragon.

"The overseer *must* be taken hostage alive and unharmed," I insisted. "And there are children in the daronpuis' compound, young boys indentured to Temple: You can't kill them."

"Those under a certain age will be spared, and those with rishi parents will be freed. We are not barbaric, Kazonvia."

I inclined my head a small way, as acceptance of her words.

The dark outlines of the myazedo along the hilltop were waiting with palpable tension for the burning signal in the distance. Wind soughed over the grass. A cur barked in the Clutch down below. Several other dogs joined the one barking in the Clutch.

And then: Thin flame-fish leapt into the air in the distance, and the black outlines along the hill began flowing down toward Xxamer Zu.

"Take my children and mother to the arbiyesku," Tansan said, turning away from me. "Guard the escoas. We'll capture Lupini Xxamer Zu unharmed."

"Wait!" I called after her as she turned and started down the hill. "Where's Ryn?"

"Here!" a thin voice cried out, and I saw three shadows some way down the hill come to a straggling halt and struggle with each other.

"Let the boy go," I ordered Tansan.

"We need a guide in the daronpuis' compound—"

"He told you all he knows. I promised no harm would come to him. Let him go. He's only a child."

Tansan pursed her lips, turned, and gestured at the struggling shadows. Shadows everywhere, pouring down the hill, across the plains, merging with the dark, drawn to the fiery beacon in the distance.

Then Tansan was a black outline loping steadily, easily into that dark, toward that fiery beacon, and Ryn was before me, shivering, and Savga's small hand was prying open one of my clenched fists and slipping, like a frightened animal into a burrow, into the shelter of my palm.

We stood on that hill and watched the brands in the distance flicker and dance. They looked harmless. Like silk ribbons of red and orange fluttering from a caparisoned dragon on parade. Then the two brands winked out.

It was silent on the hill.

Wind blew. Grass rustled. The escoas snorted. Saddle leather creaked.

It seemed impossible that we couldn't hear the metallic clang of the tin moon doors in the daronpuis' compound being shoved open by shoulders, nor the screams or pleas or gurgles of the holy wardens being swiftly, methodically murdered in their cells. We could hear no grunts of men in combat, no blades biting into bone or slicing through bedsheets. We heard no wailing of women or sobbing of children as bayen mansions were stormed and the lords within murdered.

Perhaps the invasion wasn't happening.

"Agawan has been weaned," a voice said, and for the first time I turned to look at Fwipi, who'd been present all along, but hidden by darkness. She came closer; she looked insubstantial, as if the last few days had whittled her into a nub of what she'd once been. "That was one of the ways Tansan prepared for this night. She weaned her son. If she dies, he won't sicken for want of her milk."

"Tansan won't die," I said, looking back at the dark outline of the Clutch.

"You have dragonsight too, now? It's contagious, then, like the coughing sickness."

I glanced down at Savga. Her hand was still in mine.

"You don't think Savga can see through the One Dragon's eyes." I stated it as fact.

Fwipi looked down at Agawan, asleep in the sling Fwipi wore across a shoulder and breast. A pudgy brown leg dangled free, tiny toes motionless and perfect and all but invisible in the dark. Fwipi's withered fingers gently touched those toes.

"After Tansan was conceived," she said quietly, and her words sounded sister and mother to the wind, "my greatmother took me out in the plains at night, while the other women were asleep. She did things to me. Old things. What I remember most is how I could not breathe. I could not breathe because of what was in my mouth, and I was gagging, and the pain in my belly was like fire. I expelled the child in my womb, or so I thought, and then my greatmother died. She fell with a thud at my bloody feet. I staggered back to the women's barracks. I babbled. No one could make sense of what I said, and the blood scared them. Eventually my mother followed my blood back into the fields. She did this alone, at night, a foolish thing. She was angry at her mother, and she was frightened for her. See? By the time others realized my mother had gone, the carrion wolves had gutted both her and my greatmother. The next day my belly started swelling. It swelled fast and stayed swollen for eleven long months and my eyes turned milky. Tansan was born with a great caul over her that was as thick as a dragon cocoon and dulled the midwife's knife as she cut it off. And I was old."

A whirlwind briefly swirled about us, cool and smelling of unseen starlight. Fwipi looked up at me from where she'd been gazing steadily at Agawan, stroking his small, perfect toes.

"Maybe I remember that night wrongly, or maybe, like some say, I was raped again two months after I shed the first fetus. Truth is like wind:

It blows one way; it blows another. It's never still, yet it touches everything. So maybe Savga has dragonsight and maybe she doesn't. Maybe Tansan will die tonight and maybe she'll live. Don't ask me what I believe anymore, Kazonvia. There is only death and hope and uncertainty."

The dragonmaster had been listening intently to Fwipi; he made a sound in his throat and, muttering to himself, stomped toward the dragons. He bent and started removing their hobbles.

I turned and brusquely gestured at Ryn, who was now dressed in a simple tunic. "Go help. We're leaving."

I knelt beside Savga, my back toward Fwipi. Savga was staring intently into the darkness with nostrils flared and quivering.

"Come on, Busy Ant," I said softly. "We're going home."

Keau came to collect me at dawn, with the news that the daronpuis' compound had been secured, Tansan was alive, and Lupini Xxamer Zu was being held hostage, unharmed.

One of Keau's hands was heavily swathed in fine white fabric crusted with dried blood. He held up his wounded hand and grinned through bloodied lips, revealing a mouthful of broken and missing teeth. "Lost a finger, hey, but gained a knife."

My eyes dropped to his waist. Incongruous against his simple loincloth, a gilded scabbard studded with chunks of turquoise hung from his hip. I recognized the scabbard at once. It belonged to the lordling who'd come trolling for Tansan during my second night in the arbiyesku.

"I didn't know you knew how to kill a man," I said to Keau, hating the grin on his face and my own glimmer of satisfied vengeance at knowing the lordling was dead.

Keau shrugged. His grin didn't fade in the slightest. "There were two of us to his one."

Once she knew her mother was alive, Savga agreed to remain in the arbiyesku compound and not accompany me; after all, she had much to tell Oblan and Runami about her flight upon dragonback and her adventures in the jungle. I was amazed by the innocence and resiliency of the child.

The dragonmaster, however, insisted on joining me.

Wind blew from the southwest, carrying the muddy smell of the Clutch river and the charred, ashy smell of a spent fire. Overhead, the sky was a sea of warm steel. To the southeast, the blur of the jungle mountains was shadowed by black cloud. We jogged toward the center of the Clutch, firing questions at Keau.

"How many were killed?" I asked.

Again, Keau beamed. "It was a good night; the Infinite Winged was kind. Already we pile the bodies."

"Dump 'em in the egg stables; give 'em to the brooders," the dragonmaster replied. "They need a good feed."

The smile died on Keau's face. How inconsistent that he could kill a man without guilt, but was appalled at the thought of feeding the corpse to a dragon.

I ignored the dragonmaster. "I was asking how many of the myazedo were killed."

"None." Keau clutched his hand to his chest as he loped along. He was breathing heavily and sweating profusely. His cheeks were pale, the green whorls standing out in stark contrast. He probably shouldn't have been running. "Some were wounded badly, but our attack was good. Like wolves, we were. Fast, deadly. A good attack."

Bandit warfare. People looking to plunder and rape the aristocrats. That's not what makes rebellion successful, blood-blood!

We loped across the soft, dusty grasses in silence after that, until we reached the bayen thoroughfare. We slowed to a walk.

A few windows had been smashed, and one mansion had been gutted by fire, its white stone exterior streaked with oily black, plumes of smoke rising from its roofless skull. I shivered; truly, the One Dragon had looked kindly upon us. Such a fire, throwing sparks high into the night on the windy plains, could have easily set the whole Clutch ablaze.

"An overturned lantern," Keau said. "A mistake."

"We were lucky," I said grimly.

"We are careful," Keau said, and he nodded with his chin at a group of soot-streaked men in loincloths. They wore blackened cloth over their mouths and bayen boots on their feet, and they held shovels and hoes in their grimy hands.

"Myazedo?" I asked.

"Serfs, gathered from friends and family of the myazedo."

I saw a child's face up in the window of a mansion, peering out from behind a curtain: a girl, black haired and ivory-skinned and seven years old at most. Our eyes met. She quickly disappeared.

"The bayen women and children are still in their homes?"

"Yes," Keau said. "Some of their servants stay with them; some are alone. They have food enough in their cellars, and water in their cisterns. Each of these houses has a cistern that servants must keep full; did you know?" His eyes were wide with amazement.

But for how long will their servants stay with them? I wondered.

At the far end of the thoroughfare, another group of Djimbi worked. Vultures and carrion birds flew high overhead in great, wide circles. The smell of piss and blood and death and shit wafted on the breeze. Corpses were being added to a grisly heap of bodies on the road. The corpses had been stripped of all belongings. Arms and legs jutted out from the tangle.

I wondered if the bayen child in the window could see her father's body in that heap. I fervently hoped not.

We turned down an alley and came out on the market square. A crowd had gathered near the entrance gate of the daronpuis' compound, mostly young boys and old men and women. They squatted or stood in clusters and appeared to be waiting for something with a serf's typical patience. Their eyes watched us as we approached them. Myazedo fighters with bayen steel on their hips guarded the gates from inside the daronpuis' stockade.

As we wove through the crowd, people shuffled aside, silent, watchful. One of the myazedo within nodded at Keau and swung the iron gate open. We were ushered in without question or comment.

"Why the crowd?" I asked Keau. I'd lowered my voice; I couldn't say why.

Again, another of his nonchalant shrugs. "They've heard about the liberation. Maybe they wait for the eggs and meat and grain stored in the daronpuis' cellars, or maybe their brothers or uncles have volunteered to gather bodies and they wait for the robes and boots from the dead."

Even as he spoke, an old Djimbi man crossed one of the stony bridges that humped over the dusty, nonexistent ponds within the stockade. His scrawny arms were laden with purple and ivy green vestments. I stopped to watch.

He walked up to the towering iron fence that enclosed him within the stockade. A group from the crowd outside quickly stepped forward. There was no elbowing or shouting or impatience as hands extended through the bars to receive a chasuble or robe or scapular, and the myazedo fighters guarding the fence didn't bark at anyone to move off. No. It was as civilized a distribution of plunder as I could imagine.

I turned back to Keau and the dragonmaster, the latter who hadn't bothered watching and was muttering to himself and making vigorous gestures with his hands, as if arguing a point.

"I saw an acolyte's scapular in those clothes," I murmured as we followed Keau up a cool set of smooth stone stairs. "The acolytes weren't supposed to be killed."

"Maybe that one fought," Keau said, and he stopped at the top of the stairs and looked at me with eyes that, for the first time, were weighted with the loss of life that had occurred during the night. "There was much noise, hey-o. Much shouting, much confusion. And we had to move fast, and some of us are not trained warriors and may have been afraid. We had to move so fast."

I understood, then. Those shrugs of his were not of nonchalance: He didn't want to talk about last night, was haunted by some of the things he'd seen and done.

I stepped away from a smear of dry, brown blood ground into the stone wall near my cheek and followed him to Tansan.

FIFTEEN

Only two of the seven myazedo rebels who were gathered before Tansan were seated. The rest stood, paced, gestured, and ran hands through their wild hair and over their matted beards. All of the seven wore ragged brown waistshirts and tattered breeches stained with blood, and each of them was armed with an assortment of knives, swords, and blow darts. They looked like they hadn't eaten a good meal in years, nor bathed for as long, and to a man each was fervent, intense, and sounded informed beyond the scope of the average serf.

Their eyes were battle-bright as they engaged in curt dialogue about the distribution of goods, the creation of a people's army, the necessity for [illegible]—the patronage of the people—and who amongst them should fly an escoa and try to find Chinion, their absent leader, to apprise him of their liberation of Xxamer Zu.

I had something to say about that, but I bided my time, waiting for the right moment. Watching. Calculating. Perched on the edge of an exquisitely carved mahogany table, greedily eating a dusky plum plucked from the silver metalwork fruit basin that was beside me.

Tansan watched the discussions in silence from where she was sat—not reclining, but seated as if upon a throne—on one of the many low divans in the room. She, too, was bloody, and a wound on her arm was swathed in cloth. Like her fellow warriors, she was dressed in a waistshirt and breeches. It was powerfully alluring, seeing her clothed like a man, the swell of her bosom straining against her bloodied waistshirt.

The dragonmaster had not been admitted into the room. He was waiting outside the guarded doors. Frothing.

"This suwembai kam," one of the seated rebels said, referring to the dragonmaster as a madman. He didn't look up from the knife he was using to carve dirt and dried blood from under his fingernails. "He's skilled with dragons. Do we trust him enough to take one to go look for Chinion?"

"No," said a rebel with two heavy, matted braids hanging on either side of his face. "We use the drunken herald we hold hostage instead."

"We need to send out more than one dragonflier. Chinion could be at any of our camps; we'll waste days locating him."

One of the pacing rebels made a chopping motion with a hand. His face was a tangle of black beard, and his hooked nose bore old acne scars. "Only one escoa should fly out. We don't have enough skilled dragonfliers, and I don't trust the suwembai kam."

I cleared my throat. All eyes swung toward me, swift and sharp as swords.

"How many skilled dragonfliers do we have?" I held up a hand and ticked them off. "The man you call the suwembai kam, who flew the escoas and Tansan's girl-child to your camp in the jungle. The boy Ryn, who flew alongside him. And this hostage you speak of, this drunken herald. A man who goes by the name of Kaban, if I'm guessing correctly."

By the carefully imperturbable expressions on the rebels' faces, I knew I'd guessed correctly. A point for me. "Any other dragonfliers? No? The rest killed in our takeover, hey? Fine. This is what I suggest, then. We use them all, send them all out."

An explosive snort of derision from Acne-nose. "And if something goes wrong and none of them return? We'll have no one amongst us who can fly a dragon."

"Perhaps that should have been considered before the massacre last night."

He spat and took a step toward me, eyes blazing. "Is there blood on your hands? Did you fight for your life and freedom last night? Who are you to sit there and criticize our success?"

"I'm a danku rishi via, born on Clutch Re." I kept my voice low and even and my eyes riveted on his. "My father's name was Darquel, my mother's Kavarria. She was born here, on Xxamer Zu. She named me Zarq. Some call me Zarq-the-deviant. Others call me the dragonwhore of Re. You may have heard of me."

A subtle stillness fell over the room, as if I'd reached out and lightly cupped, dagger in hand, the balls of every man present. Acne-nose looked as if he were fighting the urge to draw back a pace.

I felt some satisfaction in knowing that talk of the infamous dragonwhore of Re had reached a hidden camp of rebels isolated deep in the jungle. They'd heard of this woman Zarq who had dared defy Temple by joining a dragonmaster's apprenticeship, a woman who may or may not be demon-possessed and commit bestiality with dragons.

I looked at Tansan. "I didn't lie to you; I *am* Kazonvia, the second girl to leave my mother's womb. But now you know me also as Zarq."

"And why have you come to the myazedo, *Zarq*?" Acne-nose asked, voice hostile.

"To hatch bull wings for the rishi," I said.

Thunderous silence for half a heartbeat.

"You know how to do this?" asked the rebel who was studiously carving blood from under his nails. If he'd looked once at me, I'd not caught him at it.

"I do. I can promise you bull dragons—not just one, not just two, but several clawfuls—in as little as eight weeks' time, maybe sooner."

"How?" asked the one with two braids.

I took a bite of the plum I'd been warming in one palm and chewed. Every rebel except the one carving his nails watched me.

"Hear me out first," I said, and I wiped juice off my chin. "From what I understand, Chinion is your leader. He has several myazedo camps and he plans to use his troops of rebels, at some point in the undetermined future, to liberate several Clutches that are small and geographically isolated. This is good."

I pinned Acne-nose with my eyes. "But not good enough. It'll be only a matter of time before the liberated Clutches are once again under Temple rule. Temple stems from the Emperor, and the Emperor has legions of men. There are seven fully inhabited islands in the Archipelago, all of them under the Emperor's rule. He will never run out of soldiers. We will.

"When we have bull dragons, we end the Emperor's monopoly over dragon ownership, and instead of throwing the myazedo down the jaws of the Emperor, we'll convince the Emperor that he can't stay in Malacar, regardless of how many soldiers he has. We'll make Malacar undesirable for him. We'll drive him out. We'll end the poverty and starvation in every Clutch, all across the land."

I finished my plum with three swift bites and wiped my hands on my stained and ripped bitoo.

"A grandiloquent speech," the seated rebel with the knife murmured, without looking up.

"I'm not finished." I waited several moments, letting the silence stretch long before I continued. Not a man among them was pacing now. "I have access to a network of men who have been planning just this sort of thing for some time. They can supply us with arms on a massive scale. They can arrange the sinking of the Emperor's ships in the harbor of Lireh, and they can move us on dragonback to locations so that we can, in the course of a single night, steal the bull dragons and raid the daronpuis' quarters of several targeted Clutches. These people can help us make all that happen before the end of the month, so that the Emperor's army is drawn out across the nation and a united attack on this Clutch will not be deemed a priority by Temple. And meanwhile, if we use our own overseer to parley with Clutches Cuhan and Re—which, by the way, are now governed by our deposed overseer's half brother—we can keep *them* at bay while we're breeding bull dragons."

I turned to the fruit basin beside me, selected a pomegranate, and dug my fingernails into its thick, nubby skin. "That's why I suggest that we send out three escoas. One to find your Chinion as swiftly as possible, one to my contact in Liru, and one as a parley between Clutch Re and Ghepp, our deposed overseer. And I suggest we do it soon, because unless we move fast, Kratt and Temple will sweep down and crush us before the next full moon."

A moment of silence. Tansan leaned forward. "Who is your contact?"

"A merchant tycoon with a fleet of ships and several of his own escoas. He helped arrange my escape from Arena. He can be trusted."

I hoped.

"What is this network of men we should blindly trust?" Acne-nose said, and there was something of a sneer in his voice. He didn't like that beneath my bitoo was a woman who'd defied Temple in a far grander way than he had during his years of training for rebellion in a hidden jungle camp.

"Not blindly," I snapped. "Never blindly. I've fought in Arena and twice survived the attack of a bull dragon; I do *nothing* blindly."

I looked away from him, let him know by my body language that he wasn't worth engaging in debate. I spoke to Tansan and the rebel who sat listening to every word I said as he carved at his nails with his knife, and to the other gaunt, savage rebels who were listening and watching me intently.

"This network I speak of is comprised of foreign émigrés and merchant tycoons," I said. "Retired roshus. Paras who've defected from the Emperor's army. I think it'd be wise for your Chinion to meet one or two of them. Here, on this Clutch, on his terms, as soon as possible. We need to move fast."

"Let's say Chinion can be located and returned to this Clutch," Knife-carver said, still without looking up. "Let's say you should bring a few select men here to speak with him."

I hesitated, then took a bold guess, remembering rumors of an uprising of several Hamlets of Forsaken that had occurred when I'd been an apprentice in the dragonmaster's stables. "Chinion will be flying back here on his own dragon, yes? One of the dragons he stole from Clutch Maht last year."

Knife-carver gave a ghastly smile that sent shivers up and down my spine. "We prefer the word *liberated* to *stole*."

"How many of the Hamlets of Forsaken throughout Malacar are connected to Chinion?" I asked.

Knife-carver didn't answer me. Tansan did.

"Most Hamlets are simple farming communities. A few once supplied Chinion's camps with grain and food staples, but after Chinion's attack on Clutch Maht, Temple razed several Hamlets to the ground. Everyone within was murdered. Even the elders were not spared. Women and children were raped first. Chinion asks nothing from the Hamlets now, and they offer nothing."

"Separate entities," I said.

"To protect the Forsaken."

"The Forsaken should be alerted of what's about to happen across Malacar. They'll be Temple's easiest targets of retribution, regardless if they're uninvolved."

"We need to harry Temple enough that the Hamlets are viewed as a low priority," Two-braids said.

"The Hamlets should be forewarned nevertheless," I said. "We're creating a future for the children of this nation; we want to limit the bloodshed as much as we can."

"You dislike our methods," Knife-carver said.

I chose my words carefully. "Bayen children suffer nightmares and grief as much as any rishi child does. I'm not certain that the massacre last night was necessary. But I don't know that taking every lord hostage would have been feasible, either. What's done is done. If we can limit bloodshed in the future, we should do so."

"Sinking ships and raiding Clutch stables are not bloodless activities," Two-braids said. "A revolution creates corpses as well as a new future."

I grimaced. My hands were stained red by pomegranate juice. "I know."

Sensing a moment of weakness on my part, Acne-nose pounced. "Will you deign to tell us bloodied ones how you propose to create bull dragons from air, hey-o? Or are we supposed to merely trust that you can do such a thing, like we must trust everything else that spills from your mouth?"

If I'd had a whip in my hand, I would have cracked it against his nose and slashed that pocked skin wide open.

"I'll tell those who are worthy of telling," I said acidly.

Tansan rose from her divan. "We have work to do. If any heralds or dragonfliers arrive from other Clutches or elsewhere, they're to be brought here alive and unharmed. Zarq, you stay. We must talk further, you and I."

Acne-nose glared at me as he departed.

Knife-carver remained at his seat at the table.

I picked a ripe durian fruit from the metalwork basin beside me, rose, and placed it before him. "It'll spoil if it's not eaten soon."

He slowly looked up. His eyes were dark as wet loam and brimming with intelligence. Like the other rebels, he was haggard from undernourishment, and his beard and hair were long and unkempt. Flakes of dried blood were peeling off his forehead and cheeks in lentil-sized circles. One of his victims had sprayed under his knife last night, it seemed.

He reached out and took the durian. The peppery, urinelike smell of the fruit burst from the skin as his blade sank into it.

"Tell us who you are, Zarq," Tansan said quietly. "Tell us how you know the Wai Vaneshor."

So I did. I told her whom the man they called the suwembai kam really was, and how, in an Arena wager backed by Malaban Bri, an influential merchant tycoon, I'd unseated the Roshu of Xxamer Zu and set Ghepp as the overseer in his stead. I spoke of Daronpu Gen, now the missing Wai Vaneshor for Ghepp, and of the ancient prophecy that Gen knew of that spoke of my destiny as the Skykeeper's Daughter.

My throat went dry. I paused to drink some clove-and-orange wine from a rock crystal ewer. With the sweet wine on my lips, and my head buzzing slightly, I spoke of Waikar Re Kratt, known not only as Lupini Re, but Lupini Re-Lutche because of his recent appropriation of that Clutch. I told of the Skykeeper that Kratt wielded through my sister, Waivia, and explained that it was my mother's haunt, an insane creature created from my mother's mad obsessions, her Djimbi magics, and, circuitously, Kratt's sadism. I drank more wine.

I recounted my stay in Temple's obscure jail and of the things that had occurred to me there and how I'd played a crucial part in the rescue of both myself and Jotan Bri, sister of the merchant tycoon Malaban Bri. I spoke of venom and dragonsong, Longstride and the rite performed upon me under the jungle canopy in the dark of night. Suddenly the wine was no longer sweet enough—or perhaps was too sweet—and I pushed it away from me.

While pacing before the table where Knife-carver sat, I told them why no bull dragon had ever hatched from an egg on a Clutch, nor ever would. I told them that bull dragons didn't hatch from eggs, that they incubated within yamdalar cinaigours, the keratinous involucres a dying female dragon secretes about herself. Eight weeks the transformation from female to male takes, I said. Eight weeks. And for decades—for centuries—members of the arbiyeskus throughout Malacar had been disposing of dragon cocoons diligently every month, four weeks before the dragons within had completed their transformation into bulls. By the time I was finished, Knife-carver had eaten the durian, and the dull sunlight dribbling through the many openwork windows of fine, hard stucco cast shadows of arabesques and leaf motifs upon the tiled floor. It was well past high noon.

The dragonmaster pounded on the door and demanded entrance. Sounds of a scuffle with the guards outside. Shouted invective from the dragonmaster.

"We'll keep the suwembai kam," Knife-carver said. "As the former dragonmaster of Re, he has skills we'll need when the bulls are born."

"Be careful of him, Tansan," I warned. "He's often irrational, frequently cruel, and always impatient. Life holds no sanctity for him. None."

I didn't know what had transpired between the two in the jungle camp, but her scarred jawline was hard as she stared at the door.

"We'll use him to our ends and dispose of him when he's no longer needed," she said with a curl of her lip.

A moment of silence. We were all avoiding talking about the crucial revelation in my narrative. Knife-carver studied me from under his shag of hair.

"The calcarifer fish does this, changes from female to male," he said quietly.

"Moths, butterflies," Tansan said. "They change from worm to winged insect while inside cocoons. But I have my doubts about what you tell us, Zarq. There've been times when illness and negligence have prevented the arbiyesku from its monthly hashing in the cocoon ware-

house. Surely somewhere, over the many years, a bull dragon would have hatched from an involucre. It's too unlikely that for centuries no one has stumbled upon this secret."

I shook my head, reached for a fistful of nuts from a metalwork box inlaid with copper and gold. I wanted to rid my palate of the taste of the wine, of the sharp reminder of how inadequate a substitute anything was for venom. "Dragons are aerial creatures by nature. Think of a jungle crown, where the dragons live in the wild. Think of the cocoons on a tree branch, clinging hold tighter than any vine. Think how the involucres that are secreted around the branch are exposed to blistering sunlight, day after day."

I felt again the heat of the bonfire shriveling the skin on my arms and cheeks during Longstride's rite. "Involucres have to be exposed to heat for the transformation to be successful."

"Like eggs incubating beneath a brooder's belly," Knife-carver said quietly.

I nodded. "Exactly. It's always been the practice for brooders to be herded into a warehouse, to be kept conveniently out of the way until they appear irrefutably dead and can be ground up with impunity and used as fodder. Temple vouchsafes to protect our divine dragons during their journey down the Claw Path to death by enclosing them in a warehouse, but what Temple does, unwittingly, is deprive them of transformation and life."

Tansan gestured outside. "And during the Wet? How do bulls hatch without the heat of the Fire Season's sun?"

"I don't know." I brushed off the fibrous, papery shells of the nuts I'd been peeling. "Maybe they don't hatch during the Wet. Maybe the cocoons just rot. Maybe it's the One Dragon's way of keeping things in balance, making sure the jungle isn't overrun with bulls. I don't know."

"So we create our own heat," Knife-carver said.

"Burn any wood we can get our hands on," I said, nodding at the exquisitely carved tables throughout the room. "Keep controlled bonfires roaring night and day."

"It won't work," Tansan said flatly. "The smoke will fill the warehouse and smother everything within. Flies, carrion beetles, firetenders, whatever might be developing in the involucres. Nothing will survive."

I felt profoundly foolish. She was right. We'd be creating a smokehouse like those used to cure meat, albeit on a larger scale.

"Do we know that it's heat alone that the involucres require?" Knife-carver murmured. He leaned forward, chair creaking, and took a handful of the same nuts I was eating. "Maybe the involucres are like plants. Maybe they wither from lack of sunlight, not heat."

The rite had been held during the night, under the dark jungle canopy. Longstride and the matriarch hadn't required sunlight to perform their rite. I shook my head emphatically. "It's the heat. As for the smoke . . ."

"We knock down walls, cut holes in the roof." Knife-carver shrugged. "Simple."

"Do we know for sure that it's eight weeks the involucres require to mature into bulls?" Tansan asked.

Again, I was stumped. The gong that had rung during Longstride's rite had resounded eight times. I'd assumed it represented eight weeks. Could've meant eight months, though. I said so aloud.

"Eight months is a long time for something the size of an involucre to go unharmed in the jungle," Knife-carver said, and again he gave that humorless smile that thinned his lips and further caved in his bearded cheeks and made his eyes look sunken. "The jungle destroys anything without roots that stays motionless too long. I've lived in it long enough to know."

Tansan was still frowning, and I felt my certainty slipping away.

"I've worked in the [illegible] warehouse during Fire Season," she said finally. "The heat in there is stifling at high noon. If cocoons require only heat and time to transform into bulls, a bull would have hatched somewhere, by accident, over the centuries."

Silence a moment as all my confidence dribbled away and left me confused and uncertain.

"Sunlight must be the key," Knife-carver said. "That's the primary difference between a cocoon exposed in the jungle and one shut in a warehouse during the Fire Season. Sunlight."

Tansan nodded. "It must be so. Sunlight and heat and time. That's

what we deprive the cocoons of by placing them in a warehouse. That's what prevents the transformation from completing."

I opened my mouth to argue, then shut it again. They were wrong, I felt certain. Longstride's rite had been performed on me at *night*. And yet Tansan was right: Somewhere, by accident, an involucre should have had the opportunity to develop into a neonate bull if all that were required was heat and time.

There had to be something else. I was missing something. . . .

"We have little sunlight," Tansan said. "The Wet has begun."

"Only just," Knife-carver said. "Given enough heat, perhaps the light we have will suffice."

"We have to try," Tansan said.

I nodded but felt no confidence. I was missing something. I was sure of it now.

"Will you fly alone to your contact in Lireh?" Tansan said, switching subjects so suddenly I was momentarily without an answer.

"I didn't learn how to fly a dragon and read aerial route maps during my apprenticeship under Dragonmaster Re," I muttered. "I need Ryn to fly me."

"The turncoat acolyte?" Knife-carver said. "A boy. He won't know the way to the coast."

"He's an apprentice herald; he can read maps—"

"Take the suwembai kam, this former dragonmaster of Re."

I grudgingly acquiesced with a nod. I'd not the spirit to argue; I had the uneasy feeling, after the objections raised by Tansan, that the cocoons wouldn't transform into bulls. I was missing something.

Knife-carver slowly uncoiled from his chair. He was twice as tall as I'd expected. As tall as Longstride.

"You'll leave now," he murmured, sheathing his knife. "Bring who you like here from this network of yours, and if we can locate him, Chinion will speak with them. We'll begin the work at the arbiyesku today."

SIXTEEN

The dragonmaster pored over several impressive, ornate maps, memorizing landmarks and landing sites and choosing our aerial route with care. His goatee braid had completely unraveled and looked like dirty froth hanging from his chin. Occasionally his teeth chattered, as an excited cat's does before it pounces.

I'd never before seen an aerial route map. I realized that if the monopoly over dragon ownership were to be rendered truly obsolete, all rishi should one day not only have access to those maps, but be able to read them. I would speak with Tansan and this Chinion about the need to educate Clutch serfs.

We returned to the arbiyesku late afternoon. Already the place was a hive of activity that sounded chaotic but looked somewhat organized. Mallets rang against the brickwork of the warehouse; mortar crumbled and dust rose in acrid clouds. A stream of rishi poured steadily into the compound, carrying bayen furniture and the bamboo from abandoned shacks upon their backs. They dumped their loads onto sprawling piles of smashed tables, portrait frames, and divans.

Children ran hither and yon, aiding and disrupting. Elderly women were bent over cauldrons of yanichee, their voices raised in syncopated song, and the rich scent of the hot yolk broth wafted over the arbiyesku, mingling with the salty smell of the slabs of preserved meat soaking in steeptubs; clearly distribution of the food in the daronpuis' larders had already begun.

The escoas had been hobbled, wing bolted, and crammed into six of the mud-brick domiciles belonging to the arbiyesku men. The dragons looked unperturbed by the bustle and phlegmatically accepting of their peculiar quarters. To a dragon, they also looked overfed, their distended bellies rumbling with indigestion. The domiciles reeked of gas and maht, regurgitated dragon food, and flies buzzed over the pats of manure thick upon the floors. The escoas' saddles, reins, bridles, and saddlebags were nowhere in sight.

The dragonmaster bellowed at the children and adults gathered outside the doors of the domiciles. "Move back, move back! A dragon's a dragon, whether it has wings or not!"

Piah, Myamyo, and Keau, all from the arbiyesku contingent of the myazedo, roamed in front of the entrances of the domiciles, acting as guards. Piah wore a turban of bloodstained bandages around his head and lurched heavily from wall to wall, eyes vacant; he looked as if he should be on his back, not guarding dragons. Myamyo sported an ugly bruise around one eye, and the corresponding cheek was as fat and red as a tumor. He was dressed in some dead lord's finery: a waistshirt of fawn byssus so delicate and silky it shimmered, an extravagantly broad sash the creamy orange of a new squash, billowing green pantaloons, and white pebbleleather boots. The clash of colors emphasized the angry red bulging from his injured face.

Keau still wore his crusted bandages around his wounded hand. He looked pallid and dazed, the whorls on his face standing out starkly, but he marched with arms akimbo, his chest puffed out. No unauthorized person would get by *him* to the escoas, oh, no.

"Where's their tack? Why've they been fed so much? When were they last watered?" the dragonmaster demanded of Keau.

Keau shrugged, face impassive, eyes sliding to the savanna. He held no love for the dragonmaster.

Knife-carver was pushing through the crowd, coming toward us, Ryn at his side. Two-braids followed, prodding a giant, grizzled man before him. The man's hands were bound behind his back and he wore the maroon tunic of a herald, albeit dirty and rumpled, the green crest over his left breast stained. It took me a moment to recognize the herald as

Kaban, the drunken stablehand I'd knocked unconscious and tied up the night I'd liberated the escoas. I recalled the ugly bruises and dried blood on Ryn's legs, and my skin crawled with revulsion for the man.

"Where's the tack?" the dragonmaster shouted at Ryn.

"Under the women's barracks." Ryn's eyes were bright, and he looked like he'd slept well.

I nodded at him. "Are you ready to fly again?"

"He goes with me in search of Chinion," Knife-carver said.

"You keep him safe, make sure he returns. I vowed no harm would come to him."

"He'll fly me back."

That was as good a promise as I was going to get.

Ryn didn't look overly concerned. His night amongst the arbiyesku, and the news of the liberation of the Clutch, seemed to have erased his fearful timidity. He was standing close to Knife-carver, looking at him with the bashful idolization young boys usually reserve for war heroes and dragonmasters.

The herald Kaban was watching Ryn with equal interest, though his eyes were filled with a hostile greed that made me want to smash him, the way one smashes a louse. Ryn felt Kaban's gaze on him, and the boy's hand dropped to his waist. A crude leather sheath was belted at his slender hips.

"You've a blade," I murmured.

Ryn nodded. "I've been taught how to throw it, too." He spoke loud enough that Kaban could hear. The man sneered and spat.

"Children should know how to defend themselves," Knife-carver said, eyes steady on mine, and I could see in his stance and hear in his voice that either he'd learned how Ryn had suffered at the hands of Kaban the herald, or had guessed. "A child should know how to cut a man so that he can't rise again." In the domicile behind me, an escoa snorted. Children squealed. The novelty of seeing a winged dragon close up, combined with the thrum of activity and smells of yolk broth, had made the children highly excitable.

Crowded by onlookers, the dragonmaster, Ryn, and I saddled three escoas and slid halters over their snouts. Kaban made a caustic comment about the stupidity of flying a dragon without a nose barbell and bridle, and Two-braids slammed the butt of his knife so hard against Kaban's ear, it sounded like a nut had been smashed open with a rock.

Knife-carver stepped quietly beside the reeling man. "If a boy half your age has mastered an escoa without a barbell, what kind of herald are you if you can't?"

Knife-carver's poise and tone unnerved me. He reminded me too much of Kratt. Kaban wouldn't live the day out, I was certain; nor would he die cleanly or quickly. The knowledge made me feel tainted, when all I wanted to feel was a grim satisfaction. But I didn't say anything that might prevent the murder. No. And, placed in the same circumstances, I would certainly remain silent again.

Two old men from the tanners' clan brought us sacks of food. We loaded the sacks into our saddlebags, then led the escoas behind the compound, onto the savanna. A crowd of children followed us; as we removed the escoas' hobbles and wing bolts, more rishi gathered. We mounted; the crowd murmured. As the dragons hop-lunged across the brittle grasses and their great wings spread wide and stirred dust from the ground, a huge cheer rose from both the gathered rishi and those swarming over the arbiyesku warehouse.

To the sound of that exultant cheer, we rose into the sky and went our separate ways.

Come evenfall and a rainsquall, the dragonmaster and I landed at one of the ganotei hani, airway tracts, that are maintained—some better than others—throughout Malacar. These strips of relatively flat land are bi-annually seared of all flora and are located near a river or lake and, occasionally, one of the overland egg-train routes. The ganotei hani are used by heralds, First Citizens, Temple authorities, and militia traveling on dragonback. Once a year, the ganotei hani along the aerial routes between Clutches and Arena are swarmed with retinues of bayen gamblers, daronpuis, and dragonmaster apprentices, all of whom are accompanying bulls to and from Arena.

Needless to say, the ganotei han we camped at was not on one of the major routes. The tract of land hadn't been seared for at least a year, and we landed upon a thick growth of new ferns and fireweed, amongst old blackened tree stumps sprouting lichen and moss. As rain pelted down, I watered our escoa at the swampy lake, wading cautiously in amongst mangrove roots and thick water vines, then joined the dragonmaster in making a crude shelter of leaning fronds and branches.

Thoroughly drenched, we crunched crispy strips of vinegar-dried fish and worked at tart chunks of slii fruit leather as rain penetrated our primitive refuge and turned the ground beneath us to mud. We spoke not a word to each other, slept fitfully and miserably, and woke at dawn.

We flew long that day, resting twice for the sake of our escoa.

By late afternoon I caught my first glimpse of the ocean, a band of steel shimmering in the distance. It rose up, like a wall, to touch the clouds. I was appalled that water could stand upright like that until I realized, with a hot flush, that the water wasn't standing upright but stretching long and far into the horizon.

I shuddered and readjusted my grip on the saddle rungs. As we neared the ocean, the land below us changed into farmland and vineyards and villages. We flew up and over a two-humped mountain that had been shorn of every tree, and there, abruptly, was the bay of Lireh and the sprawl of caravansaries and taverns, factories and warehouses, smithies and ports and temples and market squares that led to the great capital city of Liru beyond.

Liru itself was wedged upon the mountainside to the north, visible as great tiers of marble mansions, sandstone palaces, and gleaming white cupolas. Rising ponderously from that grandeur were the huge triple domes of Wai-Liru Temple, obese monstrosities plated in green copperscale tiles. Torqued onion domes with lustrous purple spirals clustered around the mammoth domes, bright in the fine rain blowing off the bay.

Another escoa was circling the vast city, descending for a landing, and a second dragon, a russet-and-ivy speck, was disappearing over Liru Mountain. Under the dragonmaster's guidance, our dragon banked, circled wide over the massive ships dwarfing the dockyards, and began a slow descent.

I felt bewildered by the sprawl of the capital city, by the huge ships moored at the docks, the hundreds of little caravels bobbing around them, and the people swarming on the wharves beyond. And the smell and look of the sea! I'd never before inhaled its wild, salty tang, never before looked toward the horizon to see nothing but ever-surging ocean. The sheer size of it was terrifying, and the smells of seawater, wood, hempen rope, turpentine, coal, and the mildewed canvas of ship sails were all marvelous and foreign.

How would we ever find Malaban Bri in all that?

The dragonmaster flew our escoa to a raised stone rostrum the size of a small courtyard, situated at the edge of a wharf. A bevy of women were gathered upon the rostrum, around its outskirts; at our approach they ran for the stone ramp that descended to ground level in three precise, rectangular switchbacks.

"Damn whores, get out of the way!" the dragonmaster bellowed. Our escoa took the vertical position of landing and her wings backbeat against the air. Clawpads slid over wet stone. We landed light as chaff. I wondered how I had ever been so green as to almost fall off a dragon at landing.

Neither the dragonmaster nor I was able to dismount easily, though. My spine felt stiff as an oyster shell and my legs were as rubbery as old kelp, and the dragonmaster looked as if he were suffering the same sensations. We avoided each other's eyes in our chagrin over the limitations of our bodies.

The women who had been standing upon the rostrum prior to our landing came back up the ramp, hips swinging, bells tinkling on their ankles. Their stained blouses were cut low over dark bosoms that had been painted with clear oil.

The women grinned, some toothless, and broke into a cacophony of hawking cries, boasting of their abilities, their inexpensive charges, the heights of ecstasy they guaranteed between their legs. I gawped at them.

The dragonmaster was deaf to their enticements and efficiently bolted our escoa's wings shut. I followed him down the ramp, blushing furiously as a whore pressed her breasts against me. She reeked of woodsmoke and old ale.

Hunched against the drizzle, we started along the wharves.

The non–egg laying, dewinged dragons known as satons were everywhere, pulling wagons laden with bales of jute and tobacco leaf, barrels of oil, sheaves of rubber, and dragons' eggs packed in straw. Their drivers shouted at the throng to make way, while urchins darted in behind them, scooping up any deposited manure the moment it hit the wharves' worn planks and darting away with the fuel. Stevedores bearing incredible loads of wild-scented mahogany planks lumbered along piers and up gangplanks as wagons of iron ore rumbled past us.

Stray dogs slunk between legs. Beggars squatted along the edges of the docks. Thick-bodied, brown-skinned women—descendants from the island of Lud y Auk—slit open fish with scale-flecked knives, pale fish guts strewn about their sandaled feet.

Wide-eyed at the stew pot of goods and people clogging the wharves, I walked with one hand upon the neck of our imperturbable escoa. Her keratinous scales were cool and wet, but between them, her leathery hide was warm and soft, pulling taut, then wrinkling a little, with each shambling lunge forward. Beneath my bare feet, the wet, worn wharf was gummy and pebbled with grit.

The dragonmaster barked a question at a Djimbi seaman whose whorls were the brownish green of uprooted kelp flung upon the beach. The seaman pointed at a series of leaning wooden offices near the wharves' end. We pushed and wove through the throng toward them.

A green-streaked copper sign that had the likeness of a sextant stamped upon its center hung from two black iron chains over the turpentine-soaked timbers of one office. The hieratic for the caranku, the merchant guild clan, framed the left of the sextant; the hieratic for *Bri* framed the right. Rain softly pinged off the copper.

Shutters hung askew from the office windows. A legless beggar sitting on a board that had rusted casters beneath it was dozing against the building, protected a little by the warped eaves. Seagull guano had defaced the entire building with streaks of grayish white.

I was dismayed and alarmed. I'd expected something far, far grander from a merchant tycoon.

"Wait here with the escoa," the dragonmaster ordered, thrusting her reins at me.

"No. I'm coming with you."

"Then say good-bye to our dragon," he snapped. "Thieves abound here."

He dropped the reins and barged through the heavy wooden door beneath the copper sign.

I grumbled and waited, but felt exposed standing there alone with the escoa, so I leaned hard on the door and peered into the gloom beyond. There was the dragonmaster, standing before a massive wooden desk, behind which was seated a brawny aosogi man with a great spill of unkempt gray hair hanging about his broad shoulders. From ceiling to floor the room was surrounded by hexagonal scroll slots, each slot crammed with bamboo casings. A curled, ripped, and mildewed map hung on the wall behind the man. At his elbow sat a cold boiled renimgar, whole save for a ripped off leg—the gnawed bone of which sat near the boiled head. His desk was littered with dockets.

Both men glanced at me. Holding the escoa's reins, I stepped inside and pushed the door partially shut. The heavy door was warped and moved reluctantly.

"And that'd be the escoa you're talking about?" the brawny aosogi man said, nodding at the green snout just visible at the end of my reins, poking round the door. "I've no record of her comin' off any ship of ours."

The dragonmaster smacked his bald pate in exasperation. "Not off a boat! We flew in, flew in, yes? Two days ago, and we've been waiting for whomever it was who was supposed to retrieve the damned beast, but no one's come, and I'm telling you, I'm leaving with the escoa before nightfall if you don't send a runner to Malaban and tell him his beast is here, and burn what he paid for the dragon!"

The brawny man placed his great knuckles on the desk and slowly heaved himself out of his wooden chair. He lumbered out from behind his desk and disappeared up a creaking set of narrow stairs. Above us, the scrape of a chair being shoved back, the muted sound of voices, the creak of floorboard planks.

The brawny man reappeared, lumbering down the narrow stairs as if movement exhausted him. "We'll send word," he grunted as he descended.

"We'll wait here," the dragonmaster snapped. "I'm not wasting more coin at another cesspool that passes as a tavern in these parts. Two days we've wasted! I'll be recompensed for this, understand."

The dragonmaster's inherent vehemence made his act utterly convincing. I was hard put not to stare at him.

The brawny man lowered himself behind his desk again and waved a meaty hand in my direction. "Bring in the beggar from outside."

The dragonmaster turned and looked at me. "Go on, then."

Scowling, I heaved the door open. I stared at the mound of rags outside, uncertain as to how to address them. As if feeling my gaze, the beggar slowly looked up. His nose had been eaten entirely away by disease; puckered yellow skin and two gaping holes were all that remained.

"You're wanted inside," I said weakly.

I watched with morbid fascination as the beggar straightened to the height of my thighs and propelled himself toward me via wooden paddles he held in his hands. I stepped smartly out of the way, and my escoa snorted and tipped her head to one side as he rolled in front of her.

"Open the door, hey," the beggar growled at me. I shoved it hard with a shoulder and the beggar wheeled himself inside.

The dragonmaster's voice, querulous and tyrannical. The desk man's voice, low and weary. An eager yap from the beggar.

Moments later the beggar slid outside again and set off toward the city, arms paddling furiously, his casters clitter-clattering over the grooves between the wharves' planks.

"Make sure you say the escoa was delivered by Zarq!" I shouted after him. "Zarq, you hear?"

He disappeared between legs and ankles and cart wheels.

We waited, the dragonmaster and I, alternately pacing the wharves in the drizzling rain and taking shelter within the office, and the entire time I rode the sharp peaks of amazement at the strangeness of my surroundings, and the dark valleys of fear that our mission would be unsuccessful and that Malaban Bri wouldn't come, or if he did, he would dismiss us at best or come with Temple soldiers at worst.

Come dusk, two gaunt young men, one the dark brown of a wild boar, the other the toasted brown of a biscuit, descended from the upper floor of the office. They walked by without looking at where I stood against a wall of floor-to-ceiling hexagonal scroll cells, dripping rainwater onto the creaking wooden floor. I wondered how many descendants and immigrants from the Archipelagic isle of Lud y Auk lived in Lireh. Plenty, it seemed.

As the young men shoved the door shut behind them, the brawny deskman gave me a baleful look, wordlessly lit a smoking lantern, and continued to paw and scribble through the paperwork on his desk. Now and then he paused to lift the carcass of the boiled renimgar to his mouth and rip off a chunk of meat.

My stomach growled outrageously. I ducked outside and joined the dragonmaster and our escoa.

With twilight, the wharves had been emptied of working stevedores. Seamen and whores strolled and staggered through the gloaming, and urchins ran about, sometimes alone, sometimes in pairs, combing the docks for dropped fruit. Compared to the frantic activity of the day, the empty dockyards looked eerie, as if the dark waters lapping rhythmically against the barnacle-encrusted pylons had claimed all life to support its own. The silhouettes of the ships moored alongside the piers looked like hulking carcasses, the rigging, furled sails, and masts like great ribs and fingers. Beyond the bay, the ocean was visible as a rippling, restless black, stretching far into the distance and merging with the twilight sky.

I shivered. Malaban Bri wasn't coming.

What now? I had failed, monumentally. Perhaps we could try to locate Malaban Bri's villa, force an interview upon him—

My escoa snorted and shifted restlessly.

"Easy, now, easy," I murmured. She cocked her head toward the ghostly white blocks and blurs of Liru on the mountainside and stared intently into the dark sky.

"About time," the dragonmaster muttered. He peeled himself away from where he'd been crouched on his haunches, back against the dilapidated office building, staring moodily at the bay. His knee joints popped as he straightened.

I saw it, then: A winged dragon was approaching, flying low, coming fast. An intense rush of hot relief flushed my throat, set my ears to ringing. Somehow the legless beggar had delivered his message to Malaban Bri, and Malaban Bri had come. Alone.

The approaching dragon landed, great wings slapping the wet air like sails in a gust. The door to the office behind me shoved open with a squeal of water-swollen wood. Light spilled in a glaucous circle around me as the brawny deskman looked out, lantern held high.

The dragonflier was lithe and dressed in warm leathers, and he raised a hand in greeting to the brawny deskman behind me.

"Thank you, Shendar." The voice was high and womanly. "Lock up and return home now."

I squinted through the gloom and my heart fish-flipped in my breast. "Jotan? Jotan Bri?"

A grin from the flier. "We meet again, Zarq."

It *was* Jotan, a woman I'd last seen unconscious and near death after months of being imprisoned in Temple's most secret and nefarious of jails.

"You can *fly*?" I said, incredulous.

She shrugged expansively. "I demanded to learn how. Malaban says I've become difficult and reckless since my return. I believe he's correct. Mount up and follow me."

The dragonmaster opened and shut his mouth several times, then stalked over to my side and jerked the reins from my hands. On an impulse, I walked away from him and stood in front of Jotan's bright-eyed, feisty mount. The wind from her dragon's wings smelled as sweet and peppery as new orchids.

"Can I ride with you?" I asked.

Again a grin, and Jotan scooted back in her saddle and gestured in front of her. "Only if you lie underneath me."

Heat bloomed between my thighs. "You always did prefer being on top."

She threw back her head and laughed, and I swung up in front of her.

In her rain-speckled leathers she was as cool and slippery as a wet dragon's wings, and her breath was warm against my nape as she assumed the flying position and lowered her weight atop me. She smelled like clove-roasted plums and red wine.

"I'm glad you've come," she murmured, her lips brushing my ear.

With that, we launched into the sky.

SEVENTEEN

"Malaban's away," Jotan explained as she showed the dragonmaster and me along a corridor. Mosaics flashed by us, lustrous indigo and white tiles bright under the lantern carried by the young serving girl who scurried before us.

"Away for the night or away from Lireh?" I asked tensely.

"He's doing business with an inland Clutch, selling off containers of fur and sea elephant ivory from up north."

I cursed roundly, using one of the more colorful phrases in my vocabulary of invective—something involving the Infinite Winged and a pig. Beside me, the dragonmaster muttered vehemently to himself.

Jotan shot me a cool look. "Malaban will be back within a clawful of days."

"You need to summon him back *now*," I said. "Events are unfolding that require his immediate attention—"

"And you think I'm incapable of handling them?" Again, the cool sideways look from under her dripping leather skullcap.

I hesitated. "I don't know if you're aware of . . . certain things."

"Anything Malaban is aware of, I'm aware of."

"But . . . you were imprisoned for a long time. I don't know if you're aware of everything that transpired outside our prison walls during that time."

"And you are?" she said archly. "How well connected you've become."

I flushed. "Not so well connected, or I wouldn't be here."

"Good that you remembered that. As for me, let's say that I've made it a hobby of mine to keep very well-informed. Thank Temple for sparking such curiosity in me."

Ahead of us, the serving girl inserted a key into a door, pushed it open, and slipped inside. Jotan stopped before the open door and turned to face me. "You'll want to change and eat before we speak. I take it discussion shouldn't wait until morning."

When we'd been imprisoned together, ill health, lack of sunlight, and overexposure to venom had turned her the color of tallow; now her skin was a healthy dark tan, and I could see she had little of the Emperor's blood in her, but plenty from the Archipelagic isle of Lud y Auk. Truly, she was not fa-pim; she was not landed gentry.

Her lips were fuller and redder than I'd remembered, too, and her eyes, black as a jaguar's pelt, inflamed and addled me, despite the rivulets of blood cobwebbed in her sclera and the shards of white sparkling in her pupils. Or maybe because of those venom markings.

I remembered how she used to lie on a divan, in the quarters in which we'd been jailed, with one leg lazily hanging down to the ground and exposed to the thigh, one arm draped over the cushions above her head, her diaphanous gown sloping off a shoulder.

I remembered, too, how both of us had been so brutally, routinely violated in that jail, how our bruised and broken limbs had been heavy with lassitude, our spirits submersed under an ocean of passivity. Seeing her now, a free, healthy confident woman, brought back frightening memories of all we'd suffered.

I could see her examining me, wrestling with the same emotions, trying to reconcile the image of the woman before her with memories of the Zarq she'd known in prison.

"Zarq?" she prompted. "Can discussion wait until morn?"

"What?" Did she smell faintly of venom? "No, we should talk tonight. I have to return as soon as possible."

Beside me, the dragonmaster growled in his throat. "We can cat later. We talk now."

"Then you talk to the walls," Jotan said, turning her gaze on him. "I intend on bathing and dressing first."

A fire crackled in the hearth of the room beyond. Candles had been lit. The serving girl ducked out of the room and stood, eyes downcast, at Jotan's side. I was dismayed to see that she was Djimbi. I wondered if any Djimbi held posts of status or owned any property in Lireh.

"This way," Jotan said to the dragonmaster. "I'll show you to *your* quarters."

I went into the room and closed the door after me, then stood there, stunned by the magnificence of my surroundings.

A massive bed was the focal point of the room. Raised off the tiled floor by clawed teak dragon legs, covered by thick quilts and a profusion of pillows, the bed was a masterwork of carving. The crown of the bed was carved in the likeness of two dragons, necks arched and mouths agape, fangs bared and tongues entwined. The dewlaps of one were inflated, and as smooth and round as breasts, and beneath the scaled belly of the other was a forked phallus that penetrated the humanlike vulva of its partner. Two long teak tails trailed from the dragons and ran on either side of the mattress beneath the spill of quilts. Their tails joined and entwined at the foot of the bed.

The footboard of the bed had been carved in the likeness of two diamond-shaped tail membranes, only much larger, and the way the membranes arched against each other, pressing together like the bellies of joined lovers, was somehow more provocative than the headboard itself.

A yellow gown had been draped over the profusion of quilts. It was elegant in its simple cut and was far finer than anything I'd ever touched, let alone worn, in my life. I knew at once the neck of it would ride so low as to just cover my nipples, and that the thin material would cinch my waist and cup my hips like the hands of a greedy lover—if I were bold enough to put the gown on.

If it was intended for me. Maybe I was mistaken; maybe I would find something beneath it that was more befitting one of my status.

A knock at the door and, after a pause, two serving girls slipped in, carrying a large tin tub.

"Your bath, lady," one murmured as they set the tub on the tiles in front of the fire.

Five more women came in, ranging in age from thirteen to thirty, each carrying behind her neck two steaming pails of water at either end of a pole. While I stood there dripping on the tiles, unsure what to do, they efficiently emptied their buckets into the metal tub and departed.

The two young serving girls remained behind.

We stood in silence a good while, me at a loss as to what to do next and they waiting patiently for I knew not what. Neither would look up from the floor.

Both were Djimbi. Senemeis, I thought, recalling Savga's honey-colored skin embellished by faint whorls that looked the color of sun-bleached grass. *A hue much more pleasing than the starkly mottled shades that result from coarse piebald pairings.*

I wondered if our revolution—Nashe, as the dragonmaster called it—would affect Malaban and Jotan Bri in ways I'd not anticipated. I wondered if they were even aware of the racial bias inherent in their choice of servants. I wondered if Jotan would treat me differently if she knew I was Djimbi.

"Climb in while it's hot?" one of the serving girls finally asked.

"Can either of you read?" I asked.

Their eyes whipped up to mine, surprised, then returned to their former meek study of the tiled floor.

"No, lady," answered one.

"Are you required to submit to the wants of male guests?"

Again, startled eyes met mine. "Bayen Hacros Bri gives his guests his ebanis, lady. Do you . . . want one brought to you?"

"Certainly not." I was shamed by the flare of heat in my groin at the prospect. "Are you indentured serfs?"

Frowns. "We earn our keep, hey-o."

"You're allowed to look elsewhere for work?"

"Bayen Hacros Bri runs a good house." The one who'd answered all my questions met my eyes and gestured, pleadingly, at the bath. "You'll get in now, hey?"

"I'll scrub myself," I said. "You can leave."

I waited till they shut the door after them before stripping off and immersing myself in the steaming water. I wondered what my belly and breasts would look like with green whorls upon them.

By the time the serving girls returned with silver bowls and platters of food, I was scrubbed and dry and sheathed, uncomfortably, in the magnificent yellow gown. My hair, which I'd dried with a nutmeg-scented towel, felt light as down against my shoulders, and yes, just as I'd suspected, the scooped neck of the gown plunged so low that the edge rode just above my nipples. The serving girls set their ewers of wine and platters of food on a small table near the fire. I gawped. One of the girls announced each dish as she lifted the lid from it.

"Candied breadfruit flowers. Bananas boiled with gharial meat. Spicy roasted parrots in yolk sauce. Flying fish and roasted coranuts baked in pastry."

I was awed at the strangeness and the abundance of the food in front of me. The girls stood back, and, after a moment, I cautiously tasted a bit of the spicy parrot in yolk sauce. The spice brought tears to my eyes—but was exquisitely delicious. I attacked the rest of the meal with great vigor.

When I was done and my limbs glowed pleasantly from the wine and food I'd consumed, one girl brushed my hair while the other rubbed cream in my hands and polished my nails with beeswax. I couldn't fully enjoy either, for their attentions were too strange for me, and I was actually relieved when they finished and I was given slippers that matched the yellow of my gown and a fine shawl as black as venom. I inexpertly wrapped the shawl about me, grateful for some sort of cover for my revealing gown, and, feeling as graceless as a boar in my unfamiliar and fine surroundings, I followed one of the girls to where Jotan and the dragonmaster awaited, in a library of parchment scrolls.

Just seeing the dragonmaster's ugly, hostile face made me forget my awkwardness concerning my splendid environs and reminded me of the coarse reality behind my presence in Jotan's villa.

Jotan listened intently while I recounted everything—though I kept back, of course, the details of why bulls never hatched in captivity. I paced around the library we were ensconced in so as to avoid her distracting eyes, the look of her stunning red lips, the artful way her long black hair was held up with a dragon clip, revealing her neck. Her gown was white and sleeveless; the neckline plunged in a sharp vee to her navel, and was laced up by an indigo silk ribbon. The indigo silk against the shocking white of the gown against her dark golden brown skin, topped by her jet hair, made a stunning combination.

The dragonmaster, dressed in a plain brown tunic belted by braided leather, remained silent through most of my narrative, interrupting only occasionally with a passionate outburst when he felt more detail, or less, was required.

"I know whom to contact," Jotan said quietly when I'd finished. "I'll send a herald now."

She leaned from her chair and pulled a silken cord, then turned back to me. "You're right; Malaban needs to return immediately. I'll have him summoned. Of course, you'll stay until he returns."

"How long will that take?"

"A day for my herald to reach him, a day for Malaban to reach us."

The idea of remaining for two days in the Bri villa held much appeal. I nodded, even as the dragonmaster sputtered outrage.

Jotan turned coolly to him. "It won't be wasted time. Preparations will begin without my brother's presence: the gathering of arms and people and monies that you'll require to fortify Xxamer Zu, the scheming and planning that Zarq talks about concerning attacks on Archipelagic ships and certain Clutches. The men I'll contact will arrange all this."

"As will we," I said.

Her venom-blooded eyes turned on me. "Don't expect to be a central part of this, Zarq. Once the key players I've summoned receive my herald, they'll send their representatives to other contacts, who'll alert their operatives. There are networks and networks of people involved. . . . You heard of the Wai-Fa Paak factory skirmish? No? Of course not. You are rishi, a Clutch serf."

I bridled; she continued, aware of my indignation and enjoying it.

"It was an uprising started by a group that calls itself the Kindlers. Perhaps some of our men are involved with them, perhaps not. It doesn't matter. What matters is the unrest of the working class, the willingness of laborers to burn to the ground a factory that employed them, rather than continue to line the pockets of the Archipelagic proprietor. Many shops and tenements burned that night; the looting continued for days. There have been other uprisings, of course, always quashed by Temple soldiers. At least once a month a bridge is barricaded by the Kindler ikap-fen." Her eyes glinted wickedly. "That's Lireh's equivalent of you rishi: the laborers, the working class, the ikap-fen: the spinning spiders."

I refused to tense at her barb.

The dragonmaster, who'd been twitching and muttering and scratching at his shanks in agitation, could remain seated no longer. It must have been costing him a powerful amount of self-control to hold his tongue concerning his dream of liberating the Djimbi from years of oppression. He started pacing around the perimeter of the library, like a wildcat pacing inside the perimeter of a cage. I immediately stopped *my* pacing and dropped onto a divan, afraid we looked too much alike.

"The Wai-Fa Paak factory skirmish is the most famous uprising to date," Jotan continued, a smile playing on her crimson lips. "The Archipelagic proprietor was torn limb from limb in broad daylight, in public, by the ikap-fen who'd dragged him into the street. The proprietor's women and children were torn apart too, apparently. I wasn't there. Who can say for certain? Doesn't matter. Some of the Kindlers who were involved were later found and publicly decapitated by Auditors. Or maybe it wasn't the Kindlers who were found. Temple wasn't picky. As long as heads rolled, any heads that weren't ludu bayen, the Ashgon was satisfied."

She shrugged, stretched a little. Movement of belly and breasts beneath her indigo silk lacing.

"My point is this: All these skirmishes, whether they're spontaneous workers' affairs or assaults clandestinely orchestrated by influential men, and all the beheadings and curfews that follow, always fail to spark the Great Uprising. Now *you* arrive with the news that you can breed bulls in captivity. You, Zarq, will be the catalyst that will unleash the Great Uprising. But you are not the uprising itself."

I held my tongue—barely. If I voiced my ambition of bringing bull dragons to all Malacarite rishi and what she called the ikap-fen, I might alienate her. She was bayen; the men she intended on contacting would be bayen, too. Yes, some would be foreigners and yes, some may have risen through the social ranks from humble beginnings, and yes, all of them were driven by their own reasons toward the same goal: ending the Emperor's theocratic dictatorship of Malacar.

But few of them would wish to give their servants breeding dragons. If a servant owned either a bull or a female dragon, what need would he or she have for being a servant? This was a caste war I was fighting, too, and once my neonate bulls broke free of their cocoons . . .

If they'd break free, damn it.

The feeling nagged that no bulls would come forth, that all the efforts of the rishi who were toiling in Xxamer Zu even as I glared at the fine parquetry floors of the Bri library would come to naught. Because I was missing something.

A servant appeared. Djimbi. He kept his eyes upon the floor. I guessed him to be older than me by several years; I wondered if he had a claimed woman and children. Wondered if he was considered a spinning spider by Jotan and her ilk.

Jotan rose, went to a desk, dipped quill in ink, and scratched the quill over parchment. She blew the wet ink dry with a fan of white feathers, then rolled the parchment, slotted it into a bamboo casing as slim and short as a fresh shoot of sugarcane, and melted emerald wax over the cork bung. She stamped it with a seal, then refreshed her quill in ink and wrote two more missives, which she likewise sealed in bamboo and cork. She handed all three to the servant, who had waited with eyes cast to the floor the entire time.

"Wake the heralds Suip and Domsti," she ordered. "Suip is to deliver this scroll to House S'twe and place it in the hands of Bayen Hacros S'twe himself. He's to carry Bayen Hacros S'twe's response back to me this evening. If S'twe needs him to wait several hours in his byre before a response can be given, Suip is to wait. Understood?"

"Yes, Lady Bri."

"Herald Domsti takes *this* scroll to House Etaan. He's to return here and fly at dawn to Clutch Swensi and deliver this last scroll to Bayen Hacros Bri. Three scrolls, each to a separate person. Send the wrong scroll with the wrong herald to the wrong house and I'll have you castrated. Understood?"

"Yes, Lady Bri."

"Go then."

The servant backed out of the library. Jotan remained standing by the door and faced me and the dragonmaster. "I'd suggest that you both retire now. I'm sure you've had a long day. I know mine hasn't yet ended."

"Are you mad?" the dragonmaster cried from where he'd been pacing back and forth before the fireplace. "We've more to discuss than this!"

"Not tonight we don't."

"Where're the men of this house? I demand to speak with them."

She smoothly continued to talk through his spitting protestations, though I saw her stiffen. "Tomorrow etiquette dictates that you meet my mother, Zarq. Dragonmaster Re need not accompany us. Mother knows who you are."

Which meant that her mother knew, in all its appalling detail, of what had befallen Jotan during Jotan's imprisonment. I thought a mother ought to be spared such things. Then again, maybe not all mothers knew obsession and passion as intensely as mine had.

I recalled the great white sprawl of the villa we'd landed in, guided by Jotan, some short hours ago. It was huge, this Bri estate; it was nigh on palatial. But it rested at the foot of the Liru Mountain and was not amongst those tiers of palaces and cupolas of Liru itself. The Bris were affluent, yes, but they were not ludu bayen. They were not landed gentry of pure Archipelagic blood.

"Who else lives here besides you and Malaban and your mother?" I asked, ignoring the spluttering dragonmaster. "Aside from your servants."

Jotan gave a wintry laugh. "We're a veritable nation unto ourselves, we Bris. I have sisters, brothers, cousins, aunts, uncles, nephews . . . they all live here. But don't worry. You'll remain safe and anonymous. Only my mother need know who you are."

The dragonmaster stalked across the room and stood before us. We'd been wrong to ignore him; it had whipped him into a rage.

"I want answers!" he cried, yanking the snarled froth of his unraveled goatee braid. "I will *not* be sent off to bed while some saggy-titted via flings heralds hither and yon—"

"Dragonmaster Re," she said icily, and her venom-blooded eyes locked with his, and that was something to see, two venom addicts unafraid of death facing each other in a moment of barely repressed fury. "I am under no obligation to give you anything you ask for, and I demand that I be treated with the respect I accord you. Is that understood?"

The dragonmaster was a monkey of a man, enraged and impotent and demented and old. Yet he'd killed so frequently, and so well, that his arms were corded with death; his muscles were lubricated with murder instead of blood; his sinews were fed by slaughter; his bones had grown strong and thick from the crack of skulls beneath his fists. He launched himself at Jotan Bri a second before I launched myself at him.

We became a twelve-limbed beast devouring itself.

The thump of furniture overturning. The thud of flesh pounding flesh. Grunts, panting. No shrieks. No curses. Just blood and teeth and fists.

The crack of a brass statuette splitting bone, and the dragonmaster fell to the floor, convulsing, and I cursed and fumbled for a pillow from a divan, leaving a streak of blood upon samite, and shoved the pillow under his head. His eyes rolled. His convulsions stopped. He went limp.

Silence.

"I've killed him," Jotan said flatly. She knelt on the dragonmaster's other side. The lacing of her gown was open to her navel. A flap of torn flesh hung above a rapidly bruising left breast. The dragonmaster's rotten teeth had mauled their way through the silk of her gown.

The dragonmaster's chest fell. Remained still. Wouldn't rise. Couldn't rise.

But no: Slowly, reluctantly, it rose.

Fell . . . rose.

"He's alive," I said, and I dropped onto my rump, shaking.

"We'll end up like that one day. Deranged by venom," Jotan said, throwing the brass statuette aside. It thudded against an overturned table. Her eyes met mine. They were feral, alive, and gorgeous. She wanted me. Wanted me there, now.

So help me, Dragon, I wanted her, too.

"Wait," she said, and she licked her lips, and I froze in the act of coming toward her on my knees.

Jotan rose to her feet. Staggered over scroll casings that had clattered to the floor when backs had slammed repeatedly against wooden floor-to-ceiling hexagonal scroll cells. She reached into one cell and rifled through the bamboo casings that remained within, her arm buried to the elbow.

When she returned to me, I already knew what she held in her fist.

"Where did you get it?" I asked through a bruised and swelling lip, hating her and myself and the rock-crystal vial with its ebon contents that she held in her palm.

She unstoppered the vial.

That scent. It ravished me, and I welcomed the mauling.

Hands trembling, she slowly withdrew the stopper from the belly of the nearly empty vial. The long crystal stalactite of the vial's stopper came out tipped with venom. Under her trembling hands, the stalactite rattled on the lip of the vial.

"I plan on visiting my supplier tomorrow," she whispered. "You'll come with me."

I nodded. Yes. I'd go with her.

"Open your mouth," she whispered, and so help me I obeyed, and she slowly ran the tar-streaked stopper over my lips, over my gums, across my tongue.

She did the same to herself as heat blazed in my sinus cavities and my head turned into a ball of fire.

"Part your legs," she whispered, and again I obeyed, leaning back against a scroll case and lifting my gown to my waist. She dipped the stopper into her vial, then ran the blackened crystal over the gnarled flesh that remained from where a nun had circumcised me, and then she slid the crystal into me.

She did the same to herself while my back arched and I longed to bite her, enter her, become the soul and breast and heart and nerve center of her, as I sobbed and ached for dragonsong.

As I hated myself for once again descending back into venom's captivity.

"Now," Jotan croaked, "we will make our own motet."

And that's what we did. Deprived of the dragons' enigmatic music, we fucked and moaned and sighed and cried and made our own choral composition on the library floor.

EIGHTEEN

The Bri connate healer said the dragonmaster was in a coma, from which he would not revive.

Jotan nodded grimly. Pale and sweat-beaded from venom's ebb, she was standing beside the bed the dragonmaster had been laid in. She'd dressed in a clean gown and had hastily braided and coiled her hair. In the privacy of my room, the two silent serving girls had washed and likewise dressed me in a clean gown, and I knew I looked somewhat respectable, despite my bruises and swollen lip and the late hour.

But clean clothes and liberal doses of attar still couldn't disguise the scent of venom and sex that lingered around Jotan and I, nor the lingering sourness of bile from me; I'd been violently ill after indulging in venom with Jotan. I was appalled that I'd succumbed, so readily, to the desire for venom. I was in Lireh to spark rebellion, to start a war; I carried knowledge that could overturn centuries of oppression; and I'd vowed never to use venom again. No half measures. That had been my mantra, my motto, the principal guiding my bold confidence ever since I'd escaped Ghepp's dungeon.

But at the first sight of venom I'd weakened and succumbed. Great Dragon, how I loathed myself.

"I've had the urge to crack someone over the head like that ever since the same was done to me," Jotan said, her voice husky and low. I remembered how she'd been knocked unconscious in prison, just prior to our rescue. Her skull hadn't staved in like the mildewing shell of a hollowed gourd, though. "I suppose I should be grateful I survived."

"You suppose?"

Jotan shrugged, gestured with her chin at the supine dragonmaster. "He could smell the venom on me. That's why he attacked."

"The dragonmaster dislikes women," I murmured. "He's been losing the fight for his sanity for a long time. That's why he went wild, nothing else."

But I knew, even as I said it, that Jotan was right. The scent of venom clinging to Jotan like a supramundane musk had triggered the dragonmaster's leap over sanity's edge. What would I be like at his age?

I glanced at the long-faced connate healer. He was busy unpacking items from the trolley of drawers he'd wheeled into the dragonmaster's room, and he didn't look at all unsettled by being summoned from his bed at middle-night to tend a stranger who had been attacked by two women. By Jotan's cavalier mien, I guessed the connate healer knew about her illegal habit, too. I wondered how his silence and loyalty had been bought.

I looked back at the waxen husk of the dragonmaster. The pillow behind his head was damp with the amber-colored fluid seeping from his cracked skull. His eyes looked as if they'd been knuckled hard, and his face was peculiarly aslant, as if one half had slid slightly south of the other. He was grotesque and foreign. I found myself thinking of my mother and how she'd looked during her last days of life, her jaw shattered and her nose staved in from a boot heel.

What was I feeling? Supreme indifference? Fear? Relief? Horror?

No. Something far more familiar: anger.

I was angry that the dragonmaster had attacked Jotan, angry that his attack had provoked such a primal violence within me. Angry that he'd refused to readily succumb to our fists and teeth, and angry that he was in a coma and not likely to survive. Angry that now I'd have no dragonmaster to train my neonate bulls . . . *if* the bulls even came out of the cocoons. Angry at myself for using venom.

My head throbbed and I craved water and darkness and sleep.

The connate healer treated the wound over Jotan's left breast, where the dragonmaster had torn into her with his rotting teeth. Jotan sat stiffly on the edge of the dragonmaster's fine bed, her eyes closed, and she sucked in air, sharply, as the healer stabbed needle through flesh and pulled gut tight to close her wound. I flopped into a chair by the crackling fire

And fell asleep.

When Jotan woke me, the healer was gone. My neck was stiff. My mouth felt made of chaff. The fire had long since died in the hearth, and Jotan was dressed in a luxurious russet bitoo. The bitoo fell in many pleats and folds to the tiled floor, and the hood was equally lavish in cloth.

"We'll travel anonymously," Jotan said. Her voice still had that raw, erotic rasp from venom use and prolonged sex. She threw an armful of dove gray byssus at me and it landed with some weight in my lap and spilled about me. "Yours."

"What hour is it?" I croaked, rising to my feet.

"Well past morning."

"You should have woken me!"

"Herald Domtri is well on his way to Clutch Swensi to fetch Malaban. No, don't," she said with an arch smile as I started to slip out of the gown I was wearing. "That bitoo is an outer garment. You wear it *over* your gown, to protect yourself from inclement weather."

Flushing at my ignorance, I angrily tugged the slippery fabric over my head. It slid over me and pooled at my feet, soft and cool as snake belly skin against my bare arms.

"Why did your demon not manifest last night to subdue the dragonmaster?" Jotan asked.

I quickly looked up. I'd forgotten that while imprisoned, Jotan had once witnessed the violent power of my mother's haunt being channeled through my body.

"It's gone," I said abruptly. "The haunt's left me."

"Why?"

I adjusted the long sleeves of my bitoo to avoid her eyes. "I don't know."

"Ah." She didn't believe my poor lie but didn't know how my evasion might affect events.

Prompted by her question, I now had a question of my own. "A man known as the Wai Vaneshor of Xxamer Zu visited here not long ago—"

"The rebel Genrabi, yes. A former daronpu."

"You know him?"

"I told you: Since my imprisonment, I've made it a habit to know everything. I've trained certain servants to . . . aid me in the gathering of knowledge."

I nodded slowly. "Gen came here—"

"—with a request that Malaban find an illustrious post for a lordling being ousted from Xxamer Zu, so that the contents of the lordling's mansion might be used as barter for a destrier from Clutch Diri. An asinine scheme, if I may add, when the sale of slaves would have sufficed."

Either her spies were thorough, or Malaban shared his information freely with her. Somehow, I suspected the former. A merchant tycoon involved in sedition would not be prone to sharing all he knew with a venom addict created and wanted by Temple.

"Do you know where Gen went upon leaving here?" I asked, keeping my face blank, watching her face closely. One who gathers secrets, holds secrets. "He never returned to Xxamer Zu."

"He never left to return to Xxamer Zu." Her expression conveyed pleasure at knowing more than I did. "He flew direct to Cuhan."

"Cuhan?" I reached for the water urn on the table beside me. "Clutch Cuhan?"

"There's only the one."

I poured water and cursed my visibly trembling hands. "Did Gen say why?"

"No. Would you like my educated guess?"

I couldn't even bridle at her tone of relish. I nodded and swigged down mint-laced water.

Jotan's eyes glittered. "On the day Genrabi departed, the city was abuzz with the news that Lupini Re had flown his Djimbi Wai-ebani into Liru for safety reasons, then appropriated Clutch Cuhan for himself, on the grounds that Cuhan was harboring you, the dragonwhore, on the Cuhan estate. People love to hate you, Zarq. It's the one thing bayen and ikap-fen and Temple are united about: They all call for your death."

I sipped more water and forced my hands steady. One phrase in particular that Jotan had just uttered was making it supremely hard for me to focus on everything else she was saying: *Lupini Re had flown his Djimbi Wai-ebani into Liru for safety reasons.* My sister, Waivia, had recently been in Liru. Could be here still. Unaware of my distraction, Jotan continued. "While the reports flying from Clutch Cuhan didn't unequivocally state that you'd been captured, there *was* frequent mention of a Skykeeper. A Skykeeper! It was said that Lupini Re had summoned it for his holy mission to Cuhan. Genrabi flew to Cuhan to confirm the sightings himself. He'd many times called *you* the Skykeeper's Daughter in conversation with Malaban; he was alarmed, I think, to learn that a Skykeeper was aiding Lupini Re in a quest to find and kill the Skykeeper's Daughter."

How much did Jotan guess? How much did she know?

"And Gen's not been seen nor heard from since," I said hoarsely.

She nodded, her venom-blooded eyes devouring me.

"Did Kratt . . ." My throat was too dry for words. I sipped more water. "Did Kratt imprison him?"

"From what little I know of the man, I believe Genrabi had more wit than to announce his presence to Kratt in Cuhan. I've heard the Clutch was in a state of chaos, with heralds and Temple soldiers and Kratt's crusaders all thick in the air upon escoa and destrier. Perhaps Genrabi slipped in under cover of the confusion. He seems adept at disguise."

Very adept.

Again, I sipped more water before attempting to ask my next question. "This Djimbi Wai-ebani that Kratt flew to Liru . . . would you happen to know if she's pregnant?"

"As of two days ago, she is not. She gave birth to a bawling boy, delivered, I may add, by the same midwife one of my sisters uses."

I almost dropped my glass. "Kratt's ebani is still in Liru?"

Jotan's eyes narrowed slightly. "Yes. Why?"

"I . . . Do you know where?"

"I told you, I make it my business to stay well informed."

"Can you . . ." My heart was thudding so hard I could scarce speak. "Can you arrange a meeting between her and me?"

Jotan's eyes widened. "I fail to see why you'd wish to declare your presence to the Wai-ebani of the man who's mad-bent on seeing you dead."

I took a chance. "We're half sisters."

Astonishment parted Jotan's lips; then her face turned hard with spiteful glee. "How interesting life can be! Are others aware of this?"

"Kratt may know it by now. I'm asking for your trust and discretion that no one else learns of it."

"I see. Well. How very interesting indeed." Her eyes were dancing. "And you trust that your half sister won't deliver you direct to Kratt?"

"She won't." I said it without hesitation or doubt. If Waivia had the desire to deliver me to Kratt, she would have done so, using the might of the haunt, long before now.

"So it's to be just a brief visit of an auntie to see her new nephew?"

"Something like that," I said tightly. "Can you arrange it or not? Don't toy with me, Jotan."

She grinned, blinked basilisk eyes. "Consider it done. Would the morrow suit you for the visit? I know you're in a hurry to return to Xxamer Zu."

I nodded curtly and thanked her with as much grace as I could manage.

Jotan studied me a moment, head cocked to one side, then took a step toward me. "Zarq. You realize I have a problem."

She wasn't talking about her addiction.

"Here you arrive, a wanted woman hated by all. And you tell me you know how to breed bulls in captivity. You tell me you and a group of rishi have seized control of Xxamer Zu, a fuck-useless Clutch on the edge of nowhere that the insipid brother of Lupini Re recently won governorship of, because of a wager backed by my brother in Arena."

I set the glass down. Carefully.

"You ask for money," Jotan continued. "Arms. Protection. You want the Emperor's ships sunk, and help orchestrating attacks on other Clutches so that you can steal their bulls. You bring an insane old man who attacks me. You tell me your demon has abandoned you, for reasons unclear. But there's one thing you don't tell me. You don't tell me how you plan on breeding bulls."

I thought of the letters she'd written last night and wondered what, exactly, she'd written on them. Or if she'd even sent them.

I faced her squarely. "Am I a guest here or a prisoner?"

Her nostrils flared. "A guest."

"Until Malaban arrives and decides what to do with me."

"I don't need my brother's direction to make decisions," she said acidly.

"What do you want from me, then? I can't produce any bulls for you as proof; I need time for that—not much, just a little—and I need your help and the help of the people you know to buy me that time."

"I don't want to be made a fool of, Zarq. Understand? I don't want to be made a fool of."

It all came clear.

She knew what venom did to a person. The dragonmaster was a promise of the dementia that overcame all venom addicts. And Jotan was a venom addict. When she looked at him, she saw her own future, and it was that which she was fighting, not me. With her fierce belief in her superiority in the social hierarchy, with her intelligence and wit—she who had once been an instructor at the capital's institute for higher learning—she was terrified of losing her mind, her status, and the respect of others. Since her rescue from Temple's jail, her life had been reduced to the walls of the Bri villa; all she had left to her was her circle of spies, her quest for knowledge, her sense of superiority. If she were to be dismissed as a raving addict, she would lose all that. Venom would be the only thing remaining to her.

"What I tell you is truth," I said firmly. "I own a Clutch and I know the secret to breeding bulls."

Both half-truths.

"I won't end up back in Temple's jail," she said fiercely. "And I won't wind up a guest in Kratt's play chamber again."

So Kratt *had* romped in the fields of algolagnia with Jotan after stealing her and me from Temple's prison. I'd been convinced his intelligence would have overpowered his brutal urge to torture for pleasure. I'd been wrong.

"It won't happen again," I said.

She pointed at the dragonmaster. "I won't hesitate at doing that to you, if it comes to it. Understand?"

I nodded. I understood, all right: I had no dragonmaster, no allies save a ragged group of savage rebels, no clue as to what crucial detail I'd overlooked during the black rite performed upon me by Longstride's tribe, and Daronpu Gen—my once stalwart supporter—had correctly suspected I was not the Skykeeper's Daughter. To round it off, the woman under whose roof I was now abiding had just threatened to kill me, should she be so provoked.

Yes. I understood my situation perfectly.

I was not introduced to Jotan's mother. That had merely been a ruse of Jotan's to get me away from the dragonmaster, so that she and I could visit her venom supplier in the Ondali Wapar Liru, the Academia Well of Malacar's capital city. The ruse had been rendered unnecessary once Jotan had knocked the dragonmaster insensate.

"My supplier is a distinguished academician at the Wapar," Jotan murmured as she pulled aside one of the palanquin's curtains and peered out at the streets beyond. It was my first time within a palanquin, and I hated it. I felt ill from the rocking motion of the thing, balanced upon the shoulders of slaves, and disliked the confining, padded walls surrounding me. I tried to overcome my queasiness by concentrating on Jotan's words.

"He's one of Malacar's leading authorities on dragons and venom, but he's much disliked amongst his peers because he has no love for either the Emperor or politics. He cares only for the study of what he calls dragonscience."

"Yet he's allowed to teach," I said. "He hasn't been arrested."

"He's fa-pim, and he's a man."

"What do you give him in exchange for the venom?"

She remained looking out her window. "You'll see soon enough."

We fell silent after that. To distract myself from the rolling motion of the box we were enclosed within, I pulled back an edge of the curtain and watched the vast human beehive beyond.

Aviary keepers, musicians, astrologers, and necromancers swept along the cobbled streets, their roles of office indicated by the baskets of birds or gleaming brass instruments they carried, or the opulent gowns they wore. Bakers and confectioners and butchers worked behind fragrant shops of carved stone, and palanquins sat outside milliners' and jewelers' boutiques, their rain-soaked, half-nude bearers squatted beside them. Fa-pim bayen women with hair coiffed into outrageously tall topknots could be seen moving beyond the windows of fabric emporiums; when we paused at a corner because of traffic, I watched one woman examine herself in a mirror, passing judgement on a long brocaded robe faced with a black-speckled white fur from some northern beast.

We entered the central gate of the Wapar and crossed a garden court resplendent with flowering shrubs and tinkling fountains. The court was vast—as large as a small orchard—and tended by a clawful of Djimbi gardeners wielding shears and shovels and wheeling handbarrows. Up a flight of long, low stairs, past a saloon, a museum, a library, each grand building fronted by pillars and covered by friezes of geometric, floral, and hieratic motifs that informed the learned what lay within the fine architecture.

Jotan whispered the names of each building we passed with a mixture of reverence and bitterness. "The Pavilion of Hieratic Arts. The Royal Chamber of Music. The Hall of the Wapar Treasury. The Court of Physicians and Connate Healers. The Seat of Cinai Theologians."

It was before that last building we disembarked, and, concealing cowls up, we swept along a shadowy arcade of pointed arches, past fa-pim scholars engaged in debate and idle chat, into a cavernous corridor of carved marble screens. We passed a tight cluster of women, some brown-skinned, some aosogi, some fa-pim, but all dressed much as we were, a few—the youngest, I could tell at a glance—with their hoods boldly cast back. They paused in their murmured conversations to watch us descend a superb carved teak staircase.

The Wapar was not a place that welcomed women. I felt that in the shadows and dark spaces and the way the architecture dwarfed human life. I felt it in the spacious, austere courtyards visible beyond windows that barely let in light through dense stoneworks of arabesques. I felt it in how quietly the women had been speaking to one another, how closely they stood together, their shoulders hunched like the petals of flowers closed against rain.

I marveled at the boldness of those women, that they'd dared ventured within those cold walls to brave the Wapar's imposing masculinity, all in pursuit of knowledge. That some women even taught impressed me further. It was not hard to envision Temple soldiers marching down the stone corridors and arresting a woman on a trumped-up charge.

Just like a rishi, a bayen woman faced immense challenges, should she long to break out of the rigid confinement of Temple's patriarchal regimen.

"He's expecting me," Jotan murmured as we stopped before two great wooden doors twice our height. We were down in the bowels of the Wapar. Water dripped along the walls, and whispers ran like rats down the gloomy corridor. "He has no students today, nor entertains no visitors save me. But if someone *is* within, keep your hood up, remain silent, and follow me out at once."

The chamber beyond was shadowy and smelled of caustic soap and alcohol and sulfur. Watery light came in through the windows—high up, small, covered in perforated stone designs—and dust motes danced in the air. Our slippered feet *shushed* over the cool tiled floor, and the echoes whisked around the cavernous place. The doors squealed as Jotan shut them behind us.

Strange glassware cluttered tables alongside dripping alembics. Heavy ledgers lay alongside scrolls that were pinned open by rocks held in each of their four corners. Slates covered with chalked numbers and symbols and quantities of formulae covered the walls, between hexagonal scroll shelving and shelves laden with murky, indeterminate equipment.

"Who's this with you?" a voice barked, and I spun to face a sanguine man whose eyes swam in his head. His dark, oily hair was speckled with white, and it took me a moment to realize the white was a surfeit of dandruff. He was dressed in layers and layers of shirts and pantaloons, each layer apparent by the different colors and textures of cloth visible beneath rips and inadequate patches. Stuffed into one pocket was a wilted bouquet of hoontip blooms.

Jotan tossed back her hood. Even in the gloom I could see that her cheeks were flushed. "This is Zarq-the-deviant. Zarq, meet Komikon Sak Chidil."

Sak Chidil looked neither surprised nor perturbed to find the infamous dragonwhore from Re in his laboratory, though *my* heart thudded furiously at my identification being so glibly divulged. Jotan pulled back my hood so he could see me, and I slapped at her hand, but after a glance at me, Sak Chidil merely turned to Jotan. "Is she going to participate? I can't give you more than the usual."

"She doesn't want recompense," Jotan murmured.

"Come on, then," Sak Chidil said, and he barred the doors we'd come through by dropping a heavy piece of wood across them, then wove his way through the laboratory to the far end, pausing here and there to adjust a spigot beneath an alembic, or the position of a rubbery pipe, or to stir something with a pipette.

Jotan followed him, and, after a few moments of trying to recover from the shock of being exposed, I trailed behind.

"The infamous dragonwhore, hey-o?" Sak Chidil said. "How many times have you performed bestiality, then?"

When I didn't answer, he stopped fussing with an alembic and looked at me.

"Answer him, Zarq," Jotan murmured. "He's interested for scientific reasons. You're safe."

"Safe as anyone is," Sak Chidil barked. "Accident, illness, politics—something gets us all, in the end. Ten times? More?"

"I haven't kept count," I said frostily.

He waved the pipette he was holding at my face. "By your eyes, I'd say at least five times. That about right?"

I nodded. He looked pleased, placed his pipette down, picked up a ledger, inkpot, and quill, and turned to a small locked door. He handed Jotan the ledger and writing instruments, then withdrew a key from a dirty length of twine around his neck and inserted it into the lock.

"Inside, then," he muttered, shoving the door open. He picked up a heavy leather case that was sat beside the door like a dwarf sentinel. He waited for us to enter.

A venomous dragon resided beyond.

I knew it at once by the smell of venom, maht, manure, and hide, even before I stepped into the small stone stable. Sak Chidil locked and barred the door behind us, muttered to the shadowy form of the dragon, and crossed the room to where a second door was located. He ensured that it was barred before turning to where a rickety teapoy was shoved in a corner. He picked up the teapoy and placed it into a spot of light that was weakly streaming through the lone stonework window high up near the ceiling. Jotan placed his ledger on the teapoy, set the inkpot and quill beside it, and began to disrobe.

Sak Chidil set his heavy leather case on the ground, crouched before it, and unbuckled it. Inside lay an assortment of metal instruments and glass tubes.

"The dragon is docile," Jotan explained to me in a voice gone husky and slightly breathless. "She's both a pet and a study specimen for the theologians in the Wapar. Komikon Sak Chidil has trained her in the rite. He used whores before I came along. He's the only theologian in the Wapar who has, through his research, learned of the rite."

Her bitoo fell to the ground. Outer garment—ha! She was naked beneath.

The dragon—a placid dewinged female with clouded eyes—shuffled forward and nuzzled Jotan as if seeking a tidbit of crunchy snail or a fistful of sweet orchids. Her leathery snout bumped against one of Jotan's full, heavy breasts. Jotan pushed the dragon away, a mixture of impatience, disgust, and anticipation on her face. Her nipples were raised.

"You can have a turn after me, Zarq. Sak Chidil is interested only from a scientific perspective. Understand?"

I was staggered. Appalled. And envious. She would hear dragonsong.

Jotan lay on the floor and spread her knees wide. Sak Chidil crouched between her legs, carefully slid a steel instrument into her, then scraped what he'd gathered into a glass tube. He swabbed the inside of her mouth with another small metal spatula and slid the saliva into a bottle. He examined her eyes, smelled her breath, made notes. Jotan lay compliant, knees spread, eyes glassy, and staring straight at the high stone ceiling.

I had no idea what Sak Chidil was doing, by scraping and gathering bits of Jotan and putting them into glass tubes and bottles. Such bizarre behavior was alarming in the extreme. It reminded me, vaguely, of the methodical way potters figured out the best manner in which to make new glazes and clay types. But what, for the love of the Dragon, could Sak Chidil possibly hope to create from the bits he was gathering from Jotan?

The dragon snuffled over to her and, without preamble, went to work between Jotan's legs like a cur well trained but bored with its assignment, even as Sak Chidil kept touching Jotan's wrist, counting under his breath, and scratching quill over paper at intervals.

I whirled about and faced the door, breathing heavily, legs as soft as wet clay, and I rammed my fingers in my ears to block out Jotan's ecstatic cries and the wet snuffling of the dragon.

Afterward, Sak Chidil rewarded the dragon with the wilted bouquet of hoontip blooms he pulled from his pocket. The dragon serenely chomped them between her molars as Sak Chidil gathered more bits from Jotan's vulva, carefully inserted them into various glass tubes, and neatly labeled them. He checked the color of her eye membranes, bled her from one wrist, and carefully decanted her blood into more tubes. He took copious notes in his ledger, the scratching of his quill and the champing of the dragon's molars mingling with Jotan's weeping and ecstatic babbling.

"Your turn, now," Sak Chidil said, looking at where I stood rooted in one spot, trembling and aroused and appalled.

Would I?

Great Dragon, I wanted to hear dragonsong. I wanted it with every fiber of my being.

I stepped toward him.

Stopped.

"No," I said hoarsely.

"Are you certain?"

I wavered. . . . It took a great effort to nod.

"Too bad, then. Fresh samples always impart new information. Why not?"

"I . . ." I couldn't answer.

He shrugged, slightly annoyed, slightly disappointed, but not unduly upset. "Waste of your time coming then, wasn't it? Here, carry this back in for me. She'll be a while yet recovering."

I dumbly carried his ledger and quill and inkpot back into his laboratory. Jotan continued to writhe in ecstasy on the stable floor behind us.

"Good samples," Sak Chidil murmured in satisfaction as he carefully set his tubes of Jotan's blood and discharges in a rack on a table. "The whores' diseases taint their samples. Jotan is a superior symbiont."

"Symbiont?" I breathed. I found a stool and sat weakly upon it. I was drenched with sweat.

He glanced up at me with his swimming eyes. If he'd ever used venom himself, it must have been but once or twice. His sclera were as clear and blood-free as cooked egg white.

"A symbiont. An organism living in close physical association with another, yes? Here, roll these between your palms. I don't want the blood to coagulate yet." He handed me two stoppered vials of blood. I obeyed, dazed, overwhelmed. The warmth of the blood seeped through the glass of the vials. I was cupping a small part of Jotan between my palms.

"A symbiotic relationship is mutually advantageous to the two species involved," he continued. "There is the gilli bird and the screwbuck lizard. The remora and the shark. And the dragon and the human, yes."

He placed his remaining tubes of blood in a small, round receptacle, closed a lid on it, and began vigorously pumping a pedal with one foot. The receptacle spun around, faster than a potter's wheel. The odor of the man—unwashed hair, greasy clothes, and sulfur—wafted from his pumping leg.

"Take the gilli and the screwbuck lizard. The screwbuck has poor eyesight, moves slowly, survives on a diet of millipedes and termites. It leaches poison from its skin and digs burrows to sleep in. It requires warmth to live. The gilli bird roosts in the burrows of the screwbuck, and the screwbuck's poison wards away any egg eaters from its nest. The bird keeps the screwbuck warm during the cool Wet, and its excellent eyesight and skirl alerts the screwbuck to approaching danger. The seed eater does not compete with the lizard for food and is not affected by the lizard's poison. An ideal relationship, yes? Maybe now and then a lizard foot crushes a gilli egg. Maybe now and then the noisy gilli inadvertently alerts a mongoose to the location of a screwbuck, and the screwbuck is eaten. But mostly it's an ideal symbiosis."

He stopped pumping. The receptacle slowly whirled to a stop. He unlocked the lid and withdrew the tubes of blood. Clear amber serum had separated from the thick red during the spinning process.

"Now I ask myself, what purpose does it serve a dragon to sex a woman, hmm? So I look for answers. It's easy to see how a woman is lured into the relationship: She receives sexual gratification and is imbued with feelings of puissance from the dragon's poison. Of course, if she's not been gradually habituated to the poison, she suffers blisters, swelling, blood poisoning, skin sloughing, infection, erratic heartbeat, lowered blood pressure, eventual death. But as the poison makes for a fine hallucinogen and analgesic when diluted, a woman can readily be made tolerant of direct, undiluted doses of the dragon's venom."

He strapped a peculiar leather band around his head and screwed, above one eye, a glass lens into a round windowlike frame sewn into the leather. Carefully he lowered the bulging dome of the lens over his eye, magnifying his eye to many times its size. I stared.

"Keep rolling those vials between your palms, yes, like that." He carefully tipped a little serum onto a glass plate and smeared it thinly across the surface. "Good. So. We shall say that a woman is lured into the relationship with the dragon, even though the benefits are few and the risks are high. This is not an advantageous relationship for the human, but it is a compelling one. So perhaps the dragon is a parasite, yes? But why? What benefit is it to the dragon, all this?"

He bent and studied with his lens the sample on the glass. "Let us now examine the hallucinations a woman experiences while under the influence of venom. She is filled with empathy for the dragon. She imagines herself as a hatchling, hunted by men. She experiences maternal fear for the dragon. *Now* we are getting somewhere! Who is the main predator of dragons, hmm? Humankind. What greater way to neutralize an enemy than to make the enemy one's advocate, one's protector! So. Somehow, millennia and millennia ago, the ancestors of the Djimbi and the ancestors of the dragons began the peculiar symbiotic relationship that we frown upon today. Fascinating, yes?"

I made a breathy noise that he took as assent.

"Years ago, before I learned of the rite, I studied hatchlings," he continued, even as he scratched a quill over his ledger. "I was fascinated by the hatchlings' apparent urge to attack the human face. I did experiments, took measurements, and made a discovery. It is not the human face the hatchling instinctively shoots its not-yet-venomous tongue at: It is the human mouth. A wet, gaping, red hole. Much like the maw of a mother dragon, yes, only on a smaller scale. A food source! Maht comes from such a maw, and maht feeds a hatchling. So. When I learned of the bestial rite, I could see how the instinct of a hatchling could easily be utilized to train a dragon to insert its tongue into a woman. You have a question?"

He'd devoted his life to examining things, scrutinizing his surroundings, noticing minute changes. My face must have shown the question forming in my mind.

"You don't believe dragons are divine," I said slowly. I didn't, after all, phrase it as a question.

He snorted. "Certainly not. Nonsense inspired by venom hallucinations, promoted by the lore of primitives, upheld by scheming governments and theologians. Divinity, gah! There's no more divinity in the dragon than there is evil in the kwano snake. They are mere beasts, dumb results of change and time."

"And humankind?" I asked.

He glanced at me, one enormous goggle-eye dwarfing his lens-free one. "We are mere beasts. Dumb, with the potential for greatness, but we are incapable of achieving that greatness, will always be incapable of it. We are steered by primitive urges."

He looked pointedly at the little stable room where Jotan still moaned and wept in carnal bliss. "We are no better than humping snakes. And we never will be, dragonwhore. Never will be."

That night, long after Jotan had returned to her room, leaving me raw, naked, and musky upon my bed, I mulled over Sak Chidil's conversation.

His theories disturbed me, stole my sleep. I didn't want to believe that the dragons were as mundane as we humans, didn't want to believe that dragonsong was temporal hallucination, that the venom rite had evolved as a means of survival for the dragon.

If dragonsong were merely the hallucinations suffered by a venom-touched woman, then how come I, who had never witnessed shinchiwouk prior to entering Arena, had been able to imagine specific details of shinchiwouk in Temple's jail, upon receiving undiluted doses of venom direct within my womb? What about the magic I'd witnessed my mother perform during my youth, and the dark magics Longstride's people had performed? How could Sak Chidil explain the presence of the haunt, its ability to appear as a Skykeeper? Surely there were otherworld forces at work in our lives, and if so, why should they not involve the dragons?

Or might the haunt and my mother's pagan magics and my visions of shinchiwouk one day be described in terms as scientific as Sak Chidil had described the rite?

I didn't know.

I paced.

I fretted.

When my mind grew tired of flinging itself against the dead ends and down the dark tunnels Sak Chidil had presented it, I worried over other matters: my loss of the dragonmaster, the disappearance of Daronpu Gen, Kratt's megalomaniac crusade against me, my sister's use of the Skykeeper. As the dark hours of the night dragged toward the small hours of morning, my thoughts centered around the yamdalar cinaigours in the arbiyesku warehouse and around the rite performed upon me by Longstride.

What had I missed? I knew Tansan was right; the cocoons needed more than just heat and time to develop into neonate bulls, else over the centuries chance and circumstance would have produced, at some point, a bull.

Influenced by Sak Chidil's methodical pattern of inquiry, I stoked the fire in the hearth, dipped quill into ink, and sat before a table. I meticulously recorded every aspect of Longstride's rite, down to the detail of the musky smell of the matriarch and the raspy sound her necklaces of gold had made as she'd stooped over me. I then recorded the routines and actions of the arbiyesku, as pertaining to the cocoons. By then my inkpot was empty, my arm ached, my fingers were cramped, and I'd run out of firewood for the hearth. I lit all the candles I could find in my room and tucked myself under the quilts of my bed. The coir in the mattress groaned softly beneath my weight.

I reread what I'd written. Over and over I reread it, searching for clues. There had to be something in there, had to be. . . .

My vision began to blur. Dawn was coming. I was exhausted and thickheaded and cold. I wanted to curl up and sleep, abandon my fruitless search.

We are mere beasts. Dumb, with the potential for greatness, but we are incapable of achieving that greatness, will always be incapable of it. We are steered by primitive urges.

My eyes had closed; I jerked awake. I would *not* be a mere dumb beast. Screw Sak Chidil: A human could achieve greatness. I'd prove it to him.

I stared at the hieratics slumping and slithering across my pages, and my eyes grew heavy again.

We are no better than humping snakes.

My eyes jerked open again and I stared dully at the pages in front of me. I was getting nowhere. I needed sleep.

I was surrounded by women in snake masks. I read the hieratics I'd written without really seeing them. *The snake women surrounded the fallen dragon that was Longstride and circled her tightly.*

I woke up a little, and then woke up a lot.

I pawed through my pages. There. Yes. *The arbiyesku regularly eradicates the warehouse of any stray kwano snake that has found its way from its regular habitat in the jungle to the savanna, lured there by the fetor of the cocoons.*

I stared at the embracing dragontail membranes carved on the footboard of my bed, letting my thoughts slowly cohere, hearing again Sak Chidil's words in his laboratory.

A symbiont. An organism living in close physical association with another, yes?

Kwano snakes had breeding cycles that synchronized with a dragon's nesting habits. The suckers—the hatchling kwano snakes—lived like parasites upon a dragon until the sucker had developed the teeth and mouth of an adult snake, whereupon it detached from the dragon's skin and went about its life in the jungle canopy. This was common lore amongst all Malacarites; songs were sung about the bloodsucking kwano; the threat of the evil snake was used as a means of getting children to obey adult whim and rule; artwork depicted the evil kwano being vanquished by the One Dragon; passages recited by daronpuis in temples throughout Malacar warned of the kwano's insidious malice.

The kwano snake was a perfidious parasite. Everyone knew that.

But what if it wasn't a parasite? What if it was a symbiont?

Perhaps the yamdalar cinaigours required the presence of kwano snakes to transform into bulls, for whatever reason. Perhaps the snakes consumed the dead flesh and prevented rot. Perhaps the snakes emitted something through their skin, like how the sawbuck lizard secreted poisons to ward off its predators and in doing so protected the gilli bird. Who knew? I didn't. Perhaps one day someone like Sak Chidil would. But for now, the little I knew was enough.

Kwano snakes. Those masked women who had surrounded me during the rite had represented kwano snakes. They'd circled en masse around Longstride when she'd fallen to the ground and tucked her wings about herself to imitate a cocoon. They'd had suckers for mouths. How could I have been so obtuse?

Kwano snakes.

There was my answer.

NINETEEN

Waivia's midwife was a stocky, no-nonsense aosogi woman who was clearly annoyed at doing a First Master Lecturer of the Ondali Wapar the favor of permitting a student to accompany her on her rounds for the morning. But permit it she did, as per the request in Sak Chidil's letter I had refolded into my bitoo.

Dressed in the same dove gray outer bitoo I'd worn to the Wapar the day previous, with my fingers artfully stained with ink and a ledger crooked under one arm, I spent the morning following Waivia's midwife through the bustling streets of Liru and into the mansions of its most recently postpartum elite. Trying hard not to shoot amazed looks at the ostentatious decor of the mansions I was shown into, I instead frowned studiously at my ledger and took copious useless notes, all the while struggling to suppress my anxiety over my upcoming meeting with Waivia.

Once I'd been introduced as a student of childbirth research, I was immediately ignored by the women whose babies I made notes about, so although the disguise was a tedious one, it was sound. I was all but invisible.

Just before noon, we reached the palatial mansion of white stone in which Waivia and her infant were residing, the abode of a relative of Lupini Re's, Jotan had informed me.

We went through a court to a gate where large paras with brilliant blue facial cicatrices peremptorily stopped and questioned us. I waved my letter under their illiterate noses, and my midwife, who was known to them, vouched for my behavior. Once inside their gate, we were led by a stout eunuch into a large, dim room that reeked of heavy perfume and melting wax candles and was crowded with rugs, richly covered ottomans, and divans. At the eunuch's insistence, we pressed our thumbs upon an inkpad and imprinted them upon a sheet of parchment; then he led us outside and through another court, this one graced by a tinkling fountain, peaceful almond trees, and beds of dense hyacinths. Up a flight of stone stairs, along an overpass covered by an arcade dripping with lush red blooms. Into a tiled foyer, cool and well lit by many long, open windows. Caged songbirds trilled merrily about the perimeter of the room.

"The Wai-ebani is expecting you," the eunuch said, giving a shallow bow, and he pushed open two great teak doors and gestured for us to enter within. He didn't follow, and the doors were closed after us.

And there was Waivia, a barbaric beauty, her voluptuous figure stretched upon a divan as green as wet emeralds, a cascade of thick, tawny curls spilling lazily over her shoulders and hips. She was undeniably Djimbi, and the oil she'd used on her warm-tinted skin highlighted her sage whorls.

Upon a marble table beside her, glasses of fruit ices sweated. At her feet, in a lace confection of a bassinet, slept her babe.

The midwife kowtowed. Heart hammering, I followed suit. When I rose from the floor, I briefly swayed from the pounding of blood in my head.

Waivia's eyes were brilliant, like orbs of translucent orange-brown chalcedony, and they looked only at me. The midwife muttered an explanation about my presence, but Waivia flicked a hand at her to cut her off.

"The baby is sleeping. Wait outside in the foyer till he rouses. The student can remain with me; I've questions for her concerning her studies."

I was slightly alarmed by Waivia's careless dismissal of the midwife; Waivia should have waited for a more opportune moment to subtly arrange for us to be alone. But no, that was Waivia: twice as impatient as I, and scornful of guise. The midwife was used to the ways of the bayen women she served. She merely kowtowed, tight-lipped, and left the room.

Waivia and I stared at each other. My mind was blank.

"Thirsty?" She lazily gestured to the glasses of sweating fruit ices beside her. I was outrageously thirsty, but couldn't move from where I was stood, staring at her.

"I thought you were dead," I said, and my throat was tight and my vision was blurring with tears. My body began quaking, as if I were ill. "All this time . . . Why didn't you . . . ?"

I didn't know what to say. How to express all the anguish I'd watched our mother go through because Waivia had been sold as a sex slave to the glass spinners' clan a decade before? How to summarize the grief and suffering I'd experienced during our mother's mad attempts to buy Waivia back, the obsessive stalking the haunt had subjected me to most of my life thereafter? The guilt I'd grown up with for how Waivia had been treated compared to me; the inadequacy I felt in the face of our mother's protective love for her; the loneliness, the helplessness, the frustration, the anger . . . ?

"I was only nine," I said hoarsely, and tears spilled down my cheeks. She rose from the divan, supple and smooth, and she flowed toward me and embraced me, held me against breasts warm and full of milk, and I sobbed, and once again we were sisters.

"It wasn't your fault," she whispered against my head. "It wasn't your fault, Zarq. I'm sorry."

She was my sister. I'd known her voice while in my mother's womb. She'd carried me about upon her back when she herself was but a child; she'd taught me to walk. Every night of my youth, it was the sound of her breathing beside me that had lulled me to sleep, the gentle, rhythmic fall and rise of her chest beside me each dawn when I woke.

"It wasn't your fault," she murmured over and over, holding me in arms so familiar, rocking me slightly from side to side, as she, too, wept.

Eventually she led me to the divan and made me sit. Gave me a silk hankie to wipe my face with, then thrust a glass of fruit ice into my hand.

I gulped it down, diaphragm still spasming, sounding like the nine-year-old child I felt I was.

She sat beside me and we looked at each other. Slowly adulthood crept over me again, but how I loathed it and all it entailed. I was weary from the burden of strife and responsibility; I wanted to be held and comforted and protected by my big sister forever.

Of course, I couldn't be. She was the Wai-ebani to Kratt, a man on a mission to rid the earth of my presence.

"What are you doing in Liru, Zarq?" she asked, and the last vestige of belief that she could hold and protect me in her arms forever was driven away by the question.

"I had business here."

"Business connected to Xxamer Zu? That *is* the Clutch you live in now, isn't it?"

"I don't know that I have a place I can call home anymore." I hadn't meant to sound petulant and evasive, nor rancorous. "Will you direct mother's haunt to assist Kratt in his takeover of Xxamer Zu, the way you directed her to help him seize Clutch Cuhan?"

"I needed Cuhan for my son to govern in the future. Xxamer Zu means nothing to me."

Yet, I thought to myself.

She shifted, became all brusque business. "I have arranged passage for you on a Xxelteker ship that leaves from Liru tomorrow at dawn. You'll go with enough funds to set yourself up in Skoljk, a city port in Xxeltek that apparently rivals Lireh. What you choose to do with yourself there is up to you: have babies, own an emporium, become a midwife. As you will. Kratt will never learn where you went. You'll be safe."

The allure of it was overwhelming.

Her infant stirred and cried, and I thought of Agawan, Savga's baby brother, and I thought of our own brother, hidden by Daronpu Gen in a Hamlet of Forsaken somewhere. Our brother, a young boy who'd been torn away from our mother at birth and later used by Kratt as an object of cruel pleasures.

I wonder if Waivia even knew of his existence.

Waivia lifted her baby from the white froth of lace at her feet, smoothly bared a breast, and suckled her babe. Intense jealousy swept over me and I could barely breathe.

The babe, I immediately noticed, had skin as ivory toned and pure as the Emperor.

"Will the charm on him render him impotent?" I asked harshly.

Waivia didn't glance at me, her gaze focused on the babe pulling at her breast, his tiny hands clenched into contented fists.

"When the appropriate time comes, the charm will be lifted and he'll be as fertile as a bull," she said calmly, though I heard sharp steel behind her words. She looked up, met my eyes with her tawny agate ones. They were cold. "The ship's name is the *Zvolemein*. You must board her tonight, under cover of dark. The captain will be expecting you; use the name danku Cuhan Kaban's Kazonvia."

"You move fast, to have arranged this with such short notice of my visit."

"I saw no sense in delaying."

I glanced down at the puckered face of the swaddled infant cradled in her arms. His face was so tiny compared to her massive breast; I was gripped by a sudden urge to unwrap him, to place a cheek upon his small belly, rest his tiny feet in one of my palms.

I wondered if I'd ever see him, or Waivia, again.

I rose to my feet, throat again tight, heart hammering hard. "So. The *Zvolemein*. Thank you."

She looked up at me, eyes shuttered. She'd already shed her tears; she'd already told me it hadn't been my fault. She'd apologized for what I'd had to suffer through for her sake, and she'd arranged my safe passage out of her life.

She'd already said good-bye to me.

I turned and swiftly left the room, before my tears could fall again.

TWENTY

The Conservatory of Herpetology stank of rotting plants, algae, piss, and another smell, not entirely identifiable, but reminiscent of years' worth of guano steaming in the sun after a recent monsoon. Beside me, Malaban Bri wore a sour expression.

Malaban Bri was a barrel-chested man with eyes outlined heavily with kohl and front teeth overlaid with gold. A shadow of several days' stubble coated his cheeks, emphasizing the dark circles under his eyes. Travel-sweated and weary, he'd arrived at the Bri villa just as I'd returned from my visit with Waivia. Now he stood beside me, less than an hour later, surrounded by hundreds of glass tanks roiling with kwano snakes, while Jotan toured the dockyards for a suitable whore.

"If I could just have you press your seal here, Bayen Hacros," the conservatory superintendent murmured.

Malaban brusquely stepped toward the man's desk—a great wooden structure wet with rot—and impatiently pressed his seal into the hot wax the superintendent had drizzled onto the docket of sale.

"I want my escoas loaded promptly and ready to fly out as soon as possible," Malaban demanded as he peeled his seal from the docket. "I'm in a hurry."

"They're being loaded as we speak, Bayen Hacros." The superintendent rolled up the docket, eyes glistening in the oncoming gloom of dusk. "Such an impressive offering yours will be, with all the hundreds of snakes you intend to burn at temple. A death in the family?"

Malaban Bri gave him a cold look and didn't answer, and the superintendent colored, murmured an apology, and gestured for us to follow him up a set of algae-slick stone stairs to the roof of the conservatory.

The superintendent should have known better than to inquire into the personal reasons why a man such as Malaban had chosen to buy so many snakes direct from the conservatory, instead of from the hawkers' kiosks located around every temple within the city. Such a grand purchase usually indicated a grievous sin on behalf of the purchaser: forced sodomy, murder, theft . . . some act that required, for those who could afford it, much forgiveness from Temple and the One Dragon. The conservatory kwano snakes were sold by the hundreds each day to those wishing to earn favor in the One Dragon's eyes by paying to burn the snakes upon a temple altar. Really, the superintendent should have known discretion was required.

We ducked through a warped wooden door onto the conservatory roof. The sun was sinking in the cloud-clotted sky, and a light rain was blowing off the bay. The wet air made me shiver as it touched my nape. Dressed in the kid-leather breeches, waistshirt, and fur-lined jerkin Jotan had given me, I looked nothing like the student who'd earlier accompanied a midwife to see Wai-ebani Lupini Re. I couldn't help but glance nervously from the setting sun to Malaban.

"We'll leave before dusk," he said without looking at me, and he strode toward Lords Etaan and S'twe, who would be accompanying us back to Xxamer Zu, along with several of their heralds mounted upon escoas laden with bamboo crates of kwano snakes.

I bit my lip nervously. Where was Jotan?

As if in answer to my concern, the door behind me squealed open and Jotan came onto the rooftop, panting as if she'd run.

"I found one," she said, taking my hands into her cool ones. "Dark haired, aosogi, roughly your height. She boarded the *Zolvermein* as I watched."

My teeth chattered. "What if she loses nerve? She—"

"You'll be away from here shortly. Those escoas are fresh and strong; by the time the sun sets, you'll be long gone."

"We're unarmed. If she sends mounted paras after me . . ."

We both knew who I meant by *she*.

"Fly swiftly. Reach Xxamer Zu as soon as you can. I paid the whore well, and she seemed eager enough to start a new life under the name of danku Cuhan Kaban's Kazonvia. She knows she's to receive the monies your sister purportedly entrusted to the ship's captain, upon docking in Skoljk; that's a powerful inducement for her to keep her mouth shut and sail to Xxeltek."

I nodded and we looked at each other, realizing that this was farewell.

"Come with me," I said hoarsely. "Leave Sak Chidil behind."

"It's my choice, Zarq," she said firmly. "I know there are alternatives; your Daronpu Gen offered me one, a charmed purgative. I refused. This is my choice. Don't waste your pity on me."

Malaban Bri hailed me; the escoas had been loaded. Time to flee the city, before the sun set and darkness made flight impossible. Time to bring my precious cargo of kwano snakes to Xxamer Zu—and swiftly, too, for crammed as they were in those bamboo crates, the snakes would be dying of stress, suffocation, and cannibalism if we dallied.

"I'll send word when the dragonmaster breathes his last," Jotan said, her cold hands still in mine. The dragonmaster lay in the Bri villa, his life seeping from the crack in his skull. "Now go. Go."

We embraced, quickly, and she nipped my neck, below my right ear. Then she spun and left, and moments later I was mounted upon a frisky escoa with Malaban Bri, and the cupolas and temples and whorehouses and factories of Liru and Lireh were falling behind us.

We camped overnight at the same ganotei han the dragonmaster and I had used on our journey into the capital. In pairs, we shared watch through the night, and we left as the first greenish light cracked open the predawn sky.

Long and hard we flew that day, as the crated snakes grew lank from heat and confinement. By late noon we reached Xxamer Zu. Upon my direction we landed at the arbiyesku.

No sooner did our lathered escoas touch down upon the sun-bleached savanna behind the warehouse than we were surrounded by rishi, as well as several hostile myazedo rebels. Malaban Bri slowly dismounted, as did I. Lords Etaan and S'twe remained mounted. So did their heralds, who looked supremely uneasy at our reception.

Bonfires raged in the cocoon warehouse; I could see the flames through the gaping holes that had been knocked into the walls, and the smoke that curled up into the overcast sky through the holes that had been punched through the warehouse roof. A waste of wood, those fires. The cocoons required kwano snakes as well as heat.

I moved forward, but a rebel stepped in front of me and pointed a sword at my belly. "One step more and I'll gut you like a fish, bayen filth."

I froze. It was Alliak, and he didn't recognize me, dressed as I was in a bayen man's clothes.

Behind me, I heard Malaban Bri growl in his throat. "Do you greet all invited guests in this manner?"

"It's me: Zarq," I said hoarsely to Alliak. "I mean, Kazonvia. The hatagin komikon's roidan yin."

His suspicion left no room for him to observe the truth. "Get on your hands and knees," he growled.

"Alliak—"

"On your hands and knees!"

Slowly I obeyed. No sooner did my knees and hands touch earth than he brought the broadside of his sword across my rump. I howled in outrage and pain and leapt to my feet. He slashed the sword at me as I spun to face him, and if not for all my training as a dragonmaster's apprentice, steel would have bitten deep into my skull. As it was I barely moved in time, and the tip of his sword hissed across my cheek, slicing it open in a white-hot, thread-fine line.

"Alliak!" I bellowed. "Put your sword down!"

Malaban Bri was shouting something, the escoas were snorting and rearing, people were both surging forward and backing up, and the snakes in the crates thrashed and hissed.

Alliak shouted something at me that I couldn't understand for the roaring in my head. Malaban Bri bellowed a response. Faces. All manner of blades pointed at me: pitchforks, coraks, swords, scythes.

"Where's Tansan?" I cried. "I'm Kazonvia. I'm a *woman*." I fumbled with my jerkin to bare my breasts, but they must have thought I was going for a weapon, because as one they surged closer—

Then a voice rose above the others: "Back away from her! She speaks truth! She's a woman, and she's myazedo."

Tansan. She pushed herself to the fore and stood before me, fine, strong shoulders straight, hips balanced, arms held easily at her sides. She was dressed still in the bloodstained white shirt and dark bayen men's breeches that she'd worn during the takeover of the Clutch.

As she stood there—a formidable force of calmness and authority—I dizzily remembered what the dragonmaster had said of her: *There's more to that woman than what's apparent. I've seen the way these myazedo obey her; she uses dark magics, I'm sure of it.*

Weapons slowly lowered. Those who surrounded us moved back. I was woozy, and my head was buzzing, and my ear, where Alliak had struck me, was as hot as liquid wax. I reached a hand toward my ear; only the lower lobe remained. My ear had been cut off.

I let out a string of curses so foul eyes around me widened. For one wild moment I heartily regretted sending the unknown whore onto the *Zolvermein* in my stead. Then I clamped down on the turmoil of emotions clashing within me and shoved aside the brutal reality that I'd just been mutilated, again, for life.

Swaying, clutching the bloody place where my ear had once been, I stared with blurred vision at Tansan. "For the love of wings, who did you think we were?"

She frowned. "We almost shot you down from the skies with crossbows. Communications between Ghepp and Kratt have been tense, and when it became clear you had no intention of landing at the messenger byre—"

"Ghepp's managed to keep Kratt away?"

"Barely." Her eyes flicked to Malaban Bri. "The myazedo will have seen your arrival from the stockade. A contingent of armed rebels should arrive shortly; they'll escort you back with them."

The crowd pressing around us showed no sign of dispersing. My legs were starting to give way beneath me. Tansan turned and smoothly spoke to Alliak in Djimbi. He barked at the crowd, which reluctantly began drifting away.

Tansan turned back to me. "You need tending. Savga shouldn't see you like this."

I shook my head and almost fainted from the motion. "We first have to unload our cargo into the warehouse. The snakes won't last another night in those crates."

"Snakes?" Tansan's voice was calm, unhurried.

"Kwano snakes. The cocoons won't be able to transform into bulls without them."

Her face momentarily slew sideways, and I would've pitched groundward if Malaban Bri hadn't foreseen my swoon and moved beside me.

"Kwano snakes are deadly, Zarq-the-deviant." Tansan's voice had dropped low, and her eyes were now opaque. My news was straining the tenuous trust between us, and I could see in her face that I was bucking an age-old belief amongst Clutch rishi about the kwano being demons incarnate . . . a belief started and perpetuated by Temple.

"Not deadly. Not demons," I gasped. "In destrier stables, we decapitate kwano suckers without being harmed—"

"Adult kwano snakes are different from suckers. Adult kwano have fangs."

I mustered every ounce of conviction I could and by sheer will forced my vision and voice steady. "A kwano snakebite can cause sickness, yes, which can fester and cause death, but the snakes aren't venomous. The kwano are snakes, mere snakes, and if we don't unite them with our cocoons, in eight weeks' time nothing will emerge from those involucres but maggots."

I could see her swiftly recalling the conversation I'd last had with her, when I'd revealed to her my past and the secret to breeding bulls in captivity. I could see her remembering her own voiced doubts as to why, over time, a bull had never emerged from a cocoon by chance; could see her realize how the daily cleansing of the warehouse of any stray snake—if such a snake were necessary for the cocoon's transformation—would effectively remove the possibility of a transformation ever taking place.

As I did the night we seized Xxamer Zu from Ghepp, I forced myself to wait for her to leap over yet another hurdle and trust me.

"So we unload the snakes now," Tansan said at last, the scar on her chin gleaming white as alabaster against her dusky, whorled skin. "But we can unload the snakes without you. You need to be treated, debu via."

For the first time, *debu* didn't sound derogatory, coming from her lips.

I didn't join Malaban Bri and Lords Etaan and S'twe in their meeting with Chinion, for that night I slept soundly in the arbiyesku compound, drunk on fermented maska milk, Savga curled sweet and small at my side. Tight-lipped and shoulders stooped with worry, Fwipi had dressed my ear before I'd passed out. It was clear she was afraid of the vast changes occurring in her life.

I didn't join Malaban Bri the day following, nor the day after that. My journey to Liru, my visit with my sister, my passionate intimacy with Jotan, and my damning use of venom all left me supremely reluctant to be around talk of rebellion, or to be around Malaban Bri and his bayen cohorts. I was filled with an urge to reconnect to the Clutch serfs of Xxamer Zu and to the land itself; I felt a need to cleanse myself of the ostentatious wealth of Liru and heal myself from Waivia's resolute farewell. I wanted simplicity and hard work and camaraderie to surround me. I wanted to feel honest sweat run down my back.

I needed to purge myself of weakness.

I joined one of the tree-felling teams camped in the scrubland to the south of the Clutch, where the savanna buckled into tree-dotted hills, which, in turn, after several miles, grew into jungle-covered mountain. The felled trees were needed to keep the bonfires burning in the cocoon warehouse; working on providing that firewood was where I was most needed.

With much protestation, Savga remained behind at the arbiyesku with Fwipi and her baby brother, Agawan. Piah accompanied me to the tree-felling teams, but after several days of backbreaking labor, he decided he disliked being so far from myazedo headquarters, the messenger byres, and the exhilarating information daily arriving of the skirmishes igniting in Lireh.

Thunk of ax biting into wood. Gleaming muscles swinging steel under a brooding, heavy sky. Clank of chains as felled trees were hitched to brooders; grunts of dragon and human straining against a tonnage of deadweight. Nights sleeping beside smoldering fires on a coarse grass mat.

The daily toil of Clutch life continued alongside the upheaval of a Clutch readying itself for possible invasion. While the daronpuis' larders were systematically emptied and the goods distributed, and while hoes worked clods of parched soil at dawn and dusk, the old Xxamer Zu forge sprang into an activity that it hadn't seen for half a century. Bayen pots, jewelry basins, and metalwork of all sorts were gathered from the bayen thoroughfare and forged into crude swords, even while women gave birth, the sick and elderly died, and Ghepp sent missives to his brother while Malaban Bri and his cohorts schemed with the myazedo leaders behind closed doors.

The swing of my arms wielding an ax. The smell of sweat. My desire for venom fiercely, desperately pushed deep within me.

Piah appeared one dusk, a mere week after I'd joined the tree-felling teams. I sat alone, sucking a bitter slii stone and contemplating what I intended to start on the morrow: teaching my people. I thought I'd hold lectures each night in a different part of the Clutch, and begin educating the rishi. I was so engrossed in my thoughts that I didn't notice Piah wandering amongst the clusters of rishi that were gambling and chatting upon the tree-shorn hillock, until he stood directly before me.

His prominent larynx bobbed in his throat as he grinned widely at me. "News, hey-o."

"Of?" I asked quickly.

"The Great Uprising, what else?" He looked positively smug.

He dropped down onto the dirt in front of me, picked up a brittle grass blade, and stuck it between his lips. "Delegates were sent to Ordipti, in the Vale of Tigers jurisdiction in the east. Apparently Clutch Ordipti is well-known for hating the Emperor. They were told to gather kwano snakes and light bonfires in their cocoon warehouse, so that neonate bulls can emerge from the virile cocoons housed there. Our secret's been shared, hey-o."

Jealousy and outrage flared up in me, that *my* secret had been passed on to others. But almost at once the base emotions subsided under a flood of cold reason: We needed allies and we needed bulls; what better way to obtain a great deal of both than by widening our circle of strength to include those already opposed to the Emperor's rule?

"There's more news," Piah said, enjoying not only my rapt attention, but that of those within earshot. He raised his voice, the grass blade in his mouth bobbing up and down. "Five Archipelagic merchant ships were sunk in Lireh this week, and a dry-salter emporium owned by an Archipelagic lord was burned to the ground, the same night a Temple gaol was blasted open."

"And Chinion? Has he mobilized any of his myazedo camps into action? And what about Ghepp? Has Kratt demanded that Ghepp cede Xxamer Zu to him?"

"Kratt's been busy elsewhere, thanks to Chinion." Piah looked as if he would burst with satisfaction. "Temple ordered Kratt southwest, to Clutch Bashinn."

"Bashinn?"

"Chinion's rebels attacked Bashinn, murdered daronpuis, torched stables, liberated most of their destriers. A bloodbath, hey! They did the same in Clutch Maht, but with one big difference."

He waited. I waited. People had stopped their gambling and conversations; everyone was listening. Piah was milking the moment for all it was worth.

Alas, I've never had patience for such drama.

"For the love of wings, Piah, just tell us," I snapped.

His grin went from ear to ear, grass blade falling to the ground.

"The rebels stole Maht."

I dared breach the silence that followed. "Maht *the bull*? Chinion's myazedo rebels stole Lupini Maht's *bull dragon*?"

"Rumor has it the bull flies here tomorrow, accompanied by dragonmaster Ordipti and half his apprentices."

"Here?" I virtually squealed.

"Here."

Exclamations, cheers, and animated conversation exploded around

us. I can't remember much of the impromptu celebration that followed—dizzy dancing, maska wine suddenly appearing from hidden kegs, music from drums and bamboo pipes—but I do remember thinking this: Time to go back. Time to go home, to the arbiyesku.

The next day, I did.

It was as Piah and I were shambling through the murk of a peevish morn, down from the wood camp to Xxamer Zu, that the skies overhead came suddenly alive with wingbeats.

We stopped. Looked up. Gaped.

Looking like a small mountain encrusted with amethysts and emeralds, the massive bull dragon, Maht, slowly soared over our heads, his enormous outspread wings like rippling sheets of amber. The skies around the great bull were *clogged* with destriers that had been stolen from Clutch Bashinn and Clutch Maht, ridden by dragonmaster Ordipti and his apprentices. It was as if the firmament were a vault of jewels spilled across azure cloth; dragon after dragon winged overhead, scales like cut peridot and bloodred garnets, tourmaline and rubies, jade and red zircon, brilliant against the diamond clouds.

The sound of so many dragonwings flapping and gliding sent a shiver down my spine. It was a wet, membranous sound that was palpable, as is the memory of wind through damp hair on a twilight eve. My scalp tingled as the myriad dragons poured in a steady stream toward the center of Xxamer Zu.

Beside me, Piah breathlessly tried to count them aloud and lost track somewhere around forty.

I felt small, yet empowered. I felt elated, yet terrified. I wanted to tip back my head and expose my throat to the sky and howl. In my blood and bones I could *feel* everyone throughout Xxamer Zu stopping their morning activities to watch the jewels in the sky rain down upon our Clutch like a blessing; I could feel their awe at the massive mauve-and-beryl mountain that was mighty Maht in flight.

"When our bulls hatch, will they grow that big?" Piah murmured in wonder.

"Hush," I whispered, as if he were interrupting a supremely sacred ceremony, one that joined day with night, the world of the eye with that of the soul.

When it was over—when Maht had landed on the southwestern outskirts of Xxamer Zu, and when every destrier that had accompanied him was likewise landlocked—I felt as if I were coming out of a trance. Piah and I looked at each other, dazed and wordless, and then, slow and hot like a wind-fanned fire, grins broke across our faces. Fierce grins. Grins of determination and pride.

Grins that bespoke a fury of belief in ourselves.

Nashe—the Hatching—had begun.

TWENTY-ONE

Alliak moved fast and brought his staff down hard toward my head with an overhand swing. I spun under and away from it and, with a backhand slice, brought my own staff across his midriff. With a *woof* of air, he went down to his knees.

We'd been fighting for several furious minutes in an alley, swinging crazily, our missed blows hissing like cane switches through the night air and hammering like mallets against the ground. Flamelight from the tall torches that we'd pounded into the ground prior to our clash danced over our sweating bodies.

As I'd intended, we'd drawn a crowd.

I felled Alliak and stepped away from him. The crowd watched askance as Alliak rose with a grimace.

"The series of moves that I just used"—I panted, addressing the gathered men—"is called zahi hawass merensen: water crashing down the chute. Dragonmaster apprentices use it while fighting one another in Arena. I'll do it again, slowly, and then *you* can try it against me. If you're not afraid." I pointed to a big, broad-bellied man who looked as if he'd move as slow as setting gruel and sooner die than admit to being afraid of a woman.

Everyone was taken aback by my speech; idle spectators don't expect, nor want, to be drawn into the drama they're watching. I'd thrown them off balance, especially as I was a woman, and a woman who was fighting. They stared at me for several heartbeats; some of them hastily turned away, as if I were doing something shameful. The man I'd pointed to looked confounded; should he leave? Should he stay? Why him? What was going on?

Alliak could have nodded at the man in that noncommital way men often have with one another, but he just stood scowling at nothing in particular. He'd agreed to participate only because Tansan had strongly encouraged him to do so and, I suspect, because of the opportunity to take a few swings at me.

I raised my staff and nodded at him to attack again. He looked ill pleased and obeyed with a little more force than was necessary.

A few of our spectators left. Most moved back a bit but stayed to watch, giving themselves enough distance to readily leave should they so choose. But Alliak and I were a diversion, a good story to talk about later. Entertainment didn't happen often for rishi, so why pass it up?

More boys and men gathered, to see what the commotion was about.

As the crowd grew, Alliak's attacks seemed less of a mock fight and more like the real thing. Several times I bellowed at him to stop, so I could explain to the crowd the position a leg should be in, that a groin might be protected, or the stance of the torso, to shield the heart. He always stopped with ill grace. I'd use Piah as a sparring partner next time.

The crowd continued to swell.

When I eventually drew my chosen participant into the torchlight, I had to request that those in front crouch down, so that those in the back could see. With the larger crowd had come acceptance of the spectacle; aping a great fighter, the big man swaggered into the light, flexing his muscles to hoots of encouragement.

I took several rather heavy blows that I could have dodged, and there were many cheers and guffaws from the crowd. I parried and dodged the rest, though; with his great arms, the man was capable of crippling me. He fought stoutly, with heart but little skill; when I'd had enough, I swept his feet out from under him, and the crowd roared good-naturedly. I bowed to my opponent and held the position while he lumbered to his feet, panting. After a pause, he chose to make light of the situation, grinned, and theatrically returned the bow. He received several claps on his broad shoulders as he returned to the crowd.

"Zahi hawass merensen." I projected my voice so all could hear. The group was comprised mainly of men and boys—all rishi, Clutch serfs—but several women and young girls hovered at the back. The spectators settled down again and waited for me to continue. "Zahi hawass merensen: water crashing down the chute. Those words are comprised of seven hieratics, the first of which is water."

I approached one of our guttering torches; at its base lay several lumps of charcoal from an arbiyesku fire. I bent, picked one up, and I scribed upon the back of the nearest tenement the hieratic for water: three cursive parallel lines.

A moment of astonishment in the crowd, followed swiftly by swelling fear: The Emperor forbade all Djimbi from knowing how to read and write, and the punishment for a Djimbi doing so was decapitation.

Heart pounding, I spoke, voice clear and strong.

"We're a free people, free from hunger and Temple. Now we need to free ourselves from ignorance. A staff that can strike a blow to the body can also be used to strike a blow to the mind: We can burn the ends of our staffs and use them as quills. We won't be afraid of the scholar's art, no more than we are of the swordmaster's. In this Clutch, *our* Clutch, we'll claim the power of reading and writing for ourselves."

The silence that followed was so complete I could hear every sputter of flame from the torch warming my face, an arm's length from where I stood. Trembling a little, I turned back to the tenement wall.

"This is Nieth," I said as charcoal rasped over wood. "Nieth means things are equal. It's comprised of the symbols for bow—here—and arrow and heart—here and here—because when the heart is centered, as an arrow fits into a bow, it's balanced. Nieth."

I turned around again.

They were watching closely, realization dawning on their faces: They were learning a forbidden skill, and no one was going to stop them. No one, ever again.

They were realizing the full extent of their freedom.

Though I saw the same epiphany light other faces over the weeks that followed, it's the memory of that first night that I treasure most: my charcoal glyphs scribing the breadth, width, and depth of possibility that awaited them. It wasn't just glyphs I was drawing upon the walls. I was writing a whole new future.

Days were swallowed by nights. My sparring partners varied: Sometimes Piah accompanied me, sometimes Myamyo, sometimes Keau. Occasionally I brought old Yimtranu with me, the crone from the Poultice Zone with whom Savga and I had boarded. She was a font of medicinal lore, and the knowledge she shared with the women and children who clustered at the crowd's fringes was received like water upon a drought-blasted land. Mothers thirsted for cures for their children's festering cuts and ear infections, for ways to alleviate fevers, dull pain, ease childbirth. Yimtranu showed them what healing plants they could forage in the savanna and jungle, now that Temple daronpuis wouldn't—*couldn't*—flog them for practicing pagan arts. Sometimes old women in the crowd would remember things Yimtranu had forgotten: Slowly knowledge was resurrected. Liberated. Shared.

Each day I worked. Sometimes Savga worked alongside me, if I was in the arbiyesku. But there was so much work to be done, and I drove myself so relentlessly, I wasn't in the arbiyesku three days out of eight. Trees had to be hewn and transported from the jungle's edge. Bonfires had to be kept lit. Land had to be tilled, vegetables dug up, water fetched. Brooders that had begun secreting death wax had to be collected from the egg stables and convinced—by means of hobbles and stakes—to hunker down amongst the bonfires in the warehouse.

My debilitating venom-withdrawal attacks had to be suffered through, and my yearnings for dragonsong.

With every sleep I dreamed of Jotan Bri and the ecstasy on her face as she'd offered herself to Sak Chidil's venomous dragon. Since I'd imbibed the dragons' poison in her mansion, a hole had ripped open in my soul, and I feared—how I feared; or was it hoped?—that I would weaken, and that like Jotan I'd find some way, any way, to regularly indulge in the sensual numinosity of venom and dragonsong.

So my new addiction became this: Every day I worked, and every night I roamed the Clutch, drawing listeners as I disseminated fighting and writing skills, Yimtranu's healing lore, and my radical ideas. That's what an addict does: replaces one obsession for another. Work replaced venom. Teaching, dragonsong.

People came to see me. They came by the clawfuls. I was a curious mixture of entertainment, propaganda, novelty, and erudition. I inspired; I outraged; I educated; I empowered. Me, the aosogi-via who wore a bayen man's jerkin and leather breeches. Me, the One-eared Radical who preached against the oppression of women and Djimbi and the barbarity shown dragons.

I could *feel* the Clutch changing. Its pulse was beating faster, its muscles flexing, its bones growing stronger, straighter. The changes frightened me, even though change had been what I'd wanted. Change embraces the unknown, the unpredictable; few of us readily embrace either. I, alas, proved no different from most in this regard. So I kept busy doing what needed to be done. Yes. Yes. I was doing *good*. I kept busy and exhausted, because exhausted, I fell asleep quickly, like plummeting off a cliff, and had no time to worry, to wonder, to fear. To crave. I worked and I worked, and that work was my shield that protected me against both my base needs and the changes I was provoking. Frightening, vast changes that affected not just a Clutch, but an entire nation.

Don't think on it.

Work.

As I worked, myazedo rebels were flown in from Chinion's other camps. I saw them sometimes—gaunt, wild-haired, and keen-eyed—listening from the back of the night crowds that I drew. Sometimes I saw hard-looking aosogi men lurking there, too: ikap-fen operatives from Liru. Dragonmaster Ordipti's apprentices, when given leave from the confines of the heavily guarded destrier stables to search for female company, also squatted amongst the rishi gathered before me; the apprentices' old whip scars glistened like white snakes upon their bodies. Groups of Forsaken were brought to Xxamer Zu from their Hamlets, for their own safety and to provide the Great Uprising with much-needed labor; I saw them, too, in my crowds, telltale clay disks pierced through their lower lips.

During my nightly roving I also learned while I taught. I gleaned information about what was happening throughout our nation and beyond: Xxelteker corsairs were suddenly thick on the Derwent Sea, plundering Archipelagic ships. In the southwest and northeast of Malacar, Clutch Bashinn and Clutch Maht were harried again and again by the mysterious Chinion's myazedo rebels. Granaries and crop fields were torched. Incendiaries were hurled into the bastions where the overseers lived. Kratt was still in Bashinn upon the Ashgon's orders, and was suffering heavy losses from the rebels' attacks. And, too, I learned when the Ashgon deployed a regiment of holy soldiers to Bashinn, so Kratt could return to Re. Clutch Maht no longer had a bull dragon; the Ashgon didn't bother to send soldiers *there*. What was the point? A huge success: In essence, Clutch Maht now belonged to the myazedo leader, Chinion.

In Lireh, the rebels who called themselves Kindlers disobeyed Temple curfews and harassed Temple soldiers. Temple responded with beatings and arrests. The Kindlers rejoined with murder. In a marble palace in Liru, an ebani—her name unknown to history—poisoned the lord who kept her. Overnight no one was safe: Servants poisoned their lords and ladies with abandon, and inadvertently poisoned one another and themselves when aristocrats demanded that their domestics taste their food before they did.

Skirmish after skirmish, death after death, arson after arson: Decades of festering resentment erupted into purulent brutality in Liru and elsewhere. The nation was intoxicated by insurrection, went mad with murder.

It wasn't all *my* doing. No. It had existed before me, all that violence, that primal need for freedom. I couldn't be blamed for the deaths, the pain, the loss and grief. Please, no. Surely, no. I couldn't.

Work.

Work.

Drown my worries in exhaustion. Divert my fears. Deny my cravings.

Like a magnet I was drawn to the pottery clan of Xxamer Zu. At the time I didn't realize it, but looking back, it's clear: my night teachings took me closer and closer to flesh-and-blood family. Closer to my roots. Until one night I saw my mother in the crowd.

My mind went blank; Piah's staff connected hard against my back. I went down. Blacked out. When I came to, I'd been rolled faceup. A circle of women surrounded me, my mother amongst them.

Her hair: glossy as a wild animal's, falling to her waist. Mahogony, shot with gray. Her eyes, trapped by wrinkles. Concerned and a little frightened.

"Would you want water?" she asked. Her voice was deeper than my mother's, and raspy, as if she smoked waterpipes like a man. Indeed, I could smell oily tobacco leaf on her. "Can you sit?"

"I thought . . . You're not . . ." I struggled to gather my wits. "Who are you?"

Lips: black from a lifetime of sucking slii stones to dull hunger. Teeth: cracked or missing. A canker sore on her upper lip. Papery hands, soft on my arm. "I am Mawenab, from the danku. If you can stand, teacher, you should join us for the night. He hit you hard, hey."

She shot a withering look at Piah, hovering above the crouched women who protected me from the press of the crowd.

"Wasn't your fault, Piah," I croaked. "I wasn't paying attention. You taught us all a good lesson tonight."

He smiled gratefully and looked a question at me. Would I come back to the arbiyesku? Or stay?

I was not brave; my first instinct was to flee with him. But then I gave in to weariness, to the ache in my heart and the ache where he'd struck me.

"I'll stay in the danku tonight," I said, and my pulse sped up, for it felt as if I were divulging a shameful secret. Heat surged up my cheeks.

He nodded, and the danku women clucked about me, pushing the gawkers back, easing me upright, bashful in and honored by my presence. With an arm draped about two of the women, I was taken into the danku.

I saw a hint of my sister in the face and carriage and full-hipped sway of an adolescent girl walking before me. I saw a glimpse of my mother in the chin gestures of an old woman who had gums as wrinkled and black as raisins. I heard Mother's laugh from the woman on my left. My chest hurt so much, I was certain my heart was failing.

Up rickety wooden stairs, into the danku women's barracks. Gentle smiles, fleeting touches. Water. Food. Toddlers staring wide-eyed at me.

They didn't recognize my mother in me. I was bursting with words I was too frightened to utter: My mother was born here! You're my navel auntie, my greatmother, my niece. But I couldn't reveal my identity to them; I was the One-eared Radical, respected for how I inspired, for what I taught. They knew me and accepted me as that, and I was afraid, so afraid, of being turned away should they learn I was more—or less—than what they thought I was. I'd been turned away by kith and kin too often in the past. I wasn't brave enough to risk that happening again, even at the cost of forgoing the very family I was afraid to lose. Don't ask me where the reason is in that. There is none. Only fear.

See? I'm not brave and admirable, when stripped to my core. But I wonder: Are any of us?

"Sleep now," Mawenab rasped, her old-lady hands stroking my brow. I was stretched upon a sleeping mat; the wine I'd been given had been spiked with something. "Sleep."

"Mama," I whispered. And I slept.

I awoke late morning to shouts. I at once remembered where I was, and bolted upright with a gasp. The barracks was empty; the clamor was coming from outside. My mouth felt as sticky as drying sap.

With a thumping head I clambered to my feet, staggered to the door, and flung it open. I stopped, momentarily blinded by light; beneath my feet the stairs jiggled as someone rapidly mounted them.

"Teacher! Teacher!" A small hand grasped mine. I opened my eyes; it wasn't Savga, but a girl about her age, and her eyes glistened with excitement. "A bull has hatched! Come quickly; they're taking it into the stables; we're all going to see it!"

Women were ululating and clinging to one another, swinging around and around. Young men were vaulting off one another's backs. Old folk were beaming, weeping, lifting arms to the sky in praise of the One Dragon. Somehow, I'd come full circle back to my ninth year in the pottery clan of Clutch Re, for I'd last seen such joy and celebration when the dragonmaster had honored our clan by choosing Dono to join his apprenticeship.

Old Mawenab—my navel auntie—came partway up the steps. Tears coursed down her wrinkled cheeks. She held my hands within her soft ones. "Join us, teacher," she said quietly. "Our joy is yours. Bull wings have hatched upon Clutch Xxamer Zu."

"One of our cocoons?" I sounded as stupid as I felt.

"We are blessed, teacher. Truly."

We joined hundreds of others who were surging toward the old daronpuis' stockade. My heart pounded overloud in my ears. I was too stunned to feel the fierce triumph that was rightfully mine. A queer sort of disbelief disengaged me instead.

"I did it," I murmured as I was jostled to and fro by elbows and knees and feet. I couldn't see where we were going, not really: thatch roofs, tenement buildings, the red bricks of caravansary walls. A crush of people.

I realized we'd reached the market square only when I saw the domes of the temple looming before me. It was frightening, the surge and swell of the crowd. I felt as if I were drowning in it.

I was separated from Mawenab in the crush. For a moment I felt panicked and grief-stricken. I looked from face to unknown face, seeking her. She was gone. Lost to me.

No. Not lost. I knew where she was, knew where the danku would always be. I had met my navel kin; they'd sheltered me, fed me, accepted me. I had their respect. That was enough. My panic turned to relief. I could go celebrate my victory with my family.

And family, I now knew, is not necessarily those who share one's blood.

TWENTY-TWO

"Dance with me, Savga, dance!" I cried, whirling her around in my arms. She squealed and leaned back, legs locked around my waist, hair fanning out like black cornsilk as we giddily spun to the wild beat of drums.

I backed into someone, stumbled, and Savga and I tumbled to the ground in a fit of giggles.

The whole arbiyesku was dancing beneath the twilight sky, save those who were pounding a furious celebratory rhythm upon upturned kettles and water barrels. The elder women of our clan clapped their hands in swift syncopated time, while the old men, grinning toothlessly, whooped a peculiar song that sounded very much like a triumphant battle chant. All across Xxamer Zu, similar revelry was taking place.

Now I was bursting with fierce pride. *My* Clutch. *My* bull. I had done it.

The beat of the song changed, became slow, sensual, heavy. I looked up from where I held Savga pinned down and was tickling her. Tansan was walking into the center of the clan compound, and the others who'd been dancing fell back, giving her space.

A single woodwind pipe breathed plaintive notes into the twilight air as the smell of woodsmoke from the bonfires in the warehouse mingled with the wild, windswept smell of the savanna. Tansan started to dance.

Slowly her hips rolled one way, then the other. Her breasts were lifted high and proud, her neck tall. Her black, iconic eyes reflected the very same fierce pride that I felt, and as they fell upon me, my breath caught in my throat and a flush spread over my cheeks.

She didn't move; she *flowed*. Straight shoulders, powerful arms, smooth skin, voluptuous hips and thighs and chest . . . Her dance was arresting. Slowly she came toward me. Closer. Closer. Till I was looking up the length of her legs to where she stood above me. While still dancing, while the woodpipe plaintively cried into the wind and the drums beat like the heart of the savanna itself, she extended a hand down to me. I rose to my feet, entranced.

We moved, she and I, the heat of her body infusing my limbs with swarthy emotions, the grip of her dark eyes relentless. One by one, she chose other women of our clan to join us, and we danced.

Then I turned and saw Longstride standing at the end of the arbiyesku, near the cocoon warehouse. Longstride, with the matriarch beside her. Surrounded by her tribe.

I came to an abrupt stop.

The woman on my left bumped into me, stumbled, stopped, causing the woman beside her to likewise falter. A domino effect followed as around the circle, women stumbled to a halt. I felt, rather than saw, everyone follow my gaze. The drums and the pipe music staggered to a halt.

Tansan spoke first. "Why have they come, Zarq?"

My face must have shown something for her to ask such of me. I swallowed, shook my head.

"Don't know." I had to force the words out.

Tansan's eyes searched mine. "Is it them?"

For a moment I'd forgotten that I'd told her all about the rite enacted upon me in the jungle. I nodded.

"So. Let's go greet them, yes?" She sounded so reasonable, as if suggesting drinking bushtea with friends.

Savga's hand slipped into mine.

Surrounded by my clan—Fwipi on one side of me, little Savga and her mother on the other side—I approached Longstride and the matriarch. I wouldn't have liked to approach them alone. Longstride's amber eyes were as fierce as a wounded wildcat's. The matriarch stood beside her, swathed in a glittering, pearl-pink blanket. The blanket was covered in tiny shells, all stitched on by gold thread. Where she'd obtained such thread—or even the many gold necklaces around the matriarch's proud, straight neck—was beyond me. Behind me, my clan murmured at the sight of the fine blanket, that cascade of necklaces.

The matriarch's face was a slab of imperturbability. Beyond her stood her tribe, packs on their backs, loads borne upon travois dragged by the strongest men and women. It looked as if they'd dismantled their camp.

Some of the myazedo rebels who guarded the cocoon warehouse stood with swords unsheathed, watching tensely, keeping a distance . . . barely.

Longstride spoke, chin lifted. She was still wearing my lock of hair braided into her own.

"What did she say?" I asked. I glanced sideways at Fwipi.

Fwipi clucked. "You think there's only one Djimbi language in all this big-far land? Gah! There's clawfuls. I know them as well as you do."

"There must be someone on Xxamer Zu who speaks their language," I said.

"*Must* be?" Fwipi shook her head. "Because you will it?"

On the other side of me, Tansan shifted. "Djekid speaks a little. In the hills, his path crossed this tribe's occasionally. Piah will fetch him."

Piah peeled away into the gloaming.

We stood and waited. The bonfires in the warehouse crackled and snapped. Night settled over us. One of the arbiyesku women wondered aloud if we should offer the strange Djimbi food and drink. The notion didn't seem logical; the mood was one of a standoff. None of the matriarch's tribe had squatted onto their haunches to rest while waiting. Everyone stood, eyes upon me. None of us had sat down, either. No one seemed comfortable with the thought of sitting, let alone eating together.

In the distance we could hear the booming of kettledrums and the muted whoops of celebrants.

The waiting was interminable.

At last we heard two escoas overhead; they were barely discernible against the dark sky. They landed near the warehouse; Knife-carver and Malaban Bri dismounted from one escoa, and a richly attired aristocrat and a myazedo rebel with two long braids dismounted from the other. Malaban Bri nodded at me and faced Longstride and the matriarch.

Longstride's eyes swung to Knife-carver; she said something to the matriarch, who gave an imperceptible nod. Longstride demanded something; Knife-carver responded with a few words in Longstride's language, but Longstride cut him off with a stream of vitriol. She held her spear steady and jerked her chin disdainfully in my direction. The rebel Two-braids shifted and glanced at the aristocrat beside him.

I acknowledged the fear that had begun to grow within me: The matriarch's tribe had come to collect the debt they felt I owed them.

Knife-carver and Two-braids bent their heads together and exchanged words. They apparently both understood a little of Longstride's language. I wondered which of them was Djekid.

Knife-carver spoke again to Longstride. Again she cut him off, her bearing and tone even more contemptuous and angry. Two-braids knelt and sketched two crude dragons in the dust, one with plumes jutting from its head. He haltingly said a few words and pointed at me. Longstride scornfully lifted her chin in agreement.

Knife-carver shot me a look that chilled my guts; then he turned to Malaban Bri, who had listened as impassively as had the matriarch opposite him. The aristocrat beside Malaban remained silent, his neatly groomed beard gleaming with oil in the firelight.

"This one"—Knife-carver jerked his chin at me in unconscious imitation of Longstride—"promised the tribe a winged yearling and a neonate bull dragon, in exchange for the secret to breeding bulls in captivity. The tribe has come to collect the promised dragons."

"Is that so, Zarq?" Malaban asked, glancing at me. His kohl-encircled eyes were somber.

I had difficulty finding my voice. "I don't speak their language. Maybe a promise was implied by my participation in their rite. . . . I don't know."

Malaban nodded slowly, thick neck barely moving. He knew all about the bitter sting of rites. His sister, after all, was Jotan Bri. His huge chest slowly inflated, slowly deflated. He looked at the matriarch again.

"So." His resonant voice carried across the crowded arbiyesku compound. "We have a problem." He glanced at Knife-carver. "This tribe goes by any name?"

"They call themselves the Kwembibi Shafwai," Knife-carver said. "The Silent Slayers."

"Strong name."

"Strong people."

"Honorable?"

"We don't want them for enemies."

"Have they come to join us in our fight against the Emperor?"

Knife-carver smiled thinly. "They care for nothing but what directly concerns them. They want the bull and a yearling."

"And then?" This from the aristocrat who'd remained a silent observer up to that point.

"They'll move on, return in a year or so to the jungle mountains near here. Maybe." Knife-carver shrugged.

"But what happens to the dragons?" the aristocrat said irritably. "Do they intend on breeding them?"

Again Knife-carver smiled thinly. "They'd be hard-pressed to prevent a young bull from mounting a yearling, hey-o."

"Not acceptable." The man glared at Longstride and the matriarch. "We can't have Djimbi savages breeding dragons whenever they please."

The entire arbiyesku tensed.

"Djimbi savages?" I said.

"What I'd be interested in knowing," Malaban Bri smoothly interjected, "is how they're so certain we *have* a young bull to give them."

Knife-carver looked at me accusingly.

"I never left this Clutch to tell them," I said heatedly. "Every night I've been here, every day. I have witnesses. Hundreds."

Knife-carver posed Malaban's question to Longstride. The matriarch herself replied. Her answer was brief.

"She has dragonsight," Knife-carver translated.

"Dragonsight," Malaban Bri rumbled, and for a moment every flame in every bonfire froze, and the silence of the endless savanna swooped down on us and reduced all of us to the mere inconsequential wisps of bone and flesh that we were.

The eerie stillness was broken by the matriarch.

She stiffened, then spun about and cried out to her tribe, her voice as strident as a screaming falcon's. She flung her arms wide . . . and her tribe went berserk.

Children shrieked and ran madly for the cocoon warehouse, followed by men and women, all scattering like maddened ants. Our warehouse guards tried to stop the swarm with shouts and raised swords, but they were overwhelmed. The Silent Slayers swarmed up the sides of the warehouse, spears strapped to their backs, clambering for the roof. Longstride hefted her spear into the air and began a keening that ripped up and down every nerve in my body.

"What are they doing?" Malaban shouted at Knife-carver.

"They're screaming, 'The roof, the roof.'" He shrugged, shook his head. "I don't know."

Tansan lifted an arm and pointed into the dark skies. "Something comes."

We all stared and saw it. A shimmering blue star moving through ebon sky. Growing swiftly larger as it approached, swelling rapidly to the size of a luminescent moon. I was filled with dread presentiment. I recognized that phosphorescent blue. . . .

"No," I whispered. "No."

Above the cacophony of the tribe swarming up the sides of the cocoon warehouse, it seemed impossible that I'd been heard. But I had. Tansan's fingers bit into my arm. "What is it, Zarq?"

"A Skykeeper," I hoarsely replied.

The luminescent moon was no longer round but elliptical in shape, with two great bluish white sails projecting from either side. Wings.

"Is it yours?" Malaban knew who I was supposed to be: the Skykeeper's Daughter, the Dirwalan Babu.

I shook my head: no.

"Kratt's," he said grimly, and I marveled at the stoicism of the man, at his ability to accept the surreal even as it approached with preternatural speed.

The Skykeeper was now clearly identifiable as the massive other-world creature that it was. My clan began running for cover, shrieking. Tansan shouted at her mother to take Savga and Agawan into the women's barracks, but Ewipi was already running, Agawan in her sling, Savga's hand in one of her own. Dragonmaster apprentices and myazedo rebels likewise ran for cover, and I wanted to join them; I did. But instead I stood and watched, because Tansan stood immobile beside me, and I wouldn't run if she didn't. No.

Those of the tribe of the Silent Slayers who'd gained the roof stood shaking their weapons defiantly at the creature about to descend upon us, their children standing on the shoulders of adults with reckless bravery, raising spears to the sky. Women, too, clambered atop the shoulders of men, who stood with legs braced and calves quivering, lifting them to the sky. The Skykeeper swooped nearer—I could see the fish-belly white of its brisket, where luminescent blue feathers parted under the speed of its descent—and the Kwembibi Shafwai shrieked asinine defiance and stretched spears up to the swooping monstrosity, ignoring its massive, outstretched talons.

Tansan and I dropped to the ground and covered our heads.

The Skykeeper was upon us.

Its skirl cracked the night sky asunder, and the ground trembled, and talons the length of saplings and blazing with spectral light raked across the cocoon warehouse roof. Bricks thudded into involucres and bonfires, splattering ribbons of rotting flesh and fiery logs and branches People shrieked as talons ripped off the rooftops of domiciles. Timbers flew through the air like hurled spears; domicile thatch shuddered loose and rained to the ground. Insects showered down from their nests in the women's barracks as timbers split and crashed into buckling reed-matting walls.

The smell of necrotic flesh was thrown over Xxamer Zu like a vast and reeking caul. The Skykeeper skirled again and continued its flight over the Clutch, its extended claws shredding and cleaving and wreaking havoc and death in its path. The sound was horrific: wood screaming as it died.

No. Not my Clutch. No. My hands clenched dust and I wept in fury, afraid to raise my head and watch.

Then the otherworld creature ascended into the dark sky, rattling timbers and cracking tile with its unearthly shrieks, and was gone.

People had been injured and trapped by the shower of debris. Malaban Bri worked alongside Knife-carver and me through the night, always keeping me in sight, however surreptitiously.

The Kwembibi Shafwai did not aid in uncovering the trapped and wounded. The Silent Slayers looked after their own injured; several of those who'd gained the roof had died during the Skykeeper's assault. Come dawn, the Slayers were flensing the corpses.

"They eat their dead," Knife-carver informed us, giving one of his ghastly smiles. "To honor them."

I did not like Knife-carver and I did not like Longstride and her people. Though really, when I think of it now, there's not much difference between giving one's dead to a gharial to consume and then consuming the gharial, and merely consuming one's dead directly. It's only other people's customs that one finds repungant, never one's own.

The arbiyesku had a tally of three dead. Fwipi was amongst them. She'd been crouched over Agawan, Savga's infant brother, when a brick from the cocoon warehouse had slammed through the reed matting wall of the women's barracks and into the side of her face. Since I'd found Savga huddled beside Fwipi's body in the debris, she'd insisted on remaining by my side, Agawan strapped to her back. Tansan was keening over Fwipi's body.

The destruction in the arbiyesku compound was horribly reminiscent of that which had been wreaked in danku Re, during my youth, by a maddened yearling Kratt had flown into the pottery compound. Life goes in circles. I found myself gripped with a strong urge to hide in a small corner and rock myself to sleep.

I wondered if Mother was aware of the consequences of what she was doing. I suspected not. The haunt's obsession with protecting Waivia had multiplied with each passing year. That obsession was like a virulent growth; it had sucked everything good and humane from the haunt and left behind only destructive malignancy. At least, I hoped that was the case. The alternative was too appalling to consider: that the haunt—my mother—was aware of what she was doing, but was nonetheless obeying Kratt's desires, expressed through Waivia.

Why would Waivia wish harm upon Xxamer Zu?

Because Xxamer Zu was the seat of Nashe, the center of the Great Uprising that would end Temple's reign; and Kratt, the half bastard of a Xxelteker ebani, wanted to *become* Temple through the acquisition of as many Clutches as he could. Waivia wanted the same power and wealth for her son. It was sheer speculation, conjured by a shocked and exhausted mind. But I *knew* Waivia. I knew her determination, her mental prowess, and the vicious survival streak in her that had been exacerbated, if not created, by the cruel bigotry shown her as a child.

"You'll accompany me back to headquarters," Malaban Bri said, surveying the wreckage and the rishi toiling amidst it. It was just after dawn; Knife-carver was approaching with one of the two escoas that had run in panic, hobbled and wing bolted, at the Skykeeper's appearance. Malaban Bri and I stood side by side, soot-streaked and covered with straw and jute litter. The bonfires were still raging in the warehouse; Malaban had made it his first priority after the Skykeeper's departure to ensure that the fires remained lit, so that the few undamaged involucres remained heated.

"Zarq?" he said.

"I heard."

I glanced down at Savga, who was looking up at me with those bruised and fierce eyes of hers.

"Stay with your mother, Little Ant," I murmured, placing a sooty hand gently upon her back and pushing her away from me. I refused to think of Fwipi, of the way she'd looked when I'd found her, her head turned at an impossible angle on her broken neck, her face a bloody mess from the brick. A child should never have to witness such. But they do. They do. "I'll be back. Promise."

Shoulders hunched, Savga moved away a pace, then turned to watch me mount the escoa.

Malaban and I launched into the sky and flew toward the stockade at the center of the Clutch.

We landed in the messenger byre and I instinctively glanced at the shadowed corners, expecting Auditors to appear. Unnerved and exhausted—and drained by the image of Fwipi's crushed face that kept swimming to the fore of my mind—I silently followed Malaban into what had formerly been Xxamer Zu's Hives, the chambers where the Clutch Daron stored precious copies of Temple scrolls in the floor-to-ceiling hexagonal cells that filled the room. The smell of ink and incense and old paper mingled with the reek of tobacco.

Rutgar Re Ghepp—the erstwhile Lupini Xxamer Zu—was amongst the grim-faced men who awaited Malaban Bri and me. Ghepp looked almost as disheveled as we did.

His fawn silks looked slept in. He'd lost weight, looked sleep-deprived. But he was still beautiful, and he sat amongst his captors as if he were one of them. On second glance, I realized he *was*. The myazedo's liberation of his Clutch had worked somewhat to his advantage; thanks to my insistence that Ghepp be kept alive to parley with his brother, he was still a key player, surrounded by powerful men. Only now, others were responsible for the welfare of the Clutch, and he was free from being solely accountable for making difficult decisions.

He regarded me with thinly veiled hostility and leaned forward, a muscle working over one of his sculpted cheekbones. He reminded me of a notched and drawn arrow.

Malaban Bri summarized the night's events, including his encounter with the Kwembibi Shafwai. He listed the tribe's demands and then introduced me, giving a brief history of what he knew about me—a far less detailed summary of my life than that which I'd given Knife-carver and Tansan. Save for Malaban Bri and Ghepp, I didn't recognize anyone. I shifted uneasily. Thought of Fwipi. Thought of Savga. Pushed the thoughts away.

A neat aristocrat in lavender silk interrupted Malaban. "This rishi before us is Zarq-the-deviant?"

"That's one name she goes by," Malaban said, unperturbed. "She was introduced to me as the Dirwalan Babu. The Skykeeper's Daughter. She's onc and the same who told me the secret to breeding bulls and she learned that secret from the Kwembibi Shafwai."

A stir in the room. The eyes that regarded me held varying degrees of revulsion and shock, save for those of one swarthy lord; his eyes glinted with lust.

"She summoned that creature last night?" Lavender Silk asked, voice rising.

Malaban turned to me. "Zarq? Did you?"

"Malaban, that Skykeeper *attacked* us."

"Not at your behest."

"No!"

"Coincidence that this tribe appeared just before the Skykeeper did, and that you're known to them," Lavender Silk said.

"They didn't summon the Skykeeper. You weren't there; you didn't see—"

"You call yourself the Skykeeper's Daughter, rishi via."

"Damn it, *Kratt* sent the Skykeeper!"

"Kratt?" Lavender Silk's preened eyebrows arched. "You're saying Waikar Re Kratt controls a creature of the realm, and not you?"

My mind was spinning. "My sister controls it. She's with Kratt. It used to obey me but—"

"Now it does so no longer," Ghepp interrupted, his tone curdled. "You require the rebel daronpu to control it, and he's conveniently not present. Yet again, he's departed at our time of need."

"Gen returned? When? Why didn't someone tell me?" Confused, I looked to Malaban for answers.

He asked a question of me instead. "Can Dragonmaster Re control this Skykeeper? He turned against you in my villa; would he use the creature to get at you here?"

"The *dragonmaster*? What's he got to do with this? And he's dead by now, surely."

A pregnant silence.

"No," Malaban rumbled beside me. "His room was discovered empty two days ago, and one of my escoas gone."

Not possible.

"Jotan?" I asked.

"She was out." By his tone, I knew precisely where she'd been. "The handservant she kept in her room was found dead. Head staved in."

I remembered the malice fomenting in the dragonmaster's unnatural eyes when he'd spoken of Tansan: *No one ties me up without suffering for it.*

The dragonmaster was alive and loose.

"I suggest we appease my brother's wrath and prevent another attack from his creature," Ghepp said, addressing the men around him. "Give him this deviant."

"I don't see why she's even amongst us," Lavender Silk said. "You've done ill, Malaban, succoring this heretic."

"I'll remind you—" Malaban began tightly, but I interrupted.

"Kratt's not after me. Not now, not anymore. He thinks I'm in Skoljk. The Skykeeper's attack was a warning not to proceed against Temple."

Ghepp's beautiful nostrils flared. "I won't have my alliance with my brother ended over your presence in my Clutch."

"*Your* Clutch? *Alliance?*" I was near to tearing out my hair. "You're a hostage, you idiot, and whatever *alliance* you think you have with your brother is worth shit! He's been occupied in Bashinn, and that's the only reason he hasn't attacked us before now. Don't you see? Kratt's got his sights on governing all of Malacar; he wants to be the next Emperor, and he'll stop at nothing to achieve that. *Alliance,*" I said bitterly. "He's playing you for a fool, and using Temple's might to achieve his own ends."

A stupid outburst: Kratt had usurped Ghepp's birthright and always made Ghepp feel a fool. Ghepp flushed and his almond eyes went glassy. "Send her to my brother."

"Strange powers stir in the land," Malaban growled, and I could scarcely hear him, my heart was pounding so hard with fury. "If Zarq has the ability to influence these powers, we should deliberate long and hard before giving her to Kratt—"

"Imprison her." Ghepp's eyes were tearing me limb from limb.

I should've held my tongue. I *tried* to, for all of several heartbeats. "You will not lock me away again," I said, voice low. "You did once, and I escaped. Try it again, and I'll kill you."

Ghepp surged to his feet. His chair thudded against the floor. "You hear? This deviant bitch threatens me! Send her to my brother."

"Where's Chinion?" I cried. "Why're there no myazedo rebels in this room?" I rounded on Malaban. "We need Djimbi elders on our council, people who know and understand the old magics. Not these *flowers*."

Outbursts from several of the men; two rose to their feet in indignation.

"We're not concerned with useless paganism, rishi via!" Lavender Silk cried above the others.

"Send her to Kratt!" another shouted.

"Gentlemen!" Malaban boomed, and he slammed fists upon the table. Silence. He glared around the table. "I've not forgotten who first informed me of the secret to breeding bulls in captivity, and I expect some of you to remember who first informed *you* of it. If Zarq's to be given to Kratt, we discuss it behind closed doors."

He didn't look at Ghepp as he spoke, but Ghepp's finely chiseled nostrils went white with rage nonetheless. Ghepp knew Malaban was implying that decisions shouldn't be made with Kratt's brother present.

"We imprison her, then," Lavender Silk said.

"She's not our hostage," Malaban rumbled. "She brought us the secret."

"She's a liar and a swindler and a deviant. Someone else gave her the secret; *that's* clear to me."

"She can be kept under close surveillance until we reach a decision," Malaban Bri said, immovable. "This council will recess while Zarq and Rutgar Re Ghepp are escorted back to their quarters."

I could see how Malaban had risen in power to become the successful tycoon that he was; his commanding presence brooked no argument.

Sullenly, the lords of the council acquiesced.

TWENTY-THREE

I returned to the arbiyesku on foot, flanked by armed soldiers.

Cinereous smoke occluded the air, sludgy and dense as fear. Thatch was strewn about like batting from a gutted doll. Mud-brick huts had been butchered and fractured. The distilled sound of grief keened through clotted pockets of silence.

The Skykeeper's flight over Xxamer Zu could be precisely mapped by the trail of lacerated huts its talons had left behind. Just that, understand: a trail. Not widespread destruction. Not rampant ruin. Just that one smoking path.

A warning.

I reached the arbiyesku depleted. It was late noon; those who'd had to work the fields—regardless of death of family or friend—had picked up hoe or scythe or spade and trudged to the fields. Their backs were bent, their shoulders stooped. The damage the Skykeeper had done was much wider than that one path, after all. Fear is like the wind: invisible, invasive, unfettered by paths and trails.

The bonfires still blazed in the ruins of the cocoon warehouse, heating the few intact involucres and baking into hard ribbons the shreds of splattered cocoons. The tatters of keratin and flesh smelled peculiar as they curled in the heat. It was an aborted smell, that. The smell of necrosis charred, of decay smoked and preserved.

Instead of marching around the outskirts of the warehouse, scimitars swinging at their hips, the dragonmaster apprentices stationed as cocoon guards were hewing wood and feeding the fires. Few rishi helped; I could count how many with a swift glance. Indeed, the many rishi usually seen toiling about the arbiyesku were markedly absent.

The tribe of the Silent Slayers was not.

There they squatted, their bellies now full—if Knife-carver were to be believed—with the excised flesh of their dead. I bitterly reflected that they *could* have been assisting the arbiyesku in rebuilding huts. But as much as I resented their willful insularity, a small part of me couldn't help but grudgingly admire them for their solidarity and singularity of purpose. They'd come to collect a debt, and nothing would distract or deter them from obtaining their goal.

The children and old women of the arbiyesku were weaving jute-and-reed wall matting to replace the smashed sections of the women's barracks. At my approach their hands fell still. Savga stood up from amongst them, eyes reflecting the awful weight of her grief over the loss of her granna, Fwipi.

Throat tight, I placed a hand on her head and sat beside Agawan, asleep on the ground. My escorts stood in sentry position a few paces away from me. The old women and children looked from the soldiers to me, eyes wide with unease, afraid to move.

"Ignore them," I said wearily. "They mean no one any harm. They're here to . . . watch over me. Nothing more."

After an uncomfortable pause, Savga moved. "I'll get you water," she whispered.

She returned with water, a cold kadoob tuber as wizened as an old monkey's balls, and Tansan. Tansan wore grief for her mother like a splintered circlet upon her brow. She didn't so much as glance at the soldiers; Savga had forewarned her.

Tansan stood above me, statuesque and beautiful. "We took her body to the fields, said prayers. The vultures and hyenas will make new life from her body and bones."

"Hearts are riven when a mother dies," I murmured. My words were inadequate. I didn't know how to express what I felt over the loss of Fwipi; I'd clamped down on those emotions, had buried them beneath hard layers of anger toward my mother's haunt, and Kratt, and yes, even Waivia.

After a pause, I drank from the gourd Savga held out to me and took a bite from the kadooh. Its smoky flavor was too bitter. I preferred hunger that day.

Tansan squatted beside me, muscles in her smooth thighs bulging. "What did the council say about them?" she asked, voice pitched too low for the soldiers to hear. She was looking at the Kwembibi Shafwai.

"I didn't bring the secret of the bulls from the jungle; we owe the Kwembibi Shafwai nothing, because they're mere savages."

"Wrong thinking, that," Tansan murmured, sounding potently like Fwipi.

"What should we do?" I wasn't asking her so much as myself, but she answered anyway. Softly. I could barely hear her.

"Some of the Xxamer Zu myazedo will take an old egg layer from the brooder stables tonight, take her to the camp in the hills. They'll hew wood and prepare for when she secretes death wax about her."

A slow shiver swept over me. The cold pimples were for two reasons, the first being the mutinous theft that Tansan was planning against the council of the Great Uprising. The second reason: that she had chosen to share such information with me. It was the culmination of a tense, unsteady relationship that had started when we'd first met and she'd declared my life cursed. I was moved by her disclosure.

"You're going to hatch your own bull," I murmured.

"We intend on trying."

"The brooder stables are unguarded?"

"Some of us have been . . . gathering bayen gems and gold since the liberation of the Clutch. Some of the brooder guardian clan will be sound sleepers tonight, for these gems and gold."

"Tansan, if you're caught . . . Think of Savga, of Agawan."

Her black eyes turned opaque. "I won't get caught."

There was nothing to say against such conviction. I dropped my eyes. "May bull wings hatch for you. May you be safe." And then, irked by what felt like her abandonment of Xxamer Zu, I angrily looked up again. "We shouldn't give up. I still think we can do this."

"Do what?" She swept a hand across the compound, the Clutch, the nation. "This is no longer our battle, Zarq. This is bayen men playing games of power and wealth. They'll forget what they owe the piebald rishi of Xxamer Zu before the year is through."

"We won't allow them to forget! This is our land."

She looked again at the Kwembibi Shafwai. "If they don't give them what is theirs, they won't give us what is ours. We're one and the same to them."

Again, I couldn't argue against the bitter truth in her words. "I want to gather a group of Djimbi elders to join the Nashe council. Will you at least help me in that, Tansan?"

"A waste of time."

"So you *are* giving up."

"I didn't say I wouldn't help you. But until Chinion returns, it won't matter who we send to the council. Only Chinion can cut the truth from the fat of bayen lies and deception."

"There're some pretty tough elders on this Clutch who won't be cowed by the council lords, I'm betting."

"We're a strong people," she agreed.

"When *is* Chinion returning?"

"He'll be back."

"You're sure?"

"Yes. He promised." She smoothly rose to her feet. "Water needs to be fetched."

I watched her walk away, her dark, mottled limbs fluid as hot gravy running slow and thick from a ladle. She was a warrior, and her mother had just been killed, and she was carrying an urn upon her head to fetch water for her children and kin.

That's the definition of strength, for me.

Dusk, and clouds congregated into a hierarchy of proportion and density. A light rain fell—it would have been torrential, over the distant jungle mountains—and the bonfires in the warehouse spat and sizzled as if dashed with oil.

Piah came running into the arbiyesku, breathless: A regiment of soldiers was marching our way.

We stared, stunned and appalled. What?

"To throw them out." Piah pointed at the Kwembibi Shafwai, whose eyes shone in the dark like pearls, all of them, every man, woman, and child, focused on me and my clan.

The sound of wings overhead. Terror spurted through us, and we all tensed and flinched, but the sound was not that of a Skykeeper: escoas only, their leathery wings churning up sooty dust as they landed in the gloaming. A collective shudder of relief swept through us all.

I stiffly stood and met Malaban Bri as he dismounted. Knife-carver slid off from behind him. Two-braids, and again the bayen man from the previous night, dismounted from the second escoa. My two soldiers shadowed me.

"Is it true?" I asked Malaban. He smelled of smoke and charcoal and sweat and was covered in soot; he hadn't changed since the previous night.

He turned to face me, khol-encircled eyes grave. "It's been decided. There's no proof that we owe these people recompense for the knowledge they allegedly gave you."

"They didn't *allegedly* give it to me. It's the truth!"

His barrel chest swelled and he released his breath: "So you say."

"You doubt me?"

"*I* don't."

"But—"

"I'm sorry, Zarq." His words were final. He nodded to Knife-carver, and the two of them, followed by Two-braids and the lord, crossed the compound to where the tribe of Silent Slayers awaited payment.

I followed. Savga followed me, Agawan carried in a sling upon her back. Tansan materialized from the gloom and joined us. Alliak and Piah joined her. A slow flood of rishi followed, pressing closer, closer to me. My soldiers were hard-put to stay beside me in the crush.

Like the *scritch-scritch* of a thousand weary cockroachs moving over scree, we heard the footfalls of the approaching regiment of soldiers, coming to deal with the Kwembibi Shafwai.

Longstride and the matriarch stood. We all assumed our positions from the previous night, as if we were resuming a well-rehearsed dance.

"Tell them," Malaban Bri said shortly.

Knife-carver gave his skullish smile and began a choppy speech to the matriarch. He paused once to search for a word, head tilted like a bird of prey's; unlike the night previous, he didn't consult Two-braid, and Two-braid made no suggestions.

When he was finished, the silence was all-pervasive.

Then Longstride hissed at us. At *me*.

She drew back her lips into an impossible snarl—she wasn't human, wasn't anywhere near human—and hissed, and her hiss didn't stop; it kept flooding from her as if each droplet of blood in her body were turning into air and shooting from her mouth in a vehement stream, and I backed up a step from her, every fine hair on my nape, on my arms, rigid with horror. Either side of me, my soldiers' hands dropped to their hilts.

The matriarch spoke, baritone voice muted and confident. Knife-carver looked nonplussed as he digested her words. My skin crawled then. He was not one to allow himself to look nonplussed. With effort he wiped his expression blank and translated. "She says they will summon the creature from last night. They say that unless you fulfill the bargain, they will summon the creature every night until nothing remains here but blackened bones and burnt earth. She says she can do this, and will do this, even when claimed by death."

The matriarch turned to face her tribe and raised her arms, her exquisite waterfall of gold necklaces flashing with reflected firelight. She barked out something. At once dreadful, coarse coughs started erupting from various tribe members. Longstride continued her eerie hiss, eyes unwavering upon me.

I could barely find my voice. "Malaban, how far away are your soldiers?"

He looked at me. "Is this woman capable of doing what she says?"

"Look at the clouds."

The clouds had turned to coals, churning and clotting, edges tinged livid with fire. One man was singing—no, crooning. The sound was smooth and sinister, like a garrote slicing slowly through the neck of a victim.

"Savga," I said hoarsely. "Run."

Thank the One Dragon, she obeyed, and her flight loosed fear in the rest of the arbiyesku, and they began to scatter, slowly and uncertainly at first, but as the clouds began to sizzle like oil-splattered coals, pulsating with red, panic spread and soared. Mothers grabbed children and ran for cover, and sons helped aged greatfathers stagger into domiciles. Tansan and Piah remained beside me. As did my soldiers.

My nose began to bleed.

The matriarch bent, her magnificent pearl blanket held regally about her, and scooped up a fistful of dirt. The dirt was slaty, griseous: the color of clay. That had been the foundation of my mother's world when she was alive: clay. The matriarch straightened. Spat into her palm.

"Tell them to desist," the lord behind Malaban said, unease fat in his voice. Malaban nodded at Knife-carver to obey, and Knife-carver spoke. His words fell on deaf ears.

With the spittle-dampened clay in her hand, the matriarch began forming a figure.

"Piah," I said. "Tell the soldiers to hurry. Run."

From the corner of my vision, I watched him disappear into the dark. *Drip, drip*; crimson beads of my life fell into the dust at my feet. With trembling hands, I pinched my nostrils together to stop the bleeding.

The matriarch reached under her waterfall of fine gold necklaces and withdrew a feather. A luminescent blue feather. I remembered how her tribe had swarmed up to the roof of the warehouse the night previous as the vast feathered brisket of the Skykeeper had swooped over us; I remembered how they'd raised their spears, how women and the young had clambered onto the shoulders of men. Stupidly unafraid, I'd thought them. Uselessly defiant.

Not so. They'd had a purpose. They'd been trying to reach the Skykeeper, and they'd succeeded: They'd procured a feather.

The matriarch rammed the feather into the clay effigy. Swift as an adder, Longstride grabbed my head, wrenched it forward, and the matriarch extended her palm beneath my chin. My blood dripped onto her clay figure even as Malaban Bri shouted something and Tansan leaped toward me and my soldiers withdrew their swords.

A fiery pain blasted across my face, and the next I knew I was on my back, on the ground, watching the clay figure in the matriarch's hand grow and lengthen as a violent blue vortex enclosed it. Tansan, too, lay on the ground, still and silent beside me. My guards were likewise unconscious, their swords shattered about them as if they'd been made of glass.

The figure floated off the matriarch's hand, grew to the size of a human, and coalesced into my mother, gowned in pleated blue.

She looked ill pleased.

"Zarq." Her voice was horrible, the rattle of a finger bone prodding the loose teeth of a corpse. Her eyes found mine: her eyes, but not her eyes. Eyes that, in lieu of pupils, had roiling maggots. "How?"

She wanted to know how I'd summoned her. But I hadn't.

The matriarch spoke.

Like a sheet of moving blue water, my mother turned slowly to look, unblinkingly, at the matriarch. Slowly her blue bitoo began to fade from the waist down. In its place appeared scaled red legs, stork-thin and dripping with rot. At the matriarch's command, she was beginning the transformation into a Skykeeper.

"Don't listen to her," I said, speaking over the matriarch's chant. Somehow I was on my feet again, legs unsteady. "Mother, don't do it. This is *your* Clutch, Xxamer Zu. Remember?"

I turned to Malaban Bri. "Give them the damn bull and a yearling."

The matriarch continued to speak while the harsh, unnatural barks of the tribe of the Silent Slayers ricocheted around the night. The haunt's arms turned into wing bones.

"Mother, listen." I stepped forward. "You have kin here, the danku, the pottery clan. I've seen them. You have nephews, nieces. Your sister, she's alive. She has a daughter who looks just like Waivia."

"Waivia." My mother—the haunt, the half-formed Skykeeper—swung on me. "*You.* You threaten her safety."

"No—"

"She tells me you gather forces, you forge weapons, you want to take what's hers."

"I would never do that! She's my *sister*." Outrage gave me strength, even as I realized that somehow Waivia had learned that I hadn't taken that ship overseas. "Don't you dare accuse me of hurting Waivia. Ever."

Malaban Bri said something to Knife-carver. Knife-carver found his voice, with difficulty. He spoke in the language of the Kwembibi Shafwai. The matriarch paused; the barking paused; Longstride's hissing paused.

"Yes," Malaban said to the matriarch, stepping forward, extending the soft underside of one of his wrists. He swiftly pulled a knife from a sheath at his belt and drew it across his skin. "Blood truth. I vow it."

If the lord who'd accompanied him was still present and conscious, he did not refute Malaban's vow: the Kwembibi Shafwai would receive the neonate bull, and a young yearling to mate it to.

The matriarch needed no translation. She nodded.

The tribe began *reversing* their barks, sucking in belly-deep inhalations, while Longstride began hissing *in* air. My mother began to fade.

"Mother, listen to me." Again I stepped toward her, arms outstretched. Great Dragon, even *now* she was still my mother, still exerted a pull on my emotions, and I didn't want her to leave me. "Don't kill the children of your birth Clutch. We won't harm Waivia, I promise."

"You'll submit to her."

"I can't make that promise for Xxamer Zu. For myself . . . if you promise not to touch this Clutch or anyone on it"—I was thinking of Savga, and Oblan, and Agawan—"I will . . . I'll submit to her. Me alone. To her will alone. Yes."

"Not good enough." She was flecks of bone and necrosis in ebon air, her voice the soft rasp of powdered clay blowing over slate.

"I'm your daughter!" And I admit it, I was crying. She would always make me cry; every time she abandoned me, every fresh renouncement and abdication of her love would shatter me anew.

The haunt paused. Those chips of disintegrating bone floating in midair visibly *paused*.

"Yesss," came the hissing sigh. "My Zzzarq."

If I could have, I would have swept those chips of bone to my breast and embraced them, for I loved them, couldn't help it. I did.

"Ssso. Thisss: I will not return unlesss Waivia enters thisss Clutch. If she doesss, I will protect her, regardlesss of cost to kin. I will protect her, as I should have done long ago."

The matriarch clapped her hands together, smashing the clay effigy into dust. My mother's haunt abruptly disappeared. The matriarch blew the dust in her palm away. The Djimbi chants stopped.

I swooned and landed beside Tansan, who was just beginning to rouse.

TWENTY-FOUR

What do I remember of the days that followed the departure of our first neonate bull with the Kwembibi Shafwai? Of the weeks that followed my mother's promise to stay away from our Clutch unless Waivia entered it?

I remember the damp, silty feel of clay beneath my hands as I formed incendiary shells in an assembly line. Savga's prattle as she worked beside me, stuffing twists of straw into one of three chambers of each shell. How my eyes watered and nose ran and tongue shriveled from the stinging powder that others funneled into the clay fruits I fashioned by the hundreds.

At night: needles flashing orange in firelight as every spare hand, at every spare moment, sewed the heraldic crests of the Great Uprising: a burning yellow crown stitched upon bolts of plum-colored cloth that would be strapped upon the briskets and bellies of our destriers.

I remember the clanging ring of weapons being forged, the whoosh of pumped bellows, the metallic smell of hot iron plunged into barrels of water. I remember the smell of wood shavings, the thud of hammer and mallet, and rows and rows of great crossbows lying in the sun like the pale ribs of a herd of some slain, strange beast.

When I smell jute, hemp, and leather, I remember old men and women clustered together, knotting rope into nets, deftly attaching the nets to leather surcingles that would later be attached to saddles. A new weapon, those nets were, inspired by the Xxelteker incendiaries that we were fashioning from the firepowder and kerosene shipped in from the north and arriving by wagonfuls in Xxamer Zu. The nets held upward of eight incendiaries, and were to be slung beneath the belly of destriers, flown over the enemy, and cut loose. Takeoff ramps were designed and hammered into existence to accommodate such net-laden destriers.

I have other memories, too, formed around hard pits of emotion. Frustration: trying to convince Djimbi elders of the necessity for joining the council of the Great Uprising. But they were mistrustful and scornful and afraid, those wise old people, and why should they trust me, an aosogi-via? I wasn't one of them.

Where I failed, Tansan succeeded. With diplomacy and patience—and that supernatural presence that the dragonmaster had been so suspicious of—Tansan escorted a group of Djimbi elders into the Uprising's stockade, to consult over the weeks with the council.

I remember jealousy: Why was I working on an assembly line, instead of in the destrier stables, caring for our neonate bulls? (Because I couldn't go near venom, not for any reason. Couldn't trust myself. Knew I would plunge into addiction like an anchor dropped down into the sea.)

I remember my growing fear as the days clambered quickly over one another: Malacar was going to war. Xxamer Zu was going to war. *I* was going to war. It seemed surreal, even as I formed shell after shell for incendiaries—surreal but terrifyingly true. Like the way a nightmare can leave one unsettled for days, the residue of the unreal viscerally impressive and impossible to shake, affecting how one views every moment of the next day.

Laughter seemed sharp-edged. The sight of children at play was arresting and brought tears to the eye. Any baby that cried was quickly tended to—we all scurried to alleviate anyone's discomfort; we all treasured the touch and sound of those we loved—even while we snapped at the baby for crying. We were all shorter on patience than usual. We were preparing for war; we had no time to waste on scraped knees, on children's squabbles, on little tummies that demanded food and drink so relentlessly! Couldn't the children understand this? We were going to *war*.

The children *could* understand, and we *did* waste time on scraped knees, on children's squabbles, on hungry little tummies. The need to give and receive love and attention is never more necessary than when security is seeping away, and what was the war about, if not the future of our children?

Emotional times.

Above all of my memories, I'm ashamed to say, there is one that is strongest. It is that of a taste. A taste as bitter as unripe cranberries, starchy and omnipresent on my tongue and the back of my throat. It's the taste of the concoction Yimtranu boiled for me, from the gizzards of a boar and the roots of the evernight plant, laced with toxins from the blister toad and shavings from a gharial's tooth. A concoction meant to rid me of the debilitating withdrawal symptoms I was suffering from, to cleanse me of my increasing desire to once again hear dragonsong. Even as a fleet of Imperial war galleys sailed into Lireh and disgorged over ten thousand foot soldiers meant to crush our uprising, I fought my cravings, was haunted by memories of a dragon between my thighs. How I lusted and writhed at nights! How I trembled and sweated during the days! Yimtranu's concoction was a poor substitute for Gen's, but it did alleviate my sufferings somewhat . . . though at a cost. My fingers grew clumsy, my head clotted, my tongue thickened. Savga, with little Agawan always strapped on her back, became something of a nurse to me, mopping my brow, giving me water, explaining to others my fainting spells and bouts of poor eyesight as a difficult pregnancy.

Truth was, a life of a sorts *was* growing within me and causing the fainting. My own life.

It was Yimtranu's concoctions, see. They were weakening the threads of the charm my mother had spun about me at birth, and the real me was pressing through, like skin showing behind old fabric. It wasn't until Yimtranu accused me of not drinking the concoctions she was laboriously brewing for me that I realized what was happening.

"I *am* drinking them," I snapped at her. "You're not making them strong enough."

"Strong enough, bah! I've been curing venom-snared lords for decades; my potions have never once failed! You should be retching at the thought of dragon poison." She made angry gagging noises to demonstrate.

"Well, I'm not. You'll just have to make them stronger. Please? Yimtranu? Please?" Addicts know how to wheedle.

She turned away from me and groused at her smoking brazier. "She wants stronger, she'll get stronger. See if *this* batch will bite through her shield, hey."

Shield.

Gen's voice: *It is a most powerful enchantment that surrounds you. Like a shield, Babu! So powerful, it prevents you from being wholly you.*

That was when I knew what was happening to me each time I swallowed more of Yimtranu's brew: The stuff was weakening the enchantment. And the *me* of me, the me I'd never truly known, was starting to slip through.

Terrifying, that. Did I want to know the real me? Would my unenchanted eyes have poorer vision? Would my reflexes be slower? Would my skin be as darkly whorled as Yimtranu's, or lightly green-spattered, like Savga's?

Did I have the courage to face who I really was?

The alternative was suffering through the vicious venom-withdrawal attacks. Some days I chose Yimtranu's brew, and other days I trembled incessantly with lust for the dragon's toxin.

Despite all this, I still roamed the Clutch at night, teaching. No, I taught *because* of my sufferings. I needed the distraction; I needed to feel worthy and special. But the nights changed; the Clutch grew choked with strangers. By overland carriage, Roshu-Lupini Ordipti relocated the bayen ladies and children of his Clutch to Xxamer Zu, between caravans of grain, meat, iron ingots, and weaponry. He then flew to our Clutch the ten neonate bulls that had emerged in his cocoon warehouse, along with his adult bull, the great Ordipti, and every destrier and escoa in his stables. In that bold move, Roshu-Lupini Ordipti extended the theater of war across the entire nation and located the heart of it in Xxamer Zu, in the difficult-to-access interior of Malacar, where the mountainous jungle terrain preceding the dry savanna was unfavorable to enemy ground forces.

Combined with the neonate bulls emerging from the cocoons in our warehouse, fifteen bulls were located upon Xxamer Zu. Never before in recorded history had so many bulls simultaneously existed in one Clutch. We instantly had many allies, and Xxamer Zu burgeoned with lords, warriors, mercenaries, dragonmaster apprentices, destriers, and escoas.

Destrier squadrons were formed, air calvary comprised of lords and dragonmaster apprentices, and an infantry was created of soldiers, myazedo rebels, rishi, and mercenaries. Tansan and Piah joined a troop assigned to guard the cocoon warehouse.

We met one day, Tansan and I, by accident: I was with a throng of rishi carrying clay from the banks of the river, and she was carrying an empty urn upon her head to fetch water. Savga noticed her first.

"Mama! Look, here we are!"

I stepped out of the line of rishi walking bent double under loads of clay. The slab I was carrying upon my back via a strap across my forehead was so heavy I could feel my old rib fractures creaking with each footfall.

Tansan had grown darker and sleeker with muscle over the weeks, and she rivaled my sister for her barbaric beauty. She embraced Savga and dandled Agawan, who chuckled delightedly and kicked his chubby legs.

"Zarq and Tiwana-auntie have looked after you fine," she said, smiling at her babe, and I took the compliment as high praise. "Look how plump you are, Aga! Savga has been feeding you so well!"

Savga flushed with pride.

Tansan turned her sparkling eyes upon me. "It formed a cocoon, hey."

It took me a moment to understand that she was referring to the brooder she'd stolen and hidden in the hills.

"Who's with it?"

"Keau and a few others. They keep the bonfires lit. No need to hunt for kwano snakes; the jungle provides enough."

"So it might transform."

"It will," she said with utter confidence. "We'll have our own bull one day soon." She handed Agawan back to Savga and patted her on the head. "You be good for Zarq Kazonvia, hey."

"Will you come sleep with us tonight in the arbiyesku?" Savga asked. I felt a pang of jealousy at the yearning on her face, then disgust at myself for feeling such. Tansan was her mother, not me.

"Can't tonight, Little Ant. Clutches Re and Cuhan began marching toward us today; war draws nearer."

My heart fish-flipped. "I didn't know that."

"The news will spread like wildfire. You'll hear it a thousand times by morning. I found out at dawn."

"From Chinion?"

A troubled look briefly crossed her face. "He hasn't returned yet. But he will. He will."

I told myself that I imagined the doubt in her voice. So easy it is to convince ourselves that nothing wrong is about to occur, especially if averting the wrong means struggle and courage. I wasn't the only one guilty of playing a little of the coward's game. Tansan, too, was refusing to fully embrace the reality that perhaps, just perhaps, she was being negligent by not making contingencies for Chinion's death, by not following up on the progress of the elders we'd sent to the uprising's council.

Like me distracting myself by teaching rishi how to write and fight each night—important work, yes; I'll give myself that much credit—Tansan, too, was focusing too much on becoming a warrior, falling in love with training with a spear instead of fighting for her land.

None of us is infallible.

We went our separate ways, Agawan bawling for his mother.

Tansan was right; the news of Re and Cuhan marching upon us *did* spread like wildfire across the Clutch. As the days progressed, updates on Kratt's progress spread, too, as well as news concerning the ten-thousand-strong Imperial regiment marching on us from Lireh. I didn't then know how accurate were the rumors burning the ears and mouths of those in our Clutch, but now I know that most of the rumors had been correct.

In Liru, the downtrodden stormed shops, emporiums, warehouses, and mansions, and burned barrels of lamp oil while chanting the Votive:

In the chambers of Lireh's heart, the spider is spinning now,
And the owl hoots above the emptiness that was once filled by daronpuis.
The webs will not be swept away!

In the Village of the Eggs, the four most powerful Clutches in the nation—Lutche, Ka, Re, and Cuhan (the lords from Cuhan given little choice but to side with their usurper)—sent regiments of destrier-mounted lords to stop the rioters rampaging through Liru's outlying nashvenirs, the sacred ranches where onahmes that had been bred at Arena laid fertile eggs.

More rumors: The Imperial regiment was being haunted by a band of rebels known as the Black Sixty. Water sources were visited in advance and fouled with animal corpses; wagons of provisions were exploded by incendiaries. The profuse insects of Malacar's jungles were bestowing fever and festering rashes upon the Imperial soldiers; marching hours were decreasing as deaths in the mobile infirmaries doubled. Perhaps the regiment's commanders had been well aware of the distances in Malacar, but rumor had it that the regiment's soldiers—islanders used to short marches along smooth roads lined by well-provisioned farms—were sorely discouraged by the reality of Malacar.

I pushed myself harder, worked longer, taught later and later each night, trying to drive away the dread fear blooming within me.

One evenfall, Xxamer Zu sent out squadrons of incendiary destriers. They strafed Kratt's infantry after twilight, when crossbow archers couldn't see our fliers coming, and when cooking fires acted as a beacon. The road Kratt's infantry traveled was through the salt pans, and thus far more exposed to aerial attack than the jungle-clotted road upon which the Imperial regiment traveled.

Two nights running we strafed Kratt's army; then on the third night, enemy squadrons intercepted our fliers. Every destrier and flier Xxamer Zu sent out perished that dusk, and Kratt's army continued its advance.

Closer. Closer.

I made incendiaries frantically, and my lust for venom and dragonsong was an almost unbearable thirst, a burgeoning madness I could only temporarily douse by downing Yimtranu's brew. As feverishly as I worked, others labored: our Clutch was a frantic hive pausing for rest only during the latest hours of night.

Then came the dawn when Kratt's infantry was less than a day away.

Out on the salt pans—separated from Xxamer Zu by less than ten miles of rolling savanna—a gray smirch boiled from the sky and landed. That smirch was the armor-plated destriers and armed lords of Clutches Ka, Cuhan, Lutche, and Re. Somewhere in that roil of men and swords and dragons was Kratt himself. At his side stood my sister. When she stepped onto Xxamer Zu soil, my mother's haunt would appear.

Destriers were speedily saddled, incendiaries were loaded into nets beneath their bellies. Commanders rallied their fighters. Ranks of crossbow archers swarmed the northeasterly outskirts of Xxamer Zu, facing the enemy in the distance. The crossbows would be the first wave of our ground assault, shooting enemy destriers from the sky, then raining quarrels upon Kratt's oncoming foot soldiers.

Bandages and medicaments and surgical saws were hastily readied by proselytes of the Chanoom sect. Elderly rishi and mothers with young children prayed aloud as they flocked toward the center of the Clutch, infants and meager belongings on their backs. Many continued toward the safety of the jungle. No one stopped them.

In that turmoil, Tansan located me, where Savga and I were frantically packing clay shells with powder, kerosene, and straw. Tansan's eyes flashed with anger and urgency.

"They've made no provisions to protect us against the Skykeeper," she panted. "I've just learned that the Djimbi elders we sent to headquarters have been kept segregated all these weeks and were never once consulted."

I stared at her, appalled. "And Chinion?"

"He's still not here." The admission nearly strangled her.

"You swore he'd return!" I cried, feeling utterly panicked. Chinion was the voice of rishi and Djimbi to the council. "Tansan, you *swore* it!"

"As he swore to me," she lashed back. "But the reality is that he hasn't arrived, and our wisest elders that we sent to the Council of Seven have been scorned, and the battle is now upon us."

I wanted to shriek and pull my hair out; what in the name of the One Dragon did she expect me to *do*?

This was my Clutch. These were my people. This was my rebellion, and I'd been wrong, far wrong, to focus all my energies on educating the rishi and rely instead on the great unknown Chinion, a handful of Djimbi elders unused to political scheming, and the Council of Seven—the directors of the Great Uprising—to prepare for the Skykeeper's probable attack.

No half measures.

"Fine," I said grimly. "I'll . . . I'll . . . do something."

"What?"

"I don't know!" I cried. "Let me think—"

"Go to the stockade. Take Savga and Agawan with you." It was an order; her face brooked no argument. "Keep them in there, away from the front line."

I nodded, thoughts spinning. "I'll find Malaban."

"Go, then. May the Dragon give you strength." She turned and ran, long thighs flashing in the sun. The look on Savga's face as she watched her go just about ripped my heart out.

No time for emotion; I'd squandered my days and nights focusing on *my* wants, instead of thinking bigger. Time to get outside of myself.

I grabbed Savga's hand and ran for the center of the Clutch. Through curses and sheer will, I managed to locate Malaban Bri in the frantic hive of activity within the stockade that had once been the realm of Xxamer Zu's daronpuis. The great bear of a man looked up from a sheaf of papers as I barged into his office. He regarded me warily as heralds, lords, and commanders thronged the corridor behind me. I shut the door. Savga pressed against me, Agawan wide-eyed in the sling on her back.

"How did you get in?" he said gruffly. "Never mind, we've no time. What do you want?"

I hadn't seen him since the night I'd banished my mother's haunt from Xxamer Zu, when he'd overseen the delivery of our first neonate bull, as well as a yearling, to the departing Kwembibi Shafwai. But I knew that his report of what had occurred that night had prevented me from being delivered to Kratt.

"I want to know what provisions you've made to protect us against the Skykeeper." My lower jaw was thrust out.

He cursed under his breath and shot a look at his paper-crowded desk.

"You haven't consulted with the Djimbi elders we sent you. Malaban, you *know* what we're going up against. You witnessed—"

"I'm not on the Council of Seven; I only advise them. No lord but me saw what occurred that night. As far as the council is concerned, this talk of Skykeepers and otherworld magics is beyond the realm of war."

"It *is* the war! Our incendiaries are nothing compared to the Skykeeper!"

"Zarq, you don't understand. That council you stood before answered to another one, a higher one—"

"Take me to them."

"I can't."

"Now."

For a moment he looked like quarry being pursued by birds of prey, hounds, and hunters, all. Then he nodded, brusquely, and came out from behind his desk.

Savga and I swiftly followed him out the door.

Seven men, their ranks, names, and origins unknown to me, regarded me soberly.

They were big men, big in every way: size, confidence, experience, influence, resource, and intelligence. Their hands used pens for weapons; the steel of their coins was sharper than swords. They spun impenetrable webs between foreign émigrés, Malacarite politicians, the wealthy, and the discontent. They shaped destiny as if it were clay, using the muscles of laborers, partisans, resistance groups, serfs, tycoons, dragonmasters, and Clutch overseers. They stood at the pinnacle of the Great Uprising's pyramid, networks and armies of people as their expansive base. Not one of them, save Malaban, was from the council I'd stood in front of before.

Five of the seven were aosogi. One was the dark brown of those descendants from Lud y Auk. One was a blue-eyed, gray-haired Xxelteker.

There wasn't an ivory-hued fa-pim body in sight. But neither was there a whorled one.

Maps covered the walls: aerial maps, ground maps, and diagrams of destrier squadron formations. Half-eaten food, empty wine flagons, inkpots, quills, and parchment covered tables.

Savga waited outside the closed and guarded doors, Agawan on her lap, as I stood surrounded by those maps, before the seven of the Great Uprising. I wondered how the indefatigable men before me felt, sitting before a woman from some obscure pagan prophecy as they prepared to engage in warfare.

"You've made a mistake by spurning the council of Djimbi elders we sent you," I snapped. "We needed to make provisions to protect against Kratt's Skykeeper—"

"Tell us what it can do, what we can expect." The Xxelteker man fired off the command as if it were an arrow.

I paused, considered. "The Skykeeper is berserk. She's insane."

"She?"

"Otherworld power is heedless of gender." I didn't need to stand upon a crate box to educate whomsoever surrounded me.

One of the aosogi men unrolled a scroll of vellum. He pinned its corners down under a wine flagon, an inkwell, and two dusky plums. A sensuous female Djimbi blazed forth: the likeness of Waivia, trapped by paint. "Is that your sister? The one who stands beside Kratt and controls the Skykeeper?"

I shouldn't have been surprised. After all, the men before me could tear down and reshape a nation. "Don't hurt her."

"If your sister were captured, unharmed, then what?" asked the darkest of the seven.

"You won't succeed," I said. "The Skykeeper would perceive capture as an act of harm to Waivia. We have to keep Waivia *away* from Xxamer Zu. Only if she steps upon this Clutch will the Skykeeper attack. The Skykeeper vowed it."

"Will it hold to the vow?"

"She has thus far."

A shift in the air. The Xxelteker man stirred, his peculiar bright blue eyes surrounded by tired fish-belly-white skin. "And if this Waivia is killed, then what?"

My guts curled. "You can't kill my sister."

"This is war. People die. So tell us: What becomes of the Skykeeper if this Waivia dies?"

I remembered how, each time I'd left Clutch Re prior to the haunt finding Waivia, the haunt had become embedded within me. Would the berserk thing that was so intent on protecting Waivia become trapped within me should Waivia die?

(I'd be Mother's child at last, with Waivia gone.)

I grabbed the edge of the heavy teak table the seven sat around, appalled at myself. "If you kill my sister," I said hoarsely, "the Skykeeper will destroy every living thing on this Clutch. Me included. *Don't hurt her.*"

Did I speak the truth? I didn't know. Was I trying to protect Waivia? Most certainly.

"Does the Skykeeper view you as an enemy?" Malaban asked. "Could you draw your sister and her creature away from the battle?"

"How?"

"Those magics the Kwembibi Shafwai employed—"

"Are unknown to me," I said tartly. "Those Djimbi magics are ancient, obscure. If not for the persecution of the Djimbi, more Djimbi would know such magics, but that's not the way things are, is it? Djimbi have been reviled for what they know, not respected. The Djimbi race has been watered down, made *more pleasing,* by laws forbidding unions between Djimbi. The knowledge that you want, Malaban, now resides amongst the likes of the Kwembibi Shafwai, my sister, Daronpu Gen, and maybe a clawful of Djimbi who know the old lore. Such as the very Djimbi elders that we sent to you, and whom you've scorned to consult with."

I turned my anger from Malaban to the seated seven.

"We have to locate my sister and keep her safe and away from Xxamer Zu. Kill her and you cut your own throats. For the love of wings, is that not clear?"

"And your Djimbi elders can help us locate her, amongst all those thousands Kratt has gathered out there?" The Xxelteker's voice was cool.

"They can," I hoped.

One of the men reached for a quill, scrawled something on a corner of parchment, and handed it to Malaban Bri. "Give this to the herald outside the door. Have these Djimbi elders summoned."

My knees went weak; I could do this thing yet. I could keep Waivia alive, and safe, and away from Xxamer Zu. . . .

A noise outside in the hall.

Music that eclipsed my mind like a finespun cloud, both hirsute and silky. A green feeling slowly began pulsing through me, a raw, sappy feeling fluorescing with bud time, seed time, dew and youth. The stronger the sensation grew, the more it altered; I became buoyant, supernal, belonging to a higher world. I was lured and goaded by the sweetening infusion, a sound that incited and soothed both.

My flesh began pricking with latent memory. The sensation was akin to when one has sat too long in a still position, and then, upon moving, blood rushes painfully back into stifled limbs.

Djimbi chants. I was hearing Djimbi chants. As were the men around me.

The doors burst open and Daronpu Gen lurched in.

He was dressed in a tattered brown tunic belted by a cord of coarse jute. His massive hairy feet were bare, chafed, and blistered. His beard—snarled, black, touching his collarbone—had been cleaved in two and gave the impression of black tusks sprouting from his sunken cheeks. The black hair on his head looked like the wiry bristles of a wild boar. His skin—covered with weeping whip welts—was bark brown, the same hue as when I'd first met him, years ago, yet his cheeks were pale, as if he were drained, exhausted, as if he'd been running through jungle for days.

One of his eyes had been gouged out, was an appalling socket surrounded by weeping, puckered flesh.

"Had to use a charm on them," he said hoarsely, gesturing at the guards outside the doors. The guards stood with jaws slack, eyes glazed, and were lovingly handling themselves beneath their skirts. Gen had used that charm before, to get past those who wouldn't otherwise let him proceed. As he had done so then, Gen now shrugged. "Best charm I know."

Savga slipped in from behind him and came to my side, Agawan asleep in the sling on her back.

"Where the Dragon have you been?" one of the seven growled at Gen. "And what's happened to you?"

I looked from Gen to the man who had spoken. They knew each other?

"Gen," I said hoarsely, and he turned his grisly, one-eyed gaze on me. There was something in his look and stance that stilled the relief, the joy, and the fiery hope that had exploded within me at his appearance. I sucked in a sharp breath and actually stepped back a pace.

The dark man addressed Gen, unable to disguise his disgust. "You wield a strange power, Chinion, to get into this council."

"Chinion?" I gasped. "*You're* Chinion?"

Gen waved away the revelation as insignificant. "I've come to find the prophesied one, the Dirwalan Babu, who will win us the battle and be Temple's ruin."

A moment of silence. All eyes fell on me.

"You're not referring to Zarq," Malaban said.

Gen looked grim. "I was wrong. It's not her. That creature Kratt wields is no Skykeeper. Is it, Zarq? Temple was right: It's a demon."

"My mother is no demon," I said breathlessly, still reeling from the revelation that Chinion and Daronpu Gen were one.

"Manifestation of love, manifestation of hate . . . two sides of the same coin," Gen rasped. "The personification of passion without reason, that's what Kratt's creature is." He looked at the seven. "I went back to Cuhan, followed the traces of the Skykeeper's essence. It led me to *her*, what-hey."

He pointed a bony finger at the vellum on the table.

"Long and long I watched that woman, like a bat in the night, like a roach on the wall. Twice I was caught and twice imprisoned and tortured. But I was successful, what-hey; I witnessed that woman's interactions with the thing Kratt would have us believe is a Skykeeper." Gen's weeping eye socket turned again in my direction. "There's no doubt it's one and the same as the creature that once answered to you, is there?"

No point denying it. "It's the same."

"How long've you known you aren't the Dirwalan Babu?"

"I've wanted to believe it ever since you told me." I started to feel defiant, piqued that he'd hid his alternate identity from me. How long had he not trusted me, to hide such? "How long have *you* suspected that I'm not the Dirwalan Babu?" I snapped.

"When I learned you were unaware of the magics that veiled your heritage. A fool, I've been. Made obtuse by hope, led by self-delusion. Humbling, blood-blood!"

My throat was dry. "What am I, Gen? Now that I've started all this: What am I?"

"Remarkable. But not, I fear, the Dirwalan Babu."

"So this creature of Kratt's is not a Skykeeper?" Malaban frowned. "It's a *demon?*"

"It's a shedwen-dar, the haunt of a dead osmajani," Gen said.

"Which means?"

"Osmajani, osmajani, a . . . what would you call it? A Djimbi replete with knowledge of otherworld powers."

"Are *you* an osmajani?" I asked.

"Not," Gen said sourly, "a very good one."

"And Waivia?"

"A fearfully damn good one."

I didn't ask if I was an osmajani. Didn't need to. I already knew I possessed none of my mother's pagan skills.

"Can it be conquered?" the Xxelteker man asked. "This *thing?*"

"Unlike a Skykeeper, a shedwen-dar is not immortal. Its powers are limited. It *can* be conquered." Gen smacked his great palms together; at my side, Savga started. "Now all that remains is to discover the Dirwalan Babu."

"The battle has all but begun," the Xxelteker man said curtly.

"She'll show, man, she'll show! The prophecy foretells it: *Zafinar waskatan, bar i'shem efru mildon safa dir palfent.* The Dirwalan Babu is present the day the efru mildron clash, on the field soon to be marked by talon and blood."

"You once thought those words meant I should be present at Arena," I said, and yes, I was bitter.

Gen swung his half-blind gaze toward me. "True, true, I did. But you yourself pointed out to me that the efru mildon, the colossals, don't actually clash in Arena. No, the bull dragons don't fight one another. And you were correct, hey-o! My interpretation of the passage was wrong."

He looked at the men who were listening to him with inscrutable expressions. "Efru mildon is an old Djimbi term, used by some tribes to refer to dragons, by others to refer to any who wield great power. *We* are the efru mildon in the prophecy, we who will clash today. Our forces against Kratt's and Temple."

One of the seven rose from his chair and placed his knuckles on the table, his expression somber and intense. He waited several moments before speaking, a man used to receiving the attention of all present.

"I'd be foolish to dismiss what I've seen and heard, and I am not a foolish man. But now is the time for tangibles. We have thousands of men prepared to die today, and we need to talk strategy, deal with facts, and move fast."

Grunts of agreement.

"Tell us how this thing Kratt controls can be beaten," the man demanded of Gen. "By fire? Steel? Incendiary?"

Gen scowled. "No, no, and no! A shedwen-dar is the personification of a passion; we must eradicate the source of its passion." He pointed a bony finger, and one by one everyone looked at the rendering of my sister, Waivia.

My heart stopped.

"You can't do that," I said huskily. "The haunt won't let us get near her; it'll be like throwing ourselves into a fire."

"True." Gen looked at me with pity, and that's a powerful thing to see from a man who has recently suffered torture: pity. "But if the shedwen-dar is locked in combat with a Skykeeper—our Skykeeper, a *true* Skykeeper, one prophesied to appear—we'll be able to move in on Kratt's osmajani."

"You're talking about killing my sister," I said hoarsely, hands clenched. Gen had once been my ally, my mentor. No longer. He was not only undoing all my work to protect my sister, but was cutting me out of his circle of power completely.

"Osmajani, sister: it makes no difference," he said.

"She has a baby," I choked out. "She's a mother, a woman."

"Alas, Zarq," Gen murmured, his one eye soft with empathy, "death and otherworld power recognize no gender. Your sister must die."

TWENTY-FIVE

Once, when I was a child—no more than four, if memory serves; really, that must be right, because Waivia was about thirteen at the time—I went with my mother and father to the Grieving River. I don't remember anything of the six-day journey there, nor the trip back. I don't remember how many potters from danku Re went with us to collect clay from that river's banks, nor the reasons that I went along. All I remember is this: We were a family—mother, father, and two sisters—standing on the banks of a wide, silver-plated river at dusk. Mother was smiling at us, Father too. A cool wind blew off the great river, making me shiver.

"Go splash in it if you want to," Mother said, eager on my behalf.

Father laughed, delighted at the suggestion. "Fine idea. Splash, play!"

Waivia turned to me, grinning. "Come on, Zarq."

So much expectation around me, so many smiles.

I didn't really want to go into that dark, silver-plated water. A river at dusk to a four-year-old who has never seen a river before in her life is a daunting thing, and, too, the wind was cool. But there was Waivia, grinning at me. There was my mother, smiling and urging me on. There was my father, eager to vicariously experience my play.

So I went into the water and splashed, squealing, terrified, shivering violently, and afterward I curled up on Waivia's lap before a fire, my teeth clattering. Her arms were warm. She seemed strong, big. I could hear her heart beating against my ear.

How cold a river can be at dusk. How heavy the love of family. How sheltering the arms of a sister.

TWENTY-SIX

On the twenty-fifth day of Mwe Shwombei month, in the fifty-second year of Emperor Mak Fa-Sren's rule, the seven of the Great Uprising launched an aerial assault against the forces gathering under Temple's banner, less than ten miles to the northeast of Clutch Xxamer Zu, upon the brittle, dry Malacar-Djom savanna.

At Daronpu Gen's insistence, I'd been force-marched from my confrontation with the seven to the front line of that battle, but not before I'd first fought Gen with words, curses, fists, and teeth.

"Leave me here; I have a child and an infant to care for!" I shrieked as two soldiers wrenched me away from Gen, pinned me against a wall, and bound my wrists behind my back.

"The children'll stay here, blood-blood!" Gen roared. "It's you I need out there, not them!"

"You won't use me against my sister! I refuse."

"Then you'll damn well watch her slaughter us firsthand. See if spilled blood and dead men won't change your mind!"

Agawan wailed, and Savga's eyes shot hatred and flame at Gen. "You keep them safe!" I cried over my shoulder to the seven, as two soldiers marched me from the room. "For the love of wings, you keep them safe!"

I murmured the words again, under my breath, a short while later, from where I stood upon the rooftop of the arbiyesku's women's barracks, flanked by Gen, Malaban Bri, and the soldiers. My wrists had not been freed, and I was shivering.

Before me, on the ground, was the sprawl of men and weaponry that formed our front line: thousands of soldiers gleaming in plastrons of oiled black leather and chain-mail gauntlets; twice as many rebels, hired mercenaries, and ikap-fen operatives in a motley of clothes, armed with an assortment of weapons; and at the very back, neat rows of archers manning the great, wicked crossbows that had been carted to the front line amidst much dust and tumult. The noise of so many men—a sea of limbs, axes, lances, sickles, pitchforks, swords, maces, and more—was a ceaseless roar. I thought of a mountain slide.

Our air squadrons were located to the northwest of the Clutch, where the seven hundred destriers that made up our air force had been housed in temporary stables erected near the river. Heralds darted overhead, carrying communiqués from headquarters to the infantry, from the infantry to the air squadrons, from the air squadrons to the infantry. Their escoas wore the uprising's burning-crown crest on their briskets, and the cloth shuddered and flapped in flight.

The air smelled of steel, sweat, dragon piss, and leather.

"It's ludicrous, my being here," I gasped to Gen. "Unbind me; give me a sword, at least."

"You'll do as I say," he growled, scanning the heaving sea of foot soldiers.

"I have no skill in Djimbi magics. I don't know what you expect from me."

"I expect you to stop nattering!"

"Don't treat me like a fool, Gen!" I cried. "This is my war as much as it's yours. Now untie me!"

He turned his back on me and walked to the very edge of the roof. I spun on Malaban Bri.

"He doesn't know what he's doing—"

"Shut up, Zarq," Malaban barked. "I saw what the Kwembibi Shafwai were capable of, and I've seen what Chinion can do. If he says we're to stand in the very center of the battle, then by Dragon, that's where we'll stand!"

"He's human. He's fallible."

"As are you. Now shut up."

He turned away from me and grimly stared at the roiling gray smirch that was Kratt's gathering forces.

The air above Xxamer Zu was suddenly alive with destriers, all bearing the burning-crown crest of the uprising. In precise diamond formations, ninety-six dragons—eight squadrons of destriers laden with incendiaries—flew overhead. The raspy, metallic noise of their wings vibrated the thatch roof beneath me; crests flapped, green and rufous scales gleamed, talons flashed, and tails that had been studded with steel barbs flicked like spiked metal whips in the sky. The dragons poured overhead . . . and then were winging hard above the savanna, carrying the deadly cargo slung beneath their bellies straight toward Kratt's infantry.

A great cheer rose up from our forces, a typhoon of sound that swept over me and momentarily stilled my blood. It had begun. The bloodshed, the rebellion, that fight for liberation that I'd wanted, had begun.

I felt ill.

Several long moments passed as our squadrons grew smaller in the cloudy skies. Wind soughed over the grasslands. The roil of activity in Xxamer Zu—of hundreds of destriers being saddled, of air squadrons mounting up, of soldiers taking position around the stables where the bulls were housed on the Clutch—rumbled and pitched in the background.

I was gulping air in fits and starts.

Some of our airborne dragons suddenly turned into gouts of flame and brilliant flashes of fire. I gasped, reared back.

"Enemy crossbows," Malaban said. "Their quarrels shattered the incendiaries strapped to their bellies."

Plumes of oily black smoke spiraled earthward with the plummeting remains of corpses.

"One Dragon, have mercy," I whispered, then tried to count the plumes of smoke. "How many?"

"Hard to say. Two clawfuls, at most."

A locust swarm rose up from Kratt's forces and swept toward our squadrons. The two aerial tides met; I expected to hear the sound of the two clashing—destriers bugling, men bellowing, talons slashing hide—but no, not at that distance. Only an eerie silence, beneath which ran the ominous rumble of a Clutch ready for war.

Beneath the aerial battle in the distance, flashes of fire began leaping like crimson minnows from the ground; our squadrons were releasing their nets over Kratt's sprawling forces. Black smoke rose into the air in plumes, and I wondered whether any of dragonmaster Re's former apprentices—those with whom I'd once trained—were there, in Kratt's infantry or his air force, hearing dragons shriek and men scream as incendiaries whistled from the sky and dirt roared into the air, severing limbs and spewing guts, rock, smoke, and a fire-flash of heat into the sky.

Eight more squadrons of our incendiary fliers launched from Xxamer Zu: another ninety-six dragons. Two of those squadrons veered southeast, toward the road that led from Xxamer Zu into the mountainous jungle, the very same upon which marched the Imperial regiment. The other six flew like loosed quarrels toward Kratt's forces.

More enemy destriers boiled into the air as our squadrons approached. Our fliers went wide, flew high, tried to avoid entanglement and come in from the sides and behind. Red and orange flashed from the ground, a firework display of incendiaries. Geysers of black smoke spewed into the sky.

Eight more squadrons of our incendiary fliers launched toward Kratt's forces. Beside me, Malaban Bri grunted. "They outnumber us four to one. We have to crush them hard and fast; once they draw nearer us, we can't use the incendiaries for fear of burning Xxamer Zu to the ground."

Daronpu Gen was standing right at the edge of the roof, sucking huge drafts of air into his nostrils like a quarry-crazed hound, neck muscles taut. I wondered, briefly, if he were mad.

Another eight squadrons of our fliers launched toward the enemy, and I reflexively ducked at the typhoon of noise, at the unnatural sight of so many destriers swarming into the air. The seething aerial mass in the distance was spreading outward, growing thicker, coming closer.

Clouds of black smoke billowed from the ground as incendiaries flashed crimson and red. Parts of the aerial battle were quickly becoming obscured from view by the smoke. I bit my lip, imagining what it must be like flying into that chaos, vision obscured, the acidic smoke choking lungs and stinging eyes.

"Notch!" our crossbow commanders bellowed, and winches clanked. Our infantry was pressing forward in battle lust, toward the low, grassy hill over which Kratt's forces would soon arrive.

"If anything happens to Savga . . ." I said hoarsely, to no one who could hear me.

The skies in front of us were now clotted with rufous-and-green outspread dragon wings flashing the color of old copper, the morass of airborne destriers pressing closer, closer. . . .

Another eight squadrons of dragonfliers launched from Xxamer Zu and flew toward the approaching enemy. Just under five hundred destriers we'd sent into the skies: almost our entire air force.

"They won't be carrying incendiaries, not those," Malaban said grimly. "Too close."

The outraged trumpeting of fighting destriers carried on the air, thin and high.

"Draw!" our crossbow commanders bellowed, and the deep, resonant cries rolled like thunder down the rows of poised crossbow archers.

The mob in the skies was so close I could see some of the individual riders crouched on the backs of the dragons, could see the heraldic crests of the enemy flapping on brisket and belly, bearing the purple-and-green Ranon ki Cinai emblem of a rearing bull dragon holding a black bird upon one extended claw.

The first ragged squadron of enemy destriers burst free of the combat and came toward us. Fast, faster, close, closer . . .

"Loose!" bellowed our crossbow commanders, and a flood of quarrels screamed toward dragon bellies.

"Where is she?" Daronpu Gen roared, slapping his head.

Our rain of arrows hit several targets. Enemy dragons plummeted earthward, wing membranes shredding in the descent. My guts clenched and I recoiled with each dragon scream that told of a quarrel driving deep into its mark. So much death, so much noise!

Several enemy destriers evaded our crossbows, flew wide around the northeasterly outskirts of our Clutch, heading south.

"They're going to regroup behind us," I cried. "They'll join the Imperial regiment when it reaches us."

"Not those ones," Malaban Bri growled. "Others, maybe."

Two of our remaining squadrons launched into the air and engaged in combat with the enemy heading south.

"Notch! Draw! Loose!"

More oncoming enemies were flying wide of our Clutch, skirting far around the eastern edge, continuing south. More of them came, and more.

"Notch! Draw! Loose!"

I was finding it difficult to inhale.

"She *must* show, blood-blood! The prophecy foretells it!" Daronpu Gen roared. His one eye rolled in his head, and he was frothing as he yanked on his hair.

I turned on Malaban, shivering hard. "Untie me."

Malaban's eyes dragged away from the battle and met mine.

"I brought you the dragons' secret," I said hoarsely. "I saved your sister. Untie me."

The skies above Xxamer Zu were now thick with dragons bearing Temple's heraldic crest, and with a sound like the earth heaving asunder, Kratt's impressive infantry suddenly boiled over the grassy hillock in the near distance and surged down toward us.

"Untie me!" I shrieked, as our infantry charged toward Kratt's, bellowing insanely.

Our archers adjusted the angle of their massive crossbows; winches were cranked tight; quarrels whined into the air and showered upon the advancing enemy infantry. Men screamed and fell, but still the enemy sea poured toward us.

Malaban withdrew the dirk at his waist and sawed at the leather thong binding my wrists. "Chinion, we should move from here!"

Dragons swooped low; our archers fired from the ground, taking out individuals. Dragons screamed; winged bodies plummeted and crashed atop soldiers. The bindings around my wrists fell free.

The shadow of a dragon loomed imminent and huge overhead.

"Down!" I shrieked as I covered my head and dropped.

Talons scored thatch. The reek of agitated dragon burned my nostrils. A whip-fast tongue struck empty air. I smelled venom.

Then the dragon was gone.

I raised my head, spat gritty thatch from my mouth. Saw *things* dropping from some of the backs of airborne enemy destriers, *things* like great silky gray parasols, floating inexorably earthward, into the heart of Xxamer Zu, near its temple.

And with a bolt of terror, I at once understood their significance. I grabbed one of Malaban's arms, where he lay sprawled on the roof beside me, belly down, while dragons screamed and clashed overhead, while arrows whizzed and people died. "Malaban, look! Kratt's dropping people into Xxamer Zu."

"Our soldiers will deal with them—"

"No, you don't understand! Kratt's dropping my sister into the Clutch to provoke the appearance of his Skykeeper."

Malaban stared at the gray parasols floating down upon Xxamer Zu. Attached to ropes that dangled beneath each parasol hung a person, whether it was a soldier intent on torching tinder-dry buildings and engaging in hand-to-hand combat . . .

. . . or a woman whose very presence would provoke a mighty haunt.

A deafening skirl rent the air, and the smell of rot fell over the Clutch like a black cloud, and there she was, my mother, the haunt, splendid in her size and fury, swooping over Xxamer Zu, knocking aside airborne destriers with her body as if they were gnats, twiggy tail lashing like an impossibly huge whip, fanged beak snapping destrier wings in two. She banked, circled back, swooped down upon our infantry, talons extended, and raked bloody twin paths through that heaving sea of soldiers. Bodies and limbs were catapulted through the air by her thrashing tail.

Malaban clambered to his feet, hauled me upright. The two soldiers who'd been guarding us lay several feet away. One was headless, decapitated by dragon talon. Daronpu Gen lay sprawled facedown some few feet away from him, splattered by blood; whether his own or the soldier's, I didn't know. But he was alive, rising unsteadily to his knees. The river-roar of fighting soldiers was almost deafening.

I moved swiftly, snatched up the dead soldier's sword.

"Gen!" I shouted, and he froze midcrouch as the point of my sword touched his throat. "Listen to me! You won't harm my sister, understand? We're going to remove her from the Clutch, that's all."

"Put down the sword, Zarq!" Malaban bellowed. He still held his dirk in his hand.

The haunt ascended the skies for another pass, eviscerating several destriers with a swipe of her talons.

"We're wasting time!" I said. "Get on your feet, Gen. Slowly! Good. Now move over to the ladder."

With my sword quivering at his throat, Gen approached the crude ladder that led down from the roof.

"You can't protect her, Zarq. She's the enemy," he boomed.

"We'll find her and remove her from the Clutch," I said stubbornly.

An incendiary exploded near the arbiyesku, and the roof beneath us juddered violently.

"Chinion!" Malaban bent, snatched up the other soldier's sword, and threw it to him. Gen spun away from me, caught the sword by the hilt, and our blades rang against each other, once, twice, thrice, a dizzy flurry of clashing steel.

The blows rang down my arms and wrenched my shoulders, and my vision swam, but I'd trained with Dragonmaster Re, and Gen was weak from recent torture, so I retained my grip on my sword. The two of us broke apart and slowly circled each other.

"You're thinking with your heart, not your head, Zarq!" Gen panted. "For the love of wings, listen to how many are dying around us! Will you turn traitor and let your Clutch be captured, all for the sake of Kratt's ebani?"

"She doesn't have to die!" My voice was cracking, and I hated myself for it. "Put her on an escoa; take her into the jungle."

"You think the shendwen-dar will permit that?"

"You think she'll allow you to harm Waivia?" I fired back, and I attacked him wildly.

He was driven back several paces under the savagery of my blows, but then he rallied, counterattacked, feinted, attacked again. He was debilitated from the torture he'd suffered during his imprisonment, and his impaired vision from the loss of an eye disadvantaged him gravely. But he was still twice my size and weight, and his arms had twice the reach of mine, so despite my fighting experience in dragonmaster Re's stables, he easily held his ground against me.

We drew apart, the both of us breathing heavily. My arms trembled. My sword weighed at least a thousand pounds.

"You've no wish to kill me, Zarq," he panted. "Put down your weapon."

I felt desperate and cornered. There had to be a way to save both Waivia and my Clutch. . . .

I heard her, then.

Savga. Screaming.

And accompanying her blood-chilling shriek was the image of Agawan being laid upon a stone altar by calloused Djimbi hands, his small, chubby body being cruelly lashed onto the stone like a live sacrifice.

I gasped, and my sword slipped from my loose fingers. Reeling, I grabbed my head. Daronpu Gen was instantly at my side.

"I could've killed you with one blow," he growled, planting a foot over my sword as Savga's screams and Agawan's wails ricocheted round my head.

"What is it?" he said sharply.

I looked at him, wild eyed, my skin pimpled from chill. "Can't you hear?"

He opened his mouth, then went rigid. Scented the air wildly, great nostrils flaring. "What is it? Where? Flavor of the otherworld in the air—"

My vision slid sidewise, Daronpu Gen disappeared from my view, and instead I saw Agawan bawling on the stone altar again, and saw Savga this time, too, thrashing, squirming, screaming, in the grip of Djimbi arms.

My vision cleared. The screams were abruptly cut off. I was gazing into the distance, toward the center of the Clutch, at the three white domes of the temple.

"Someone has Savga and Agawan," I said hoarsely. "In the temple. They're going to sacrifice them on the altar."

He frowned. "What?"

Malaban was at my other side, sheathing his dirk, looking a question at Gen, which Gen was ignoring. Gen jerked rigid again; then his whole rangy body started quivering like a hound's about to be unleashed for the hunt. "Yes, there, a whiff of Elsewhere in the air . . ."

I wrenched away from him and started for the ladder. "We have to go to the temple, now."

"Wait!" Gen cried, and I paused, one foot on the ladder rung.

He bent, picked up my sword. "You forgot something. You'll need it if we run into any of Kratt's soldiers. But raise it against me again, and I'll kill you."

We sprinted along a grassy path, heading toward the center of Clutch Xxamer Zu. Buildings were afire; people were running, carrying goods with them; a string of rishi were hurling buckets of dirt and water upon the flames. Timbers groaned and crackled, and soldiers—ours and Kratt's—clashed here and there in pockets.

Two soldiers stepped out from behind a mud-brick building with cries of, "Temple!"

"Nashe!" Gen roared in answer, and I breathlessly echoed his cry as I brought up my own sword.

I parried a blow, lunged, spun, felt steel glance across my thigh, as soft and cool as a shadow. The man fighting me was huge, and furious, and with each blow he bellowed, "Temple! Temple!" with increased energy.

I caught a ringing blow that drove me to my knees. The soldier raised his sword—

—and Malaban Bri stepped under his arm and buried his dirk into the man's chest, in the gap in his leather uniform that existed beneath the soldier's armpit.

The soldier gave a strangled howl and backed up, Malaban's dirk still buried to the hilt within him. Two-handed, the soldier swung wildly at Malaban, and cut him halfway through the torso.

With a cry, I leapt to my feet and hacked and hewed at the soldier, until he was a bloody, twitching mess at my feet. A hand wrenched me off my butchering. Gen.

"He's dead. Leave him."

I glanced at Malaban. He was on his back, staring sightless at the sky. I'd saved his sister from death. He'd saved me from the same.

"To the temple," I said hoarsely. Gen curtly nodded.

We ran past clan barracks, past empty granaries, weaving through people and soldiers. All was chaos around us: screaming people, smoke. We reached the temple market square. Clots of bayen women and children were running across it and gathering at the closed stockade gates, shaking them and clamoring to be let into the austere stone edifices.

I ran through the confusion. A panicked bayen woman barreled into me; we both went sprawling. I tried to clamber to my feet, was knocked to my knees by someone else. An incendiary dropped with a dreadful whine from the skies, right into the market square, and the ground heaved and buckled and I was thrown onto my back. Dust and screams everywhere, and thick, hot smoke. I staggered to my feet, looked for my sword, couldn't find it. Could see, through plumes of smoke and waves of heat, the temple. I lurched toward it, weaponless.

A mangy bitch ran past me, wild eyed, a pup in her jaws.

I staggered up sandstone stairs and reeled into the temple. I paused, one hand braced against a pillar for support, as my eyes adjusted to the dimness of the sunken central amphitheater. Slowly my vision resolved.

There, standing on the tiled floor of the amphitheater, was Savga, struggling against the hands that gripped her. Hands that belonged to my sister, Waivia.

There was Agawan, bawling upon the central altar, lashed to it by leather thongs. A bald Djimbi man was tightening the last of those cords.

To one side stood Kratt, his clear blue eyes almost ghostly white in the gloom. He was looking directly at me.

He spoke; I heard him not for the roaring in my head and the chaos beyond the temple. All eyes looked up at me. My sister's face was a mask, carved from polished brown stone, her eyes cold carnelian. I couldn't look at Savga, lest I become undone.

I began descending the temple tiers to the amphitheater below. I felt, rather than heard or saw, Gen appear alongside me, sword at his side. I moved carefully, deliberately.

"I told you she'd come when properly provoked," the Djimbi man cackled to Waivia, and I recognized him, then. Dragonmaster Re. His narrow, green-whorled face was grossly disfigured, as if half had slid south of the rest. One eye ran northwest to southeast instead of on a horizontal plane, and his nose was a cleaved and wizened fig. One half of his mouth hung slack, in a drooling frown. Even the tangled spill of beard beneath his chin was uneven, half reaching his collarbone, the other half encroaching in snarls about his chest. He was a gross parody of a human.

"Summon the other one now," he demanded of Waivia. "A bargain's a bargain."

"I summoned her when I called Zarq." Waivia didn't turn her eyes to the dragonmaster while she spoke, looked only at me. "She'll be here soon."

Beside me, Gen stirred. "Release the children, osmajani, and no harm will come to your own son after you've lost the war! You can't escape; soldiers will surround us soon—"

"My haunt is destroying your soldiers even as we speak," my sister said, cutting him off, and to give weight to her words, the haunt skirled above the temple, and the ground trembled, and mortar from the temple dome briefly showered upon us. Waivia's tiger-banded eyes flashed at Gen as I descended the last step to the amphitheater floor. "You impress me, though. I didn't think you'd survive my beloved's play room."

My eyes flicked to Kratt. He was standing at ease, leaning against a pillar. His expression would have been one of languid amusement if his diamond eyes had not betrayed him, glittering with a frightening excitement. I found it hard to breathe, looking at him.

"Kratt," I said hoarsely. I forced myself to not look away from his cruel eyes as I moved closer to Waivia. Closer. "I'm here; you have what you want. Now release the children."

"I think not."

"*I'm* the one you want—"

"Ah, but I must keep my word to the dragonmaster. He promised me you, and in return I promised him vengeance. And look, how timely: His opportunity for such has arrived." He looked up the dark rows of tiers beyond me.

"Mama!" Savga screamed, and she threw herself forward, wrenched herself form Waivia's grasp, and went hurtling up the amphitheater tiers. Waivia moved after her, raising a hand that spat green sparks like chips of peridot, but I leaped in front of Waivia.

"Let her go!"

We were inches apart, yet aeons away from each other. We'd never embrace again.

"You should have boarded that ship, Zarq."

"Don't turn yourself into Mother," I said quietly. "Don't damn your child with your madness."

"What I do, I do *because* of my child. He won't suffer as I did, won't be taunted and despised, abused and starved."

"Perhaps not." I refused to flinch before her pain and fury. Not this time. Not anymore. "But if you stay this course, he'll suffer as *I* did. I know what it's like to be at the mercy of a mother's madness."

"You know nothing about being a mother!"

"I know everything about being a helpless child."

Tansan hove into my view, statuesque, sweated, raked with sword cuts. I saw her deliberately lay her bloodied spear on one of the tiers halfway down the amphitheater before continuing her approach.

When she reached the ground floor, she and Waivia faced each other. Tansan was taller, straighter, all strength and vigor held still. Waivia was all dusky curves and fury, a flame-eyed virago crouched to spring.

"Release my baby," Tansan said.

"Come and get him." The dragonmaster cackled, and he held a dagger against the soft folds of the bound baby's neck. "Yes! Yes! Come and get your by-blow."

Tansan looked at me with eyes as black and dense as venom. "Savga, go with Zarq."

"Mama, don't—"

"Now."

Kratt stepped away from his pillar. "Zarq will be coming with me."

Daronpu Gen shifted, raised his sword. "Stand down, Kratt!"

"Gen!" I shouted. "It's me he wants. Waivia . . ." I turned to her. "Release the baby. He's not that much older than yours. You're not an infant killer. Don't do this. Let the baby go. Tansan will go with the dragonmaster, but *let her baby go*."

"I told you once before, Zarq: You take what's mine, I hurt you," Waivia said.

"Hurt me, then. Hurt *me*. But not a baby."

Her nostrils flared. Agawan was crying in hoarse spasms, his tiny ribs heaving against the leather that bound him so cruelly. His hands were clenched into small red fists. His cries had started Waivia's milk flowing; the front of her bitoo was damp in two spreading patches.

Waivia's eyes flickered at the baby, then back to me. They were cold, hard. "Go stand beside Kratt."

"Sweetling," Kratt said, voice hard as iron. "The baby stays where it is."

A look of revulsion crossed Waivia's face, and I knew, with utter surety, that she held neither love nor respect for her claimer. He was a tool she used, nothing more.

"The baby," she said tightly, "is unnecessary. You have Zarq."

"Gen, take Agawan and Savga and go," I said breathlessly.

An unbearably tense moment followed, broken when Waivia moved to the altar. She spoke a word; viper-green light flashed, and a cloud of smoke puffed above the altar. Then she was lifting Agawan from the stone slab, severed cords trailing from his unharmed body.

Gen's one-eyed gaze met mine. Sorrow, frustration, and admiration were in his look. He nodded once, lowered his sword but didn't release it, and approached Waivia. Another tense moment as they stood before each other: two enemies, one armed with a sword, the other with an infant. Gen growled, dropped his sword to the ground, and took the baby from her.

In that moment, while we all watched Tansan's child being placed in the rebel holy warden's arms, the dragonmaster moved. Swift as an eel, he slid from his place behind the altar and placed his dagger at Tansan's neck.

Since then, I've often wondered if she saw him coming, but forced herself to stand still and defenseless. She was a warrior; she would have sensed him moving, surely. But no, she chose to stand still. I'm not surprised. After all, I'd seen her give herself away without a fight before, to two drunken bayen men, just to keep a promise to one of her children.

"Mama!" Savga cried, breaking free from Daronpu Gen.

"Don't come closer, Savga!" Tansan barked, and her voice was harsh, bloodless.

Savga stopped, went rigid.

"Brother, put the blade down!" Gen shouted. "She's one of us—"

"Fool," the dragonmaster shouted. "Arrogant, blind dupe! Zarq's not the one; I told you all along!"

"Put down the knife," Gen boomed.

The haunt skirled; a dragon screamed. The attacked dragon must have plummeted into a building outside; there was a dull crash just beyond the temple, and thatch and bricks exploded into the air outside.

"The puling kitten is the one!" the dragonmaster shrieked. *"Here's* your cursed Skykeeper!"

He drew his knife hard, deep, and fast across Tansan's throat.

I screamed, Savga screamed, the baby in Gen's arms screamed. We surged forward as the dragonmaster released Tansan with a shove. She staggered forward—one step, two steps—hands going to her throat. Swayed.

Blood pumped down her neck, red as flame. Where her lifeblood gushed, fire ignited. Behind her, the dragonmaster shrieked triumphantly and held his hands above his head. "Nashe! Nashe!" he screamed. You'll die now, Kratt, and Temple along with you! Triumph the Djimbi!"

Kratt's face was alabaster as he realized he'd been double-crossed. He moved forward, as if to hew the dragonmaster down, but Tansan was now engulfed in flame, and Kratt threw up an arm to shield his face from the fierce heat and thought better of going after the dragonmaster.

With eyes upon the growing cyclone of flame that had been Tansan, my sister slowly backstepped, hands weaving jade symbols in the air, some of which shattered into shards from the heat, others that snaked toward the vortex of flame.

Daronpu Gen leapt toward Savga, grabbed her by the back of her nape as if she were a small cat, and, with Agawan tucked like a gourd under one of his rangy arms, scooped Savga up and threw her, shrieking and kicking, over one shoulder.

"Nashe!" the dragonmaster cackled, knees jerking into the air in a macabre parody of a dance. Flames began to consume him, too. "Nashe!"

Overhead, my mother's haunt skirled, and men and dragons died.

The flames grew, and the dragonmaster gave a gurgling shriek and ran in circles, arms windmilling as he uselessly tried to bat out the flames devouring him. I staggered back, away.

"Get the children out of here!" I screamed at Gen.

"Zarq, run!" Daronpu Gen bellowed at me, and for the last time our eyes met. Then he turned and lumbered up the amphitheater's tiers, Savga slung over one shoulder, Agawan tucked under his other arm.

I ran, too.

But not after Gen. No. I had a debt to settle.

I dove for the sword Gen had dropped to the ground, that he could accept Tansan's babe. The heat from the expanding maelstrom of flame that had been Tansan scorched my cheek. I grabbed the hilt of the sword, rolled, came up against the cool stone of the lowermost tier, and rose unsteadily to my feet.

In the unnatural blaze of orange light thrown from the column of fire that now towered to the very apex of the central dome, Kratt's eyes met mine. They weren't pale blue in that light, but shimmered like opals.

They were focused exclusively on me.

He raised his sword. I raised mine. We drew closer to each other.

Without removing his eyes from me, Kratt sidestepped up onto a tier. I moved as if his mirror image. Up another tier, up another, each time putting distance between ourselves and the fiery cyclone that had been Tansan. From the corner of my eye I was vaguely aware of Waivia standing her ground near the heat-sundered altar, partially shielded by a dense green light. Her bitoo billowed about her in the heat, smoking, flames licking over it here and there but soon dying beneath the necrotic green light she commanded.

Whatever spells Waivia was weaving were preventing Tansan—a

Skykeeper in the fiery throes of birth—from bursting from the cyclone of flame and exploding through the temple's dome, into life and freedom beyond.

Kratt attacked.

Our swords crossed, crossed again. I staggered back, my entire spine whiplashed from the blows. I summoned every gout of fury I'd ever felt against him, channeled all my years of suffering and hatred and craving for dragonsong into a rage as fiery and powerful as the otherworld cyclone towering above me.

"For my father!" I bellowed, and I ducked under one of Kratt's swings and slashed my sword low, at his calves. Felt the sword tip drag slightly as it cut cloth, caught flesh. "For my brother! For my mother!"

He'd been trained by swordmasters since childhood, whereas I'd had but a year of discipline from a venom-addled dragonmaster, using a wooden cudgel instead of a sword. My rage, although briefly potent, could not overcome his skill, even as blood ran from the slash I'd dealt his leg.

I barely stopped a crashing blow meant to cleave my shoulder from my body, lost my footing, teetered on the lip of a tier . . .

. . . and fell.

I landed hard, on my back, sword clattering to the tier below me.

Kratt paused, a cruel smile playing on his face as he stood above me, savoring his victory.

Beyond him, I saw that Daronpu Gen had deposited Savga upon the uppermost tier of the temple; she held Agawan in her arms. They were small silhouettes, backlit by white, smoky light. For a second Savga paused. Then she turned and ran, away from the temple, away from my death, her baby brother clutched against her.

Gen himself had bounded back down the tiers, had retrieved the spear Tansan had set down upon one of them. He had it raised above his head. Aimed at my sister.

"No!" I shrieked.

Gen was a better osmajani than he'd given himself credit for.

He hurled the spear while bellowing a word that was an explosion of Djimbi magics, a starburst of pagan power, and his magic-borne spear flew with unnatural speed and strength. The force of it picked Waivia off her feet, drove her through the cyclone of fire, and impaled her upon a great wooden carving of a dragon hanging on the far wall.

Someone screamed, and I was running, stumbling, clambering down tiers. The emerald ropes of magic that had trapped the Skykeeper within the fires of its birth began to shatter.

I reached Waivia.

Tried to pull the blood-slick spear from her back. Couldn't.

No. No. No.

I stroked her sooty cheek, where she was impaled face-first against the great wooden face of a dragon. Her bitoo was a diaphanous gown of char; her hair was a smoking snarl. Her eyes were lifeless.

No. My sister, my sister. No.

A movement beside me.

Kratt.

He stood swaying. I must have wounded him on the chest, too; blood was flowering across his waistshirt.

Vain thing, I thought inanely; he should have worn armor.

He raised his sword to kill me.

Two things happened then, simultaneously.

A hideous sound blasted through the temple, on a wind rank with the stench of necrosis. I looked away from Kratt, away from his bloodied sword, looked up the many tiers of temple, and saw . . .

. . . an impossible thing beyond them. A massive beaked maw lined with razor-sharp teeth, growing larger, faster. I could see the trembling muscles lining that rot-corrugated throat.

My mother.

Coming for her dead child.

And in that exact moment, the last of my sister's insidious green ropes binding the cyclone of fire to the earth shattered, and Tansan—the Skykeeper—burst through the dome of the temple and out into the white skies beyond.

Glass tesserae and plaster and ceramic shattered in a great cloud of dust as the pillars of the temple were blasted apart, and the ground beneath me shook, and an avalanche of crumbling dome and walls roared around me, and I dropped to the heaving ground and covered my head and bellowed fear and anguish.

And then there was silence.

Stillness.

Smoke.

Slowly I raised my head.

My sister's lifeless body was gone. The great carving she'd been impaled upon was gone. Kratt was gone. Gen was gone. The temple we'd been within—the mortar and pillars that had supported it, and the gilded spire that had topped its three white, smooth domes, and the great stone altar that had been the center of it—was entirely gone.

I stood in a crater, a great blasted hole of corrugated, scorched earth.

And within me, railing and roiling in grief, and powerless without Waivia, was my mother's haunt. She'd protected me, in the end.

I clambered out of that crater, through a thick sea of cindery smoke, the black earth beneath my hands and knees and feet as hot as smoldering coals. My skin blistered, burst, and wept from the heat.

I reached the lip of the crater, pulled myself out. Lay there, faceup, as the Skykeeper soared through the shifting smoke above.

Its flaming wingspan seemed to engulf the sky, and contrails streamed in its wake. It was a true Skykeeper; had she still existed outside of me, my mother's haunt would have been dwarfed by it. Not just by size, but by the crackling potency, the sheer *imminence* of it.

Instead of reeking of death, it smelled of molten copper, of new-forged steel. Its sapling-sized talons gleamed like brass. Lightning licked and crackled over its blue wings. Its smoking beak was massive, made of gold and serrated knives, and its eyes were pools of lava that bubbled and spewed forth molten rock. Its tail was not the thin, whiplike thing that the haunt had had, but a great plume of fiery blue feathers streaming behind it. It loosed a cry that sounded like the scream of a typhoon, and the earth beneath me heaved as if it were an ocean swell.

Savga appeared by my head. She studied me a moment from a sooty face, eyes grave. Agawan was silent in her arms, staring wide-eyed at the Skykeeper wheeling high above.

"Can she be ridden?" I croaked.

"If I ask her."

"Ask her."

Savga opened her mouth and sang. Dragonsong.

I stoppered my ears to block out the exquisitely painful pleasure that Savga's unearthly song provoked within me. It was terrible, such hedonic power coming from a child's lips. I couldn't watch her, either. I focused my gaze on the Skykeeper instead.

At once, the immortal creature began descending.

Lightning forked over her wings and sizzled down the length of her great body. Trapped against her, black clouds swirled and clashed in miniature typhoons. As she swooped lower, the glare from her golden beak brightened smoke into gilded fog and obliterated everything from sight, much the way a brilliant flash of lightning momentarily erases everything visual.

In that eerie yellow fog of nothing, the Skykeeper landed, settling within the crater as if it were a nest. I slowly sat up, every part of me aching.

The Skykeeper was enormous. Two pools of bubbling lava that were eyes, each the size of a small dragon, dripped lumps of molten rock to the ground, and the heave and ebb of her blue-feathered breast sounded like the swell and crash of mighty waves breaking against miles of cliff. Her two legs were scaled ruby spires, and her tail fanned above her, larger than any rainbow, scintillating various hues of blue: turquoise, sapphire, the color of sunlit blue glass and of small, powdery flowers. Heat and cool billowed off her, as if she were all seasons at once, and she smelled both metallic and coal-like, as if forged from the core of the earth.

"She'll burn Xxamer Zu to the ground with that dripping lava!" I shouted above the din of her breathing. "Can that be stopped?"

Savga shot me a reproachful look. "Those are *tears*. She's crying."

"Then you have to talk to her, soothe her grief. Tell her . . ." I paused, unsure of what the Dirwalan Babu should tell the immortal deity that had birthed her.

I might not know what the Dirwalan Babu should say, but I did know what *I* wished I'd had the chance to say, as a child, to my mother.

"Tell her you'll grow strong and live long, despite losing her," I said. "Tell her that you're her child and will never forget her, but she must let you go, as you have to release her. Tell her . . . tell her you love her."

Lower lip trembling, eyes laden with unshed tears, Savga sang.

A massive claw at the end of a towering, crimson leg ponderously moved. In a cloud of brilliant yellow smoke and dust, the fires licking from the puddles of lava were stomped out of existence. Molten rock stopped dripping from those lava-pool eyes.

"Can we mount her?" I shouted.

Savga sang my request to the Skykeeper, and again I hastily screwed my fingers into my ears. But still I could hear. Great Dragon, I could! I thought I'd go mad if Savga didn't soon stop her otherwordly song, knew I would hurl myself in a rage of excruciating ecstasy into those storms that roiled and clashed over the Skykeeper's oceanic body.

After a pause, a belt of green materialized from the tip of the Skykeeper's beak and ran, like a path of foliage, up to the Skykeeper's head. Ponderously, the great creature lowered its beak to the ground, as if she were a bird about to sip water from a pond.

Savga stopped singing. With Agawan still in her arms, she hurtled toward the Skykeeper.

My hoarse cry of alarm went unheard.

But Savga—almost whitewashed from existence by the radiance of the Skykeeper—stepped unharmed onto that green trail on the Skykeeper's beak and clambered up the creature's head.

After a moment I followed, squinting against the brilliant light.

It *was* a belt of green foliage that had appeared on the Skykeeper's head. It smelled verdant and fresh, astringent with bud sap. Cautiously I stepped onto the grassy trail on the Skykeeper. The soles of my feet tingled.

Taking a deep breath, I climbed the lush knoll that was the Skykeeper's head. I could feel each swell of her breath and the surge of her immortal blood as if I were walking over the surface of a rushing river. The weeping blisters on my hands, knees, and feet healed.

Just beyond the crest of the Skykeeper's head, Savga had sat down. Velvety vines had entwined about her legs and torso. She beamed up at me.

"Look what Mama can do!" she said, patting the vines about her. "Look what she made for Agawan!"

A cradle of vines. The toddler was, impossibly, peacefully asleep in it.

But I was alarmed and disturbed by the vines that strapped Savga down, and it must have shown on my face, for Savga looked annoyed. "How else are we going to stay on when she flies, hey-o?"

Vines began to slither about me, velveteen and warm. Their sinuous movements were uncomfortably sensual as they twined up my calves and reached for my thighs.

Those slinky vines were an extension of the Skykeeper, and the Skykeeper had once been Tansan, a woman I'd lusted for. Her firm, intimate touch brought a flush to my cheeks.

The network of vines soon enclosed me up to my collarbone and braced my neck, extending around me in thick buttresses.

"Hold on, now!" Savga shouted. "You're going to love this!"

I tensed myself for the ascent, and then I and my two children rode a Guardian of the Celestial Realm to freedom and victory.

EPILOGUE

Under my direction—relayed through Savga—the Skykeeper routed Kratt's infantry and the remains of his air force. The enemy's retreat was ragged and swift, and the sound of their retreat horns was the sound of the Great Uprising's victory.

The first thing the Imperial army saw as it descended from the scrubland surrounding the jungle was the Skykeeper and Temple's retreating forces. With only some slight resistance, the Imperial army surrendered to our waiting soldiers.

At my request, the Skykeeper then hovered over the roofs of the daronpuis' stockade, whence the Council of Seven, from within their glass observatory, watched Savga, and me holding a sleepy and content Agawan, descend down the verdant ramp on the Skykeeper's lowered neck and beak.

The Skykeeper didn't ascend into the skies. No. Within a blink she was suddenly gone, and with her, every fire that was blazing over Xxamer Zu was extinguished.

Savga wept bitterly and clung to me.

We never saw the Skykeeper after that. Rather, no one but Savga saw her, and then Savga saw her only in her dreams.

I would like to say that Malacar was radically changed for the better after so many died that day, but life isn't like that. People's beliefs and wants vary for a myriad of reasons: upbringing, status, health, perceived needs. Culture, personal quirks, family foibles. Fears. Boundaries. Experiences, or lack thereof. People react strongly and uniquely to situations for all the above reasons, and emotions are triggered. And so people disagree and disagree vehemently.

Life is change. Growth is optional. One must choose wisely.

Two weeks after the Great Uprising, the Ashgon fled Lireh. His departure sparked an exodus of landed gentry returning to the Archipelago.

Political factions sprang up. Over the next eight years Malacar teetered again and again on the brink of civil war. Perhaps it will continue to do so for decades yet to come. I don't know. Perhaps I might hear how my poor, beleaguered country is faring, from wherever it is that I decide to disembark from this Xxelteker merchant ship as it plies its trade up and down the Xxeltek coast. But for now, I'm content to know nothing.

I earn my keep as a sailor, and I write, in moments of calm on the ocean, this history that some would call a memoir. This ship, and the captain who sails her—an astounding Xxelteker woman introduced to me, years ago, by Jotan Bri—have become my home.

Savga and Agawan chose to stay behind in the Skykeeper's Dragoncote, which is what Xxamer Zu was renamed. Of all the things I've experienced in my life, only two I consider an indisputable success: raising Savga and Agawan, and securing Xxamer Zu as a Djimbi-governed egg-production estate, one free of any Temple influence.

Leaving Savga behind ripped a part of my soul out of me, and I cradle that ache, for it is mine and mine alone and I have every right to feel it. But she would not come with me—willful young woman that she is—and I could not stay. If it had been left to me, I *would* have stayed in Malacar, and descended into venom madness and died as violently as Jotan Bri did last year, but Savga screamed at me to go, demanded that I tell her I loved her and then . . . set her free.

She had no wish to watch me further battle my need for venom, understand. She had no wish to watch me lose that battle one last, devastating time.

And that may have been my fate. Yes, I admit it: I knew, at the end, that unless I fled from dragons and dragonsong, I would die as Jotan Bri had.

Until her descent into madness and her brutal suicide last year, Jotan had been a formidable ally to me. Her network of spies, her wealth, her intelligence, and the influence she wielded through her century-established family connections, all aided me mightily in my dedication—addiction, you could say—to securing Xxamer Zu as the self-governed commune it is today. It was also through her that the Council of Seven, which renamed itself the Iron Fist, heard my views, again and again, as they tried to create a new foundation upon which to build a nation. Three of the original seven have been assassinated, over the years. Some say by fellow members of the Fist.

But despite the grief and uneven support the Fist has given me in my determination to secure Xxamer Zu as a self-governed dragoncote, that mighty political party has done some good for my people, the Djimbi. Not out of empathy or compassion. No. Where's the profit in that? But because of the power they witnessed a young Djimbi girl summon from the skies, and because of the powers my sister, Waivia, had exercised while partnered with Kratt.

I am Djimbi now, too. Finally, some years ago, I found the courage to eradicate the enchantment my mother spun around me at birth. My skin is the brown of a water vole, whorled with green as dark as wet ivy. It still takes me by surprise every time I glimpse myself in mirror or water. But it is me, nonetheless. Zarq Kavarria Darquel. Zarq of my mother, Kavarria, and my father, Darquel.

As for the Fist: It has begun a clever eradication and assimilation program, whereby the symbols, dates, and rituals of Dragon Temple are being slowly and irrevocably converted into a fusion of new and ancient Malacarite *and* Djimbi religious practices. This transmogrification will, over the years, help eradicate Temple's presence in Malacar and unite Malacar under a single religion.

Or so is the hope.

And what of dragons? What of the fifteen bulls that so many people died protecting the day the efru mildon clashed? I'll answer the latter first: They were taken from us. As Tansan had predicted.

When Xxamer Zu's allies departed, the Council of Seven took every bull with them. But the old brooder that Tansan had stolen from Xxamer

Zu's egg stables prior to the war and force-marched into the hills produced a neonate bull. That's all we needed: a single bull. From that single bull and the brooders left to us, the dragoncote grew. Several more bulls were produced over the years, and those that we could afford to give away, were given away wisely, to two small Clutches that proved open to certain radical ideas, such as refraining from amputating the wings of brooders and not shackling them for life in egg stables. Ideas such as overturning the barbarous laws that prohibit pairings between Djimbi. Ideas such as teaching rishi—male and female, Djimbi and otherwise—how to read and write.

I'd hoped to change a nation. Some would say I failed. But I *did* change certain practices on three Clutches—Xxamer Zu, Diri, and Pera—and perhaps the seeds I sowed during my teachings as the One-eared Radical will someday take root and spread across Malacar. Who knows? We now live in an epoch in which the solid ground of tradition and preconceived ideas shakes daily under our feet, and that, to me is a good thing.

Are dragons divine? Most Djimbi say that they are. Rishi believe that they are. Jotan Bri was certain that they are *not,* and Sak Chidil is determined that they are no more divine than any other lizard or winged creature on earth.

As for me, I believe that both Sak Chidil's and the Djimbi views are correct. I believe—no, I *know*—that divinity rests within all living things. Life is sacred, and we are alive. Ergo, we all are sacred.

Even the creature trapped within me.

The irony is not lost on me that just when I'd found the strength and conviction to say good-bye to my mother forever, I discovered that not until my own death would I be freed of the entity that grew from my mother's obsession with Waivia. Through whatever obscure powers she wielded when alive, Mother rooted herself to the earthly realm through me when she died in Convent Tieron, when I was but nine. Now that angry, grieving, powerless entity is trapped within me until I myself die.

But somewhere in that anger and grief, buried beneath those sweet and sour memories she forces me to relive some nights, lies my mother. The mother who turned the blood of her body to milk for me to suckle as an infant. The mother who molded with her power and art the soft and yielding heart of a child, a child who became a woman who shook an entire nation.

A mother who taught me that failure is not the falling down, but the staying down.

In my journey on these foreign seas, I hope the two of us—mother and daughter—can finally make peace with each other. I know it won't be easy; little between a mother and her child ever is. But the bond between us both is there. Forged in flesh, secured in spirit, and buried in our experiences, the bond remains.

All that is left is for the two of us to exhume and heal that bond together.

ABOUT THE AUTHOR

Janine Cross has published short fiction in various Canadian magazines and was nominated for an Aurora Award in 2002. Her nonspeculative fiction has appeared in newspapers and a local anthology, *Shorelines*. She has also published a literary novel.